Breaking All My Rules

Also by Trice Hickman

Unexpected Interruptions

Keeping Secrets and Telling Lies

Playing the Hand You're Dealt

Published by Dafina Books

BREAKING ALL MY RULES

Trice Hickman

Kensington Publishing Corp.
http://www.kensingtonbooks.com

DAFINA BOOKS are published by

Kensington Publishing Corp.
119 West 40th Street
New York, NY 10018

All Kensington Titles, Imprints, and Distributed Lines are available at special quantity discounts for bulk purchases for sales promotions, premiums, fund-raising, and educational or institutional use. Special book excerpts or customized printings can also be created to fit specific needs. For details, write or phone the office of the Kensington special sales manager: Kensington Publishing Corp., 119 West 40th Street, New York, NY 10018, attn: Special Sales Department, Phone: 1-800-221-2647.

Dafina and the Dafina logo Reg. U.S. Pat. & TM Off.

ISBN-13: 978-0-7582-8720-5
ISBN-10: 0-7582-8720-8

First Dafina trade paperback printing: March 2013

10 9 8 7 6 5 4 3 2 1

Printed in the United States of America

b2027175x

Dedication

This book is dedicated to everyone who has ever dared to step outside their comfort zone, take a risk, and follow their dreams. For those who haven't, don't be afraid to try something new. You are more powerful than you know.

Acknowledgments

I'm an author. I love words. But it's hard to find the right ones to adequately express how happy, thankful, and appreciative I am to have completed another novel! God has blessed me, healed me, and loved me through many storms, guiding me toward splendid sunshine. Thank you, Lord! I continue to be humbled by Your grace and mercy.

Publishing another book is like a dream come true all over again! I'm so grateful for this opportunity, and again, there are many people to thank. In my previous novels I thanked individual family members and loved ones, friends, fellow authors, book clubs, and industry professionals who have helped, supported, and encouraged me along this wondrous journey. Each time I have inevitably missed someone, not on purpose, but because God has surrounded me with so many awesome people that it's hard to keep up with everyone. So as not to leave out anyone, this time around I will simply say, "Thank you! I love you all!"

Abundant Blessings,

Chapter 1

"*Nooooo!*" Erica screamed over and over, gasping for breath, drowning in fear. She was falling. Falling fast. Her slender arms and thick legs flailed through the air as if she were on a runaway roller coaster. Her mouth gaped open and her eyes bulged wide when she realized what was next to come.

She knew it would only be a matter of seconds before she hit the hard, rugged earth below. Death was near. She could feel it. Hear it calling her name. Smell it invading her nostrils. The bitter taste of it filling her mouth as she screamed. Then, suddenly, her panic and fear vanished into the whisper-thin air around her. She couldn't explain her newfound sense of calm, or what had caused the shift, so she did the only thing that was left to do at such a terrifying moment—she obeyed it.

She stopped struggling.

She relaxed her tired limbs and welcomed the uncomfortable peace spreading through every inch of her flaccid body—the kind of peace that only death could bring. *This is it,* Erica thought as she swallowed hard. She closed her eyes, anticipated the rough gravel and dirt that lay mere inches away, and readied herself for the fatal impact.

Bonk! Beep! Bonk! Beep! Bonk!

Erica shot straight up in her bed and fumbled as she reached over to silence the alarm clock blaring loudly near her head. Her chest heaved up and down with rapid speed as her lungs fought for air. She took two deep breaths, closed her eyes tightly, and began to slowly count backward from ten until her body no longer trembled with fear.

She breathed in and out as her heart searched for its natural rhythm. After several minutes she was finally able to inhale and exhale at a normal pace. "Thank you, God," she whispered, covering her parched mouth with her trembling hand. The exercise had worked again, just as it had so many other nights and mornings in the past.

Erica slumped her tense shoulders and shook her head, falling back onto her pillow. Waking up like this made her wish she could end her day before it began.

It was Friday morning, and despite the fact that the weatherman had forecast a bright, beautiful day to start what promised to be a picturesque weekend, Erica felt as if dark clouds were hovering directly above her head, ready to drench her at any moment.

"*Aggghhhh,*" she moaned.

Erica Stanford was normally an upbeat, optimistic go-getter who always looked on the cheery side of things, no matter how bleak. If she had a bad day at work, she didn't sweat it, because she knew the next day would be better. If she missed out on a business contract, she didn't get discouraged, because she was confident that a much better opportunity would be waiting around the corner. Whatever the situation, she always tried to change her way of thinking so that she felt empowered rather than trapped by the challenges that faced her. But lately her state of mind had been steering counter to her character, and she couldn't seem to shake the funk it brought in its wake.

She knew she should adopt a better outlook and operate from a more hopeful place. After all, she'd learned long ago that negative thoughts led only to negative outcomes. But no matter how hard she tried to conjure up her usual glass-half-full, rainbow-laden optimism, she couldn't run from her haunting dreams or the seemingly bad luck that was bearing down on her.

This was the second nightmare she'd had this month, and she could feel the heavy weight of her past pressing into her here and now.

Erica turned over again and shifted her body against her dampened Egyptian cotton sheets as she adjusted her purple gown, which now clung to her skin. She wiped her perfectly arched brow, thinking about how her frightful dreams were always accompanied by unsparing panic and horrid night sweats.

Whenever she felt stressed, unsure, anxious, or confused, the nightmares would return. Some nights she was chased through winding, narrow streets that never seemed to end. At other times she was hiding from faceless assailants whose footsteps nipped at her heels. And in her darkest, most alarming dreams, she was completely helpless and without a way to protect herself. Those were the dreams she feared most, like the one she'd just had—falling powerlessly from the sky without a soul to help save her.

But no matter the particulars of her dreams, the results were always the same; she was fighting for her life, awaking just in the nick of time to save herself from a fatal ending. It had been that way for the last twenty-five years, and it had all started the night of her tenth birthday.

After a whirlwind day of fun, laughter, and gifts that had been capped off with chocolate cake and vanilla ice cream to celebrate her first double-digit birthday, Erica and her family had settled in for the evening. A peaceful quiet rested over their large brick and stucco home as her mother finished cleaning the kitchen and her father read in his study. Erica and Nelson, her twelve-year-old brother, were walking upstairs to their bedrooms when they heard frightening sounds that froze their feet into place.

From out of nowhere, a thunderous crash of glass, followed by the terrifying sound of gunshots, sliced through the still night. What happened next raced by so fast that neither young Erica nor Nelson had time to react as they stood motionless, watching the violent scene unfold before their helpless eyes.

In the span of the few seconds that it took her mother to dial 911, Erica's father was shot twice after racing from his study to defend his family. But despite his wounds he managed to break the would-be thief's arm, bust open his nose and lip, and leave him a bloody mess before the man hastily limped away through the broken glass of their patio door to a getaway car that had been parked down the street.

The intruder, a drug-hazed career criminal, was apprehended the very next day. Thankfully, Erica's father survived the brutal attack. It

took months for the wounds to his right shoulder and upper ab-
domen to heal, but the emotional scars lingered with the family for
long after. It was especially hard for Erica, a sensitive child who wore
her emotions on her sleeve.

The violent home invasion had traumatized her on a day that had
been otherwise filled with nothing but goodness.

Erica learned many things on that fateful night. She learned how
strong and fearless her father was. How calm and levelheaded her
mother was. How resilient and determined her brother was. And how
painfully fragile she was. But most of all, she learned that no matter
how wonderful your day started out, everything could change after
the sun went down.

Chapter 2

Looking at her alarm clock for a second time, Erica considered crawling back under her luxuriously soft bedsheets. But instead of giving in to the urge to hug her mattress and block out the world, she willed herself to stand up, put one foot in front of the other, and lumber her way downstairs to her kitchen to make a cup of coffee.

Erica knew what her problem was, and she'd been thinking about this day ever since she had looked at the calendar last Tuesday and realized its significance.

She wanted to pull herself out of the dreary place where she was stuck, because it was like being locked inside a room without a key. But try as she might, lately it seemed as if every time her mind took one step forward, something would go wrong and pull her back two paces. And this morning she felt as though the gun had sounded but she was still hunched over the starting block, already behind in the race.

"You've got to get it together, sister," Erica whispered to herself as she rubbed sleep from her tired eyes.

One of the reasons for her less than enthusiastic mood was the fact that she had to report to D.C. Superior Court for jury duty by 8:00 a.m., which meant she had to leave soon. She had a jam-packed workweek ahead, filled with a million and one things she had to do at Opulence, the high-end bath and body care boutique she owned. The next three weeks were crucial for her business's future growth.

Through a combination of networking, planning, and being in the right place at the right time, she'd managed to score a game-changing business opportunity. Opulence products were going to be included in the coveted swag bags at the highly anticipated Tracy Reese fashion show during New York City's famed Fashion Week. Erica was ecstatic about the stroke of good fortune, because she knew it was going to catapult her small company to an entirely new level.

But ever since she'd signed the contract eight months ago to seal the sweet deal, everything that could go wrong had. From a mix-up with her chemical formulations for Paradise, the new body butter she planned to debut at Fashion Week, to a breakdown in price negotiations with a longtime supplier, to one of her employees abruptly quitting two days ago, leaving her short staffed, Erica had been scrambling to hold things together.

Her days were rushed, her nights were long, and the last thing she needed at this pivotal juncture was an all-day trip to the courthouse.

But the other source of her frustration, and what felt like a subtle blow to the pit of her stomach, could be summed up in three small, but painful words . . . Claude Daniel Richardson. Or as her best friend, Ashley, not so affectionately called him, Lucifer!

Today made exactly six months since Erica and Claude had broken up, bringing their two-year romance to a crushing end. Erica knew that she shouldn't let a failed relationship have this kind of effect on her, especially since breaking up with Claude had been for the best. But she hadn't met a decent man worth mentioning since their split, or even gone on a date, and now her gloomy love life only added to her already dampened spirits.

Her breakup with Claude had been just one in a long string of disappointments that she'd experienced with men, and now she was what she'd secretly feared—a statistic. She was one of the reported 42.4 percent of single black women who had yet to marry. And worse still, she didn't see her prospects for matrimony getting any better, because one needed to actually meet and date men for that to happen, and right now things were looking fairly dim.

But what concerned Erica even more was the thought that she might reach over to the ugly side of that dreaded statistic and become the stereotypical bitter, angry black woman who ranted about all of life's woes and the sorry, no-good men who'd dogged her, yet didn't have an amiable disposition to attract anything different. That was why she was always mindful to be pleasant and kind to everyone she met.

Erica shook her head when she thought about her ex. Claude Richardson was supposed to have remedied her statistical fears. He was supposed to have been "the one." She'd thought he was her black prince, the man who would give her the two kids, the dog, and the big, beautiful home that most women dreamed of, and that she'd been accustomed to growing up.

Claude was the man who all her family and friends, sans Ashley, had referred to as a good catch. He was a successful investment banker who owned a sprawling home in the wealthy Palisades neighborhood of northwest Washington, D.C. He was handsome, successful, educated, well mannered, and responsible. He opened doors, always remembered special occasions and holidays, and showered Erica with thoughtful gifts and any material thing she desired.

After their split, Erica had received condolences and a strong show of support from her girlfriends, who had said things like, "I'm so sorry to hear about you and Claude. He was one of the good ones," and "I can't believe you and Claude called it quits! You two were absolutely perfect together." But within days, the very friends who had shared drinks with her, offering sympathetic words of comfort, had added Claude to their phones' speed dial and had linked up with him through various social networking sites. The murky, shark-infested waters of the D.C. dating scene were brutal, and it was all about survival of the craftiest.

Erica opened the cabinet over her sink and reached in for her Winston-Salem State University coffee mug. "Damn, why can't I at least go out on a decent date?" she mumbled to herself, thinking about her crappy luck with men. But she knew the answer to that question before she'd asked it. The real truth was that her work schedule and her underlying fear of being disappointed again were both blocking her way.

She inhaled the sweet aroma of hazelnut-flavored coffee and watched as her Keurig machine produced a liquid stream of black gold that filled her ceramic mug. She shook her head again, remembering how much Claude's lying ass loved a piping hot cup of coffee first thing in the morning. "Why didn't I see it coming?" Erica asked herself.

On the surface, Erica and Claude had been the ideal couple. They had both graduated in the top 10 percent of their class from Winston-Salem State University, loyally following in the tradition of both their parents and grandparents by attending a historically black college. They had each earned advanced degrees from Ivy League schools, Erica's in fine arts from Columbia, and Claude's in business from Yale. Even their backgrounds growing up had been similar. They each hailed from well-connected, old-money families and had been raised in affluent suburban neighborhoods—she in Maryland, he in Pennsylvania. As everyone had said, they were great together. At least on paper.

Erica had met Claude at a cocktail fund-raiser for a popular D.C. councilman who'd been running for reelection. She had attended the swank downtown affair at the urging of Ashley, a gregarious but pragmatic prosecutor who was in the know about all things social. "This event is not to be missed," she'd raved to Erica. "Everyone who's anyone will be at Councilman Perry's fund-raiser, so put on your best dress and sexiest heels, 'cause, girl, that party is the place to be!"

Claude and Erica had locked eyes from the moment she entered the hotel's lavish ballroom. Her confident stride and natural beauty had instantly attracted him. From her shapely figure and curvy hips, which she swayed like a gentle breeze, to her radiant chestnut-brown skin, which looked dewy to the touch, to her full, kissable lips painted in burgundy blush, to the neatly trimmed shoulder-length bob she sported with fierce style, Erica had captivated him.

Even though they shared the same undergraduate alma mater, they'd never formally met before that night. They were a few years apart in age, so by the time Erica had entered WSSU as an eager freshman, Claude was a graduating senior and an established big man on campus.

Erica had heard all the buzz about Claude during her first week of classes. She and Ashley had been roommates, but they'd shared completely different views on the handsome upperclassman. Erica thought he was amazing, while Ashley thought he was, as she often smirked, a slick-ass phony. But despite Ashley's negative feelings about him, Erica managed to get her best friend to tag along with her to social events where Claude would be. Admiring him from afar became her hobby.

Claude had been a star quarterback, a university scholar, a popular fraternity hunk, and the object of desire in nearly every young coed's fantasies, as well as some of the faculty members'. A knee injury during an end-of-the-season play-off game had sidelined his hopes of an NFL career, but his brains and strategic planning landed him in business school and then led him straight into a lucrative career with a prestigious investment banking firm.

Initially, Claude hadn't had a clue as to who the gorgeous brown beauty was when he'd spied Erica gracefully sipping champagne by a buffet table with an attractive woman, who he later learned was Ashley—the only woman he'd ever met who couldn't be lulled by his charms. But Erica had known exactly who he was, and she was looking forward to becoming better acquainted.

Once Claude introduced himself, they exercised the standard Q & A etiquette that available singles in their social milieu practiced. They quickly established a connection, and despite not wanting to swoon over him, Erica was hooked at their first hello.

Claude was everything she had wanted in a man. His handsome good looks and commanding presence had ignited a smoldering flame inside her that hadn't been sparked since she'd ended her last relationship the previous year. He was well over six feet tall, with broad shoulders and toned muscles, and looking at Claude was like experiencing a dash of charming wrapped in a bundle of sexiness. And although his college athletic days were well behind him, he was still in tip-top condition.

Now, finally meeting the famed Claude Richardson face-to-face, Erica knew she'd struck gold. She could also see that Claude was still a highly sought-after commodity, as was evidenced by the women sprinkled throughout the room who leveled envious stares in her direction each time he gently touched her arm during their conversation or smiled with interest as she spoke.

Erica liked the fact that Claude's moves were purposeful and deliberate, meant to demonstrate a point. His actions made it clear to her and everyone else at the event that she was the only woman who was getting his undivided attention. From that night forward, they were a couple. A power couple.

Claude's hotshot corporate bravado contrasted to and yet complimented Erica's easygoing entrepreneurial spirit. She took pleasure in the fact that her handsome boyfriend was a seasoned professional who was socially connected and well respected in the right circles. And for his part, Claude was proud to boast that his beautiful girlfriend was the accomplished owner of an upscale, ultrachic bath and body care boutique that catered to some of D.C.'s most sophisticated clientele.

The first few months of their courtship were so blissful that Erica thought she was living in a waking dream. Claude was kind, attentive, and the epitome of what a good boyfriend should be. Their sex life was strong, and their bond outside the bedroom was just as solid. Erica was in heaven!

They went to all the best restaurants, attended all the "happening" parties and social events, and held front-row seats at the most coveted performances at the Kennedy Center. They spent four out of seven nights a week together and were practically inseparable. Their relationship was quickly shaping up to resemble something that looked like it was leading toward the yellow brick road to marriage.

They had been dating for one year when Claude proposed to Erica at her favorite restaurant on the anniversary of the night they met. It was a traditional and very romantic candlelit moment. When Erica ordered her favorite dessert, a flawless two-and-a-half-carat diamond in a dazzling platinum setting accompanied the piece of cake, all served on an antique silver platter, surrounded by red rose petals. It took her only a half second to say yes, cementing their intent to walk down the aisle. Her father gave his blessings, her brother wished her luck, and her mother shed tears of joy when she told them her happy news.

But a curious thing happened shortly after Erica accepted his proposal. Slowly, very slowly, things began to change right before her eyes.

What she had initially thought was Claude's commanding presence eventually revealed itself to be a hugely inflated ego. What she'd thought was pride in his personal appearance was really his extreme vanity in motion. And even his thoughtfulness turned out to be nothing more than skilled manipulation and calculated strategy. He had pretended to be considerate, when all along his acts of kindness and generosity had been motivated by what he could get from them in return. But it wasn't until one of Claude's disgruntled exes sent her an anonymous e-mail detailing his shady ways, that Erica finally learned just how dishonest he really was.

She learned that his monthly out-of-town business meetings with one of his prime accounts had really been time spent in the company of an exotic dancer named Chocolate Kiss. The twenty-five-thousand-dollar engagement ring he'd supposedly bought her was really a complimentary gift he received from one of his wealthy international clients who was connected to the blood diamond trade. And the nephew he visited every so often down in North Carolina turned out to be the child he'd fathered ten years ago—the result of a one-night stand with an old college flame during a homecoming weekend.

After that explosive e-mail, Erica came to see that everything about Claude was a big mirage. Because of many disastrous relationships, she'd wanted a prince so badly that she put up with more than she should have, losing sight of the fact that she was a queen, deserving of much more. He was all show and flash on the outside, and as hollow as a drum within. And to her great disappointment, the very things that had drawn her to Claude turned into deficits that eventually bankrupted her feelings for him.

"Bullshit mind games and straight-up triflin'!" is what Ashley had said about him.

Soon after Erica's eyes had been opened to the real man behind the facade, her relationship with Claude died a quick death. Never having been rejected by a woman, he'd been livid when she broke up with him, prompting harsh words and high emotions that she still remembered to this day.

As Erica stirred a teaspoon of brown sugar into her coffee, she realized that Claude was another reminder of how things could start out well but end in disaster.

Erica drank her coffee, pushing both Claude and her disappointing love life out of her mind. She knew she didn't have time to think about either, because she had so many other challenges to juggle.

She had postponed her obligation to report for jury duty three months ago, when she'd received the notice, which had come during the time she had the formulation disaster with the Paradise body butter she planned to include in the swag bags for Fashion Week. It had been a trying and frustrating time. But she couldn't get out of her civic responsibility this go-round, because it was mandatory by law. She had a gargantuan amount of work to do at Opulence in preparation for the boutique's debut on the national stage, and spending her day at D.C. Superior Court was only going to put her further behind.

Erica finished her coffee and headed back upstairs so she could get going. After she showered and did her hair and makeup, she milled through the neatly lined garments in her spacious walk-in closet. As she looked at the abundance of expensive clothes, shoes, and jewelry she owned, she thought about what a blessing and a curse her life had turned out to be. She was happy, thrilled even, about her professional success. But lately, her long hours and demanding schedule made it difficult to achieve what she longed for just as much as her career accomplishments—a loving mate to come home to and share in her good fortune.

She held a candy apple red–colored wrap dress up against her body, inspecting herself in the gilded full-length mirror in front of her. It was an outfit more fitting for a hot date out on the town than a day in court. But she needed to boost her spirits, so she removed it from the silk-padded hanger and slipped it on. "I guess sometimes you've got to break the rules," she whispered, pulling the dress over her hips. She stood back, admiring how nicely the dress complimented her curves. She wished that she really was getting ready to go on a date instead of to court. "Why don't they ever tell you about this part of the fairy tale?" Erica asked out loud. "Prince Charming my ass! It's all a sham."

But before she started feeling sorry for herself again, she shook off her negative thoughts and concentrated on all the great things she had to be thankful for: her loving family, fantastic friends, and good physical health. And the fact that she owned her own business and was living her professional dreams was a blessing she didn't take for granted. Being able to do what she loved gave her purpose.

★ ★ ★

Ever since she was a small child, Erica had had a love affair with lotions, oils, and perfumes. When she was six years old, she baked her first cake in her Easy-Bake Oven, and later that evening she raided her mother's vanity tray, spraying and rubbing every kind of perfume, powder, lotion, cream, and oil she could get her small hands on, all over her tiny body.

Although her mother had been less than thrilled, and had taken Erica straight to the bathroom to wash it all off, it was then that Erica developed her passion for body care products and fragrances. And as her love for skin care grew, she quickly realized that cooking food, like the cake she'd baked, and creating luscious body products required similar skills—the right ingredients, precise measurements, and careful attention to detail.

When she was in high school, she experimented with recipes in her mother's kitchen, mixing creams, oils, and lotions to create ambrosia-like scents and silky textures that made her smooth, soft-to-the-touch skin the envy of her classmates. By the time she graduated from college, she was creating her own body oils, just like the African vendors at the local flea market had taught her. She'd also perfected her skills by developing scents that were so hypnotic, men often stopped her on the street to ask what she was wearing.

Armed with a degree in business and a talent for making products that could put the formulations at any department store's beauty counter to shame, Erica knew it was time to set out on a path that would put her on the road to fulfilling her dream of starting her own boutique.

She knew that in order to be successful, she had to plan, research, and save her money before she took the leap of opening her own store. After years of studying the market as well as her competition, mastering her own original concoctions through trial and error, and squirreling away the lucrative salary she earned as a senior beauty editor at *Washington Woman,* a local magazine, Erica stepped out on faith and opened the doors of Opulence.

Over the past five years Opulence had grown into a premier destination for discriminating customers, offering high-end, all-natural bath and body care products that left one's skin smelling good, looking radiant, and feeling silky to the touch.

Erica was very particular about how she wanted her boutique, as well as her employees, to look. Sophisticated, elegant, and of course, opulent—that was the brand she had built and had become known for. Opulence was all things rich and luxurious, from the super-emollient body creams customers loved to the amethyst-colored designer aprons that each employee wore over a crisp white shirt and stylish black pants. Erica had cultivated her boutique to reflect who she was and what she wanted out of life.

Erica raised her wrist, looked at her stainless-steel Patek Philippe, and let out a deep sigh when she realized the time. "I better get going," she said as she slipped on her heels and grabbed her handbag from the upholstered sitting bench at the foot of her king-size bed.

For a split second she thought about skipping jury duty altogether, but she knew that the penalty for not showing up was a price she wasn't willing to pay. So, like many things in her life, she swallowed her discomfort, put a smile on her face, and headed out the door to face her day.

Chapter 3

Erica scrolled through her phone as she sat at the front of the crowded room on the third floor of the D.C. Superior Court building. She was impatiently waiting in the same uncomfortable chair that she'd claimed when she first arrived several hours ago. She wanted to get up and move around, but the room was so packed, she stayed where she was for fear of losing her seat and having to stand on her three-and-a-half-inch heels.

She sighed when she noted that it was early afternoon and she still hadn't heard from the graphic artist she'd hired to create a new signature design that she wanted imprinted on the container jars for her Paradise body butter. He was supposed to have sent her the final design file two weeks ago. Now she feared that even if she received it today, her container supplier wouldn't have enough time to manufacture the product and have it back in time to meet her shipping deadline for the swag bags.

"I'm screwed," Erica mumbled to herself. But she knew the lion's share of the blame rested squarely on her slim shoulders. Instead of using the trusted company she had done business with for years, she'd decided to give a new start-up a try. She figured that if the organizers of Tracy Reese's fashion show could give a virtual unknown like her a chance, it was only fitting that she return the favor for another young entrepreneur. Christopher, one of her employees, had highly recommended the graphic artist in question, and after meeting him,

Erica had felt confident that the young man could do the job. But instead of her generosity being rewarded, it looked as though she was going to end up with the short end of the stick. *No good deed goes unpunished,* she thought.

She was half listening and half checking her e-mails as the clerk called off a long list of names, directing the selected individuals to step into the hallway outside. This was the first step in deciding which lucky public citizens would receive the honor of serving as a juror at an upcoming trial.

"Stanford one-four-five," the diminutive woman called out in a large voice that didn't match her small frame.

The sound of Erica's last name jarred her from her phone, but her mouth didn't open and her feet didn't move.

"Stanford *one-four-five,* are you present?" the woman repeated, this time with slight annoyance.

"Damn," Erica whispered under her breath, realizing that the last name and accompanying numbers belonged to her. A small twinge of angst seized her stomach. She was hoping her luck would turn around and that she would be given at least one small victory this week, even if it was just the chance to avoid being selected to serve at a trial. After listening to Ashley talk about her court cases over the years, Erica knew how time-consuming a jury trial could be, and with a minicrisis brewing at work, she couldn't afford to be pulled away from her business.

Reluctantly, Erica opened her mouth and said, "Um, yes, I'm here."

Less than a minute later she walked out into the hallway, joining others as they trickled out of the room. Once everyone was assembled, Erica counted nearly sixty people, all standing in a neat, orderly row. *This is gonna be fun,* she thought as she planted her feet behind a cheery-looking older woman, who turned and offered her a warm smile. Erica gave the woman a cordial nod in return, a gesture that put her in a little bit of a better mood.

She was about to resume her task of responding to e-mails on her phone when her attention was snatched away without her permission. The only word and thought that came to her mind was *incredible.* He was simply incredible!

He was a stealth black panther, elegant and sleek. Then, on second thought, Erica decided that he was more like a Great Dane on two legs: bold, beautiful, and powerfully seductive.

At six foot two, he seemed to claim every ounce of air and space around him. His skin was smooth like crushed velvet and was the color of melted dark chocolate. His clean-shaven face and gleaming bald head only added to his intoxicating allure. As he walked toward the straight, obedient line in which Erica was standing, his eyes landed on hers, giving her a deep, penetrating stare.

She thought he had the kind of eyes that could move through your soul, learn all your secrets, and then make them his own. She couldn't hold his direct stare for long without feeling flushed, so she lowered her eyes and watched him carefully behind her own set of baby browns, willing herself not to give away what she was feeling at that moment—intense heat that chilled her to the bone.

Erica raised her phone closer in front of her face in an attempt to appear unaffected by his presence, but try as she might, she couldn't ignore the fact that the man drawing near was unlike any specimen she'd ever seen.

As the Great Dane came closer, she went out on a limb and attempted what she hoped would be a quick, innocent glance. She smiled, admiring his effortless stride and strong aura. His smooth cadence bore witness to a type of swagger that made everyone around him take notice that a *man* was coming their way.

A bright, warm sensation tickled Erica's skin as he walked past her. She thought he must have read her mind, because he smiled slightly as he headed toward the very back of the line. She wanted so badly to turn around and steal another glimpse of him, but she dared not make such a daring move.

Erica shifted her feet, resting her right one on the heel of her stylish crocodile stilettos. She was glad she had decided to wear a formfitting dress and sexy platform heels, which she affectionately called her Dorothy shoes. Whenever she wore them, they always led her down a road to good fortune, just like the character in the magical movie *The Wizard of Oz*. They brought her good luck, and on a day like today, she needed something good, maybe even great, to happen.

As she stood in line, not seeing, but feeling the Great Dane's eyes leveled on the back of her head, she thought for the first time in a long while that her luck just might be changing for the better.

"Please follow me," the clerk announced as she led the line into a large courtroom. "This is the beginning of the voir dire process," she explained. "The formal set of questions that you're about to be asked will determine whether you will be selected to serve as a juror on one of the court's upcoming cases."

Erica didn't pay much attention to the clerk's words. She knew the drill all too well because she'd heard Ashley describe the process in detail many times. The defense wanted people with a heart, the prosecution wanted people with an edge, and both sides wanted individuals who would side with their client. Erica had already made up her mind that she didn't want any part in the entire process.

After she settled into her chair in the room, she noticed that the Great Dane was now sitting just five seats down from her in the very same row. She was thankful for her keen peripheral vision, which allowed her to study him discreetly, without being noticed. She crossed her shapely legs and began her inspection, starting from the bottom and working her way up, beginning with his feet.

Now that she had the time and opportunity to appraise him, she noticed things that she had obviously overlooked when he'd strode past her only moments ago. She saw that he was wearing work boots, and that they looked as though they'd been put to use on a daily basis. And even though he was sitting down, she could tell that his faded jeans were a perfect fit, not too baggy or drooping off his butt, like the style a lot of men were wearing, a trend she despised. His solid blue long-sleeve shirt also had a most complimentary fit, as if it had been made especially for him. His attire was neat and clean, simple and basic. But since he was dressed so casually during the middle of business hours, it led her to believe that he was a working-class man, perhaps in a profession that called for him to use his hands, which she could see were large and rough looking.

Erica also noticed that he wasn't wearing a wedding band, which made her perk up. But what made her pause with skepticism was his bare wrist, which was a bad sign for her. She remembered the words her father had always told her. "Erica, a man who doesn't wear a watch has no sense of, or respect for, time. And if he has no respect for time, he obviously has no place to be and probably doesn't have a job, or if by chance he's employed, it's a job and position requiring no real level of responsibility."

Erica's father, Joseph Stanford, was CEO of Eastern Electric, the largest utility company in the D.C. metro area, serving nearly two million residents. He was a well-respected, powerful man with equally powerful friends in both the business and government sectors, and Erica clung to his words on most things as gospel, despite his personal foibles. He was a loving father, and just like her mother, he'd always been the rock she could lean on for support and solid advice.

But in this case she didn't want to make snap judgments, because, after all, her father was old school, and most people nowadays relied on their cell phones to keep up with time. And besides, she had learned long ago that just because a book cover painted a certain picture, the story inside could be very different once you turned the pages and read the words. But even with this knowledge, after seeing the Great Dane's blue-collar attire and lack of accompanying timepiece, she turned her full attention back to the court clerk.

One by one the defense and prosecuting attorneys called out the names of those who were free to go, relieving them of what everyone in the room seemed to be dreading, except the bubbly older woman who had first greeted Erica in line and was now sitting beside her. No one wanted jury duty!

"This is exciting," the plump, silver-haired lady said, leaning over as she whispered to Erica. "Think you'll get picked?"

"I sure hope not." Erica sighed.

"I've always wanted to serve on a jury trial but in all the years that I've been summonsed, I've never been chosen. I'm hoping this will be my lucky day," the woman said with enthusiasm.

Erica wondered if the kind old lady was a little bit off her rocker. She couldn't imagine why anyone would want to sit through hours of testimony every day, listening to people plead their case for the alleged crime they were accused of committing. But as she looked at the woman, Erica could see that she was sincere and seemingly stable. *Just a lonely old soul who needs something to fill her day,* Erica supposed.

"I retired ten years ago," the woman said. "I worked for the D.C. public schools for thirty-five years, and let me tell you, the stuff I saw people do. . . . Well, let's just say it should've been tried in a court of law." She chuckled and winked. "But I have to admit, I miss the excitement. I bet sitting on the jury of one of these cases will be full of drama! I sure do hope I get picked."

Erica smiled. "I have enough drama in my life, so I hope I get to leave." She glanced down at her lucky shoes and said to herself, "Feet, don't fail me now."

Two hours later Erica's dread became reality. "I can't believe I have to serve on a criminal jury trial," she said to Ashley, switching her phone from her right ear to her left as she descended the escalator, headed toward the courthouse exit.

"You make it sound like you just got sentenced to prison," Ashley said and laughed.

"Very funny, Ash. You know I don't want jury duty."

"It's not that bad. Hell, I'm in a courtroom all the time."

"Because you're a prosecutor. It's your job."

"True, but really, it's not that bad. You might even find it fascinating."

Erica shook her head. "I doubt it, especially with all the headaches I'm facing at the store."

"Since when did my bright, cheery best friend become such a pessimist?"

"Since problems started piling up by the shitload."

"What's wrong?" Ashley asked with concern.

"There're so many things I have to do in order to prepare for Fashion Week. It's three weeks away, and the graphic artist I hired still hasn't gotten the new design to me for Paradise."

"What? Oh, no, that's not good. Have you called him?"

"Yep, and I e-mailed him, too. As a matter of fact, I sent him a message this morning, right before I reported to court."

"I guess you're going to have to sue his ass. Fax over his contract and let me take a look at it. I'll get the ball rolling."

Erica was silent for a moment, wanting to kick herself. She'd been a business owner for five years, and in all that time she'd never entered into a service agreement without a signed contract. But after meeting

Pierre St. James, the quirky, kindhearted designer she'd hired in good faith, she had a great feeling about him and believed he'd do a fantastic job. Their lunch meeting had turned into a creative design session, with him capturing the concept of what she'd pictured in her mind. From there, it was pretty much a done deal—sans a formal contract, which she never got around to executing, and now wished she had.

"Erica, I know you signed a contract with that man, didn't you?"

"Um, I really messed up this one."

"Girl, you never do business without a contract. You want me to get involved?"

"Thanks, but that's okay. I talked to my dad about it the other day, and he's made a few phone calls for me. I also contacted the design firm I normally use, and they're going to get some samples to me early next week. I just hope it'll come in time. I'm up against the gun. Plus, one of my employees just quit, so I have to review applications and hire someone right away."

"Wow, I'm sorry to hear that."

"So you see why jury duty is the last thing I need right now."

"Well, just look at it like this. You're fulfilling your civic duty."

"Thanks. That makes me feel much better."

"Okay, hold up. I know work has you stressed the hell out, but you always handle everything in stride. This attitude isn't you, my friend. What's really going on?"

"Just tired, I guess," Erica said, taking a deep breath. "I haven't been sleeping well."

"Nightmares again?"

"Yeah."

"Oh, Erica. When did they start back?"

Erica tilted her head and sighed. "Just this week."

"You want to talk about it?"

Erica was temporarily distracted when she spotted the Great Dane in the distance. She eyed him as she stepped off the escalator just in time to see him walk out of the courthouse's massive glass doors.

She continued to study him as she moved closer, inspecting him from a spot-on angle. She admired his handsome face and smooth, blemish-free skin, which let her know he put time into grooming himself. His deep-set, sexy brown eyes were piercing as they stared straight ahead, and his full, tantalizing lips looked perfect for kissing. Erica found herself smiling as she took in his squared shoulders, which looked broad and strong. His sculpted chest and toned arms were visible through the cotton fabric of his shirt, grabbing her attention in a whole new way, drawing her eyes down to his jeans. She bit her lower lip, thinking that denim had never looked so good, and it made her want to see what was underneath the material.

Erica slowed her steps as she approached the glass door, realizing that he had come to a stop right outside the building. He was standing just a few feet away from her, talking on his phone as she approached. *Is that a flip phone?* she wondered as she peered closely. *Who uses those anymore?* She glanced back at her reflection in the glass door and quickly checked her profile, making sure she looked good—for him. *What am I doing?*

"Erica, are you there? Can you hear me?" Ashley asked.

"Um, yeah. I'm here."

"You sound like you could use a drink. Let's meet up at The Spot for happy hour."

Erica refocused her mind on her conversation with her friend. "You mean, *you* need a drink, 'cause you know I don't indulge," she said with a chuckle.

"Who you tellin'!" Ashley laughed. "There's a pomegranate martini up in there that's been calling my name since Monday."

"You and Jason aren't hanging out tonight?"

Ashley huffed deeply through the phone. "No, he's got to work late on a project for a pain-in-the-ass client who flew in from Las Vegas today."

"Oh, that's a bummer."

"Tell me about it. The guy thinks he can breeze into town and make everyone answer to his beck and call. But, hey, when you're a gazillionaire, I guess you can."

"You know what they say. Money talks."

"You got that right. So, you gonna hang with me tonight or what?"

"I don't know, Ash. I've got so much to do and—"

"You always have something to do. Forget about your worries for tonight, and hang with me. Let's meet there and then go to Vidalia for dinner."

Erica's mood immediately brightened. Vidalia, with its calming and elegant ambiance, was her favorite restaurant. Despite the fact that it had been the scene of Claude's ill-intentioned marriage proposal, Erica was a frequent patron whom some of the staff even knew by name.

"I have to admit that dinner does sound divine, and I haven't eaten a thing since this morning. But I need to stop by the boutique first. Then I'll meet you there."

"Okay, that works for me. See you in a few," Ashley said.

"Perfect."

Erica ended the call and walked to the edge of the curb, raising her arm to hail a taxi. She looked back quickly to get another glimpse of the Great Dane, but to her disappointment, he was gone. It was as if he had vanished in plain sight. With slightly dashed spirits, she settled into the backseat of the taxi and thought about her day. Even though she didn't want to serve on a trial she had to admit that Ashley was probably right. Jury duty wasn't going to be so bad, especially since the Great Dane had been selected to serve, too.

Erica paid the cabdriver and hopped out of the car in front of her boutique. No matter how many times she walked through its large mahogany and glass front door, she was in awe, and eternally thankful that her dreams had come true.

Six years ago, when she'd purchased the building, which had been in need of major repair, her vision for the two-thousand-square-foot structure had been grand, and she knew she needed to work hard to make it own up to its lavish name. After nine months of meticulous renovations, sleepless nights, threatening phone calls to contractors, and lots of prayer, Opulence was a premier boutique unlike any other in the area.

"Hey, kiddo. How's your day been going?" Cindy bellowed in her deep, Lauren Bacall–sounding voice as Erica walked inside.

"You don't even want to know," Erica answered, surveying the lush ambiance of her boutique store. She repositioned a jar of body oil on one of the shelves as she spoke. "I got selected to serve on a criminal trial."

"No!"

"Yes, and it starts Monday."

"You couldn't get out of it?"

"No, I even told them about the pressing matters with the store, but they weren't trying to hear it."

"Poor baby." Cindy frowned, shaking her head. "Well, better you than me."

"Yeah, I guess you're right," Erica agreed. She knew that Cindy's comment wasn't just something to say. It was the honest truth. At times, she felt a little sad when she looked at the thin, five-foot-two-inch, attractive but hard-faced woman, who, to her surprise, had become one of her most trusted friends. Cindy was one of those poor souls whose impartiality and belief in the general goodness of humanity had been beaten out of her over the years.

Cindy Bernstein was a conscientious store manager, a dedicated and loyal employee, and over the past five years that she'd been working for Erica, the sixty-year-old ex-socialite had become like family. She was also a woman who had been through many ups and downs since Leonard, her husband of two decades, committed suicide ten years ago.

Leonard Bernstein had been a prominent Wall Street stockbroker who took no prisoners. His shrewd business acumen had earned him a solid reputation in the financial industry, affording him and Cindy a life of luxury.

But things went sour when an FBI investigation into Leonard's independently owned and privately held firm proved fatal for his career. The government's findings exposed decades of his shady dealings, from insider trading to deep ties with organized crime. The scandal and financial ruin had been too much for him to handle, so he ended it all one night with the smooth taste of vintage sherry on his tongue and the steel barrel of a gun against his right temple.

Cindy was left brokenhearted. And to add insult to injury, Leonard's body hadn't even grown cold before his debtors came after his estate. Once the dust had settled, Cindy was left without a dime to her name. The social invitations to Manhattan's best parties stopped coming, and the requests for afternoon teas dried up. She was dropped from guest lists all over her Upper East Side stomping grounds, and the people whom she had mistaken for friends quickly retreated, no longer answering her phone calls. With no children and virtually no family to speak of, she stood exactly as she had before she met her husband—all alone.

Cindy spent the first five years after Leonard's death drifting from job to job, man to man, and bottle to bottle, all in her attempts to find her place in the world. At fifty-five years old, and with her status and connections gone and her good looks on the verge of following, she decided to leave New York City and head to Washington, D.C. She didn't know anyone there, but that was just fine with her, because she was looking for a place where she could make a fresh start.

After moving to D.C. she'd managed to carve out a new life for herself, and even though she didn't outwardly show it, and she would never confess it, she desperately wanted to trust, and even fall in love again. Thankfully, her job at Opulence and her unlikely friendship with Erica were the two things that gave her hope.

"This couldn't have come at a worse time." Erica sighed. "The judge said the trial could last for an entire week or longer."

"Who knows? Maybe it'll end early."

"Ha! With my luck it'll probably drag on into next month."

Cindy narrowed her small grayish blue eyes on Erica and shook her head. "Wow, kiddo. What happened to the optimistic, pie-in-the-sky person I work for? You sound like me, and we definitely can't have that!"

"You're not so bad." Erica winked and smiled. "I keep trying to convince you that you're just a big softy under all that heavy armor."

Cindy looked over at the neatly displayed body products on the shelf beside her but didn't say a word.

"You know I'm right," Erica persisted.

Cindy tucked a stray hair from her perfectly coiffed blond bob behind her ear as she sighed. "So, you said the trial starts Monday, huh?"

Erica knew her friend was uncomfortable with that truth, so she moved on and let the comment go. "Yeah, and I have to report to court at nine a.m."

"Like I said, better you than me."

Erica breathed out heavily, tension wrinkling her smooth forehead. "I have so much on my mind and so much to do."

"Have you heard from that flake that Christopher hooked you up

with?" Cindy asked, referring to the graphic designer who was causing Erica's stress.

"No, but I called our regular guy at Four Dimension Design, and
they're on the case. I just pray he can get something to me by early
next week. Otherwise, I'll have to use the jars we have in stock."

"That's not so bad. We've got some of the best packaging in the
industry. It's right up there with the little blue box," Cindy said en-
couragingly, referring to Tiffany & Co.'s signature trademark. "When
people see our royal purple jars, they know it's an Opulence product,
and that translates into quality and style."

"Yeah, but Paradise is in a category all its own. It's the best, most
luxurious body butter I've ever produced, and I need a design that's
just as fabulous," Erica said as she held up a bottle of shower gel.
"Don't forget, we're talking about the Tracy Reese show, the same
designer who dressed the First Lady of the United States. Everything's
got to be tight."

"Everything will be just fine."

"I've got to make it happen. I'd planned to meet Ashley for drinks
tonight, but on second thought, I think I need to stay here and get
some work done. Besides, I still have to look over applications so we
can fill Tara's position, since she up and left us high and dry."

"I've already started reviewing them, and I'll have my top picks
on your desk Monday afternoon, when you get out of court."

Erica nodded. "I might have to come in this Saturday to fill the
void."

Cindy walked over to where Erica stood. "I've already taken care
of the schedule, so that won't be necessary. I think you're just looking
for excuses to bury yourself in your work."

Just as Cindy had avoided Erica's earlier assessment, Erica was
now the one slipping into denial. She hated to admit that she was
purposely drowning herself in work, which she preferred to the
sobering reality she didn't want to face: that she was single, lonely, and
getting older by the day.

"Keep this up," Cindy warned, wagging her short index finger,
"and you're going to run yourself into the ground. You work nonstop
as it is. You need a break."

Erica shrugged. "I wish I could, but Fashion Week is right around the corner, and I've got to make sure we're ready for it."

"Don't worry about the fashion show. I've got you covered with that, too."

"Cindy, this is the single biggest event we've ever done. This show can take Opulence to an entirely new stratosphere!"

Through long days and even longer nights of blood, sweat, and tears, Erica had managed to turn what had started out as a small business in the basement of her home into the lush boutique she now owned in Georgetown, which was prime D.C. real estate.

Ever the business-savvy entrepreneur, Erica had called on the industry contacts she'd cultivated from her days as a beauty magazine editor to help her get started. She'd enlisted their aid to get Opulence featured in newspaper ads, radio commercials, and on hip and sophisticated blog sites that targeted a distinguished and discriminating clientele. That was how she had landed the opportunity to get her boutique's products placed in the swag bags for Tracy Reese's sold-out show.

Once fashion's who's who and Hollywood's hottest celebrities got a sampling of Paradise, Erica knew it would be the ticket that would put her business on the map.

"I know," Cindy replied, nodding. "But like I said, I've got you covered. The shipment of new products just arrived this morning, and as soon as Christopher gets here in another hour, we'll start sorting through everything. There's no need to worry. I'm on the case."

Erica thought about it for a moment. She knew that Cindy was capable, and she also knew that she needed to take a break from work, if just for tonight. So she decided to concede. "What would I do without you?" Erica smiled.

"Hell, I don't know . . . panic, bite your nails, probably lose your mind."

"Oh, you've got jokes!"

Cindy winked. "A few."

"Now that you've talked me away from the edge of the cliff, I guess I'll make a few phone calls and then head out to meet Ashley. You want to join us? We're going to The Spot, and I know you love their martinis."

"Can't. I've got to close."

Erica looked at her watch. "You've been here all day. Get Christopher to close. He and LaWan can handle the store tonight."

"LaWan called in sick."

"She did?"

"Yeah, and I could hardly believe it."

Erica immediately became concerned. LaWan was one of her best employees, and she couldn't remember a time when the young woman had missed a day of work. Much like Cindy, she was efficient and prompt, qualities that Erica prided herself in as well.

"I hope she's okay."

"She sounded really tired, not like herself at all. I told her to stay home and get some rest."

"Good. Christopher is still on the schedule, right?"

"Yes, but he can't close by himself. He gets flustered too easily. If a customer upsets him, he'll melt into a puddle of soft goo."

Erica shook her head, knowing that Cindy was right. Christopher was a senior at Georgetown University, majoring in English. He attended classes during the day and worked at Opulence in the evenings and on weekends. He was a great employee, but he didn't handle life's harshness well. Rude customers had been known to make him cry.

"Christopher needs me here for backup," Cindy said. "You know how demanding our snooty customers can be. The richer they are, the worse they act."

"I'm going to have a talk with him . . . again," Erica said, shaking her head. "He's got to man up. It's a hard world, and the sooner he learns how to handle it, the better off he'll be."

Again, Cindy didn't say a word. She simply looked at Erica and kept her thoughts to herself. She knew that after Erica's frustrating day at the courthouse, and her worries about the swag bags for the fashion show, the last thing she wanted to hear was that no amount of talking was going to change Christopher. Cindy knew this because life had taught her that people changed only when they were ready, not when you wanted them to be.

Chapter 4

"I'm *soooo* glad it's Friday," Ashley said, taking a sip of her pomegranate martini.

Erica nodded, raising her glass of ginger ale to her burgundy-colored lips. "Tell me about it. Technically, I shouldn't even be here right now, because I have so much work to do. But as everyone keeps telling me, a girl's got to have a life, right?"

"Absolutely. Especially since said girl's social calendar has bitten the dust."

"Please don't start."

"You know I'm right, Erica. I'm the only date you've had in months, and you look way too hot in that dress to be wasting it on me."

"Very funny."

"Actually, it isn't. It's a damn shame."

"Hey, I'd love to go out on a date, and I was just thinking about that this morning," Erica said, then sighed. "I never thought I'd say this, but right now I just don't have the time."

"Hell, make time!"

Erica twisted her round bottom atop her stiff bar stool. "Why? So I can be disappointed again?"

"You really shouldn't think that way."

"Oh, you're right, especially since my track record has been so stellar." Erica shook her head. "Let's see . . . my illustrious dating career began with a bed wetter and recently ended with an asshole, not to mention weirdos and commitment-phobic mama's boys sprinkled in between."

Ashley took a deep breath and rolled her eyes. "There will be no pity parties tonight. Just because you've kissed a few toads doesn't mean you won't find your Prince Charming. Hell, look at me," she said with a smile, leaning forward on her bar stool as she crossed her hands over her abundant cleavage. "Who would've thought that not only would a hell-raising bachelorette like me find a wonderful man, but that I'd actually be engaged to commit matrimony, of all things!"

Erica laughed at her vivacious friend. Ashley was the kind of woman whom one could describe as a pistol, fully loaded. She was a gutsy fighter who wore her five-foot-eleven-inch, size eighteen frame with unapologetic flair. Her hair and make-up were always meticulously styled, even when she was lounging around the house. She was sexy, bold, and superconfident, the latter attribute serving her well and earning her a reputation as one of the smartest and toughest prosecutors around.

She'd caught her new fiancé's eye during a law convention. He'd spied her in several sessions, and she'd smiled politely each time he said hello. On the last day of the convention, they'd both attended the closing party that evening. Ashley had been standing at the edge of the dance floor, swaying her voluptuous hips to the DJ's music, when he came up beside her. He held a beat, then took her hand in his and boldly led her to the dance floor. They'd been dancing together ever since.

"That's because you're finally allowing Jason to make an honest woman of you," Erica said as she smiled.

"I know! Can you believe it? I've officially turned in my playerette card."

"How does it feel?"

A wide smile slowly spread across Ashley's pretty face. "Freakin' fantastic!"

Erica was thrilled that after years of dating and dumping more men than she could count, her best friend had finally settled down and was now happier than she'd ever seen her.

Erica and Ashley had been friends since they met as neighbors at the tender age of seven. The two quickly became inseparable over games of pick-up sticks, hopscotch, and weekend sleepovers. They were like sisters born of different parents.

But unlike Erica, Ashley didn't hail from a family filled with generations of educated, well-to-do relatives who held elite membership in the black bourgeoisie. Her parents, George and Mamie Jackson, had started from very humble beginnings. They'd been a working-class couple, struggling to find a way to make ends meet and provide for their four children.

But the Jackson family's fortune changed one eventful evening, when George and Mamie sat in front of their small black-and-white television and watched as the numbers on the lottery ticket that Mamie held in her hand slowly tumbled across the screen one by one. They were the sole winners of a twenty-million-dollar jackpot.

The Jacksons moved from their cramped two-bedroom apartment in one of Washington, D.C.'s roughest neighborhoods into a large, seven-bedroom brick home in a gated community in the highly sought-after suburb of Prince George's County, Maryland—home to some of the wealthiest black families on the East Coast. Almost overnight Ashley was swept from a life of poverty to one filled with material abundance and nearly everything her young heart desired, all just two houses down from Erica.

"How are the wedding plans coming?" Erica asked, looking at the huge, brilliant-cut diamond ring on Ashley's finger.

"Girl, it's a certified hot mess."

"Oh, no!"

"Oh, yes! I love my folks, but I think we might end up falling out over this wedding. They still don't realize that I'm a grown woman who can make my own decisions."

Erica nodded. "Let me guess. They're trying to tell you who you can invite, what colors you should use, who should cater the reception, and—"

"Nope," Ashley said, taking a generous sip of her drink. "Try, *who* I should marry."

Although Ashley's family had come into money, had moved from the "hood," and had used their lottery winnings to build a successful hair salon empire—which always landed them a yearly mention in national magazines, like *Ebony, Essence,* and *Black Enterprise*—the entire Jackson clan, including Ashley, was a rough bunch. "We keep it real," her oldest brother, Russell, always said. Ashley held a law degree from Howard University and was highly respected in her field, but she could curse you out in five different languages while writing a legal brief using perfect English.

Her parents had taught her how to be kind, but tough. She was their youngest child, their only girl, and the only one of their four children who had graduated from college. And even though she didn't follow the path of her older brothers by joining the family's famed hair salon business, they beamed with pride at her accomplishments. But their pride had been laced with disappointment ever since she'd started dating Jason, her husband to be.

Jason Butterfield was a successful attorney and philanthropist. He'd started his own private practice a few years ago, specializing in providing financial legal services for a select client base. Born into a wealthy northern Virginia family right outside the D.C. beltway, the Butterfields were a clan who honored tradition and old-fashioned values. Jason had been taught by his father to walk the walk and talk the talk of a perfect Southern gentleman. He was kindhearted, generous, and had an easy way about him that could put even the most ardent curmudgeon at ease. His six-foot-three-inch, athletic build and boy-next-door good looks had made him quite the ladies' man in his day.

But after meeting and falling in love with Ashley, Jason had settled down and committed himself to her completely. Once they starting dating exclusively, the only women's numbers that could be found in his phone's contact list were those of either colleagues or relatives.

He was the kind of man who most parents would love their daughter to bring home. But not the Jacksons. From the moment they met Jason, they'd prayed that Ashley would come to her senses and find another suitor more aligned with her melanin. Jason was white, and they weren't having it.

Erica frowned, sucking on an ice cube from her glass. "I know that in the beginning your parents were a little tepid about you and Jason, but I can't believe they're still resistant."

"*Resistant* is putting it mildly. Try horrified."

"But the wedding is in less than six months."

"And?"

"But Jason's so sweet. He's the most caring and sincere guy you've ever dated."

"He's white, Erica."

"I know that, but—"

"But, nothing. You know how my family is. Backwards as hell."

Erica nodded. "I'm glad you said it and not me."

"Mama and Daddy are so old school, still stuck in that pre-integration mentality. And my brothers . . . girl, I don't even want to tell you the stupid-ass comment that Russell made the other day," Ashley huffed.

Erica could only imagine what had come out of Russell's mouth. She remembered that shortly after Ashley's engagement party he'd stated, quite matter-of-factly, that if his sister actually went through with marrying Jason, she'd be contributing to the downfall of the race. "She gettin' ready to marry the enemy," he'd said.

"Surely Ms. Mamie isn't still having problems with the fact that Jason's white?" Erica asked. "Your mother's one of the most understanding people I know."

Ashley smirked. "Yeah, she is, but not about this. For some reason she's in my father's camp. I love my family, but sometimes I wish I could trade them in for a more progressive model."

"Yeah, but just remember that when it comes down to it, family's all you've got."

"That's easy for you to say. Your parents support everything you do and every decision you've ever made, whether it's been right or wrong."

Erica nodded in agreement because Ashley was right. Joseph and Maureen Stanford were her two biggest cheerleaders, and even her brother, Nelson, always had her back. She couldn't remember a time when they weren't by her side, giving their unconditional support through every trouble or triumph she experienced. Her father always sent her flowers in celebration when things went well, and in encouragement when they didn't. All of them had been right there for her after she'd called off her engagement with Claude, reassuring her that if she felt that strongly about it, she'd done the right thing. She'd even received roses from Joseph the next day.

Thinking about how fortunate she was to have her family in her corner, Erica tried to offer up a few comforting words to her best friend. "I'm sure that by the time you and Jason walk down the aisle, they'll be on board. I mean, my goodness, they've got to see that you two are perfect for each other."

Ashley raised her glass to the bartender to signal for another drink. "I'm glad you think so, but as it stands, that's going to take a miracle. Daddy had the nerve to say I should just go ahead and stab him in the heart with a knife, because that's what me marrying Jason would be like."

"Stop lyin'! Mr. George did not say that!"

"Oh, yes, he did."

Erica put her hand to her mouth, completely stunned.

"Last night I went over to the house because I needed to talk to them about the guest list. You wanna know what he told me?"

"I'm almost afraid to ask, but go ahead and tell me," Erica replied, holding her breath.

"He said I might as well order a coffin for him along with my wedding cake."

Erica gasped as she swallowed an ice cube, whole. "I just don't understand. I mean, I know your folks are old school, and they came up during a time when things were a lot different than they are now. But, damn, they act like you're marrying a murderer or something."

"Tell me about it."

Erica looked at her beautiful, feisty friend, and for the first time she saw a hint of sadness rimming Ashley's wide-set eyes. She was shocked and appalled that the Jacksons were acting this way in the face of their daughter's obvious love for Jason, and his for her. Erica knew that if she was thrown for a loop, Ashley must be completely unsettled by her family's behavior. Then a thought occurred to her. She and Ashley were as close as Siamese twins and had shared their most intimate secrets. They were trusted sisters. So she wondered why Ashley was just now sharing this news with her.

Erica leaned in close and asked, "Why haven't you mentioned a word of this before now?"

Ashley took a quick sip of her second martini before she answered. "Well, honestly, I've been hoping they'd come to their senses. And frankly, it's downright embarrassing. I know my family has said and done some crazy shit over the years, but I never thought they'd act like this."

Erica gently put her hand on top of Ashley's. "Don't ever be embarrassed because of other people's shortcomings, especially your family's. I know things are difficult now, but trust me, it'll get better."

"You think so?"

"I know so, my friend."

"I hope you're right, because my folks are only half the battle. Jason's family is just as bad."

Erica wasn't surprised by this bit of information, especially after having met the Butterfields at Ashley and Jason's engagement party three months ago. She'd seen the way his family had interacted with cautious smiles and refrained celebration.

"Jason's family is old money," Ashley said, fiddling with her cocktail napkin. "Old Southern money at that, and I'm not blind to the fact that they don't want their youngest prodigy to marry a black woman."

"Have they said anything inappropriate to you?"

"Not yet. His father's really cool and very nice, but his mother?" Ashley rolled her eyes. "I know that woman is itching to say something. I can tell by the way she cuts her eyes at me from head to toe every time we're in the same room. She's probably wondering why Jason didn't pick a petite, blond, debutante-type white woman like her, instead of a tall, plus-size, big-boned black woman like me."

Erica squeezed Ashley's hand reassuringly. "Jason picked you because he loves you, and you're a beautiful, smart, loving woman, Ashley Jackson. His mother is lucky to have the good fortune of adding you as a daughter-in-law, and if she can't see that, it's her problem."

"Awww, thanks, sis. I really needed to hear that."

"Ash, it's the truth."

"This was supposed to be a fun night out, meant to cheer you up from all the stress you're going through with Opulence, plus the nightmares that have returned. And now look at me. I'm the one who's down in the dumps."

Erica wriggled off her bar stool and stood to her feet. "Like you said, no pity parties tonight. Let's go eat a good meal and enjoy ourselves."

Ashley slid off her bar stool, smoothing down the crease in her herringbone skirt. "Vidalia, here we come."

Erica smiled. "Now you're talking." She was ready to remove the tiny cloud that had tried to force itself over their evening, but little did she know that in less than thirty minutes, that tiny cloud would balloon into a full-blown storm.

Chapter 5

Erica and Ashley sipped from their glasses of sparkling water as they chatted and waited for their entrées to arrive. The soft lighting and elegant decor of the restaurant were just what Erica needed to calm her anxiety. After nightmares, work-related stress, an entire day spent at the courthouse, and then hearing her best friend's woes, she was more than ready to relax with a good meal. She was in mid-sentence when she noticed the smile on Ashley's face take a fatal nosedive.

"What's wrong?" Erica asked, but she didn't have to guess for long. As her eyes followed the direction of Ashley's death stare, the reason for her friend's shift in mood became glaringly clear.

"Are you gonna be able to handle this?" Ashley asked.

Erica sat ramrod straight against the back of her chair as she stared into the eyes of her ex-fiancé. Claude was walking into the restaurant, arm in arm with a woman who was grinning from ear to ear.

Even though they traveled in some of the same circles, this was only the second time that Erica had seen Claude since their breakup. A few weeks after their split she'd spied him walking down the aisles at a CVS store. He hadn't seen her, though, and she was glad, because she didn't know how a conversation with him might go. The last time they'd spoken, which was by phone, caustic words had been leveled from both their ends. Erica later found out that he'd told people he had no idea why she'd called off their engagement, leading them to believe he'd been wronged by her in some way.

Seeing Claude tonight, it was clear to her that he'd rebounded from his supposed hurt, not missing a beat. As she sat across from Ashley, drinking water in a candlelit restaurant, a part of her wished she was sipping champagne with a handsome man whom she could flaunt at her side.

Erica leaned forward in her chair as she watched the maître d' seat Claude and his date at a table just a stone's throw away.

"She's not even cute," Ashley smirked, sucking her teeth in exasperation.

"You don't think?" Erica asked, knowing that Ashley was right.

For months Erica had been preparing herself for the day that she would run into Claude, and in particular, when she'd run into him with another woman on his arm. She had fully expected any woman he was dating to be attractive, successful, stylish, and sophisticated. She knew those were the primary reasons he'd dated her. As she'd learned over time, Claude was all about the outside, instead of what really mattered on the inside.

But as she discreetly inspected her ex and his date, she had to retract her judgment. On a scale of physical beauty from one to ten, Erica estimated that the woman peaked around the five mark, and that was being gracious. She was middle-of-the-road average at best. Not unattractive, but definitely not a woman who made men's heads turn.

"See, why do they go from sugar to shit, caviar to hot dogs?" Ashley said.

Erica shrugged. "Maybe she's good to him."

"Yeah, good and ugly."

"Stop being mean. She might be a little plain, but she's not ugly."

"See, that's why I'm glad you're my best friend. You're so nice about every damn thing. Erica, you know that heffa ain't cute!"

Erica shook her head. "You need to stop."

"I know the kind of superficial, first-class asshole Claude is. But I'll give it to him. Even back in college, I never knew him to date a woman who wasn't a knockout. So since his date over there isn't beautiful, like you, I'm willing to bet you all the money in my wallet that she's filthy rich and well connected. Trust me, there's something in it for him," Ashley said with authority.

"Well, you do have a point. Claude was always concerned about status."

"Like I said, a superficial asshole."

Erica sat back in her chair as their server brought their food to the table. She tried not to look over in the direction of Claude and his date, but the more she tried to ignore them, the more her eyes strained to examine the couple.

From what she could see, they were very affectionate with each other, which surprised her. When she and Claude had dated, public displays of affection had been limited to him opening her door and pulling out her chair. He'd been averse to hand-holding and, God forbid, kissing or hugging too closely out in the open. That was one of the reasons why she'd been thrown off guard when she saw him walk in with his date's arm locked with his.

Ashley immediately dove into her veal porterhouse, but Erica didn't have time to take a bite of her seared sea scallops, because just as she lifted her fork, Claude rose from his table and came walking her way.

"I know he's not tryin' to come over here," Ashley hissed under her breath through a bite of veal.

Erica attempted to prepare herself, but it was too late. He was already there.

"I thought that was you," Claude said, grinning with his mega-watt Hollywood smile. "What a pleasant surprise to see you both this evening."

His words sounded sincere, but they were obviously untrue, because it was no secret that he loathed Ashley almost as much as she despised him. Erica wasn't surprised that he'd started off his greeting with a lie. It was yet another thing that she'd learned about Claude's MO—he wasn't a purveyor of truth.

"How are you, Claude?" Erica asked, speaking in the most cordial tone she could manage.

Ashley remained defiantly silent but did have the wherewithal to nod her greeting.

"I've been well," Claude responded, looking down into Erica's eyes. "You look great, by the way."

"Thank you, Claude. That's very kind of you to say."

"I always speak nothing but the truth."

Ashley gave him a slight roll of her eyes. "So, Claude, what have you been up to?"

Claude folded his arms in front of him and smiled. "You know me. Just keeping busy with work and a few other projects I've recently started."

"Is she one of them?" Erica asked, looking at Claude's date, who was fighting a losing battle of trying not to stare in their direction. Erica hated that she'd let her thoughts leap from her mouth before she could stop them. She didn't want to give Claude a sliver of a thought that she cared about his love life, although she had to admit, she was curious about the extent of his new relationship. And again, she wished that she was out with a handsome man instead of her gal pal.

Claude smiled slyly, tossing Erica a look that she couldn't quite decipher. "She happens to be a colleague—"

"Stop tryin' to front like you're out on a business dinner," Ashley said, cutting in. "That woman is staring at this table like we owe her money, so why don't you slide back over to your new girlfriend before somethin' jumps off up in here!"

Claude shook his head from side to side. "Ashley, I see you haven't changed a bit. Still your, um, *one-of-a-kind* self."

"Claude," Erica said, "it's okay that you're on a date. I hope you two enjoy your evening."

Claude cleared his throat, changing his smile from one of charm to one of seriousness. "Okay, for the record, yes, we're on a date. But she's also a colleague I'm working with on a new account. She's with Willkie Farr, and she just moved here to the D.C. office a couple months ago. Three, to be exact."

Erica knew that he'd thrown in the last bit of unnecessary information for two reasons. The first was to make it known that his date wasn't just a colleague. She was a colleague with the behemoth, globally recognized law firm Willkie Farr & Gallagher LLP, which was impressive on many levels. And secondly, he was making it clear that the woman had been in town only a short while, which meant he hadn't begun his new relationship until after his and Erica's breakup.

Neither Erica nor Ashley commented, and now Erica wanted her ex to go away, because Ashley was right. His date looked as if they owed her something and she was ready to come over and collect.

"Well, Claude, it was good seeing you." That was Erica's signal for him to move along.

"It was good seeing you, too," Claude said, this time making sure he excluded Ashley completely. "Enjoy the rest of your evening."

He hadn't taken more than two steps away from their table before Ashley started in. "Can you believe that bastard had the nerve to come over here and try to hit on you while his date is sitting over there all by herself, looking mad as hell?"

"You think he was trying to hit on me?"

"Uh, *yeah!* Don't you?"

Erica bit into a scallop and tried to regain her composure as she spoke. "No, I don't. I mean, we've been broken up for a while now."

"Yeah, it's been a minute."

"Today makes exactly six months."

Ashley stopped eating and sat her knife and fork to the side.

"What's wrong?" Erica asked.

"You've been counting the days on your calendar?"

Erica looked away, not wanting to admit that she had.

"Please tell me that you're over him. You're not seriously still into him, are you?"

Erica fidgeted with her napkin, admitting a painful truth. "As crazy and as pitiful as it sounds, I still think about him from time to time, especially when I get lonely. Well, maybe not him, but the idea of having somebody special in my life. He was my last somebody."

"And he was a complete nobody, too!"

"I don't want him back, that's for sure. I know that our relationship is a thing of the past."

Ashley was about to ask another question when her expression changed again. "What the hell?" she whispered in a low voice, narrowing her eyes as she looked across the room.

Erica looked toward the entrance of the restaurant's dining room to see Jason strolling in. Beside him was a striking blond-haired woman whose stylish comportment made her appear as though she'd just leapt from the pages of a magazine.

Erica and Ashley looked on with heightened curiosity as Jason and the pretty woman walked in their direction under the guidance of a hostess. Erica glanced at her friend's expression as she thought about their conversation earlier that day. According to what Ashley had told her, Jason was supposed to be working late tonight on an important project for a client who'd just flown into town, yet there he was, with a woman, and nothing about their appearance seemed business like.

As Erica scrutinized the two more closely, she made a biting observation that she hoped Ashley hadn't already drawn—that Jason and the mystery woman looked like a perfect couple, completely in sync. They were both attractive and slim, and they shared the same blond hair and green eyes. There was also a natural comfort between them that was obvious, which was affirmed by their relaxed body language and the engaging smiles they tossed back and forth between them.

As the two approached, Erica couldn't help but notice the mixture of excitement, surprise, and a bit of discomfort in Jason's eyes when he spotted them.

Lord, please don't let this turn into a scene, Erica silently prayed to herself. Given Ashley's temperament and history, she knew it wasn't far from the realm of possibility that her friend might show out, not bad enough to get arrested, but just enough to warrant them having to leave, and not under their own volition.

"Ash, be calm," she whispered.

"Hey!" Jason smiled as he and the woman walked over to Erica and Ashley's table. "I didn't know you and Erica were having dinner here. Your text said you two were going to The Spot tonight."

Ashley leaned forward and flipped her long black tresses off her shoulder as she formed her lips into a smile. "And your text said you'd be working late on a project for a new client," she said, giving her attention to the woman at her man's side.

Jason nodded. "Yes, and actually, I still am . . . sort of."

Erica shot Ashley a look that reiterated what she'd just said, "Be calm!"

"Where are my manners?" Jason smiled apologetically. "This is my client, Danni Stevens." He made a quick gesture toward the attractive woman. "And, Danni, this is my beautiful fiancée, Ashley Jackson, and her lovely friend Erica Stanford."

Erica wished she'd had her phone handy so she could snap a quick picture to capture what true shock really looked like. The expression on the woman's face made it clear that she was flabbergasted and had had no idea that Jason was engaged, let alone to a black woman. Erica knew this because she'd seen similar looks in the eyes of others—both black and white—when she'd been out with Ashley and Jason in the past and people had realized they were a couple. But even then, those observers had had the good sense to try to tame their real emotions, so as not to offend. But this woman seemed flat out stupefied. Erica also saw that Ashley had picked up on the same vibe, because she'd pursed her lips with a look of irritation.

"Danni and I just cleared up a major hurdle on her project," Jason continued, "and since neither of us has eaten, Danni suggested Vidalia."

"How nice!" the hostess said, oblivious to the tension beginning to rise. "Since you all know each other, would you like to dine together this evening? I can have two extra chairs brought out."

Jason looked at Danni. "Do you mind?"

Erica could see that the she devil's cold eyes said, "Hell, yeah, I mind!" But after she took a moment to gather herself, the manufactured smile she forced her lips to concoct made her mouth say, "That would be lovely."

Chapter 6

Erica, Ashley, Jason, and Danni sat around their small table, trying to stomach the uncomfortable conversation, which was limping and struggling along like a snail with one leg stuck in quicksand. To say the atmosphere was uncomfortable would be an understatement.

Erica could see by Jason's cautious facial expressions that he was keenly aware of the restive mood surrounding them, and for his part, he tried to break the ice by talking about the beautiful fall weather, the newest exhibit at the National Gallery of Art, and anything else he thought would be safe territory for a table of seemingly discontented women. She and Ashley were listening with cordial smiles when, from out of nowhere, Danni chimed in about her company. She apparently wanted to move on to more interesting subjects—such as herself.

She explained that her family's business, Sobelle Cosmetics, one of the largest and best known over-the-counter cosmetics companies in the country, was branching out into new territory, aiming its sights on hair care products. She'd been running the new products division for the last six months, and now she had enlisted Jason's services to assist in the negotiations of a top-secret merger with another cosmetics company of equal standing. If the deal went through, it would position Sobelle to compete with major brands like Pantene, Garnier, and L'Oréal.

"We've been keeping talks about the merger under a shroud of secrecy because of the proprietary sensitivity of the market. The hair care business is a very profitable slice of the pie," Danni said. "Men and women alike want to make sure their hair looks its best."

Ashley smiled and nodded. "Yes, I know all about the hair care business."

"Oh, really?" Danni said, seemingly startled as she zeroed in on the top of Ashley's head. "What do you know about hair care?"

Erica was taken aback by the flippant tone in which the she devil had asked the question—as if Ashley didn't and couldn't know anything about how to care for or manage her own hair. Erica also thought the comment came off as particularly rude, given that Ashley sported a long, shiny, healthy mane that was free of chemicals.

Unlike Erica, Ashley didn't relax her luxurious hair. Once a week she went to one of her family's salons for a nutrient-rich shampoo and penetrating deep conditioner, followed by a gentle blow-dry and a silky smooth flat-iron treatment. The result was nothing less than beautiful, shampoo commercial–worthy hair.

Ashley squinted her eyes and craned her neck. "My family owns several salons in the D.C. metro area. I've been immersed in the hair care business all my life," she said with a flip of her shiny hair. "So I know a thing or two about the business structure and the industry."

"Yes, Danni," Jason said, chiming in. "I haven't been able to discuss this, because of legal issues with our project, but now that it's out in the open, Ashley's family owns M&G Salons, the largest African American–owned hair salon chain in the area. I'm sure you heard of it while doing your market research," he said proudly.

Danni shrugged dismissively. "Can't say that I have. As Jason knows, we're primarily focused on major brands, and the black—um, excuse me—African American market isn't really on our radar."

"Well, it should be," Erica blurted out. She'd been trying to control her tongue, especially since Ashley had been exercising such amazingly disciplined restraint. But now she was pissed and couldn't hold back any longer. "We blacks, as you say, spend a fortune on our hair. Ignoring us is a great way to ensure that your new products division will experience very limited success . . . at best."

A big gray cloud rumbled over the table after Erica's pronouncement. Everyone looked disturbed except Danni, who continued to
smile as if the sun was shining bright.

"So," Ashley said, moving the conversation in a different direction, "Jason tells me that you're from Vegas."

"Yes, born and bred," Danni responded, never dropping her
painted-on smile. "But my Southern accent is compliments of my
parents' upbringing in Tennessee, and the fact that I spent all my sum-
mers there when I was growing up. I love the South. It's so . . .
charming. Everybody knows their place."

Erica nearly yelled out when she felt Ashley's foot kick hers
under the table. She knew that Ashley hadn't raised the roof of the
building only because of Jason. Even though the she devil was a bitch,
she was still Jason's client, and a wealthy one at that.

"I guess so, but I wouldn't know a thing about that," Ashley
quipped. "How do you like D.C.?"

Danni took a deep breath as she picked over her salad, which
she'd barely touched. "Unfortunately, I haven't seen much of the city.
Jason and I have been locked away in his office all day . . . working, of
course." She said the last part with a sly grin as she half winked at
Jason.

Erica's eyes grew big with indignation, but Ashley didn't flinch.
Instead she simply asked, "This isn't your first visit to our fair city,
is it?"

"Well, no, it isn't. But sadly, and I'm ashamed to say, my last trip to
D.C. was when my parents brought me here as a small child. I've traveled all around the world, from Austria to Hong Kong, but I've yet to
fully explore the beautiful capital of our great country. I'm going to
make sure I change that," she said, smiling again at Jason.

Erica was surprised that Ashley had continued to remain so calm
for so long. From the moment the she devil's behind hit the seat of
her chair, she'd been tossing out flirtatious innuendos, boasting about
her wealth, and glaring incredulously in Ashley's direction, all while
managing to throw out not-so-well-disguised insults.

Erica knew it was only a matter of time before Ashley put the
woman in her place. She just hoped it wouldn't involve high decibels
or, at this point, a police siren.

"Really?" Ashley said, without a trace of a smile. "For someone who hasn't dined in D.C. since she was in ponytails, you picked an excellent restaurant for the evening. Jason did say that it was your idea to come here, right?" she asked, keeping her eyes leveled on Danni's.

Bingo! Erica shouted in her head. She knew that Ashley's prosecutorial skills were in full effect.

Danni held Ashley's stare, looking at her with a cold gaze. "Actually, the concierge at my hotel suggested this place. But quite frankly, I've had better. As you can see, I've barely touched my salad." She smiled and cleared her throat. "But I see you must love it here. Your plate is nearly clean, and you're obviously not missing any meals."

Oh, no, the hell she didn't! Erica's inner voice screamed.

In a restaurant full of clanking dishes and noisy chatter, a blanket of stillness spread across their table. No one reached for their glass, used their fork, or made a move. Erica was so angry at the way the woman had blatantly disrespected her friend that she was ready to speak up again. But she knew she needed to let Ashley handle her own business. And as if on cue, Ashley leaned forward and pointed her well-manicured index finger in the she devil's direction. She was about to unleash her fury when Jason reached for her hand and gently guided it back to her lap.

"Danni, you're finished with your meal?" Jason asked in a voice as calm as still water.

Ashley cut Jason a look but held her tongue.

"Yes, I guess I am. Like I said, this just isn't my cup of tea. But maybe dessert will be better."

Jason shook his head. "Perhaps you'll find a more suitable selection on the dessert menu at your hotel. I'll walk you to the front so they can get you a cab."

The she devil looked confused. "I don't understand."

"It's obvious an uncomfortable situation is brewing, and before anyone says anything to cause further insult, I think it's best that you leave."

"But, Jason, it's just friendly banter between us girls."

"Girls?" Ashley quipped. "I haven't been a girl since I was ten."

"Okay," Jason said, motioning toward Danni. "Let's go. I'll make sure they get a cab out front."

The she devil looked down at her lap and ran her slender hand over her linen napkin before placing it on the table. Slowly, she gave Ashley what looked like an apologetic nod. "Ashley, I'm sorry if I made this an *uncomfortable situation,* as Jason said. Please forgive me. I guess I'm just a little jet-lagged and tired. I hope you can still find a way to enjoy what's left of your evening." And with that she rose from the table, clutching her Hermès bag as Jason led her to the front of the restaurant.

Erica and Ashley sat in silence for a moment before Erica finally spoke. "I'm almost at a loss for words. I've never experienced any foolishness quite like this. But I have to give it to you, you were the epitome of calm and cool. I'm proud of you."

Ashley didn't say a word. She simply nodded.

"I know you're pissed, but Jason handled it. Girl, your man stepped up to the plate and took care of that arrogant heifer."

Again, Ashley nodded silently.

"Say something, Ash."

Ashley sat back in her chair and stared straight ahead. "This is the shit my mother was talking about. It's exactly what she told me I'll have to put up with for as long as Jason and I are together."

"What do mean?"

"That woman," Ashley said. "She looked at me and all she saw was a plus-size, copper-colored black woman, who, in her mind, has no business being with a man like Jason. A man who she obviously thinks should be with her."

"Well, she's not and you are, so that's that."

"She's not alone in her opinion."

"That's some bullshit," Erica hissed.

"No, my friend, that's some real shit I'm talkin', and you know it."

"Who cares what that woman thinks? I know Jason doesn't, 'cause he just walked her out of here and he's putting her in a cab as we speak. And guess what? Once she's on her way back to her hotel, he's coming back in here to be with you."

"This isn't the first time something like this has happened. It's just the first time someone's been bold enough to clown me to my face." Ashley took a deep breath and sighed heavily. "It doesn't matter that I graduated number one in my law school class, or that I just received the D.C. Young Woman of the Year Award, or that I have a great sense of humor, or that I'm loyal to my friends, or that I'm a good person. All they see is my size and my skin tone, and then they wonder why Jason is with the plump niggress."

If the she devil had been stunned earlier, Erica was bewildered now. From the first day she met Ashley, she'd admired her friend's gutsy confidence. She was what people called big and beautiful, brainy and brazen, sexy and saucy, and she wore every inch of who she was with pride. Her deep copper-colored skin was luminous, and her full lips added softness to her face. She'd been known to literally make brothahs pause in mid-sentence when she walked by, strutting her forty-six-inch hips like a kite gliding in the wind.

George and Mamie had taught Ashley to be confident and self-aware. But looking at the beautiful, buxom bombshell, Erica could see that her friend's resolve had been tested tonight, and she was on the brink of defeat.

"Ash, c'mon. I know you're not letting what people think affect you. Especially not that ill-mannered Jezebel."

Ashley shook her head and chuckled. "Jezebel? Girl, please, that woman is a bitch. One hundred percent through and through."

"Yes, she is, and that's exactly why you don't need to let anything she said upset you."

Ashley sat quietly, with a faraway expression, retreating into silence again.

"Ashley Jackson, I can't believe you're letting this get to you."

"You're not on the receiving end of the kinds of looks I've gotten over the past year, since I've been dating Jason. You don't see the expression in people's eyes that spells out the snide comments they don't have the guts to say."

"I've seen the reactions when I've been out with you two, but you're right. I haven't personally experienced the things you have. But I also haven't experienced what it feels like to have a good man like Jason who loves me unconditionally, and who could care less about any of that nonsense."

Erica looked over to where Claude and his date were sitting, and she could see that his attention was aimed in her direction. She shook her head. "When Claude and I were together, we looked great on the outside, a perfect match from head to toe. But we were paper thin where it counted. So trust me, my friend. I may not have had your experience, but what you've got is so much more than you realize."

"But, Erica . . ."

"I wake up in an empty bed every single morning, and I end my day the very same way every night. I'd trade foolish looks for real love any day of the week."

Ashley nodded. "It's just hard sometimes. I mean, this isn't the freakin' eighteen hundreds. When is the madness going to end?"

Erica reached over and put her hand atop Ashley's. "I know what you're saying, and I'm not going to sit here and try to minimize your hurt, because what you're feeling is real. I just want you to see what you have, and believe me, what you have in your hand far outweighs anything in the distance."

Ashley smiled. "You're right. This is the second time tonight that you've thrown me a lifeline," Ashley said.

Just then, Jason returned to the table. "That's what I like to see! My beautiful wife-to-be with a smile on her face." He took Ashley's hand in his. "I'm so sorry about my client's behavior." He looked over at Erica and then back at Ashley. "Her attitude and comments were completely unacceptable, and I told her so when we were waiting for her cab."

"What did she say?" Ashley asked.

Jason paused for what seemed like a long moment before responding. "Nothing, really. She just kept apologizing. But enough about her. Do you ladies want to order dessert?"

Ashley shook her head. "None for me."

Although Erica wanted to order the caramel layer cake so badly she could practically taste the brown-sugar treat on her tongue, she refrained. After the night they'd had, she knew that Ashley and Jason needed to leave so they could talk in private. Plus, she could see that Jason's expression had changed from one of comfort to one of anxiety after Ashley asked him about the she devil's response.

A few moments later they stood outside the restaurant's front entrance as Erica gave Ashley and Jason a hug good night. She turned down their offer to drop her off at home and instead slipped into the back of the cab that Jason had hailed for her.

As the cab pulled away from the curb, Erica looked out the window at Ashley and Jason. They were walking away in the distance, holding hands. Ashley's head was leaned tenderly against the side of Jason's shoulder as they headed to the parking garage. Erica smiled, knowing that no matter what anyone said, the two lovers were a perfect match for each other.

"I hope Ashley realizes what she's got," Erica whispered to herself as she relaxed her legs across the backseat, preparing to go home, alone.

Chapter 7

Jerome removed his dark sunglasses from his face and stretched his lean, muscular body as he surveyed the bright sky above. The sun was beaming, and the clouds looked like giant puffs of cotton that he could reach out and touch. Working outside was always iffy, so he was grateful that Mother Nature had agreed to go along with the forecast that the local weatherperson had issued.

"Can't ask for a better day than this," Jerome said aloud. A small trickle of sweat traveled down the side of his chiseled face as he wiped his brow and inhaled a cleansing breath of fresh air. He smiled slightly, thinking about her, the woman in red, who'd been on his mind since yesterday. He couldn't shake the vision of her or the sweet smell of her skin when he passed her in the hallway at the courthouse. Even though the work he was now doing required his total concentration, he was stuck because every little thing reminded him of her beauty and elegance.

As he stood atop the roof of the house on which he'd been working since shortly after the sun rose, Jerome turned his attention to the large plot of land below. *This is the kind of crib I'm gonna have one day,* he thought, gulping the last drop of water from his bottle. *I bet she lives in a place just like this.*

Jerome looked out over the home's expansive backyard, with its custom-built deck, gourmet outdoor kitchen, and beautifully landscaped stone and marble walkway. The mosaic tile pool had been drained and covered in preparation for the fall days just ahead. As he scanned the rest of the street, admiring the mammoth-size houses sitting on majestic green lots, he wondered about the lives of the people residing inside them. What did they do for a living? What kinds of vacations did they take? What kinds of vehicles rested behind the doors of their four-car garages, and how had they come into their wealth?

Jerome almost laughed at his inquisitive thoughts, because there was a time when he didn't give a damn about what other people had or did. But now his life and its trajectory were both on a very different path. He was a man on a mission.

"I better stop daydreaming and finish laying these shingles," he said aloud. "I need to knock this out so I can get on up outta here."

Normally, as with most every weekend, Jerome wouldn't have minded working first thing on a Saturday morning or even late into the evening, but today was different. Today was his son, Jamel's, thirteenth birthday, ushering his only child into young manhood.

Jerome had originally planned to spend the entire day hanging out with Jamel. Fresh haircuts at the barbershop, followed by breakfast at IHOP, and then a quick game of pick-up basketball before ending the day at the party that Kelisha—his ex-girlfriend and Jamel's mother—was throwing for him at a neighborhood community center later that afternoon. That was how Jerome had planned to spend his Saturday. But instead he was working on a last-minute home repair project.

He'd heard the slight disappointment in Jamel's voice when he called to tell his son that he had to work and would be able to spend time with him only at his birthday party. "We'll hang together all day Sunday, okay?" Jerome had told him, offering the small consolation.

He knew that Jamel understood, because that was the kind of easygoing kid he was, but he hated letting his son down and not keeping his word. "A man's word is his bond," he'd always told Jamel.

Jerome wanted to instill a sense of responsibility and honor in his son, and he wanted to do it by setting the example. But when the opportunity for extra work came along, he felt he had to take it, especially since this particular job was so important to Jamel's future. The small last-minute home repair project Jerome was working on this morning was going to pay off in big ways.

A client for whom he'd done a spectacular kitchen remodeling job had referred him to the current client on whose roof he now stood, and this new client just happened to be a commercial real estate developer with considerable wealth and influence, and a big name in the building trade. Jerome knew that this powerful man could lead him to more business, and in particular, to large-scale projects that would put him on the road to achieving his goal of owning his own business.

He wanted to quit the city government job he'd held in the Department of Public Works for the past ten years so he could start his own contracting company. Picking up and hauling trash paid the bills and afforded him a modest living, but more important, it provided him with good benefits and reliable health care for his son. Jerome felt as though he was dying a slow death every morning he had to report in to work at the crack of dawn, handling the discarded remnants of other people's lives until his shift ended in the early afternoon. But when he picked up his tool belt, hammered a nail, laid a brick, or repaired something that was broken, he felt complete satisfaction.

Jerome loved working with his hands, and in many ways his talent made him feel like an artist, building and creating just about anything he envisioned. It was a gift he'd been blessed with since he was a little boy, putting together model airplanes and boxcars, and repairing things around the broken-down apartment he shared with his mother and older sister. But it was a talent that he'd ignored in favor of the streets, and now he hated that he'd wasted so much time on the wrong things.

And again, that was why this job was so important. He knew he was fortunate to have gotten this referral, and he planned to make the most of it. When he was just a young teenager, he'd learned how important it was to know the right people. But what he'd only recently discovered was that it was what those right people knew about you that really mattered. And for his part, Jerome made sure his work reputation was nothing less than stellar.

But it hadn't always been that way. His name had once been associated with wrongdoing, illegal activity, and street violence. It had been hard for him to remove that stain, and in some circles it still remained. But he'd vanquished that old life years ago, and the people and places that occupied his world today were very different. That was how he'd ended up where he was at the moment, laying twelve-by-thirty-six-inch shingles atop a roof, which was going to lead him to more business than he could handle.

One referral leads to another, was his steadfast motto, and it was how he'd managed to grow his home repair business over the past two years.

Jerome wanted his son to have more opportunities than he'd had growing up, and he was determined to provide Jamel with the financial and emotional resources he'd never received from his own father growing up. So if it meant sacrificing a few hours of his time today, he would gladly do it.

Jerome smiled to himself as he envisioned his future, one that until ten years ago he wouldn't have thought possible.

Jerome Kimbrough was a man of many talents and dreams, and equally as many hardships. He was born and raised in southeast Washington, D.C.—the wrong side of the tracks—in one of the city's most notorious housing projects, nicknamed The Hole, because once you lived there, getting out was like trying to climb out of a bottomless pit. Each day spent in his neighborhood was a test of one's will. Living was a game of survival for every resident, young and old, weak or strong, shiftless or determined. One had to be on the lookout for trouble at all times, because one was either avoiding it or in the middle of it. Jerome usually found himself mixed up in the latter.

By the time he'd turned nine, he was skilled at shooting craps and was an aficionado at three-card monte. When he reached his son's age, he'd graduated to running drugs for the neighborhood dealer, before moving on to selling on his own. His mother had worried day and night about his safety, hoping he wouldn't succumb to the deadly streets. Mabel Kimbrough had been the only person in Jerome's life besides his sister, Clarice, who he felt truly cared about what happened to him.

But despite his mother's prayers for him to clean up his act, and his desire not to disappoint her, the streets and their dangerous allure had held Jerome in their grasp. His father had been largely absent from his life until just a few years ago, so he'd never had a male figure to look up to. The only role model he'd had was the neighborhood pusher, who'd steered him to the way of wrong. So he continued on a course leading to certain disaster.

The death of his sister, the birth of his son, and the promise he made to his mother a few years later were the events that had finally changed him. It had been a rainy Wednesday afternoon, and Jerome was supposed to pick up his then three-year-old son from day care. But instead, he was at a buddy's house, smoking a joint, trying to erase the pain of losing his sister to cancer just one month earlier. Because he was nowhere to be found, his mother had to shoulder the responsibility of picking up Jamel. On their way back home a truck slammed into them on the slick road, spinning grandmother and grandchild head-on into oncoming traffic.

By the time Jerome arrived at the hospital later that evening, blurry eyed and with alcohol on his breath, his son had just finished getting the cut on his right leg stitched, and his mother was coming out of emergency surgery.

That night, after sobering up on weak-tasting hospital coffee, he stood over the bed where his mother lay with tubes leading to her nose, mouth, and arms, and made a promise to get his life together. Ever since that day he'd been faithful to his word.

Every now and then when Jerome looked back on the things he'd done over the years, he wished he'd made different choices in his life. He knew if he had, he wouldn't be so far behind today. But he also realized that life was about the slow and steady race, not the quick and easy finish. Quick and easy had led him down dark alleys and into unseemly situations with unsavory characters. But taking things slow and steady had pulled him up from a life that was heading nowhere and had put him on a path that, he now knew, was full of infinite possibilities.

He was excited about what his future held, about the new people he was destined to meet, the faraway places he planned to travel to, and the exciting things he was going to learn. As he thought about a world teeming with new experiences, his mind once again took him back to yesterday, and to the woman in red who had mesmerized him at first sight. He hadn't wanted to serve on jury duty, but after encountering her, a pack of wild dogs couldn't keep him from being the first one at the courthouse Monday morning. She was part of what he envisioned in his new world of possibilities, and he was anxious to see where it would lead.

Several hours later it was early afternoon, and Jerome had just re-placed the last shingle on the roof. He was glad that he'd finished so quickly, but more important, he was pleased with the job he'd done. He prided himself on the detailed craftsmanship of his work, and he knew his clients would be impressed.

Jerome reached in his pocket and pulled out a small tin of cinnamon-flavored Altoids. He popped one in his mouth and then walked across the roof to double-check that he hadn't missed anything. After surveying his work one last time, he packed up his equipment and carefully made his way down the extension ladder, descending to the ground. But once his size thirteen Timberlands hit the grass, he was startled to see the lady of the house standing just a few feet away from where he'd landed.

He was normally very observant about his surroundings—the streets had trained him to be—but he hadn't seen her on his way down, and it seemed as though she'd popped up from out of nowhere. He hoped she wasn't going to bombard him with a million questions about the work he'd performed, or ask to climb the ladder to inspect it for herself. He was used to overbearing clients and knew exactly how to handle them with his calm and relaxed manner. But today he didn't have the time or patience for it, because he needed to hit the road so he could go home and change clothes before heading to Jamel's birthday party.

He was prepared to tell the woman that if she wanted to view his work, she and her husband could easily gain access to the roof through their skylight. But he didn't have to say a word, because her lips held a smile, rather than the inquisition he'd expected. He was about to return her friendly gesture, but then he quickly stopped himself. Apprehension spread through his mind when he noticed the gleam in her eye and her outstretched hand holding an ice-cold glass of lemonade.

"I thought you might be thirsty after being on the roof all day," the woman said with a come-hither smile.

Jerome recognized trouble when he saw it, and he knew that the woman standing in front of him, holding the refreshing beverage, was danger and drama all mixed up into one deadly concoction. Her husband had left shortly after Jerome had arrived, so he knew she was home alone, which put him on alert. He immediately felt uneasy and looked around to see who else was within eye- or earshot, just in case he needed witnesses if something funky went down.

He'd seen the woman watching him when he came over to inspect the roof and do a repair estimate a few days ago, and then again when he first arrived this morning. But both times she had stayed in the background, letting her husband run the show and give direction. But now that she was all alone, she'd decided to come out and play. Jerome knew he had to proceed with extreme caution.

"It's not freshly squeezed," she said, "but it's all-natural, organic." This time she licked her thin, pink-colored lips as she made the offer.

"That's very hospitable of you, but no thank you," Jerome responded. "I was just about to let you know that I'm finished repairing your roof. Your husband said the check would be ready when I'm done." He chose his words carefully, and spoke without a smile or any gesture of nicety, because he didn't want to engage the desperate housewife beyond what was strictly business.

The coy look that she aimed at him confirmed what he suspected. *Damn,* he said to himself. She was bolder than he'd thought, and he didn't like it.

Jerome had encountered her type before: lonely suburban housewives who saw him as fresh eye candy they could have a little fun with on the side. He watched her eyes as they traveled over his smooth face, roamed across his broad chest, swirled around his bulging biceps, and ventured down to his slim waist, before finally resting on an even lower region, which she had no chance of reaching.

She was attractive, he would give her that, and he could see by the way her knee-length skirt and cotton shirt fit that she was in good physical shape. But as much as her body belied her age, the subtle streaks of gray in her stylish strawberry blond hair, the tiny crow's-feet that flanked the sides of her blue eyes, and the faint age spots dotting the tiny hand holding the lemonade were all telltale signs that she'd been intimate with Father Time. Jerome also knew that not only did she have a little age on her, but she also had a lot of experience under her belt as a woman who was used to getting what she wanted.

"You sure you don't want to taste just one sip? I promise it'll be the best you've ever had," she purred seductively.

Jerome shook his head. "I'm good. All I need is my check."

The woman pouted her thin lips. "Oh, come on. Just take a little sip. I know you've got to be thirsty."

Jerome was always cool under pressure, but the brazen woman was starting to make him lose patience. He didn't like the game she was playing, so he decided to end it right then and there. "I know your husband left a few hours ago. Should I call him to get my payment? Because I really need to get going." He reached for his phone and pulled it out of its leather holster.

The woman frowned and quickly changed her approach. "He left it with me. Why don't you come inside and I'll get it for you."

Jerome followed her up to the back door, but once she opened it, he didn't go any farther. "I'll wait out here."

He could tell that she was becoming frustrated, and that she wanted him to give in to her demands.

"You're perfectly welcome to come inside," she said with a cunning smile. She paused, leaned against the doorjamb, and eyed him. "As a matter of fact, there's some other work I'd like you to do for me. A few things that need fixing with a personal touch," she said and had the nerve to wink as she gave him a seductive smile. "I think you know what I mean and what I want. And don't worry. What you and I do will be our little secret."

Jerome wanted to tell her that there was no way in hell they'd be sharing any kind of secret, and that he was completely uninterested. But again, he knew he had to handle this situation with a calm, level head. "Like I said, I'll wait out here. If you'd like me to do additional work for you *and* your husband, I'll be happy to come by at another time, take a look around, and then give you an estimate."

The woman pursed her lips, threw her head back, and chuckled. "Well, I guess I'll go and get that check now."

Chapter 8

Jerome was in his truck, headed back to his apartment with a nice-size check in his wallet. He was tired but happy because he had finished the job early and would have enough time to shower and take a quick nap before going over to Jamel's birthday party.

He turned up the volume on the radio and sang along with Al Green's "Let's Stay Together." He knew he'd just been very lucky, dodging a deadly bullet in the form of a wealthy housewife with an appetite for trouble. She wasn't the first woman he'd worked for who had come on to him, and he knew she wouldn't be the last. Jerome hoped he wouldn't have to deal with her again, but he had a feeling she'd soon be ringing his phone with another request for work. She was just that bold. "Son of a bitch," he said aloud. "I'm not gonna let her trip me up into some bullshit."

Women had been both a source of strength and weakness in Jerome's life. There were many times he could point to when women had been at the center of some of his greatest highs and scariest lows. From the wonder of his son being born, to the deranged lover turned stalker who'd left him in the hospital with a near-fatal bullet wound, women had played a major role in his past and present. And although he was currently unattached and was not seeing anyone at the moment, he was ready for that situation to change.

He chuckled to himself, thinking about life's irony. At thirty-five years old, he was finally ready to settle down in a serious relationship, yet he was alone. Even though the state of his love life was by choice and no other reason, he longed for someone special who could walk with him on his new journey. He wanted a soldier by his side. A ride-or-die partner who had his back. A woman whom he could grow with and share life's sweet experiences.

Part of the example Jerome wanted to set for Jamel, in addition to being a man of his word, was to show him what a healthy, loving relationship between a man and a woman looked like. Jerome had never seen that growing up, and he knew that if he had, he would have probably been a better boyfriend to the many women he'd dated. He didn't want drama or dysfunction in his life, because he'd had enough of that with Kelisha. Their up-and-down relationship had been plagued by strife and doom from the very beginning.

Kelisha was a hotheaded, badass, round-the-way girl who popped off at the mouth without the least bit of provocation or care. Usually opposites attracted, and many times worked to balance people out, but Kelisha's loud mouth and fiery temperament had never jived with Jerome's cool, calm demeanor.

But Jerome had to acknowledge that he'd played a big part in his and Kelisha's troubled relationship. He had been unfaithful more than a few times, and he'd continued to run the streets with his boys, despite the fact that just like his mother, Kelisha had begged him not to.

He'd done many things he wasn't proud of, but he had few regrets because he knew all his decisions and their outcomes had led him to his present state, a place he was learning to appreciate more and more each day. He was ready to experience so many things, and he wanted a good woman in his life to share them with.

As Jerome thought about his ideal partner, his ride-or-die soldier, his mind returned to the woman in red. Stanford 145 was imprinted on his brain. He remembered every sensual inch of her, and especially her scent, which was soft and bold at the same time. Never had a woman impacted him so completely without even a simple hello. He didn't know her full name, where she was from, where she lived, how old she was, or even if she had a man. All he knew was that she'd made him want Monday morning to skip past Sunday so he could see her again.

"Damn, she was fine!" he said out loud, his mind taking him back to yesterday.

Being summoned for jury duty was something he had been dreading. Like most black males he knew, Jerome had a serious aversion to police officers and white men in black robes sitting in courtrooms. But when the juror notification came in the mail, he couldn't ignore it—by law.

Missing a day of work from his job of picking up smelly trash and hauling away overstuffed super cans had actually been a welcome reprieve for him. But he hadn't wanted to be stuck at court all day, either, and he'd hoped they would release him early so he could finish up a repair job for another client.

Jerome had shown up at D.C. Superior Court a half hour later than the 8:00 a.m. printed time on his summons. Being prompt wasn't one of his strong suits, and it was one of the shortcomings he was working to erase. He'd been sitting in the back of the room, bored out of his mind, when a woman spoke up, answering the court clerk's roll call. She had instantly grabbed his attention and hadn't let go. Her sweet-sounding voice and the confidence in her tone had held him in a state of intrigue.

Even though her back was facing him, Jerome knew by her crisp diction, erect posture, and sophisticated hairstyle that she was a woman of class and distinction. He wanted her to turn to the side so he could at least see her profile, but she didn't budge an inch. She simply bent her head down, concentrating on whatever she appeared to be reading in front of her.

His name had already been called, so he knew he'd get a chance to see her once the clerk finished the list, because they'd all have to step outside. He was prepared to wait patiently, but to his surprise and relief, he didn't have to. Less than thirty seconds after the thought had crossed his mind, the woman in red stood up and blew him away. He thought she was nothing less than stunning.

Jerome quickly studied her, taking in everything from the rise of her perky breasts peeking out beneath the base of her V-cut neckline, to the gentle curve of her round ass and full hips, which hugged the delicate material of her dress. He could tell she was above average in height, even without the sexy high heels she sported as she breezed by the aisle where he sat. He inhaled her sensual smell, which awakened his senses.

He watched her closely as she walked toward the back of the room, making her way outside. Her graceful stride was seductive, and her femininity appealed to his manhood. He knew she was a self-assured woman, given the fact that she'd chosen to wear a sexy bright red dress to a place as drab, conservative, and uninviting as a courthouse. That simple act let him know that she wasn't one to conform to the rules, and that maybe she was on her own journey, too.

As he slowly rose from his seat, he thought about his next move, anticipating what he would say or do if he had the opportunity to interact with her once he was in the hall. Given that he'd pegged her to be a sophisticated woman, he knew he couldn't approach her without having something interesting to say.

Jerome walked into the hall and spotted her right away. He focused in and locked eyes with her as he approached the line where she stood. The closer he got, the more he couldn't believe how nervous he felt inside, much like he had when he was eleven years old and asked a girl for his first real kiss. He became excited when he saw Stanford 145 give him a slight smile, but as soon as she'd graced him with what felt like sunshine, she turned her attention back to whatever she was reading on her phone.

He wasn't a man who was easily swayed or impressed, but the woman in red had literally left him enraptured. He wanted to say hello and grab her attention again, but somehow his mouth wouldn't cooperate with his brain. The only connection his body was able to make was the one that resulted in a hot sensation below his waist. *I can't believe this woman has me trippin' like this,* he thought.

Jerome was no stranger to beautiful women, or to the art of approaching and seducing them. He was a handsome, naturally confident man who'd possessed a certain type of magnetic sway since he was a young boy. As he'd grown into manhood, he'd delighted and indulged in the fact that women from eight to eighty couldn't get enough of him. He'd had his share of them across the board—women of varying sizes, shapes, colors, and ages. So the fact that the woman in red made him feel slightly nervous was as unsettling as it was exciting.

Relax. She's just a female, he told himself. But deep beyond the surface of his practiced machismo, Jerome knew she wasn't just any fe-male. There was something special and very different about Stanford 145. He knew that by the gentle look in her eyes, the soft expression that had formed at her lips when she smiled, and the way his heart beat like the ticking of a clock at the thought of her.

Once they were seated inside the courtroom, he was a little dis-appointed that he was a full five seats away from her. But, he reasoned, it was best. That way he could check her out in a more discreet man-ner.

When she crossed her long, shapely legs, revealing smooth skin and thick thighs, he felt the hot sensation return below his waist. He had to will himself mentally not to give in to the feeling or the urge to move closer to her. He took a deep breath, regained his compo-sure, and refocused his eyes, directing them up to her face. She was a naturally beautiful woman whose dewy brown skin was flawless. Her profile was regal; her features all aligned in perfect symmetry. He knew that as fine as she was, she had to have a man.

He looked down at her left hand and didn't see any hardware on her ring finger. That observation gave him hope, but it didn't remove the fact that she might still have a man. Gazing at her, he honestly didn't see how she could not.

As Jerome continued to study her, his mind led him to a place he didn't want to go, but he had to be real with himself. Given the type of woman she appeared to be—educated, wealthy, and cultured—even if she didn't have a man, he wondered if he really stood a shot with her.

Self-reflection wasn't a new concept for him. Ever since he made the promise to clean up his life ten years ago, he'd read countless books and watched dozens of DVDs that put him on a road to self-discovery and personal understanding. But even though he was a real-ist, he still surprised himself with the thought that he might not measure up in a woman's eyes. He had never questioned or been inse-cure about his desirability to the opposite sex until that very moment.

Thanks to his good looks, natural charm, and sex appeal, Jerome had never wanted for female attention, and he'd never shied away from it, either. But now he felt unwelcome insecurity slowly invade his mind.

He examined the beautiful woman's expensive-looking handbag, sparkling diamond tennis bracelet, and the sophisticated manner in which she carried herself. Those were all signs that she had high standards and certain expectations. *She goes into a nice, cushy office every day, probably runnin' things,* he thought. *She ain't about to fool with a brothah who hauls trash and works with his hands.*

Jerome leaned back in his seat and quietly took another deep breath, inhaling her scent to inject some needed clarity into his thoughts. He had to remind himself of who he was and not who he wasn't. He wasn't the knucklehead who'd dropped out of high school his eleventh grade year. He wasn't the irresponsible player who'd run through women like springwater. He wasn't the stubborn street hustler who'd almost gotten himself killed over some rocks in a back alley. Those lowly days were long behind him. He was a new man. He was determined to get his contracting license and start his own business. He was studying late each night to earn his GED. He was a dedicated father. He was a good son. He was a loyal friend. And he, too, had high standards and expectations.

He loved a challenge, but to be with a woman like Stanford 145, he knew he had to be correct and precise in his approach.

Just as he began to believe he had a chance with her, something happened that further erased his insecurities. He glimpsed at Stanford 145 and saw that she was looking at him, too. She tried to hide the fact that she was checking him out from the corner of her eye, but he caught her red-handed.

Then, suddenly, just as she'd dropped her smile out in the hallway and turned her attention back to her phone, she moved her eyes away from his direction and concentrated on the instructions being given by the court clerk.

What's up with this woman? he thought. She was quickly becoming a puzzle that he wanted to solve.

Bringing his mind back to the present, Jerome turned his large truck onto his crowded street in search of a parking space. Finding a place to park on a Saturday afternoon was like trying to find a doughnut at a fashion show. It was damn near impossible. After securing a spot around the corner from his building, Jerome walked up to his unit. Once he reached his door, he slipped his key into the lock and went inside his apartment.

Standing in the middle of his living room, looking around at all 650 square feet of his two-bedroom apartment, Jerome wondered what the woman in red would think of his living conditions. "I know her crib is tight," he said to himself. But just as he'd done yesterday in court, he took a deep breath and realigned his thoughts. Right now he couldn't focus on Stanford 145, because he needed to get ready to see his son.

Jamel's party was set to start in another three hours, giving him just enough time to make a tuna sandwich, take a shower, grab a quick nap, and get dressed before heading out the door.

The thought of having a teenage son made Jerome's chest puff with pride, especially given that Jamel was growing into such a fine young man. Even though Kelisha was loud as hell and as obnoxious as a pit bull, Jerome had to give her credit; she was a good mother to their son, and her demeanor hadn't rubbed off on him. At thirteen, Jamel was more responsible and mature than some adults Jerome knew. He made good grades at the private school he attended on scholarship, he was respectful to authority figures, and he was kind to his peers. Jamel was the kid he wished he had been at that age.

Twenty minutes later and fresh from the shower, Jerome set the alarm clock beside his bed and settled in for a nap. As he drifted off to sleep, he thought about the surprised look that he knew would come to Jamel's face when he opened the gift he'd gotten him, his very own checkbook, linked to an account with his name on it that had $250 as its balance.

"That's my boy," Jerome whispered to himself. He turned over, doubled his thin pillow beneath his head, and closed his eyes, preparing to drift off into the clouds. As his thoughts faded to a faraway sleep land, the last thing his waking mind remembered was seeing a beautiful woman standing before him in a bright red dress.

Chapter 9

It was early afternoon, and Erica was immersed in her usual Sunday routine, sitting at her desk, going over paperwork so she could get a jump on the week ahead. She was trying to take her mind off deadlines, swag bags, and her frustration about her lonely love life.

Ever since Friday night she'd been thinking about the endearing image she had seen—Ashley and Jason walking hand in hand off into the distance. It was a moment that had touched her and made her heart fill with happiness for her best friend. But it had also struck a chord of melancholy within her soul when she thought about the fact that out of all the men she'd dated, she couldn't think of a single relationship that had made her feel the love expressed in Ashley and Jason's simple gesture.

"Just once, I'd like to know love," Erica whispered, feeling a sorrowful catch in her throat.

But she knew she couldn't sit around moping and feeling sorry for herself, so she turned her thoughts from what she wanted and aimed them toward what she needed to do. She had to get to work so she could smooth out the problems at Opulence that would be facing her this week. In addition to tackling the issue with the swag bags, she had to conduct interviews so she could replace the employee who had quit last week without notice.

An hour later, Erica was still busy working when her phone rang, jolting her from the stack of papers on her desk. Her face lit up when she saw that it was Ashley. She hadn't spoken with her friend since their near-disastrous girls' night out at Vidalia. She had been wanting to know how the rest of the evening played out after they left the restaurant, but she knew she needed to give Ashley time to recalibrate and sort things out in her mind.

"How's it going?" Erica asked, bypassing her usual hello.

"Honestly, I'm really not sure."

Ashley explained that she and Jason had gone back to his house and had spent the rest of the night talking about the reality of their present and their hopes for their future—together. They had verbalized some hard truths and had revealed some deep-seated insecurities and hang-ups about race, family, and expectations on both their parts. By the time the sun rose the next morning, they were lying in each other's arms with a mixture of hope and trepidation for what they were about to get themselves into.

"Sounds like you two are approaching things the right way," Erica said. "Being up-front and honest now will save you a lot of heartache on the back end."

"Yes, and that's what I'm worried about. The back end. I'm not sure there's going to be one."

"Do you love him? I mean, really, really love him?"

Ashley took a moment, pausing as she let out a long, heavy sigh. "Jason is the only man I've ever been with who's made me even consider the idea of marriage, let alone make a formal commitment to do it. So yes, I love him. But I also know that it takes more than just love to make a marriage work."

Erica nodded on her end of the phone. "I'm convinced that everything happens for a reason, and even though that incident Friday night was messy, it spurred a conversation that you two obviously needed to have."

"That's the same thing I was thinking. And, Erica, I want to thank you for what you said to me. I needed to hear those words and reaffirm who I am."

"You're a fantastic person, and I hope you know that."

"Of course I do! And by the way, you left out that I'm awesome, beautiful, and fierce!" Ashley laughed. "But all jokes aside, sometimes we can lose sight of things . . . lose our way. Sometimes we have to be reminded of how special we are. Girl, I'm so glad you did that for me."

"I'm always gonna have your back, just like you always have mine. You helped me through everything that happened with Claude, and I'll never be able to repay you for that."

Ashley let out an exasperated breath. "I still can't believe his fake ass had the nerve to slither up to our table while he was on a date, and then lie about it."

"Well, he did eventually come clean and admit that she was more than a colleague."

"Yeah, but only after you busted him for trying to front. Deceitful bastard!"

"I'm sorry I mentioned his name."

"That makes two of us. And while we're on the subject—"

Erica cut her off in mid-sentence. "Before you say another word or ask again, I'm over him for real. I just get lonely sometimes. But I'm not walking back across that bridge. He's clearly moved on, and I need to as well."

"When, Erica?"

"Now."

Ashley sucked her teeth and sighed again. "How can you do that when you won't even make time to clear your schedule for a date, or go out someplace where you'll meet someone?"

"I told you about everything that's going on at Opulence and the deadline I'm under for Fashion Week. I need to take care of business first. Then I'll worry about finding a date."

"At the end of the day everything is going to work out just fine. The swag bags will be a tremendous hit, you'll get beaucoup orders from coast to coast for Paradise, which will become the hot new must-have beauty item, you'll be featured in a national magazine that'll have a big picture of you cheesin' in front of Opulence, and guess what?"

"What?" Erica asked excitedly, thinking about all the great things that were about to come.

"After all the accolades and frenzy, you'll end up doing exactly what I know you're doing right now, which is sitting behind that big ol' desk in your home office on a lonely afternoon, all by yourself, with no one to share your accomplishments with except your spread-sheets."

There was a brief moment of silence.

"Ouch, Ash. That really hurt."

"It was supposed to. You need tough love, and I'm going to give it to you because I love you." Ashley paused before she said her next words. "Please don't live a life full of regrets. You're much too brilliant and fabulous to fall into that trap."

That evening, as Erica sat on her couch, eating a bowl of mint chocolate-chip ice cream all by herself, she thought long and hard about her life, and it occurred to her that she didn't like being alone. During the day, when she was out and about at Opulence, attending meetings, running errands, or hanging out with friends, she was sur-rounded by liveliness and fun. But when she came home to her castle of a row house in the trendy Dupont Circle neighborhood at the end of the day, there was nothing. No one to talk to. No one to laugh with. And no one to hold.

"I've got to make a change," Erica whispered aloud. She rose from the couch and dumped her ice cream down the sink before heading upstairs to her bedroom.

After a quick shower she was in bed, setting her alarm clock. She knew that change could be unpredictable and full of ups and downs, so if she was going to start a new journey, she needed a good night's sleep to prepare for it. She turned onto her side and snuggled her head against her fluffy pillow as she drifted off into dreamland, envi-sioning a new life for herself and the beautiful Great Dane, whom she hoped would be a part of it.

Chapter 10

Erica rose from bed before her alarm had a chance to make a sound. She was glad that on this predawn Monday morning, her excitement, rather than a wretched nightmare, had called her from her slumber. In fact, she was so eager for the day to begin that she practically leapt out of bed. Starting off the day with hope instead of night sweats was a welcome change.

Erica had been secretly excited about today since last Friday afternoon, but she'd refused to acknowledge it or give in to the emotion until her phone conversation with Ashley yesterday afternoon.

Ashley's pointed yet caring words were still lingering in Erica's mind as she walked into her kitchen and turned on her coffee machine. Instead of thinking about Claude and lamenting their failed relationship, she thought about the tall, dark, handsome stranger she'd encountered last week. Knowing she would see him again in just a few hours made her tingle inside. But then, suddenly, her smile went flat when she thought about something that until now had not crossed her mind. There was a very real possibility that he had a girlfriend, or maybe even a wife.

"Damn!" Erica hissed aloud.

She didn't remember seeing a wedding band on his finger, but she knew that didn't mean a hill of beans. Plenty of married men walked around not wearing their wedding ring. But even if he wasn't married, she knew that a man as chocolaty handsome and devastatingly fine as the Great Dane probably had more women than he could handle. There were plenty of women out there who were still into man sharing and wouldn't mind splitting his time with others so long as they got their slice.

"What was I thinking?" Erica asked herself. She finished her coffee and slowly walked back to her bedroom. She felt slightly disappointed, but she knew she had to keep the faith, because even if the beautiful Great Dane wasn't the man for her, there was someone out there who was.

Erica strode with focus, her head held high, as she made her way toward the jury room. She was glad that she was the first juror to arrive. She was always prompt in everything she did, a character trait she had inherited from her father. She knew that being there bright and early would give her time to settle in, compose her thoughts, and prepare for the day ahead, and more important, it would allow her to buttress her resolve to keep her desire for the Great Dane in check.

Erica looked up when she heard the door open.

"Well, look at us. Aren't we the early birds!" the old woman practically chirped as she walked inside. She took a seat right beside Erica, smelling like lavender talcum powder. "I didn't get a chance to formally introduce myself last week. My name is Maudelene Feinstein, but my friends call me Maude."

Erica smiled and extended her hand. "I'm Erica Stanford. It's nice to meet you, Ms. Maude."

"Likewise. I know you're not too excited about being here, but I sure am. I've been looking forward to this all weekend. It's gonna be so interesting."

"I hope you're right."

Maude winked. "Honey, I know I am. Matter of fact, I bet there'll be just as much excitement in this jury room as there will be in the courtroom."

Erica raised her brow.

"From my thirty-five years of experience in the classroom, I know what happens when you put a bunch of different people together in one room. Everyone has a different opinion, and everyone thinks theirs is right. What will make this interesting is that we all have to come to the same conclusion. You can't help but have some excitement from that."

Erica nodded in agreement. "I hadn't thought about it that way, Ms. Maude. I guess you're right."

Erica and Maude continued to chat as one by one, the other jurors slowly began to fill the small room, taking their places around the conference table set for twelve. Each time the door opened and a new person walked in, Erica felt her heart jump a tiny bit, thinking it might be him. And each time it wasn't, she felt a small tug in her stomach, mixed with something she couldn't place. Finally, nearly twenty minutes after the time they were supposed to have arrived for duty, the Great Dane walked through the heavy wooden door.

Although Erica had been bracing herself for his entrance and willing her emotions to remain calm, he managed to hijack the breath straight out of her lungs. Her heart quickened with excitement. Her hands trembled with anticipation. And despite her best efforts to control them, she felt the same butterflies that had stirred inside her when she first laid eyes on him last Friday.

She watched the beautiful man as he walked into the room, slow and self-assured, as if he were right on time and not a minute late. His bold confidence made her smile to herself as she leaned back in her chair, taking inventory of him.

Today he wore tan khakis that moved with him when he walked, fitting every inch of his tight behind and long legs like a man's pants should, not too loose and not too tight, but oh, so right! His crisp white shirt was tucked into his pants, exposing a slim waistline, which she knew had to contain a sexy six-pack. He switched his black jacket from his left arm to his right as he moved through the tight space around several chairs. He glanced around the room, looking for a seat, until he found the last empty one.

Erica glanced down at her watch and once again thought about her father's take on men who didn't wear one. She noticed that the Great Dane's wrist was still bare, and that his tardiness didn't seem to faze him one bit. She didn't want to discount him, but already things weren't looking good. *Damn!* she thought.

"Good morning," the Great Dane said, nodding his greeting to everyone before claiming the seat at the end of the long conference table.

Erica watched him as he scanned everyone, and when his eyes finally connected with hers, she felt a jolt of energy that her morning cup of coffee couldn't match. And his voice! It was the first time she'd heard him speak, and his simple "good morning" sounded like thunder and music all at once. She closed her eyes for a brief moment and locked it into her memory for safekeeping. She'd always listened to her father's wise words, but she decided this was one case in which she was going to forfeit his advice. She had always trusted her gut, and right now her gut was quietly telling her to take a chance.

Once everyone was assembled, they quickly went around the room and introduced themselves. Jerome Kimbrough was his name. *Jerome,* she said to herself, rolling his name around inside her head.

Erica thought his name suited him perfectly. Jerome was a bad boy name, rugged and tough with a biting edge of sexiness. And Kimbrough sounded like a strong family name, uncommon and distinctive. She thought all these things were exactly who he appeared to be, and she wondered if she would get a chance to find out for sure.

Minutes later, the court clerk began to line up the jurors, preparing them for the order in which they would enter the courtroom. Ironically, Erica stood sandwiched between Maude, who was in front of her, and Jerome, who was causing earthquakes and tidal waves behind her. They were in the hallway just outside the courtroom, waiting to make their entrance so the trial could begin.

Erica was glad to have the old woman's bubbly, enthusiastic energy to balance out the unsettling, if not intense heat she felt from just being near Jerome. As he stood behind her, close enough to reach out and touch her shoulder, she hoped she would be able to contain the wanton desires that kept surging through her body. It was one thing to think about him, but it was another thing entirely to have to sit next to him in a jury box all day long.

She tried to focus her mind on the instructions the court clerk had given them and on the task at hand, which was a huge responsibility. They were charged with determining whether a woman would walk free or be locked away for five to ten years. Erica hoped that civic charge of duty would help her concentrate her thoughts on where they needed to be.

A few minutes later, Erica and the other jurors were seated inside the jury box, listening to the opening arguments from both the prosecution and the defense. Right away, she knew that Ms. Maude was correct—this was going to be an interesting trial.

The unlikely defendant was a short, mildly attractive African American woman of considerable girth who appeared to be in her mid-thirties. Erica watched the woman as she pushed her small glasses up the faint bridge of her wide nose, looking frightened behind her thick lenses. Her hands looked as though they were shaking as she raked her stubby fingers through her long hair weave, which was a bit of a mess. Looking at her, Erica couldn't imagine the timid woman jaywalking, let alone committing a felony.

The woman stood accused of embezzling three hundred thousand dollars from her employer, Allsource Inc., a large consulting firm that specialized in representing government hospital insurance claims. She had been hired by the firm two years ago as a case manager in their patient advocacy department. Her position was one in which she worked from home on a company-issued laptop and was paid by billing the firm for her time, which they calculated from the weekly time sheets she submitted. She recorded the number of hours she worked each week, whether it was more or less than the standard forty. And therein was the problem.

The defendant's time sheets showed excessive overtime, earning her well over three hundred thousand dollars in the last two years, and that was in addition to her modest fifty-five-thousand-dollar-a-year salary. There had apparently been no oversight of office procedures or forms, but when a new CEO was appointed last year, everything changed. A probe had been conducted in relative secret so as not to alert any wrongdoers. Once enough evidence had been gathered, they moved in and started making arrests, and that was how the defendant found herself staring down a possible decade-long prison sentence.

What made the defendant's situation even more serious was that not only was she charged with dozens of counts of embezzlement, they were federal charges because she'd submitted her time sheets electronically.

Erica crossed her legs, perched her small writing pad on her thigh, and began to take notes. She tried to concentrate on listening to the current witness on the stand. She wanted to absorb as many details as she could. But she found it difficult to focus because her mind kept moving to her right, just six inches away, where Jerome sat by her side.

She inhaled deeply, letting the sensual musk scent of his cologne tickle her nose and excite her senses. She wanted to lean over, nestle up to the side of his neck, and breathe. Erica knew that she was attracted to him, for sure. But until that very moment she hadn't realized how much she wanted him. Then another thought occurred to her. She was enthralled by him, but she wondered what he thought of her. Beyond their brief stares and slight smiles, she couldn't tell if he was attracted to her, or if he was just being polite.

Erica knew she was an attractive woman. She'd been told that enough to know it was true, plus her mirror gave her living proof every day. She had the kind of face that men found beautiful and the kind of body that made them take a second, and sometimes third, look. She was smart, kind, and successful, all attributes that went above the superficial surface of her obvious good looks. These things made her confident in her ability to attract a man.

She didn't doubt that Jerome had taken notice of her beauty, but she wondered if a man like him would be interested in a woman like her. Judging from what she'd observed of him, she wasn't so sure she was his type. She had deduced that he was definitely a blue-collar, low-maintenance kind of brother—given the type of clothes he wore, his lack of accoutrements, and the subtle gangsta street swagger he exuded—which probably made him more comfortable with women of his same social ilk.

This is one time I hope my analytical mind is way off base, Erica thought. There was something about this man that she liked, and she wanted him to like her, too.

She shifted her body in her seat, silently examining herself. She brushed a small speck of lint from the hem of her slim black pencil skirt and adjusted the sleeve of her off-white blouse. She looked down at her red manicured toes, which teased the open space of her black patent leather peep-toe heels. She thought her outfit looked good, and that her double-strand cultured pearl necklace, medium-size silver hoop earrings, and diamond tennis bracelet, which her father had given her five years ago for her thirtieth birthday, all accessorized her clothes nicely. Her outfit was simple with a hint of sexy, but she wondered if Jerome thought so, too. Erica sighed to herself, hoping he did.

Chapter 11

Erica sat back in her chair, trying to clear her mind. She knew that she couldn't let her curiosity about Jerome, or his possible thoughts about her, disrupt her concentration. She needed to once again remain focused on the task at hand, which at the moment was the testimony being given by a new witness the prosecution had just called to the stand. But just as she was about to dive back into the details of the case, she noticed something that struck her as very odd. Jerome wasn't taking any notes.

She looked at his writing pad and saw that it was empty, void of a single word, even a scribble. Although she had allowed her mind to wander momentarily, she had been paying enough attention to record pertinent information. But in the nearly two hours that they had been sitting in the jury box, he hadn't captured a thing, at least not on paper. She knew that everyone around them had been taking notes, because she could see the busy hands of her fellow jurors at work, writing feverishly, and she could hear the scratchy sound of pencils gliding across paper made by those behind her.

Just as she was about to look into Jerome's face to try to figure out what he must be thinking, the judge announced that the court was going to take its first break of the day.

Erica and her fellow jurors rose to be dismissed and filed out of the courtroom in the same neat, orderly fashion in which they had entered. Once they were in the back hallway, they dispersed to different areas for their brief reprieve. Erica knew she had to put Jerome out of her mind, because the man had consumed her thoughts all morning. She reminded herself that she had a business to run, dead-lines to meet, personnel to hire, and problems to solve, so she quickly hurried back to the jury room so she could check her e-mail and phone messages.

Time was of the essence if she had any hopes of having a new de-sign to showcase her exclusive new body butter, so she prayed that the graphic artist she'd always used in the past would come through on such short notice. Erica took a deep breath as she powered on her phone and vowed she would never again take the risk of hiring some-one who had no proven track record.

To her disappointment, Erica hadn't received the message she'd been looking for. She didn't want to, but at this point she had to face the possibility that she'd have to go with the regular Opulence design, which appeared on all the other products. No matter how much she wanted to make a splashy show, nothing was worth missing out on the Fashion Week opportunity.

She quickly sent a few e-mails, cleared out some spam messages, and scrolled through the *Huffington Post's* latest headlines. She was about to read an article when she noticed Jerome at the edge of the table, quietly staring straight ahead at nothing in particular. For a mo-ment she sat frozen, in awe of how sexy he was. *This man is fine as hell!* she thought. His dark chocolate skin looked rich enough to taste, and his smooth bald head gleamed with a high shine, which made her want to run her fingers over its surface. And those lips! He had the kind that she imagined felt good on any part of her body.

Erica was traveling in thought when the court clerk startled her with the announcement. Just as quickly as their break had come, it had ended, and before she knew it, she was standing in the same line, in the same order, ready to go back into the courtroom. This time as they waited in the hallway, she could feel Jerome standing at a slightly farther distance behind her. She wondered if it was intentional, and she felt unsettled by the fact that she wanted him closer, much closer.

Erica looked at her watch. It wasn't even 11:00 a.m., but she was already feeling tired. Dealing with business pressure had become sec-ond nature for her, and over the years she had learned how to handle it with a fair amount of efficiency. But feeling so conflicted about a man she desired, but didn't even know, wasn't as easy, and it was draining her faster than her worries about Opulence.

After another two hours of intense testimony from witnesses, and of sitting beside Jerome, who seemed to be preoccupied with things other than the trial—evidenced by his blank writing pad—Erica gladly jumped from her seat when the judge recessed the court for lunch.

As they walked back to the jury room, she had to admit that she was beginning to feel sorry for the defendant. Each person who had been called to testify against the frightened-looking woman seemed to have it in for the accomplished sister, who reminded Erica a lot of herself. They were both in their mid-thirties, single, educated, having earned master's degrees, well spoken, hardworking, and ambitious.

Erica knew there was still a week's worth of testimony to go and documented evidence that had yet to be presented, but at this point she was leaning toward the defendant's innocence.

She knew how dishonest and greedy some employees could be. She had had to fire a few who stole money from the register at Opulence and even tried to sneak products home in their handbags. But she'd also worked in corporate America, and she knew how easy it was to set someone up for a fall. More than once the jealous, mean girls at the magazine she'd worked for had intentionally sabotaged her work, and in one case, they'd falsified documents to make her look bad. But thankfully, she'd been smart enough to record in detail everything she did, creating an airtight paper trail, which made them back off.

Erica knew that she needed to be impartial and that she shouldn't exercise bias, but looking at the defendant, who could have easily been a girlfriend, cousin, or sister, Erica hoped the bespectacled woman hadn't really done what she was being accused of.

Once they were back in the jury room, everyone gathered their things and began to leave so they could make the most of the fifty-seven minutes and counting they had left for lunch. Ms. Maude was meeting one of her friends at a restaurant down the street from the courthouse, and she invited Erica to join them.

"I have to respond to e-mails and make some phone calls. But thanks, anyway," Erica said.

"Okay, but make sure you break away from that phone long enough to eat something. It's going to be a long afternoon," Ms. Maude advised.

"You can say that again."

As the room began to empty, Erica noticed that Jerome was still lingering at the end of the table. Finally, it was just the two of them.

"Erica, right?" he said as he walked toward her chair.

Erica sat her phone on the table and tapped a button on her iPad to clear the screen. She wanted to concentrate on what he was saying, so she removed any distractions. "Yes, and you're Jerome, right?"

"Yes."

They both nodded and smiled.

"So, um, what're you doin' for lunch?" he asked, his voice sounding rich and deep.

"I'm afraid I'm doing it. I have a lot of work to do, and being out of pocket this morning has thrown me even further behind."

"Too far behind to eat?"

She laughed and shook her head. "I know it sounds crazy, but if you knew what I was up against, you'd understand. . . . Lots of important deadlines."

"Nothing's more important than taking care of yourself."

Erica didn't know how to respond. His comment sounded so rational and, beyond that, so caring. It wasn't necessarily his words, but rather his tone and the look in his eyes that made her perceive what she thought was genuine concern on his part. "Yes, I suppose you're right."

"Well, I won't interrupt your work. I hope you get it all done."

"Thanks."

Erica watched as Jerome strolled out of the room with the same quiet ease with which he'd entered earlier that morning. His words had been few, but their impact had shaken her.

It wasn't until he closed the door that Erica realized he'd wanted to have lunch with her. He had stayed in the room until everyone left, and then he'd asked what she was doing for lunch. "Damn. What's wrong with me?" Erica quietly admonished herself for her fumble. She hadn't had an offer to dine with a man in months, and now here it was, she'd had a fine man asking her to eat with him, and the only reaction she'd had was to return to her smartphone and iPad so she could check her messages.

"Ashley is right," Erica whispered to herself. She was so focused on work that she let an opportunity to get to know Jerome slip through her fingers. She wanted to run out the door and go find him, but she knew he was probably long gone.

As Erica sat all by herself in the jury room, her mind took her back to what Ashley had told her yesterday—that at the end of the day she would find herself all alone, just as she was right now. And then she thought about the change she'd promised to make in her life.

Erica knew she couldn't undo what had already been done. Jerome was gone. But right then and there, sitting all by herself in the small, empty room, she made up her mind that the next time the opportunity came to do something with Jerome, she was going to grab it, ride it, and never look back.

Chapter 12

Jerome put on his jacket as he walked out of the courthouse and into the cool, sunny day outside. His mind was swimming so fast, he could barely keep up with all the ripples and waves surging through his head. He'd known from the moment he entered the jury room earlier that morning that the feeling he'd gotten last week about the woman in red had been right on target. And now, after having sat close beside her in the jury box for several hours, looking into her gorgeous brown eyes just moments ago, and listening to her gentle-sounding voice, it was official. She was the one. She was the woman he wanted.

He knew on the surface that it sounded ridiculous, bordered on crazy, that he would be experiencing these feelings for someone he'd just met. Before last week, if anyone had told him that he'd be this caught up in a woman whom he didn't even know, he would have laughed in their face. He wasn't the type of man who fell in love on a whim or acted impulsively. He was always calm and sometimes even reserved with his feelings. He didn't believe in bullshit like love at first sight, or falling head over heels after just one encounter. That kind of fantasy was for fools and daydreamers, and he was neither. In his experience, it took time to build a relationship, and even longer to fall in love.

But he had to change his thinking about that when it came to Erica. Never had he felt the kind of instant attraction and intense desire for a woman that welled up inside him when she was near. She had an alluring energy that drew him to her, wrapping him in a time that stood still. When his mind gave him free moments, she filled it with her vibrant smile and curvaceous body, and today was no different. She was the kind of woman who made him glad he was a man, in a very raw, animal sense.

He had been eager to get to court early this morning so he could see her. He'd already determined from her businesslike demeanor last week that she was the type of person who was punctual, so he'd planned to arrive with enough time to introduce himself and maybe even talk a little before the court opened session.

But he had gotten off to a late start. He was used to rising at the crack of dawn Monday through Friday because people's trash had to be picked up early. But after working from sunup to sundown every day last week, getting up early for the roof repair job Saturday morning, celebrating the festivities of Jamel's birthday party later that evening, and then spending all day with his son yesterday, Jerome was beat. When he hit the snooze button on his alarm clock at 6:00 a.m., he didn't realize that he'd actually hit the off button instead.

When he awoke to the sound of a loud scream, he looked at the clock and jumped out of bed in a rush. It was one of the few times that living in a noisy neighborhood had proven to be an advantage, because if it hadn't been for the young couple yelling back and forth in the middle of the street outside his window, he would have probably slept for another couple hours. He quickly showered, dressed, and sprinted to the metro station to catch the train.

Now, as Jerome crossed the street, headed to one of the eateries near the courthouse, all he could think about was how much he wanted her. "Erica Stanford," he whispered to himself.

He walked inside the restaurant and thought about the fact that he was getting ready to go out on a limb, but he had to trust his instincts. His gut told him that getting her lunch was the right thing to do. At first, he was hesitant, because even though she hadn't been wearing a ring, that didn't mean she wasn't attached. But after observing and talking with her, he was 99 percent sure that she didn't have a boyfriend. And the way she responded when he asked her what she was doing for lunch convinced him even more. When she said she was going to spend her lunchtime working, there was a loneliness resting in her voice, which told him there was no one special in her life to help fill her time.

Jerome walked up to the counter and scanned the menu board. He'd never eaten at Au Bon Pain, but judging from the large crowd, he knew the food must be good. He found what he wanted; then he tried to figure out what Erica might like. He wanted to take care of her, and this was his first step and opportunity to show her that he could, regardless of his station in life. He knew that everyone shared the same basic needs, and food was one of them. Everybody had to eat.

I need to get her something that's healthy and tastes good, Jerome thought. There were so many choices, and with what seemed like a hundred different bread selections, getting her a sandwich was going to be more complicated than he'd thought. After careful consideration, he settled on the same turkey sandwich and vegetable soup that he'd ordered for himself.

He knew she was up to her neck in work, so he wasn't going to take up her time, especially when there'd be other opportunities for that down the road. So for now, this was a way to break the ice and let her know that he was interested in her.

His legs couldn't carry him fast enough as he hurried across the street back to the courthouse. If it were not for the fact that he was ready for love, Jerome would have been scared shitless by the feelings that were commanding him at will. But that wasn't the case, because he was more than ready. He was complete. He was sure of who he was and what he wanted. And as he stood in the security line to reenter the building, he hoped that Erica was ready, too.

Five minutes later he was back in the jury room. He saw Erica with her phone pinned to her ear and her eyes glued to her iPad. Without saying a word, he removed her sandwich and soup, a napkin, and a bottle of water from the bag, sat them in front of her, and then turned to walk away.

"I'll call you back," Erica quickly said to whomever she'd been talking to. "This is for me?" she asked with surprise.

Jerome stopped and turned to face her. "You have to eat, right? I hope what I got you is okay."

Erica looked at the food before her. "You didn't have to do this."

"I wanted to."

He saw her smile turn into what looked like a soft blush, which made him smile in return. *Damn, this woman is sexy.*

"Why don't you join me?"

"That's okay. I know you have work to do. I just didn't want you to have to do it on an empty stomach."

"Jerome," she said softly as she smiled again, "maybe I wasn't clear. I would very much like for you to eat lunch with me."

Her quiet, yet forceful invitation both startled and charged him. He hadn't anticipated her wanting him to eat with her, and from the beginning he hadn't wanted to disturb her work, but he wasn't going to turn down this opportunity, either. He smiled, walked over to the table, and took a seat beside her.

"This was really thoughtful of you," Erica said, taking a bite of her turkey sandwich. "Au Bon Pain is one of my favorite places."

"Good. I'm glad I made the right choice."

She smiled. "Me too."

They shared an easy laugh between them as they dug into their food. Jerome was glad that he'd trusted his instincts, and as he sat beside Erica, sharing what he knew was the first of many meals they'd enjoy together, a profound realization came to him. Finding Erica and knowing that she was the one wasn't a coincidence. It was fate.

He had initially deferred his jury duty summons a month ago because he'd been working to finish the kitchen remodeling job, which led to the job he'd done last weekend. He almost laughed to himself when he thought about the fact that his busy life had actually cleared a path for the woman in front of him.

"I needed this," Erica said, breaking Jerome's thoughts. "If you hadn't been kind enough to get me lunch, I probably wouldn't have eaten anything until I finished with work later tonight."

"You work a lot of long hours, huh?"

"You have no idea. I work harder now than I ever did when I worked for someone else."

"So, what is it that you do?"

"Have you ever heard of Opulence?"

Jerome thought for a moment, then shook his head. "No, can't say I have. But I like the name."

"Really?" Erica smiled with what he could see was curiosity in her eyes. "Tell me what you like about the name."

"It sounds . . . I don't know . . . rich, real classy."

She nodded her head. "Opulence is a bath and body care boutique, and I own it."

"Get outta here."

"Yeah, I do. We specialize in high-end body products that make your skin feel and smell amazing."

No wonder she smells so good. Her smooth skin looked soft to the touch, and he couldn't wait to do just that.

Erica leaned over, reached into her large handbag, and handed him a postcard-size flyer. "This is my baby. She's five years old."

Jerome looked at the sleek advertisement. To say that he was impressed was an understatement. He knew that Erica had to be an accomplished woman in whatever she did, but he had no idea she owned her own business. From what he could see from the four different snapshots featured on the flyer, her boutique was first class all the way. Being a craftsman, he recognized quality in design when he saw it. He studied the elegant exterior of her store, with its intricately carved mahogany and glass front door, and the expensively packaged products sitting on the custom-made shelves inside. She had a successful and thriving business.

"This is real nice." Jerome said. "I'm very impressed."

"Thank you. Some days it's a headache, but honestly, I wouldn't trade it for anything in the world. It's my dream, and I'm living it."

She was doing exactly what he wanted to do: start his own business and live his dream, too. Jerome knew there was a reason he'd been attracted to Erica beyond her physical beauty and the light in her eyes. It was the passion inside her that he'd connected with. It was the same passion that rested inside him—the desire to achieve, be his own boss, live and pursue his ambition on his own terms.

As Jerome watched Erica eat, he had an incredible urge to remove her soupspoon from her mouth, lean into her, and kiss her berry-stained lips. He'd finally met someone who was exactly where he wanted to be, and the thought made him feel more confident than ever that this was fate.

"So, Jerome, tell me about yourself," Erica said.

Jerome hesitated for a moment. He felt that neither his story nor his life was nearly as interesting as hers. And besides, he wanted to know everything about the woman who'd invaded his mind, and he wasn't going to let another minute go by without learning as much as he could about her. "Let's stick to you right now. I find you very interesting," he said with honesty.

Erica blushed again. "Really? You think I'm interesting?"

"Yes, I do. And I want to know more about you."

Jerome ate his food and listened as the most exciting, beautiful, and genuinely sweet woman he'd ever met revealed pieces of who she was. He asked questions, and she didn't seem to mind answering them.

The more he asked, the more she shared, and the more she shared, the more he fell into complete rapture over her wholesomeness and gentle strength. He thought everything about her was new and refreshing, from her approach in business to her approach in life. He was used to people with an edge—hard, tough, streetwise folks who had to be that way in order to survive. But Erica was none of that. Her view on life was optimistic and hopeful, and he admired that approach because it made him feel that anything was possible, including love.

He could also see that he'd been right about her romantic status. Except for when she talked about her family, each time she spoke of her personal life, it was with a singular focus. He wondered when her last serious relationship was, how long they'd stayed together, and if anyone was trying to date her now. He knew that a woman as fine as Erica wouldn't stay single for long. *She probably has her pick of men at the country club,* he thought, because he was fairly certain she belonged to one.

Her background was almost foreign to him. He knew that people like Erica, black folks in particular, existed. But until engaging in conversation with her, sharing a turkey sandwich and vegetable soup, he'd never met anyone who'd grown up in the type of affluence she had.

Gated communities and private schools were make-believe worlds for rich white people he'd seen on TV when he was growing up. But for Erica, it was the way things were. No big deal.

Another thing he found nearly unbelievable was that she came from a two-parent home, and from what he could piece together, she and her brother had the same mother and father, who were still married to each other. Most people in his circle were lucky if they knew the identity of one parent, let alone two, and if they did know both their mother and father, it was almost guaranteed that only one parent resided in the home.

Jerome was both fascinated and slightly intimidated the more Erica spoke. It was clear to him that she was a woman of means, position, and growing power. Her expensive-looking clothes and the classy way she carried herself said it all. He knew that she easily made ten or more times the money he earned from his regular job and his side construction projects combined.

Even though the thought intimidated him, Jerome refused to let it scare him away. Running scared had cost him so much in his life. Part of the promise he'd made to himself several years ago was that he wouldn't let fear keep him from the things he wanted. He wanted Erica, and he was going to do what it took to be with her.

"Tell me what it's like to run your own business," Jerome said.

Erica moved her empty container of soup to the side and tilted her head as she took a deep breath and smiled. "It's a combination of sun and clouds. Some days it's like heaven shining down on me, and some days it's completely chaotic with no rhyme or reason."

"I can imagine. It must be very intense."

"Yes, it can be. But I honestly have to say that even with the mess and headaches I'm dealing with right now, I still love what I do."

"What are you dealing with?"

Erica told Jerome about the dilemma that the flaky, unreliable graphic artist had caused, and that she was short staffed and needed to find a new salesperson quickly.

"I've decided that if I have to go with my old packaging, I will," she concluded. "Nothing is going to keep me from getting my products into those swag bags for Fashion Week."

Jerome looked at the flyer again, paying close attention to the colorful products displayed on her boutique's shelves. "These are the jars you'll have to use, right?"

"Yep."

"They look nice to me. I know you want to have something different to go along with your new product, but I guarantee you, once those people use that new body butter you talked about, they won't be thinking about the design on the jar. All they'll want to know is how they can buy more."

Erica leaned back in her seat and smiled. "Thank you for saying that, Jerome. You just boosted my spirits more than you know."

"I'm just speaking the truth."

There was a slight pause before Erica said, "You're not just throwing me lines to make me feel good, are you?"

Jerome shook his head and became serious. "I wouldn't do that, Erica. I'm telling you what I believe is true based on what you've shown me. I know you got skills."

"Oh, you do?" she said with a girlish laugh.

Jerome returned her laugh with an intense stare. "I'm good about stuff like that. Plus, the fact that you gave a young brother with no experience an opportunity tells me a lot about you."

"I'm not so sure about that. Giving him a chance was a big mistake, because look at me now."

"I don't think it was a mistake."

"Really?"

"No. What you did was give someone a break, just like someone gave you a break when you were just starting your business. You went out on a limb to pull somebody up. You gave this guy a chance, but you can't shoot his jump shot for him. He messed up a great opportunity, but who knows? He might just come through. And even if he doesn't, you're gonna be just fine. The positive energy you put out there when you tried to help him is gonna come back to you twofold."

"Wow, that's very insightful."

"Like I said, I'm just speaking the truth."

Their conversation continued to flow like water, gently and with ease. Jerome was excited that Erica seemed to be enjoying his company just as much as he was enjoying hers. He could tell she was a genuine person by the way she looked him squarely in his eyes when she spoke. He liked that about her and thought it said volumes about her trustworthiness. He knew shady people had a problem with eye contact.

Things were going great when suddenly they were interrupted by Erica's buzzing phone.

"You need to get that?" Jerome asked.

Erica didn't even glance in her phone's direction. "Nope. I'm talking to you. Whoever it is can wait."

Jerome sat back in his chair, trying to control the big grin that was about to burst at the edges of his lips. He had been turned on last week by her body-hugging red dress and sexy high heels, and then again today by her black skirt, which outlined her curvy hips, and the soft white blouse that fell gently against her breasts. But nothing she wore either day was more sexy to him than the words she'd just spoken. She was into him, and it turned him on. But he tempered his excitement and fought to keep his voice even as he spoke. "You sure? I know you're a busy woman with a lot goin' on."

"I'm sure."

"It could be that designer you've been waiting to hear from."

Erica let out a small laugh.

"Did I say something funny?" he asked with a smile, not sure if he really had.

"No, it's just that, well, I've been waiting for that message to come through since last week. But at the moment, I'm not really concerned. I recently made a promise to myself, and somehow I know it will all work out."

"I know exactly where you're coming from. I did the same thing."

"It's exciting and scary, isn't it?"

Jerome nodded. "I guess you could say that. But in my case, it was necessary. I had no other choice."

"Sounds deep. Have things worked out for you?"

"Better than I could've ever imagined."

"Well, then, that gives me hope."

"What promise did you make?" he asked.

Erica smiled but didn't answer his question. "We've talked about me this whole time. Now it's your turn. I want to know about you."

Just then the door opened and Ms. Maude came walking in with two other jurors trailing behind her. Jerome felt relieved. He wanted Erica to know who he was, but he also wanted time to think about how he would explain his life to her, since a lot of it was still unfolding.

He was sure that she'd never dated anyone like him. He didn't have a degree, let alone a high school diploma. Given that she owned her own business, he was pretty sure that she owned her own home, too. When he thought about the two-bedroom apartment he rented in a dicey neighborhood, tucked inside a questionable part of town, he wondered what she would think. Would she feel like she was settling if she started dating him?

Jerome felt that Erica was open-minded and kind, but he wasn't blind to the fact that their differences, and in particular his lifestyle, might be too much for her.

For the first time in his thirty-five years, Jerome's emotions were so up and down that he didn't trust what he might say next, so he decided to shut down their conversation. "Looks like our time is up. We'll have to go back into the courtroom soon."

Erica wagged her finger playfully. "You're not getting off the hook that easily."

"Oh, really?"

"That's right. This is to be continued tomorrow. Same time, same place."

Jerome smiled as he watched Erica gather their empty food containers and clear the table as the room began to fill with people. "So, you wanna have lunch with me tomorrow?" he asked.

"Yes, of course. And this time it'll be my treat."

Before Jerome could object, Erica shook her head and spoke in a lower tone. "It would be my pleasure."

Despite the insecurities that had just crept into his mind, Erica's comment made him want to lay her across his bed and show her what real pleasure was. But he controlled the thought and the urge because he could see that the other jurors were beginning to stare. He adjusted the seat of his pants, put on his game face, and prayed for strength.

Moments later, as Jerome stood behind Erica, preparing to walk back into the courtroom to resume the trial, he thought about the time he'd spent with her. It had been the most stimulating conversation he could ever remember having. Then he thought about tomorrow. It would be his turn to tell her all about himself. He would have to expose his life and answer her questions, just as she'd done for him.

He knew that conversations like the one they'd just had were important, because that was what people did at the start of a relationship in order to get to know each other. But as he settled into his seat beside her in the jury box, he wondered if she would be able to handle the life he'd lived, and he hoped she'd want to be a part of the one he was trying to build.

Chapter 13

Erica could hardly contain the electric buzz she felt from head to toe as she walked out of the courthouse with Jerome by her side. She'd enjoyed their lunch, and now their conversation was cruising on easy as they chatted about the beautiful, crisp afternoon and the cool weather that had descended on them in recent days. She wished they could talk the rest of the evening, but their day together was drawing to a quick close. He was headed to catch the train, and she was headed to catch a cab. She wanted to ask him where he was on his way to and if she could join him, but she knew it would be a completely outrageous question to ask and request to make, especially since she'd only just met the man.

"Are you heading to your boutique to do some work?" Jerome asked.

"Yeah, I need to check in since I've been gone all day. How about you?" She was glad he'd opened that door.

"There's a project I'm working on that I have to finish tonight. Then I'm heading home after that."

Erica wanted to ask him what kind of project he was working on and, for that matter, where he worked. He knew a lot about her, but she realized that aside from the fact that he was so handsome it was a sin and so sexy he made her panties wet, she didn't know a thing about him.

The expression on her face must have conveyed her question, because before she could ask, Jerome answered.

"I work for the city during the day, and I do odd jobs on the side in the evenings and on weekends. I'm working toward starting my own business, too."

"That's fantastic, Jerome!" Erica said, smiling with deep interest. She wanted to know what kind of business he was trying to start and in what industry, but she sensed a hesitation in his tone, which told her he didn't want to go into details beyond what he'd just revealed. So she decided to listen to her gut, and instead of launching into a million questions, she tilted her head to the side and told him, "I can't wait to hear more about it over lunch tomorrow."

"Good. I'm looking forward to it. I'll see you tomorrow, bright and early this time."

"Okay, see you." She gave him a smile and turned to walk away.

"Oh, and, Erica?"

"Yes?"

"You smell like heaven."

He was staring at her as if he could devour her whole, causing a tingling sensation between her legs. "Why thank you," she said as she began to walk away. "My products must be doing their job." She was pretty sure he was still standing there, watching her sashay down the sidewalk, and when she turned around, she saw that she was right. She smiled again and then practically skipped to the end of the street to hail a cab.

Erica looked out the backseat window as the car headed toward Opulence. Normally, she would have been clicking away on her phone or trying to estimate how much time the drive would take given the afternoon traffic. But today she wasn't doing either, and it gave her a sense of relief. She sat back and enjoyed the ride as she thought about her day.

She was proud of the small changes she'd already begun to make, all because of the tiny promise she'd committed to last night and then reminded herself of this afternoon. She grinned from ear to ear as she thought about Jerome and the sweet gesture he'd made. It had only been a turkey sandwich and a small container of soup, but to her, it had tasted better than any meal she'd ever eaten at Vidalia.

As her cab approached the swank exterior of her boutique, she smiled to herself, knowing that once she walked through the door, her day would get even better. After talking with Jerome and hearing the encouraging things he'd said about her business, she knew that no matter what worries or headaches arose, everything would work out just fine.

"Hey, Ms. E," LaWan said with a smile as Erica walked through the door.

Erica was glad to see LaWan, who was one of her best employees. She had hired the exuberant young woman a year ago and had promoted her to assistant manager just recently. Last Friday was the first day she'd called in sick since she'd been working there.

"How're you feeling?" Erica asked. "I was worried about you when Cindy told me you called in sick last week. Is everything okay?"

LaWan waved her hand in the air as if shooing a fly. "I'm doing great. Actually, I was just a little exhausted. I woke up and could barely get out of bed."

Erica stared at LaWan with concern. The pretty young woman's eyes looked heavy, as though she hadn't slept in days, and her light brown skin appeared ashen, void of its usual luminous glow. When she turned her head, Erica noticed that LaWan's thick, Afro-like natural hair looked dry, lacking its normal high glossy shine.

"LaWan, are you sure you're okay?"

"I'm not one hundred percent, but I feel a lot better than I did last week."

"Maybe you need to go see your doctor."

LaWan shook her head as she walked from behind the glass and granite counter. "I'm good, really. I'm off tomorrow, and I plan to spend all day in bed." She smiled, shaking her head as a small giggle escaped her full lips.

Erica took careful inventory of LaWan's appearance, from the smile wrapped around her mouth, down to her size seven feet, which shifted back and forth and couldn't stay still. Erica knew exactly what her blushing employee was suffering from.

"Um, I think I know what your problem is."

LaWan gave her a goofy grin. "You do?"

"How old are you again?"

"Twenty-four, but I've got a birthday coming next month."

"All right, birthday girl. Make sure your new man lets you get some rest tomorrow." Erica winked, knowing the deal.

"Damn, I'm busted."

"I've been there, LaWan. But let me give you a little advice."

The young girl widened her eyes eagerly. "Okay?"

"Don't allow any man to let you lose your focus. And, for heaven's sake, don't allow him to have you dragging in here looking like you just rolled out of bed sideways," Erica said, walking over to LaWan, adjusting the collar of her white shirt, which didn't look as if it had been ironed. "Come with me."

Erica took LaWan by the hand and led her back around to the counter. She reached into one of the cabinets and removed a small bottle of coconut-scented jojoba oil. She rubbed a quarter-size dollop in the palms of her hands and then into LaWan's unruly hair, finger combing it as she went along.

"I think the world of you," Erica continued, "but you know my policy and my standards. Part of Opulence's image lies not only in the products we sell, but in the people who sell them. You know my business motto, right?"

"Yes, Ms. E. Perception is reality."

"That's right, honey. So please don't come in here lookin' all jacked up again."

And as if on cue, Erica lit up with a radiant smile and walked over to a group of customers to greet them.

After selling four sets of shower gels, body scrubs, and creamy lotions to the enthusiastic group of customers she'd just greeted, Erica walked down the small, narrow hall toward the back of her boutique. She peeked into the break room and saw Christopher's head buried in a thick novel. He'd been avoiding her for the past few weeks because he'd heard about the product design fiasco.

Her first thought was to say something to him about his trifling friend Pierre, who hadn't followed through on his business commitment, but she quickly aborted the idea. She knew it wasn't Christopher's fault. It was hers. Plus, she was afraid Christopher might burst into tears if she spoke the words that were sitting on the edge of her tongue. She didn't want to deal with sobbing, since her afternoon had been going so well.

So instead of getting both of them worked up into a small frenzy, she walked a few more steps down the hall to her office and flipped on the light. Unlike most small retail stores, which housed one common area, serving as both an office and a break room space for all the employees, Erica had made sure, as with most other things, that Opulence was different from the rest.

The moderate-size break room was outfitted with a microwave, refrigerator, and sink, along with an art deco style dining table and high-back chairs. The potted plants, soft lighting, sage-green-colored walls, and large zebra-print rug gave it an elegant feel. And Erica's small, but very chic office continued the lavish look with its ruby-red-colored walls, golden bronze accents, and framed pictures of vintage perfume and lotion bottles.

Erica sat behind her desk to dig through the mountain load of work that awaited her. She hadn't looked at her e-mail since lunchtime today, so she braced herself as she turned on her computer.

She quickly scanned her in-box and saw an e-mail from Pierre. She leaned forward in her chair and opened it.

Hello Erica,
I apologize for getting back to you at such a late date. I had a family emergency that required my immediate attention. I know my personal crisis in no way excuses my lack of professionalism, and I am truly sorry. I have attached a design that I came up with that I hope you will find satisfactory, and captures the look and feel of your wonderful new product. Again, my sincere apologies.
Best,
Pierre St. James

Erica wanted to be understanding, because she knew how important family was. If anything ever happened to her mother, father, brother, or Ashley, she knew she wouldn't hesitate to drop everything at Opulence in order to take care of them. But at the same time, she was still annoyed that two full weeks had gone by without Pierre taking so much as a quick minute to respond to her dozens of e-mail and phone messages.

She clicked on the paper clip to open the attached file and had to blink twice when she saw the design. After carefully perusing Pierre's portfolio of work, she'd known that he was talented, but she had had no idea he was a genius! The new graphic he had designed was absolutely brilliant. He'd taken the concept she had given him, listened to her vision, sampled the product, and created an elegant, sophisticated art design that captured not only the richness of Paradise, but also the very essence of Opulence's brand.

Erica was so ecstatic she let out a loud, whopping scream that bounced off the walls and down the hall. She rose from behind her desk and went down to the break room.

"Christopher!" she called out.

Christopher jumped backward and dropped his book, looking startled and afraid at the sound of Erica's voice. "I apologize for the way things have turned out with Pierre. I just don't know what to say."

Erica let out a sigh and shook her head. *A twenty-two-year-old man shouldn't be acting like a frightened child,* she thought as she looked at Christopher fumbling to pick his book up off the floor. She wanted to tell him to get a grip and grow some balls, but at the moment she was too happy to be irritated.

"Pierre just sent me the design, and it's so completely fantastic, I'm speechless!"

Relief washed over Christopher's angular face as a smile slowly came to his lips. He closed his eyes and raised his head toward the ceiling and said, "Thank God he came through!"

"Not only did Pierre come through, but he also set a gold standard. I'm going to send the file over to our supplier right now. They can do a rush order that will get the new jars here by the end of the week."

"That's fabulous, Erica." Christopher stood, leaving his book on the table as he walked over to her. "We should celebrate."

"We will once Fashion Week is over."

"And speaking of Fashion Week!" Christopher smiled wide with excitement, adjusting his sterling silver cuff links as he spoke.

"You're not on my list for Fashion Week, Christopher."

"But . . ."

"Sorry, but that's final."

Erica knew he'd been angling to go, but there was no way she was going to let him tag along. The fashion world was beautiful, but it was also full of hard-core ugly attitudes. All it would take was for one bitchy designer to yell at him and Christopher would be shaking in his black loafers. Erica was nice, but she was also firm, and right now she didn't have time to deal with whining, because she had to e-mail the design file to her supplier. She reached over for a Kleenex, told Christopher to grab ahold of himself, and then marched back to her office.

As she sat behind her desk and pressed the send button, Erica thought about Jerome. He was right. Pierre had come through. She wished she could pick up the phone and share her good news or enjoy the moment with him over a delicious meal. Instead, she quietly celebrated all alone in the confines of her beautifully decorated office.

Now she knew exactly what Ashley had meant about having someone to share her success with, and it made her think about the classic line that Billy Dee Williams had delivered to Dianna Ross in the 1970s movie *Mahogany*. "Success is nothing without someone you love to share it with."

Two hours later, Erica called it a day and headed home. She walked one block to the parking garage down the street and slid into her car, letting out a relaxing yawn as she settled into the plush leather seat. After taking cabs to and from downtown to avoid the headache of trying to find a place to park her vehicle on the crowded streets, she was glad to be behind the wheel, headed home.

As she rode down the street, listening to Audra McDonald's Tony Award–winning voice piped through her car's sound system, her mind fell on Jerome again. She wondered what he would think about her taste in music, movies, books, food, and life in general. It was obvious to her that they came from different backgrounds, but that was also one of the things about him that she found appealing, and she was looking forward to stepping into his world.

Chapter 14

When Erica finally arrived home, she went straight to her bedroom, undressed, pulled on her soft terry-cloth robe, and then walked back downstairs to make a hot cup of herbal tea before she called Ashley.

"Hey, girlie," Ashley answered in a playful voice on the first ring. "What'cha up to?"

"I just got home. How about you?"

"I'm in Baltimore. I had a late meeting with a client, and now I'm in my car, headed home. I'm glad you called to keep me company on my ride back. How did your first day of court go?"

"It was great!" Erica said, taking a small sip of tea as she walked back upstairs to her bedroom. "And I can't wait to get back tomorrow."

"Hold up. Who are you, and what have you done with my best friend, Erica Stanford?"

Erica let out a laugh. "I know, right? Who would've thought I'd be anxiously awaiting another day of jury duty?"

"Not me, that's for sure. What brought about your change of heart?"

Erica quickly told Ashley about Jerome. She started with seeing him for the first time last week and went up to their impromptu lunch today. "Ash, this man is so handsome and sexy and . . . *mmm*, girl! I could just gobble him up!"

"Thank goodness! It's about time you met someone who piques your interest. See, I told you jury duty might be more fascinating than you thought. And a fine-ass man definitely raises things up a notch."

"Not only is he fine, but he's kind and thoughtful. He has this re-served strength and rugged edge that just make me want to melt."

"You're such a hopeless romantic."

"I know. Always have been and always will be."

Erica had always loved fairy tales. Growing up, she and Ashley could never watch the same movies together. Erica's choice always in-volved princesses and enchanted kingdoms, whereas Ashley's involved car chases and explosions. But that was one of the things that made their friendship click into place like building blocks. Erica's softness smoothed out Ashley's sharp edge. And Ashley's pragmatism saved Erica from floating into the clouds.

Ashley chuckled. "He sounds really nice, Erica. And I have to admit, I've never heard you sound so geeked up over a guy you just met."

"I guess it's because I've never met anyone quite like him," Erica said. "Jerome is the first man who has ever really listened to me. With most of the guys I've dated, it's always been about their résumés, who they know, what clubs or organizations they're members of, what kind of house they live in and car they drive. But with him it's different. We spent our entire lunch break with me as the center of attention."

"You did?"

"Yeah. He made me feel so special. He wanted to know every-thing about me . . . all about my life, my business, and my family and friends."

"Uh-oh."

"What do you mean, *uh-oh?*"

Ashley cleared her throat. "Girl, it sounds to me like you just might've found yourself a stalker."

"You're such a prosecutor."

"I'm a realist."

Erica sat her teacup on the side of her vanity table, took a seat in the chair, and looked in the mirror as she dabbed night cream on her face. "I think I'd know if he was a stalker. I've had enough experience dating lunatics to spot one."

"You've dated some assholes, but trust me, you don't know what real crazy looks like."

"Jerome's not crazy."

"How do you know? You just met him."

"I have a good feeling about him, and I always trust my gut."

"My dear, sweet, trusting friend." Ashley sighed. "You're really too nice sometimes and, dare I say, a bit naive."

"Just because I don't automatically assume the worse about everyone doesn't mean I'm naive."

"Okay, where is this guy from?"

"I'm not sure."

"What does he do for a living?"

Erica thought for a moment. She didn't know what he did, but she knew where he was employed. "He works for the city."

"Doing what?"

"Um, I don't know. But he told me that he's trying to start his own business. He does side projects at night and on the weekends. As a matter of fact, he was on his way to finish up a project this afternoon, when we left court."

"What kind of business is he trying to start?"

Erica paused for a second. "He didn't say. But I'll find out tomorrow, when we have lunch again."

"So for all you know, his fine ass could indeed be a stalker, or at the very least, a little crazy."

"Why does a man who shows a genuine interest in me have to be a crazy stalker?" Erica's voice cranked up a slight octave.

"Calm down. I didn't say he was. I merely suggested that he could be."

Erica rose from the soft chair at her vanity table, picked up her now lukewarm cup of tea, and walked over to her bed. "Aren't you the one who told me that I needed to meet someone and start dating again?"

"Yes, but I didn't mean just anybody."

"Jerome isn't just anybody."

"Erica, beyond his name, you don't know *who* he is."

Erica closed her eyes and took a deep breath. She knew Ashley would be skeptical because that was the cut-and-try, practical, no-nonsense type of person her friend had always been. But she hadn't anticipated such a negative response to her good news. "I don't understand why you're being such a Debbie Downer."

"Because this is real life. I deal with the criminal element in my line of work, and I see it all, and right now I don't like what I'm hearing."

"What you're hearing?" Erica balked. "I've been telling you how happy I am and how wonderful Jerome is since we started this conversation. What's there not to like about that?"

"I'm looking at the other side of it."

"What side?"

"The dark side of life, which you never seem to want to admit exists. Erica, you spent practically all day with this man and you don't know a thing about him, yet he knows everything about you, down to who your friends are. Don't you find that strange?"

Erica had to admit that she thought it was odd, too. But she'd been so caught up in her conversation with Jerome and the giddy way he made her feel that she'd glossed over it, figuring she'd find out all she needed to know in due time. Now Ashley was beginning to make her doubtful.

"Did you ask him any questions?" Ashley continued.

"No, well . . . yes, I did. I told him that we'd talked enough about me and that I wanted to know about him. But he said he found me really interesting, and somehow the conversation never got back around to him."

"See, that's what I'm talking about. Sweetie, in my experience, people who don't talk about themselves have something to hide."

Erica closed her eyes tight and thought for a minute. "The fact that he's able to serve on a jury in a court of law has got to mean something. If he was crazy or had a criminal past or something, they'd never let him serve on a criminal trial jury, right?"

"Not necessarily," Ashley responded. "Only people who have a pending felony criminal charge or who've been convicted of certain types of felonies are rejected. And as far as the crazy part, unless the court has documented papers that state he's got a mental disability, he's free to serve."

"So you're saying a person can be a crazy criminal and still make the cut?"

"Unfortunately, yes. My uncle Maynard has stabbed at least two people that I know of, and he's crazier than hell. But he had jury duty last year, and he got on my last freakin' nerve, asking me so many questions about 'the system.' "

By now, Erica was under her warm comforter, with the sheets pulled up to her chest. Her whimsical thoughts of a romance with Jerome were sinking faster than a makeshift raft. She hated to admit it, but Ashley was right. "So you think he's a crazy stalker?"

"Like I said, he could be. I just don't like the fact that he knows so much about you and you don't know a thing about him. You didn't tell him where you live, did you?"

"Of course not." Then a thought came rushing to Erica's mind. "Damn!"

"What?"

"Ash, he knows where I work. I gave him an Opulence flyer."

"Then he knows where you live, too. One Google search in the public records of deeds will link your name to both your business and home addresses. He's probably on his computer, doing a search, as we speak."

"I'm gonna do one, too." Erica hopped out of bed and walked down the hall to her home office. "I'm Googling him right now."

Erica typed in Jerome's name, but nothing appeared. She hit the back space key and attempted several different spellings, but still, nothing on Jerome Kimbrough came up on her screen.

"Did you find anything?" Ashley asked.

"Nothing," Erica answered. "It's like he doesn't exist. Nowadays, who doesn't have a presence on the Internet?"

"Somebody who doesn't want to be found."

Erica put her hand to her head, felling a dull ache play at her right temple. After she told Ashley her exciting news about Jerome, she'd planned to let her know about the beautiful design for Paradise, but now all she wanted to do was go back to her bed and hide under her fluffy sheets. But she knew she couldn't do that. She quickly jumped up from her desk chair and headed downstairs.

"You're breathing hard," Ashley said. "What are you doing?"

"Making sure my alarm is on. I don't think I set it before I came upstairs."

"Erica, I didn't mean to scare you. I just want you to be aware."

"I know. And you're right. All the things you said make perfect sense. I feel like such an idiot. I mean, who falls for someone they don't even know? And to think, he got me to tell him all my business."

Erica pressed a button to activate the alarm system's "no entry delay" feature. She looked out her back kitchen window, peering as far as she could beyond her covered garage. "You always hear stories about unsuspecting victims who never thought a terrible crime could happen to them. Well, I'm not going to be one of them."

Ashley shifted her voice to a gentler tone. "All I'm saying is that I want you to be careful with this guy. If you're still interested in him, find out everything you can about his background. But if he clams up or won't tell you anything, stop your communication immediately."

"I definitely will." Erica sighed heavily and bit her lower lip. "You know, ever since my dad was shot all those years ago, I've always made a conscious effort to fight against the feeling of being scared of my own shadow. I don't want to live in fear. That's why I give people the benefit of the doubt and look at the bright side of life, because trust me, despite what you think, I do know about the dark side. I've seen it."

"I know you have, sweetie," Ashley said softly. "In the meantime, I'll run a background check on him when I get in my office in the morning. What's his last name?"

"Kimbrough."

"And he works for the city, right?"

"Yes."

"Okay, if he has a criminal record, it should come up in our database. But sometimes, things can be expunged or can drop off for a variety of reasons, so I'll get my guy Sam to run an under-the-table check on him. Sam's good at what he does, and if this guy has any dirt on him, Sam will find it."

Erica breathed with a combination of anxiety and relief. "Thanks, Ash. I really appreciate it."

"Anytime. That's what I'm here for."

Later that night, as Erica lay awake in bed, she trembled inside. But unlike earlier today, the sensation wasn't a result of butterflies and wistful fantasies of love. It was a punch in the gut, rooted in the fear of what she hadn't seen coming.

Chapter 15

Erica quickened her pace as she turned the corner in the opposite direction of the courthouse, headed toward the parking garage several blocks in the distance. The rain had begun to pour, but she knew if she could just make it to the building, the parking attendant would be able to help her. She was almost there, but her breathing went shallow and the soft hairs on her arms rose when she realized that the foot traffic on the street was unusually sparse, with not another soul in sight. She swallowed hard, knowing what that meant.

She looked from side to side, walking as fast as her three-and-a-half-inch Jimmy Choos would allow under the conditions. The cold rain poured heavily as she took quick but measured steps, crunching the uneven pavement under her heels with a determined force of stride.

Then she heard him! His hard-bottom shoes made a *click-clack* noise behind her as he advanced.

Erica was too frightened to look back, and she knew if she did, it would only slow her down, and perhaps cause her to stumble on the slick sidewalk running under her feet. She tried not to panic as she soldiered on, increasing her speed. The sound of the footsteps was growing closer. Her heartbeat accelerated as the hard *click-clacking* of his shoes thundered in her ears, louder than the falling rain.

She could see the garage less than a hundred feet away, but she could also hear him gaining on her, advancing at a pace that would seal her fate in the next five seconds. She knew this was do or die. She had to make a move. With a determined focus, Erica breathed in and out, pumped her arms, and lifted her legs high into the wind as she dashed ahead.

But it was too late.

With a crushing force, she felt a hand the size of a baseball mitt wrap itself around the middle of her slender waist, while the other gripped her throat, at the base of her larynx, in a vicious death hold. It took only a few seconds to silence her. The scream she wanted to make became lodged deep in her trachea, unable to fight its way past her quivering lips.

She kicked and pulled and jerked and wrestled and clawed and fought. But her efforts only proved to rob her of precious energy, making her weaker as she expended the last traces of oxygen left in her lungs.

His hold became tighter. Her body began to grow limp. Erica could see death standing at the end of the deserted street, where the garage had been only moments ago. It was patiently waiting for her arrival. It beckoned her. It wanted her. So she stopped resisting.

She closed her eyes, letting her head drop against the pair of broad shoulders behind her. Listless and defeated, she opened her mouth, tasted the last drop of life upon her tongue, and waited for the end as the heavy rain stopped falling.

"*Nooooo!*" Erica screamed. She bolted straight up, wide awake, drenched in sweat, sitting in the middle of her tousled bed. Her chest heaved violently, her eyes were wet with saltwater tears, and her body quaked like an aftershock. She tried to remember her exercise, tried to breathe in and out to calm herself. But it wouldn't work this time. She couldn't focus, and she didn't care to. All she wanted to do was hide and make her nightmares go away.

Finally, she concentrated, slowing her breathing with controlled silence until she was no longer gasping for air. She reached over to her nightstand and turned off her alarm clock, which had yet to reach the hour of its sound. With slow and heavy steps, Erica pushed herself toward her bathroom and splashed cold water on her face.

Looking at herself in the beautifully appointed French provincial–style mirror hanging over her vessel sink, all Erica could think about was the change she wanted, and the fear that it might never come.

Chapter 16

Jerome felt as though he was walking on air as he approached the jury room. He switched the bag he was carrying to his left hand as he opened the door with his right. When he entered the quiet room, he was glad to see that he was the first person there. He'd set his alarm clock an hour early to make sure he wouldn't be late—that was how much he was looking forward to seeing Erica.

He shook his head and smiled, remembering yesterday and the way her tantalizingly curvy hips had teased him as she walked away, leaving him standing near the metro station in awe. Then, later that night, as he lay in bed, he wished she was there beside him so he could spoon her from behind.

He wanted to be close to Erica and to spend time getting to know her. He'd learned a lot about her yesterday, but he craved more. If he owned a computer, he would have used it last night to satisfy his curiosity. Jamel had been on him about getting a laptop for more than two years. Jerome had bought Jamel one so he could complete his homework assignments, but he hadn't seen much need to own one for himself. However, now that he was about to receive his GED and start JK Contracting, he knew he had to join the modern world. Hell, he didn't even have an e-mail account.

Jerome looked at the clock on the opposite side of the wall. In fifteen minutes his fellow jurors would start arriving. He knew Erica would be early, because he sensed that promptness was part of her nature, and the anticipation of seeing her walk through the door made his heart beat fast.

In an effort to busy himself, Jerome opened the bag he'd been carrying, removed the two cups of coffee he'd gotten for himself and Erica, and placed them on the table in front of him. He hoped she was a coffee drinker, and in case she was, he'd filled the bag with a variety of flavored creams and sugar for her choosing. He pulled out the chair beside him and placed his jacket in the seat to save it for Erica when she arrived.

When the door opened and Maude Feinstein walked in, Jerome was slightly disappointed. He thought the cheerful old lady was nice, but he was longing for Erica.

Maude greeted him with a warm hello as she looked at the two cups sitting on the table in front of him. "For me? Oh, you shouldn't have!" she teased.

I didn't, Jerome almost said. He smiled and nodded. "Sorry. I'll be sure to bring you a cup tomorrow."

"Oh, don't bother, honey. I was just kidding. I know who that coffee is for."

Jerome looked at the wise old lady and chuckled. "I'm sure you do."

"You two make a nice-looking couple."

"Um, we're not a couple." *Yet*, he wanted to say.

Maude winked. "You will be."

They both turned when they heard the door open, and three people walked in, but none of them were Erica. As the minutes ticked by, the room began to fill, but there was no sign of Stanford 145. Jerome began to worry, and he wished he had her phone number so he could call and make sure everything was okay.

He pulled back the small flap on the lid of his coffee and took a sip, drinking it straight, no sugar, no cream. He looked up when he felt a light tap on his shoulder.

"Mind if I sit here?"

Jerome stared into the eyes of Sasha Moore.

Sasha was tall and slim, with a pretty face and catlike eyes that were made more prominent by the green-colored contact lenses she wore. Her caramel-hued skin was smooth, complimenting the blond highlights that crowned the top of her dusty brown, shoulder-length hair. Jerome had heard a few of the other male jurors salivating over her during their break yesterday. They'd all said she was hot. But he knew what they'd really been thinking was that she looked like an easy lay.

Jerome knew he could easily sleep with Sasha if he wanted to. She'd been flashing him hints of her interest since last Friday, during jury selection. But her advances had gone unanswered on his part, which made her try even harder. He could tell she was the kind of woman who was used to getting attention from men, but for him, she held no interest. Her ass was way too flat for his taste. He was firmly in favor of juicy asses, curvy hips, and thick thighs.

Jerome was primed to tell Sasha that the seat was already taken, but before he could get the words out, she leaned over, brushed her heavy DD-cup breasts against his shoulder, and removed his jacket without warning. She wriggled her nonexistent hips into the seat and smiled. "How was your weekend?" she asked innocently.

Jerome was instantly annoyed. He knew that Sasha understood the deal—that he'd been saving the seat for Erica. He'd seen the tall temptress shoot Erica a nasty look yesterday, when she came into the room as they were finishing their lunch. She'd even trailed close behind them as they left the building at the end of the day. And now she was moving in, trying to stake her claim. He'd already dealt with a deadly stalker once in his life, so he knew how to spot crazy when he saw it.

Jerome looked into Sasha's eyes and read something unsettling behind her artificially colored lenses. It wasn't a stalker kind of crazy, but it was troubling just the same. He couldn't put his finger on it, but his instincts told him that just like the desperate housewife last weekend, the woman who'd just hijacked the chair beside him was nothing but trouble.

Just as Jerome was going to ask Sasha to move, Erica walked through the door. Once again, his breath was stolen from him, held hostage against his will. But very quickly he sensed that something was wrong.

He watched as Erica silently walked toward the table, barely looking his way. She took a seat across from him without saying a word. He studied her as she removed her large handbag from her shoulder and peeled out of her purple jacket. He noticed that her hair was pinned high on her head, exposing the same silver hoops that had danced at her lobes yesterday. She looked in Maude's direction, said hello, and smiled. But she didn't allow her deep brown eyes to travel the three feet that separated him from her.

By now all the jurors had arrived and the room was full. Various conversations were going on all at once, but Jerome didn't insert himself into any of them, because his mind was on Erica. He didn't know what to make of her distant behavior. She wouldn't even make eye contact with him. He wanted to get her attention, so he held up the cup of coffee he'd bought her and motioned it in her direction. "Erica, want a cup?" he said.

Erica barely looked at him, offering a half smile. "I had some on my way in, but thank you, anyway."

If Jerome's skin had been pale, he'd have probably turned as red as a crayon. He was glad the others were so caught up in their conversations that they hadn't noticed the dis that Erica had just sent flying his way.

"I'll take it. I haven't had a thing all morning," Sasha said as she took the cup from Jerome's hand. "You got any cream and sugar in that bag?"

Jerome lied and said he didn't. His mind was in a tailspin as he tried to figure out what in the hell was going on. He remembered how Erica had run hot and cold last week when he'd first seen her, looking at him one minute, smiling with light in her eyes, then shutting him down the next without even so much as a glance in his direction.

Damn. Maybe she's crazy, Jerome thought. In his mind there was no other explanation for her erratic behavior. He knew she was the creative, artsy type, and in his experience, those kinds of people usually had far-out personalities and could have serious mood swings. He wondered if she might have a dual personality and hadn't taken her meds.

As Jerome looked at Erica, examining her face, he noticed a tired look rimming her eyes. She covered her mouth and yawned, as if struggling to fight sleep. He knew that something was definitely wrong.

Moments later they got in line, standing in the quiet hallway as they waited to enter the courtroom. Jerome's body was so close to Erica's that he could reach out and hug her.

"Are you okay?" he whispered.

"Yes, I'm fine," she whispered back without turning around.

"No, you're not. What's wrong?"

"I said I'm fine."

"You sure?"

Erica slowly turned around and stepped to within a few inches of his face as she spoke in a low voice. "Why would I lie? I'm not the one with anything to hide. So if I say I'm fine, it means exactly that. . . . *I'm fine.*"

Fine and crazy as hell, Jerome said to himself. Now he was really puzzled. "Listen, I don't know what your problem is or what happened to you between yesterday and this morning. All I know is that you're acting like I've offended you, when the only thing I want to do is make sure you're okay."

He'd said his words forcefully, but also with a pleading emotion so tender that it startled even him. The weight of it made him dizzy with questions he couldn't answer.

He saw a softness wash over Erica's tired eyes, changing the expression on her face back to one of the woman he remembered. She was about to speak when the announcement came that it was time to enter the courtroom.

She nodded. "Let's talk at the break." And without another word, she turned and marched in line through the courtroom door.

Jerome felt conflicted. His gut, along with all the crazy love-struck emotions he'd been feeling, told him that Erica was special. But his practical mind and his life experience told him that something about her wasn't right. There was a hidden piece behind the softness in her eyes that led him to that feeling. And now, as he sat in the jury box, listening to the first witness who'd been called to the stand, he didn't know which way to go or what to believe. He leaned back in his seat, glanced over at Erica, and wondered what the hell he'd gotten himself into.

Chapter 17

Erica sat in the jury box, her writing pad getting a workout from her pen as she jotted down notes while the witness rattled off his testimony. She was doing a good job of concentrating, but then she was suddenly thrown off track by the feel of Jerome's knee against her leg.

"Excuse me," he whispered in his deep baritone, never taking his eyes off the witness stand to the right of them.

He had shifted in his seat and had accidentally brushed his knee against her upper thigh. Even though he was wearing relaxed dark denims and she was business casual in a pair of tan trousers, the heat from his contact made Erica feel as though they'd touched skin to skin. She fiddled with her pen and sighed, quietly wishing she could explain herself and her actions to Jerome.

She regretted prejudging him and jumping to conclusions. But after her conversation with Ashley last night, and then the horrible nightmare she'd awakened to at three this morning, she wasn't thinking straight. She knew Jerome had done nothing to warrant her cool treatment in the jury room, and she was embarrassed by her actions. She'd barely looked at him today, but after hearing the worry in his voice just moments ago and seeing the confusion mixed with genuine concern on his face, she knew he was simply a thoughtful man who was trying to get to know her, not a stalker.

Erica wanted their break to come, but time inched along so slowly, she feared she might fall asleep. She thought about the coffee

Jerome had offered her, and wished so badly that she'd accepted it, especially after the skinny, colored-contacts-wearing woman drank it. Getting her coffee had been another sweet gesture on his part, and again, she felt embarrassed about her actions.

Finally, after what seemed like an eternity, the judge dismissed them for their morning break. It took Erica a little effort to rise, and when she did, she felt the weight of her sleepless night fall down on her. With slow movements, she walked in line until she reached the hallway.

"You gonna be okay?" Jerome asked.

"Yes, I'm just a little tired. Um, do you mind if we talk?"

Jerome led the way to a stairwell on the other side of the hall from the jury room. Standing alone with him in the quiet space, Erica thought about how she'd regarded Jerome with apprehension and skepticism last night. But now she felt perfectly safe with him. As a matter of fact, a quick burst of excitement made her perk up, despite her sleep-deprived fatigue. Being close to him outside the jury room felt good, and she was glad he'd taken her to this private place.

Erica shifted her feet, feeling Jerome's eyes on her. She thought about how she must appear to him, given the distant reserve and frosty attitude she'd displayed. Then she thought about her appearance.

I must look a hot mess! Erica smoothed down a few wayward strands of hair on the top of her head. She wished she'd had time to use her flatiron this morning. But after the rough night she'd had, it was all she could do to run a small amount of oil cream through her tresses, brush them back into a neat chignon, and make herself presentable before she walked out the door.

As Jerome's eyes continued to hold her in a steady gaze, she wasn't quite sure where to begin, but since she knew their break would whizz by, she jumped straight in. "I'm sorry for the way I acted this morning. My behavior was uncalled for, and I apologize."

She waited for a reaction, but he gave her nothing—at least not verbally. His tightly crossed arms and piercing eyes told her that he wanted more in the way of an explanation, so she continued. "I was a little leery of you, and I didn't know what to think because—"

"Leery of me?" Jerome repeated, cutting her off in mid-sentence.

"I thought we were really vibin'. What did I do to make you feel that way?"

Erica let out a sigh and fiddled with her notepad. "During our conversation yesterday you found out a lot about me, but I walked away knowing absolutely nothing about you. Then, when I asked, you avoided giving me any answers. The more I thought about it, the more it made me think you had something to hide. Then I started thinking all kinds of things."

"Like what?"

"Like, maybe you were a crazy stalker and you were just trying to get information on me."

"You actually thought I was trying to stalk you?"

"Hey, it's not such a stretch. People are crazy nowadays."

Jerome laughed.

"You think that's funny?"

"No, Erica. I don't think it's funny." Jerome took a deep breath and shook his head. "Let me assure you. I'm not a stalker. The only reason I asked so many questions was because I wanted to get to know you. I'm feelin' you, and I'd like to take you out."

There was a long pause between them. A shy smile slid across Erica's toasted bronze–colored lips. "Really?"

"Yeah . . . really."

Jerome opened the door for Erica, and they entered Cosi restaurant. She would have preferred a quieter, more intimate setting, but since the eatery was across the street from the courthouse, it fit into their lunch schedule. Plus, she and Jerome had decided they should dine outside the jury room or the court cafeteria to avoid the prying eyes and gossipy tongues of their fellow jurors.

Despite Erica's protest, Jerome insisted on paying for their meal.

"But you treated yesterday, so now it's my turn. Plus, you agreed to it," she said.

"Number one, I don't keep score of stuff like that. And number two, I never agreed to anything. I just listened to what you had to say," he said with a smile.

Jerome found an empty table along the wall and led Erica to it.

Once they settled in, they didn't waste any time with their food or their conversation.

"Have you ever done speed dating?" Erica asked.

"Uh, no. But I've heard about it. Why?"

"This break will fly by super fast, so I figured we can pretend this is a speed-dating session and I can find out more about you."

"So you've done speed dating?"

Erica shook her head. "You can only answer questions. I'm doing all the asking this time."

Jerome smiled and bit into his chicken pesto flat bread sandwich. "Okay, I'm game."

"Where are you from?"

"Right here in the good ol' nation's capital. I was born at Howard University Hospital."

Erica smiled. "Okay. Where did you go to school?"

"Ballou High."

She waited for him to continue, but when she saw him avert his eyes to the bag of chips in front of him, she knew he'd completed his response, and that twelfth grade had been his stopping point. She took a sip of her double expresso and then continued. "What do you do for the city?"

"I've been with the Department of Public Works for ten years."

"Doing what?"

"I work in the sanitation division."

"Well, what do you do in the sanitation division?"

Jerome put down his sandwich and wiped his mouth with his paper napkin. He took a deep breath and looked into Erica's eyes. "Can we stop this speed-dating thing and just talk?"

Chapter 18

Erica returned Jerome's stare, trying to figure out if she had offended him. "I'm sorry. I didn't mean to make you feel uncomfortable with my questions. I just want to know more about you, and our time is limited."

"During court hours it is. But we don't have to limit ourselves to communicating here, unless that's what you want."

"It depends on what I find out."

"You're a straight shooter. I like that."

Erica smiled, fiddling with her napkin. "Okay, let's talk."

Just as their entire lunch conversation yesterday had centered around Erica, Jerome took the spotlight today. "I'm a sanitation worker," he began, "which means I pick up people's trash. I have a route in Northwest. My job isn't glamorous, but it's honest work and it pays the bills. I dropped out of high school in eleventh grade. It was a stupid thing to do and one of the biggest mistakes I've ever made. But I'm about to get my GED next month, and I'm studying for the test now."

Erica continued to listen as Jerome emptied the contents of his life onto the table. She learned that he had a thirteen-year-old son who was an honor student and the pride of his life. As he'd alluded to yesterday, he was also laying the groundwork to start JK Contracting. And since his son was also gifted with his hands, Jerome hoped one day to pass the business along to him.

Erica sat patiently, listening and nodding, but not once did she interrupt or make a further inquiry as Jerome spoke. She didn't want to be one of those high-minded, judgmental, bourgeois black folk who looked down their nose at those who weren't members of the talented tenth. But as she discovered more about Jerome's background, and in particular, his current life, she realized that certain parts of his existence made her uncomfortable.

She'd always dated a certain type of man, and Jerome definitely wasn't it. Every man she'd ever been involved with had had a bachelor's degree at minimum. Their work uniforms consisted of a suit and tie, not coveralls with their name spelled out on the upper left-hand side of their chest. And the only rental properties they'd had any interest in were the ones they owned and leased to their tenants. Then there was the drug thing. Erica knew that a couple of her college boyfriends had smoked weed in their off-campus apartments, but they'd never been involved in the selling and distribution side of it, and for her part, she'd never personally ingested an illegal substance in her life.

But here sat Jerome, a high school dropout who picked up trash for a living, rented a small apartment in a bad neighborhood, and happened to be an ex-drug dealer with what she gleaned was a little baby mama drama thrown in to round out the list of no-no's she'd always avoided.

It was a lot for Erica to digest at once. Dating a man like Jerome Kimbrough went against all her rules and all the advice her father had given her about men. She generally followed Joseph's advice because he had always been a loving father, an excellent provider, and had warned her against becoming involved with the wrong type of man.

She knew that if she sketched out Jerome's life on a sheet of paper, her parents—who had always supported her, no matter the situation—would ball it up and toss it in the wastebasket. And her brother, Nelson, would gently ask her if she was going through something, and then recommend a professional whom she could talk to. Even Ashley, who was already shaky on him, would ask her if she'd officially lost her mind!

"So, that's who I am in a nutshell," Jerome said, ending his mini biography.

Erica nodded in silence.

"Listen, you're a straight shooter, and so am I, so I'll cut right to it. I know I'm not anything like the type of dudes you're used to dating. I don't have a fancy degree, a prestigious job, or a big house. But I'm a hardworkin' brothah, tryin' to start my own business so I can build a better life for me and my son. I've made my share of mistakes that have come back to bite me, and I accept responsibility for them."

Erica nodded again but still didn't say anything.

Jerome gave her a slight smile and then shook his head.

"What?" Erica finally said.

"I can't believe I'm doing this." His voice grew quieter as he spoke. "I think you're smart, talented, sincere, and very beautiful. You're the kind of woman that any man would be proud to have by his side. I already told you that I'm feelin' you and I'd like us to go out, so unless you have a man you haven't told me about, either you're feelin' me, too, or you're not. Simple as that."

"Simple as that?" Erica said, snapping her fingers for emphasis.

"Yeah, it is. A woman knows within the first five minutes of conversation with a brothah whether she's gonna give him a chance. We've been talking way longer than that, so I know you've already made up your mind." Jerome paused and leaned forward in his chair, cutting the distance between them in half. "I don't want to waste your time or mine, so let me know what it's gonna be, 'cause I'm putting the ball in your court."

Erica had to admit that Jerome was right, although it had actually taken her ten minutes to finally make up her mind instead of five. She leaned forward over their small table, removing the last bit of space between them, until they were close enough to graze each other's lips. "Why don't you call me tonight so we can continue this conversation?"

Erica paced back and forth in her galley kitchen with her phone pressed tightly against her ear. "What did you find out?" she asked Ashley.

"Your boy had a little trouble back in the day, but for the last decade or so he seems to have cleaned up his act."

"Drugs, right?"

"You already knew?"

"Yes, we had a long talk during lunch. He told me that he'd done things he wasn't proud of and that he'd sold drugs at one point. How serious was it? Did he spend time in prison?" Erica was hoping to Jesus he hadn't.

"He had two separate arrests for possession of an illegal substance about twelve years ago, but neither resulted in convictions. My guess is that those drugs bought him a damn good lawyer who got him off."

"I see."

"Then there's the aggravated assault and murder charges."

"What!" Erica nearly screamed. She stopped pacing the floor and leaned against her granite countertop. "Why didn't you tell me that first? Oh, my God!"

"Girl, calm down," Ashley said. "The charges weren't *against* him. They were made *by* him."

Erica held her hand to her mouth as she listened.

"About eleven years ago he filed a stay-away order against a Tawanna Jones, and then six months later he filed aggravated assault and attempted murder charges against the same woman. Seems she shot him."

"Good Lord in heaven."

"I know, and get a load of this. The report says he was hospitalized for nine days with a gunshot wound to the chest that missed his heart by just one inch. That woman was trying to kill him. Interestingly, though, there's not a lot in the report about the particulars surrounding what brought on the attack. I'm thinking it was probably a lovers' quarrel, and shit went south fast."

"Damn!" Jerome had been through more than Erica had thought. "Does the report say anything else?"

"No, not the official report. But the unauthorized one I was able to get has the real four-one-one. Seems that Mr. Jerome used to be a street hustler, who, as you know, ran drugs. But it looks like he ran women even harder. The report links him to too many women to follow up on. He's had his fair amount of hood drama. The whole shooting incident smells of it. But I have to say in his defense that it looks like he's left that life behind. He makes regular child support payments, he visits his parents once a week, and last year he even received an employee-of-the-month award. . . . Ain't that impressive?"

Erica could hear the sarcasm nestled inside Ashley's last comment, but she chose to ignore it. "How did you find out all this stuff?"

Ashley laughed. "I told you, my guy Sam is good. He knows people in high and low places."

"Well, at least I have a better understanding of his life now. Thanks for doing this for me, Ash. I really appreciate it."

"You're not seriously still interested in this guy, are you?"

Erica was prepared for Ashley's skepticism, and she had to admit that on the surface, if Ashley had met someone like Jerome, caution would be her advice to her friend, too. Drama had always been a part of both their relationships in the past, but never did their romances involve drugs or violence. Erica also knew that Ashley was probably less than impressed with Jerome's profession, as well.

But Erica knew this wasn't anyone's decision to make except her own. She'd allowed Ashley to work her up into a frenzy last night, and as it turned out, it had all been for naught. So she decided she wouldn't let that happen again.

"Yes, I'm very interested in him," Erica replied. "As a matter of fact, I need to go because I'm expecting Jerome's call any minute."

Erica walked up to her bedroom, changed into her nightgown, and relaxed under her soft sateen sheets. She was trying not to feel upset about her conversation with Ashley, because, after all, she knew her friend wanted only the best for her and was concerned about her emotional safety. But sometimes Ashley got on her last nerve with her elitist attitude. "Of all people, she should know better," Erica mumbled out loud.

Although Ashley and her immediate family were nearly thirty years removed from the housing project out of which they'd ascended to the affluence of suburban Prince George's County, Maryland's gated Hill Crest Manor, a large number of her relatives still lived in the hood, from D.C. to the Bronx. So given Ashley's background, Erica found it ironic that her friend would look down on anyone, in any capacity.

As she lay in her comfortable bed, waiting for Jerome's call, her phone chimed from her nightstand. Her heart beat fast and her lips snaked into a sunny smile when she looked at the time on her digital clock, which read nine on the dot! Jerome had called right at the very moment they'd agreed upon earlier that afternoon. Erica saw this as a very good sign and was glad he was already becoming more time conscious.

She reached over and clicked on her phone. "Hey! You called right on time."

"I did?"

Erica's eyes widened when she heard Claude's voice on the other end. *That's what I get for not looking at the damn caller ID before I answer the phone!* "Claude, why are you calling me?"

"Well, it's nice to hear your voice, too," he said.

Erica sat silently, waiting for him to answer her question.

"I've been thinking about you since I saw you at Vidalia last Friday. I can't get you out of my mind, Erica. Have you been thinking about me?"

"I don't mean to repeat myself, but again, why are you calling me?"

"I just told you. I've been thinking about you, and I miss you."

"Try thinking about your girlfriend."

"She's not my girlfriend. We've been on a few dates, but that's all. It's not even like that."

"Oh, just like the little chocolate treat you had on the side wasn't like that, and the son you passed off as your nephew wasn't like that, either?"

"I was wrong for that, and I said and did a lot of hurtful things that I shouldn't have. But let's put all that behind us and look forward."

Again, Erica refrained from words, letting her silence speak her response.

"Erica, I still love you, and if you can find it in your heart to forgive me and put the past behind us, where it belongs, I know we can build a great life together."

Erica was growing more suspicious by the minute. Claude wasn't the begging type, because his ego was simply too huge to entertain the thought. So she wondered why in the world he wanted them to get back together, especially since despite what he'd said, he had a new woman in his life who had an important job with an even more important company.

Erica let out a deep sigh. "I'm not interested in the past or building a future with you. What we had ended a long time before we actually broke up."

"*We* didn't break up. It was you who broke up with me."

"I thought you said what was in the past was in the past. You lie so much, you don't even know what you're saying or doing."

"Why are you trying to make this difficult?"

Erica was starting to get frustrated. "Listen, I'm not sure what the real reason is for this call, but whatever the case, I'm not interested." And with that, she hung up the phone.

She was pissed that Claude had had the nerve to call and sour her evening. But more than that, she was disappointed that the clock was ticking and she still hadn't heard from Jerome.

Chapter 19

Jerome rushed through his front door in such a hurry, he nearly stumbled over his own feet. He sat his heavy tool belt on the floor at the edge of the living room, which led back to his bedroom, and then quickly removed his work boots. He had to be fast because he was running late. It was almost 10:00 p.m., and he was supposed to have called Erica an hour ago.

After he and Erica had finished lunch, they'd exchanged phone numbers. They both had commitments that evening—she needed to check in at Opulence and he needed to repair a leaky faucet for a client—so they agreed to talk at 9:00 p.m.. "I'll call you," he'd told her.

Jerome had every intention of calling Erica at their agreed-upon time, but he ran into unexpected problems. Instead of repairing the faucet, he had to replace it, which required a trip to Home Depot. But the store he went to didn't have the style or model his client wanted, so he had to go to another location, then double back to his client's house to finish the work. Then Jamel called and talked to him until he arrived at his apartment building. He hadn't realized it was 9:55 p.m. until he parked his truck and looked at the time displayed on the dashboard.

With speed equivalent to light, Jerome undressed, took a quick shower, and then dialed Erica's number.

"Hello." She answered on the third ring.

"Hey, I'm sorry I'm a little late."

"A little? You were supposed to call me over an hour ago."

"I know, and I'm really sorry. The repair job took a lot longer than I had expected. Then my son called, and we had to discuss a few things. As soon as I hung up with him, I walked through my door, took a shower, and then called you."

After they got off to a rocky start this morning, their lunch conversation had helped them rebound and had put them at ease. But now, hearing the disappointment in Erica's voice, Jerome wondered whether they were headed right back to how their day had begun. He definitely wasn't interested in revisiting that uncomfortable place.

He knew that calling Erica an hour later than he'd said he would wasn't a good way to kick off their first phone conversation. He had always tried to be a man of his word, but when his word involved promptness, he battled a challenge he had yet to conquer. He wished he could see Erica's pretty face right now. That way he'd know exactly what she was thinking. He'd already discovered that her feelings rested behind the glimmer of her brown eyes and the pout of her soft-looking lips.

"Jerome," she began. "I'm sorry you ran into problems, but in the future, if you see that you're going to be late, please give me a quick call or send me a text to let me know. It only takes a minute."

Jerome withstood her chiding because he knew she was right and, more important, because she'd just said she wanted to have future conversations with him. "Okay, I'll do that."

"So, did you fix the problem for your client?"

"Yes, even though it took forever. How are things at your boutique? Did you ever hear from that designer?"

Erica's voice perked up with excitement. "Yes. I can't believe I forgot to tell you! I received the file yesterday afternoon, and the design turned out better than I ever could have imagined."

"That's great news."

"Yes, it is. I'm so pleased that things are finally starting to fall into place. I even have a couple of good applicants lined up for interviews so I can replace my employee who quit without warning last week."

"I'm real happy for you, Erica," Jerome said as he walked back to his bedroom.

"Thanks. I really appreciate you saying that. It feels like it's been a long time coming." She let out a heavy breath as she finished her last words.

"Are you sleepy? I know you didn't get much rest last night."

"No, surprisingly I'm good. What you heard was an exhale of relief."

"That's good." Jerome stretched his long body across his queen-size bed, closed his eyes, and pictured her face in his mind. "So, what are you doing now?"

"Nothing. Just lying in bed, talking to you."

The image of her lying in bed excited him, but he knew it was too early in their relationship to take the conversation to the level he desired, so he kept it tame. "You said you wanted to continue our conversation from earlier today, right?"

"Yes, and actually, I'm glad you brought that up."

"Okay, let's talk. I'm ready."

"Before we do, there's something I need to tell you."

Damn! he thought. It wasn't what she'd said, but rather it was the tone in which she'd said it, that let Jerome know something was up. He hoped Erica wasn't going to confess to having a boyfriend, or worse, tell him that she was married and it was "complicated." He'd been out with a few women who'd pulled that kind of bullshit.

Erica cleared her throat. "I've been in more failed relationships than I can count, and aside from being wrong for one another, one of the main reasons things never worked out was a lack of communication. If you and I start seeing each other, I want us to be open and honest about our past, our present, and what we want for our future."

"I agree, and I can do that."

"Good. Now that I've said that, I have something I want to confess."

I knew it! Shit! He wanted to say something, but he remained deathly silent, listening to his heart beat drums inside his chest.

"Jerome, are you still there?"

"Yes, I'm listening."

"Oh, o-okay," Erica stammered. "Remember when I told you that I thought you might be a stalker?"

"Yeah?" Now Jerome's eyes were wide open, staring out into the darkness of his room.

"I have a friend who has some connections, and she had a background check done on you."

Jerome didn't know what to say, because he didn't know how much she already knew. He'd told her that he used to sell drugs and that he'd dropped out of high school. But beyond that, there wasn't a lot more to tell, at least not in his mind.

Erica went on. "I know about your arrests and a few other things from your past, and that's what I want to have an open and honest discussion about."

"What other things from my past?"

Erica paused. "Your personal life. Specifically, known associations and relationships," she said in a politically correct–sounding voice.

Jerome sat up and kicked his long legs around the edge of his bed. "I can't say that I blame you for having me checked out. You're a single woman and you have to protect yourself, so I'm cool with that. But the way I see it, getting to know each other is a process. And every process has steps and takes time."

"Yes, you're right. I'm ready to take that first step."

"Good."

They talked like friends who were catching up on old times. Jerome told Erica about his arrests for possession, his near-fatal shooting at the hands of a woman who'd become obsessed with him, and the crazy, dysfunctional, up-and-down relationship he'd finally ended with Kelisha two years ago. Then Erica poured out the bittersweet details of her first broken heart, the painful dissolution of her broken engagement with Claude, and the very real fear she harbored deep inside that she might never find the happily-ever-after she'd always been searching for.

"Finding love is just so hard, you know?" Erica said.

Jerome thought for a moment. "I don't think you find love. Love finds its own way. It comes to you."

"Hmm, I guess you're right. It makes me think of that old saying 'Love comes when you're not looking for it.' "

"Bingo." That was exactly how he felt about her. Erica had come to him without him searching for her.

During the course of their conversation they laughed, paused, asked questions, told jokes, expressed dreams, and discovered new and shiny details about each other's lives. Finally, their lids began to feel the stretch of their long day, so they said good night.

Several minutes after they ended their call, Jerome lay in bed with the phone still at his ear, holding on to the memory of Erica's voice until he fell asleep.

Erica smiled like a little girl and felt as excited as one, too, as she sat next to Jerome. They were the first to arrive at the jury room. Last night they'd agreed to get there early so they would have extra moments of quiet time before the other jurors arrived. And just as he'd done yesterday, Jerome brought coffee for the two of them, and this time Erica willingly accepted her cup.

They were both a little groggy, a result of their long conversation last night, which had crawled over into the wee hours of the morning. It had been two days since Erica had had a decent night's sleep, but looking at her, one would never be able to tell, because she seemed as bright and lively as she always did, with hair and make-up done to effortless perfection. Under any other conditions it would have been hard for her to function, but to her surprise, she was managing well.

She smiled to herself, knowing the newness of her budding relationship with Jerome was in large part responsible for her current state. After having a frustrating conversation with Ashley, and then an irritating one with Claude, Jerome's voice had been the soothing remedy she'd needed.

Erica had awakened mere hours after falling asleep, with Jerome on her mind and the anticipation of seeing him. Now, as she sat close beside him, smelling his vanilla- and wood-scented cologne, all she could think about was how much she wanted things to work between the two of them.

After last night Erica felt as though she'd known Jerome for years instead of just a few days. She thought he was the most fascinating man she'd ever met, and had she not known he'd completed only eleventh grade, she would have thought he held an advanced degree. She discovered that he was very smart, quick-witted, and well read on a variety of subjects. They'd discussed everything from relationships to politics, and Erica was impressed that he approached each topic from a thoughtful, well-informed perspective.

"I'll be glad when this trial is over," Jerome said, bringing Erica's mind back to the moment at hand.

"You know, as ironic as it may sound, I look forward to it each day."

"I look forward to seeing you every day, but other than that, I'm ready for it to end."

Erica found the cases that both the prosecution and the defense were building to be quite fascinating, but she could tell that Jerome was completely uninterested, given that he'd yet to take a single note. She was curious about it, so she asked.

"You never write down what the witnesses are saying during testimony. Why haven't you taken any notes?"

Jerome took a big gulp of his coffee. "I haven't seen much need to. After the first five minutes I already knew the deal with this case."

Erica shook her head and chuckled. "There you go again with your infamous five-minute rule."

"Go 'head and laugh," he said, playfully nudging her with his elbow. "It doesn't take a lot of time to sum up things. Nonverbal communication speaks just as loud as words and can paint a picture that someone's mouth may not speak. I watch a person's actions to get the real story, and that's what I'm doing for this case. I looked at that woman, and I figured things out. It's not hard to read what's going on."

"Yes, I know what you mean. Poor Ms. Slater," Erica said, referring to the plain-faced defendant whom she'd quietly come to champion.

"What?" Jerome shook his head as he moved his empty cup to the side. "Erica, that woman is guilty as hell."

Erica stopped sipping her coffee. "What makes you say that?"

"Everything about her looks guilty."

"You can't base someone's guilt or innocence on how they look."

"I'm not talking about the woman's physical appearance. I'm looking at other stuff."

"Like what?"

Jerome reached in his jacket pocket and pulled out a tin of cinnamon Altoids. "You want one?"

"No. Just an answer, please." She smiled.

Jerome smiled back and popped the cinnamon-flavored mint in his mouth as he continued. "Like the fact that she's trying way too hard. I believe she's frightened about the possibility of going to prison, 'cause trust me, I know how scary that thought can be. But she sits at that defendant's table, looking like she just walked out of a haunted house, eyes all big, shaking like somebody just carjacked her or something. That's some straight-up acting."

Erica frowned. "I disagree. She looks that way because, like you said, she's frightened. Not everyone can put up a strong front. If she was guilty, she'd probably be as cool as a fan, because that's how slick criminals think."

"What do you know about how criminals think?"

Erica didn't have a good answer. She had to admit that she didn't have up close and personal experience in matters of criminal activity other than the police dramas she'd seen on TV. But she trusted her gut, and just as her gut told her that Jerome was a good man, it told her that Ms. Slater was an innocent woman. "I know what my gut tells me."

"It's important to trust your instincts. That's how I make most of my decisions. But my instincts tell me she's guilty. Have you noticed that she's never, and I mean not once, looked into the eyes of one single person on this jury? She barely turns her head our way."

"That's not true. She looked at me the very first day of the trial, during opening arguments."

"You sure she looked at you or just in your direction?"

Erica thought for a moment, her mind churning as she replayed the courtroom scenes from the last two days. She remembered the defendant looking her way, but she couldn't say with certainty that she'd seen Ms. Slater make direct eye contact with her or any of the members of the jury.

"Think about it," Jerome continued. "When people have something to hide, they usually can't look you in the eye. Plus, there's other things she's done that got me suspicious."

"Like what?" By now Erica had abandoned her coffee and was listening intently to Jerome's assessment.

"When the prosecution witnesses are testifying, every now and then she'll start nervously tapping her pen on the pad in front of her.

I think it's because what they're saying is true and she wants them to shut up."

Erica hadn't noticed that detail, but she made a mental note to look for the gesture from this point forward. "Is that the only other thing?"

"No. I've also noticed that she stares down every eyewitness the prosecution calls."

"But I thought you said a person who has something to hide can't look you in the eyes."

Jerome smiled. "See, that's where a criminal mind comes into play. She ain't gonna look at us, because she wants us to believe the lie she's hiding. But those people who worked with her, who are testifying against her, she already knows that they know her ass is lyin', so she can look at them 'cause she don't give a damn about what they think."

"You make some good points. But, Jerome, I believe her. Some of the electronic time sheets that the prosecution says she turned in could've been doctored by someone in her department, or they could've had someone in IT do it. You can do anything with a computer. And trust me, I know how easy it is for people to set a trap for you on the job."

"Okay, I'll give you that. But even if they changed up her time sheets to make it look like she was double billing, why did she accept all that overtime money if she knew she didn't earn it? The records showed that a fat direct deposit went into her bank account every month, and she knew it was more than she was supposed to be gettin'."

Erica had to admit it was a question she'd asked herself. "I guess she felt like, 'Hey, I'll give it back if I get caught, but if I don't, then I'm gonna keep it.' I know that's not ethical, but it's also not illegal, and it's not embezzlement or deliberate fraud, which is what they're trying to pin on this poor woman."

Erica was expecting a quick rebuff. She'd learned last night that Jerome was quite the debater, and she loved hearing his point of view. But instead of responding to what she'd just said, he was silent.

"You're not saying anything?"

Jerome leaned in close. "I like that you see the good in people.

That's a real nice quality." He moved a little closer, placing his mouth so close to her ear, she could feel his warm breath on her skin. He breathed in deeply, and then exhaled. "I love the way you smell."

Erica nearly melted in her seat. His warm, cinnamon-scented breath was intoxicating. She drank in his dark, clean-shaven face, which was as handsome as any magazine model's, and his penetrating eyes, which made her feel shamelessly horny. She wanted to brush her tongue across his full lips and taste the cherry-flavored ChapStick she'd watched him apply when they first arrived this morning. She could feel the heat rising between them, but all of a sudden their moment was stolen when the door opened.

"Well, good morning, you two," Maude said with a generous smile.

Erica quickly sat back in her chair, pulling herself away from the kiss she'd fantasized about placing on Jerome's mouthwatering lips.

"Good morning, Ms. Maude," they both said in union.

"How's it going?" Erica asked.

"Wonderful! I'm really looking forward to today's testimonies. I thought I had a pretty good idea about how things were shaping up until yesterday afternoon. But now I just don't know what to think. One thing's for sure. This case has surely proven that there can be two very different sides to the same story."

Just then, four other jurors arrived, with Sasha leading the way. The brazen bombshell walked around the table, casting her sights on Jerome. Erica knew what the woman was up to, and she didn't appreciate the bold show of disrespect one bit. She'd read the woman's sneaky intentions from day one, and she knew that Sasha was a shark swimming in the tank, looking for smaller fish to devour. And although Erica found her to be overly made up and a bit obnoxious, she knew that men, particularly those on the jury, found her attractive. She looked at Sasha's overflowing breasts and slim features from head to toe and wondered if Jerome found her attractive, too.

Just as jealousy's serpent was about to roar, Erica's question was answered when Jerome focused his eyes and attention on her, leaned in near her ear, and softly whispered, "Did I tell you that I'm really feelin' you?"

Chapter 20

Erica took copious notes as she listened closely to the eyewitness currently testifying for the prosecution. The prim middle-aged woman was delivering damaging information, alleging that Ms. Slater had routinely goofed off on the one day a week that she came into the office at the company's downtown D.C. location. According to the witness, shoe shopping, Facebooking, tweeting, and games of solitaire were the defendant's work assignments of choice during the morning, before taking a two-and-a-half-hour lunch and then leaving an hour early to round out her workday.

"If those were her work habits when she come into the office, I can only imagine what she did at home," the woman said.

"Leading!" the defense attorney objected.

As Ms. Maude wrote vigorously, taking in the details of the defense's cross-examination, Erica studied the placid look on Ms. Slater's face. She searched for subtle gestures and body language that would give clues to the woman's guilt or innocence. She thought about what Jerome had said, and he was right. Ms. Slater was looking dead on into the eyes of her former coworker on the stand, but not once had she even glanced in the direction of the jury box.

Erica remembered Ashley once telling her that attorneys often instructed their clients to try to make some kind of connection with the jury. That way they became a person, and not just a defendant. "It's easier to convict a defendant whom you don't know, versus a person who may be innocent," she had said. Ms. Slater hadn't looked at one single member of the twelve-person jury all morning, yet her eyes were glued like a laser on the witness sitting on the stand.

Erica felt conflicted, because although Ms. Slater now appeared to be less than credible, there was still the possibility that she was innocent. In Erica's mind, there were just too many variables to draw a definitive conclusion at this point, and she now understood what Ms. Maude had said earlier—she didn't know what to think, either.

Just as Erica was about to flip to the next page of her notepad, she felt Jerome's leg graze hers and then rest there for a moment. She had to stop herself from smiling. She glanced to her right to look at him and was startled when she saw something scribbled on his clean white notepad, which he'd tilted in her direction. She focused in on his surprisingly neat penmanship and read the words, *Told you so!*

It was early Friday afternoon, and after a week's worth of documents, evidence, and testimonies, nearly every juror, except Ms. Maude, was pissed. They were ready to wrap up the case and move on with their regular day-to-day lives, but Ms. Slater had thrown a kink into their plans.

Shortly before their lunch recess, Ms. Slater had been scheduled to take the stand in her defense. Everyone on the jury had anxiously been anticipating her testimony, which would be the last of the trial, before closing arguments were made. But that wasn't to happen, because just as Ms. Slater rose from the defendant's table to take the stand, her legs became like Twizzlers sticks beneath her, giving way as she collapsed to the floor. She landed on her back, swept her hand across her forehead, and cried, "Oh, Lord, be with me, Father God! Oh, Father God!"

The attorneys for both sides rose from their seats, and Ms. Slater's lawyer quickly dashed to her side. A few of the jurors gasped at the sight of the woman sprawled out on the floor, calling on the Lord. The bailiff rushed to the spot where Ms. Slater lay, and within a few minutes paramedics were removing her from the courtroom on a gurney.

The judge ordered the court recessed until they were able to determine when Ms. Slater would be able to take the stand again. "The court will be in contact with you," he said before banging his gavel and dismissing the jurors.

Back in the jury room, a ruckus started to brew.

"Did you see that fake shit?" one of the jurors said, throwing his notepad down on the table. "She didn't want to take the stand, because she knows she's guilty as hell."

"Watch your mouth, young man," Ms. Maude said. "That woman could be experiencing a very serious medical emergency. Don't be so quick to judge, especially when you don't have any facts or knowledge of her health status. Remember, innocent until proven guilty."

Sasha rolled her eyes. "I agree with him. It looked fake to me, too. She fell down like a no-talent actress in a B grade movie. She even laid her hand across her head and pushed back the front of that jacked-up weave she's wearing."

"She should be ashamed of herself for pulling God into that stunt," another juror chimed in.

Ms. Maude shook her head in frustration. It didn't take long before a heated debate ensued as juror after juror loudly voiced their opinion about Ms. Slater's sudden attack. Erica was afraid they might soon need a referee, because tempers were escalating by the minute.

"Let's all calm down," Jerome said. His deep voice boomed against the walls, and his commanding authority silenced every person in the room. "We all have our individual views, so let's be respectful of that. The only thing we can all agree on at this moment is the fact that none of us has any real proof of Ms. Slater's current medical condition. All we can do at this point is wait for a call from the court about when the trial will resume. Outside of that, we all need to leave and enjoy an early start to our weekend."

By the time Jerome delivered his last word, Erica was so turned on, she wanted him to take her right there on the jury table. His short speech had settled everyone down, but it had fired her up!

The jurors began to quickly gather their things in preparation to leave. Erica walked over to Ms. Maude to check on her because she still seemed a little upset. She knew that the dear old lady was the only person who'd been noticeably invested in the trial from the start. "Are you okay?" she asked.

As Erica listened to Ms. Maude's lament over the case, she looked out the corner of her eye and saw Sasha slither across the room to where Jerome was standing.

She watched as Sasha smiled coyly, tilting her head to the side as she gazed up at Jerome through heavily frosted, amber-colored eyelids. Her move was classic seductress style, and Erica recognized it because she'd seen Ashley lure man after man with the same not-so-innocent gesture.

"You can't judge when you don't have all the facts," Ms. Maude said. "That was at the top of the list of instructions they gave us on the first day."

Erica smiled and nodded her head, but she was only half listening, because her attention was mostly focused on the interaction across the room between Jerome and Sasha. She watched Jerome as he smiled politely and then looked in her direction, as though he'd been caught cheating on a test. As soon as their eyes met briefly, he looked away, turning his attention back to the woman in front of him.

Erica immediately remembered the discussion they'd had earlier in the week about how a guilty person couldn't look you in the eye. If that was the case, she wondered what he was hiding.

Just as she'd made a mental note to check out Jerome's courtroom observations, she made one to remind herself to ask him about Sasha. Her gut, along with his body language, told her that there was definitely more to their interaction than what met the eye.

Jerome was glad he'd been able to calm the flaring tempers in the jury room, but when Sasha walked up to him, he sensed a new kind of trouble was about to erupt.

It wasn't until yesterday that he'd finally put his finger on why she had unsettled him from her first hello, and now he wanted nothing more than to get the hell away from her. But he knew he had to be as polite as possible because anything could pop off when dealing with a woman like Sasha Moore. Plus, he was all too aware of Erica's watchful eyes. Even though she appeared to be talking with Ms. Maude, he knew she was watching his every move from across the room.

"Since it's lunchtime, why don't we grab a quick bite?" Sasha suggested. "My treat."

Jerome smiled and shook his head. "Sorry. I won't be able to do that."

"Why not?"

"Because I can't."

Sasha folded her arms as her lips grew into a pout. "That's not a reason."

"It's the only one I've got."

"I'm not good enough for you to eat with?"

"I didn't say that."

He had a feeling that she knew he'd figured out who she was, and within seconds she opened her mouth and confirmed his hunch.

"Why you tryin' to play me, Jerome? I could tell you didn't remember me at first, but I know you do now."

Jerome wasn't one to stress, not even in tense situations that would have sent most men into a sweat. He always tried to remain in control of his emotions, no matter the challenge facing him, including the one in front of him now. The only problem was that he couldn't control Sasha's actions.

He hoped she had matured over the years and that she wouldn't show her ass in public, which, from what he could remember, she was very capable of doing. But in the unfortunate event that she did go off, Jerome knew they were in the right place, because he'd just take the escalator downstairs and file a compliant against her quicker than she could blink.

"Well?" she said, waiting for his response.

"Yes, Sasha, I remember you. But that doesn't change my answer."

"Oh, I see. Now that you got a job with the city and a little construction hustle on the side, you think you all that. You ain't got no love for a neighborhood chick, huh?" She rolled her eyes and clicked her tongue against her teeth. "You tryin' to roll uptown now," she smirked, glancing in Erica's direction.

She'd just let him know that either she'd done some checking around about his current status or she'd never lost touch with his life's movements. Whatever the case, Sasha was trouble, and he didn't want any part of it.

Jerome held her gaze with a slightly hard edge. "What I do and who I choose to do it with are my business, and no concern of yours.

I'm trying to be respectful, so let's just leave it at that and wish each other a good weekend."

Instead of getting loud and drawing attention to them, as he'd thought she might do, Sasha took a deep breath and formed her lips into a vindictive smile. "You're still the same smooth-talkin', two-timin', triflin' muthafucka who drove my cousin crazy."

"Tawanna was a nut job before I met her. And by the way, she's the one who came after me, remember?"

"Only because you tricked her into thinking you loved her, and then your sorry ass betrayed her, and that's what drove her crazy. You've never loved nobody but yourself."

"You don't know anything about me."

"I know more than you think. You just like all the other dogs out there, always chasin' behind a new bitch."

Jerome's voice grew quiet as he spoke. "You don't know shit about me, so I'ma straighten you out about a few things right now. The last time I laid eyes on you, you were in—what? Tenth or eleventh grade?"

Sasha looked away, then down toward the floor.

He went on. "Yeah, I remember you alright, you were on my tip even back then. So don't try to act all righteous, like you were so concerned about your cousin."

"Yo ass ain't all that."

"Maybe not. But like I said, who I am or what I do isn't your concern."

"You couldn't handle a woman like me, anyway," Sasha smirked, flipping her long tresses with her hand.

"I overlooked you back then because you were just a girl, and I'ma do the same thing now because you still are. So now that we've both laid down our piece, why don't we let it go at that?"

They stood in silence for a brief moment, almost as if they were battling in a standoff. With every ticking second that Sasha stood in front of him, Jerome could feel Erica's eyes questioning what was going on. Finally, Sasha relaxed her stance, gave him a nasty look, and then walked away.

Jerome was glad he'd just dodged an embarrassing scene. *Just my luck,* he thought. He had to shake his head, because what were the odds? Just as he was about to embark upon a relationship with Erica, which he was confident would finally bring him happiness, he was being pulled back into one of the most chaotic times of his life, a time that had involved so much illegal activity and moral wrongdoing that he cringed at the memory of some of the things he'd done.

He didn't know why this was happening now, but he did know the first thing he needed to do was talk to Erica, because he could only imagine what must be going through her mind.

Chapter 21

Erica nodded in the direction of her fellow jurors as they said their good-byes, leaving the room one by one. It was twelve noon, and thanks to Ms. Slater's collapse, they were free to go. Erica wanted to leave as well, but there were two pressing matters holding her in place. One was Ms. Maude, who was giving her an earful about juror protocol, and the other was Jerome, who was causing her brow to wrinkle with questions about the exchange he'd just had with Sasha. Erica knew the two had traded unpleasant words, because the woman had walked away looking pissed to high heaven.

"I guess I'll stop bending your ear so you can get out of here and enjoy the rest of this beautiful fall day," Ms. Maude said. "You're such a sweet girl, Erica. Thanks for listening to an old lady babble on and on."

Erica felt bad because she hadn't really given Ms. Maude her full attention. She'd been too busy trying to see what was happening between Jerome and Sasha, and even now she was wondering what was on Jerome's mind as he casually sat in a chair a few feet away, waiting for her to finish her conversation.

"Ms. Maude, you don't have to thank me for anything. I know how important this trial is to you."

Maude looked in Jerome's direction and smiled. "I see something that's important to you, too, so I'm going to go home now and leave you to it." The old lady gave Erica a mischievous wink, then wrapped her body in her lightweight coat and grabbed her handbag. "You two have a nice weekend."

After the door closed behind Ms. Maude, Erica and Jerome were all alone. She walked over to where he was sitting and pulled out the seat beside him. She was about to question him, but the bailiff came in to clear the room. She knew it was probably best that they discuss things outside the courthouse. She had a feeling it was going to be a long story.

"You want to go to lunch now?" Jerome asked as he and Erica walked down the hall leading to the escalator.

"Sure, and now that we don't have to rush back, let's go someplace where we can sit down and relax."

Jerome smiled, making Erica nearly forget she had concerns. "Sounds good to me."

As they headed out the courthouse doors, Erica hoped that he wouldn't tell her something she didn't want to hear.

Erica and Jerome perused their menus at Clyde's. It was a popular, well-established restaurant adjacent to the high-end Shops at Georgetown Park, which was prime real estate located right around the corner from Opulence.

As Erica surveyed the rustic hardwood floors and the vintage paintings populating the walls, she realized how good it felt to be out with Jerome in a place other than the jury room, the jury box, or a sandwich shop. She wasn't sure if it was their change of environment or the fact that she wanted him so badly, but he looked even finer and sexier under the restaurant's low lighting. She also knew that despite her growing desires, she needed to get to the bottom of what was up between him and Sasha. She'd been through deception and lies with Claude, and she wasn't about to go down that kind of painful road again.

Once they made their selections—spring ravioli for her, and fish and chips for him—they handed their menus to their server and sipped on their glasses of water. Erica was once again about to question Jerome, but she was halted when he spoke up without prompting.

"Sasha's from the old neighborhood," he said. "Remember that crazy chick who stalked me? Well, Sasha is her cousin."

He went on to tell Erica about Tawanna Jones, the lunatic of a woman who'd stalked him for six months before shooting him in a near-fatal attack. He explained, with what looked like a fair amount of discomfort, that he'd dated the woman for two months. She'd lost it when he broke up with her shortly before she discovered that he'd slept with one of her girlfriends. Even though he knew what he'd done was beyond the pale, she forgave him for having cheated on her and she tried desperately to reconcile their relationship. But when he resisted, choosing to date her girlfriend instead, Tawanna became obsessed with him—and more important, obsessed about getting revenge.

She began to show up at his apartment unannounced, banging on his door all hours of the night. She left notes on his windshield that wavered between passive pleas of love and menacing threats of violence. And she started following his every move by tailing close behind him in her car, riding up on his bumper, and smiling at him when he saw her in his rearview mirror.

But the tipping point was when she casually walked into Jamel's day-care center one sunny afternoon and tried to take the one-year-old home. After Jerome found out, he was livid, and so was Kelisha. "You better put a stop to that crazy bitch, or I will!" a furious Kelisha had said. When Jerome went to confront the lunatic, she had a bullet waiting with his name on it, ready and primed to greet him.

"Erica, I'm not proud of my behavior back then," Jerome confessed. "I was reckless and foolish. But I want you to know that the man sitting in front of you today is very different from the knuckle-head I used to be."

At that moment, Erica realized that she really had no claim to Jerome. He was explaining himself as if it was his duty, yet he wasn't her boyfriend or her lover, and she didn't know if they could even be classified as seeing each other. It was true that they talked every night on the phone and ate lunch together every day, but that had only been for the length of the five days she'd known him. But again, he'd just explained himself, which was what people in relationships did, and it made her wonder if they were in one and she just didn't know it.

"Thank you for being so forthcoming. I really appreciate your openness and honesty."

"I had to be. I didn't want you thinking there was anything going on between Sasha and me."

Erica nodded. "I figured you two had some kind of relationship, based on the way she looked at you all week and how familiar she seemed with you this afternoon."

"That's my fault, too."

"What do you mean?"

"It's all because of my past. She thought she could push up on me because, hey, in her mind I'm still the same dude who slept with my girlfriend's girlfriend. That's some scandalous shit. Pardon my French," Jerome said as he shook his head. "She was probably thinking that I'm still down for whatever. Sometimes it's hard to shake a reputation."

Erica wasn't sure what to say. On one hand, Jerome's honesty and frankness were refreshing, and it made her trust him. But on the other, it seemed that the more she discovered about him, the more drama she uncovered, and it made her question what kinds of things from his past would continue to crop up in his present. However, she knew that everyone deserved a second chance, and sometimes three or four. Life wasn't rosy—this she'd known since she was ten years old. So she decided to clear her mind of doubts and focus on possibilities.

As they ate their food, they talked about their pasts, their families, their experiences in failed relationships, and the lessons they'd learned from them. The natural comfort and red-hot chemistry they shared led them to flirt and tease. The suggestive innuendos they tossed back and forth made both of them curious and more than a little aroused. They did all this with ease, but the one subject they hadn't ventured to discuss was the future and, more specifically, a future together.

Erica knew it was soon, but she'd felt closer to Jerome in the five days she'd known him than she had to any man she'd ever dated for any length of time. He was honest with her, and he'd endeared himself to her heart by the little things he did: bringing her coffee in the morning, pulling out her chair so she could sit, opening the door for her, and gently pulling her to the other side of him when they walked down the street to protect her from harm's way. He asked her questions about her life because he was genuinely interested in getting to know her and how she felt. He cheered her business success and told her that he was proud of her. And he looked into her eyes when he spoke so she would know his words were sincere.

For all those reasons, Erica wanted to know where she and Jerome were headed. She hated always being the one in her relationships who brought up the dreaded "Where is this going?" topic. But she wanted to know. She was tired of playing the role of a casual bystander in her relationships, and now that she'd made a promise to herself to go after her own happiness, she couldn't sit back and leave things blowing in the wind, waiting to see where ,love would eventually land. If there was one thing that being an entrepreneur had taught her, it was that if she wanted something, she had to go for it and not worry about how things looked or what anyone thought of her decision.

Erica pierced a plump piece of ravioli with her fork and dredged it through the rich palomino sauce as she spoke. "You've said you're really feelin' me, right?"

"Yes, I am."

"What exactly does that mean?"

Jerome chewed slowly, looking as though he was trying to translate her words into another language.

"I know it means you like me," Erica continued, "and, for lack of a better phrase, that you're into me."

He smiled. "Yes, it does."

"But beyond that, what does it mean in terms of a relationship?"

"It means I definitely want a relationship with you, and who knows where that will lead us?"

Erica decided she didn't have anything to lose, so she laid all her cards down on the table. "I already know what I want. Do you?"

Jerome nodded. "As a matter of fact, I do. But ladies first."

"Okay. I want a relationship that's going to lead to marriage. I'm thirty-five years old, I've never been married, never had any kids, and my clock is ticking ten beats per second. I'm busy with my career, but I want someone to share it with. I don't have time for games, playing it safe, or holding back my true desires. I want something meaningful and real. Something that I can rely on and believe in. I want a happily ever after."

Erica had never been that brutally honest with a man, for fear she'd scare him away too quickly. But she knew there was no time to be afraid. She had to jump through windows, leap from buildings, and walk fearlessly to claim what she wanted. She knew if she could do it with Opulence and be successful, she needed to start exercising that same strength in her personal life. She was giving Jerome a choice. He could either stand in the comfort of "feelin' her" or he could walk out to the edge of the cliff and take a leap toward something more solid. Her eyes challenged him to answer.

Jerome moved his clean plate to the side and smiled. He leaned forward, put his hand on top of hers, and looked her in the eyes. "If you can trust in me, I can give you all those things and more, because I want them, too. And I want them with you."

And just like that, Erica no longer had to wonder. She and Jerome were officially dating, seeing each other, and most of all, they were in a relationship that just might lead her to a happily ever after.

Chapter 22

Three hours had scurried by before they realized it. Jerome liked how easy it was to talk with Erica. She was funny, insightful, sweet, and smart. He also liked that she was a good listener and gave him time to express his thoughts, which didn't always come easy. Most of the women he'd dated in the past were loud and barely let him get two words in, so her easy way made him appreciate her even more.

He was glad that he'd matured to this point, and that he was ready for a woman like Erica. There was a time when he would have never disclosed to a woman whom he was dating all the trifling things he'd done in previous relationships. He'd lied his way from woman to woman for so long that it had become a habit. But now, being up front and honest was his style of choice, and he felt good wearing the new look. He was proud that he could hold his head up high and not have to worry about hiding the truth or dodging bullets.

"Can you believe it's four o'clock?" Erica asked.

"Get out of here. It can't be four already." He gently reached for her wrist and looked at her watch. "Wow, it sure is. I'm having such a good time with you, it doesn't even matter."

Erica looked down at his hand, gently resting on her wrist. "Can I ask you a question?"

"Sure. Go for it."

"Why don't you wear a watch?"

Jerome had to think about her question. No one had ever asked him that, and he'd never thought about it.

Time had never been important to him. During his days in the streets life happened whenever and however he wanted it to. When he needed to make a run, drop off a load of product or pick up some, he'd call his contact, set a time to meet, and they'd do business. After he gave up the hustle and started working for the city, he used his alarm clock to wake him every morning. And when he had a repair job on the side, he'd arrive straight after work or, if it was a weekend, whenever he got there. On more than one occasion his clients had been upset by his tardiness, but because he produced excellent results, their attitudes faded under the light of his craftsmanship.

Jerome looked at Erica's wrist again. He could tell that the watch she was wearing probably cost as much as his truck. "I've never had much of a need for one."

"Maybe not before, but you do now."

"Occasionally. But to be honest, I feel like life's too short to always be worried about the time."

Erica shook her head. "Worrying about the time and having a healthy respect for it are two different things. You work every day, and you have a growing business. Life as an entrepreneur is about managing what's on your plate so you can stay on top of your game."

Jerome nodded. "I have to admit that lately I've been pressed with so much going on. But if I want to know the time, I usually look at my phone. And if I want to communicate with clients, we do it the old-fashioned way by actually talking to each other."

Erica looked down at his phone and sighed.

"What?"

She smiled, tilted her head, and said, "Brother, you need a smartphone."

Jerome looked at his small black flip phone and shrugged. "I know my phone is outdated, but it suits my needs. As long as I can make and receive calls and look at the time, I'm good to go."

"I'm going to show you something," Erica said as she reached for her phone.

Jerome listened as she gave him a quick tutorial. She showed him how to set a calendar alert for upcoming appointments, how to program names with speed dial and ringtones so that identifying callers was easier, as well as a host of other things she thought might be helpful to him, all in just five short minutes.

"You're good for me," Jerome told her. He finally knew what it was like to be with someone who complimented him both personally and professionally, and the feeling gave him a high that no drug he'd ever taken could come close to touching.

"What about your computer?" she asked. "Have you downloaded business software that can help you with your business, like accounting programs and bill pay?"

"Uh, no. I don't have one."

Erica's expression was one of complete disbelief. "I can see we need to get you upgraded, and quick!"

"Hey, I'm a man who's willing to learn."

They continued to talk, flirt, laugh, and flirt some more. When the happy hour crowd started to file in, Jerome knew it was time to leave.

"You want to see my boutique?" Erica asked.

"Sure. How far is it from here?"

"Two blocks around the corner."

"Let's roll."

After threatening to pick Erica up and carry her out of the restaurant unless she let him pay the bill, Jerome reached into his wallet and did the honors.

Erica thanked him. "I appreciate that, Jerome. But you don't always have to pay. Let me treat you some time."

"This is what a man's supposed to do when he's pursuing and dating a woman. There will be times when you'll do your part and I'll do mine. But for now, I got you. I want to take care of you. Besides, you are my treat."

Jerome felt good being able to buy Erica lunch every day this week, even if the places they'd eaten hadn't been the kind of fancy restaurants he knew she was used to. He knew she had had a wealthy upbringing, and he could tell by the tailored clothes she wore, the expensive jewelry with which she adorned herself, and the luxury car she drove that she was used to having fine things and living a privileged life. It was a fact that she could afford to buy herself whatever she wanted, and that she didn't need him for material possessions. So his goal wasn't to win her over with gifts or decadent meals at fancy places. Instead, he planned to work hard to give her whatever her heart desired, which was something that didn't have a price tag.

As they left Clyde's and walked down the street, side by side, Jerome reached over, slid his hand into Erica's, and smiled. When he saw her blush and smile back at him, it was the second best highlight of his day, next to strolling hand in hand through the bustling Friday afternoon crowd with his new girlfriend.

When Erica walked into Opulence, she was glad to see customers buzzing about, browsing, and making purchases. The beginning of spring and fall were always great for business, because people were switching to new fragrances and products to fit the coming season. And now that she had a new body butter to present, Erica was even more excited. She was also proud to show Jerome the company she'd built from the ground up—her very own exclusive boutique that had started in the basement of her row house.

Cindy was heading to the back of the store when Erica spotted her. "Cindy, do you have a minute?" she called out in a voice so cheery she was sure it made Cindy nauseous. She knew that cheeriness aggravated Cindy to no end, and glee often made her downright annoyed. But Erica was over-the-top happy, and she wanted to spread the good feeling around.

Cindy walked toward her, carrying a small box. "Here's what you've been waiting for, the new jars of Paradise." She thrust the open package toward Erica and even managed to wrestle up a half smile.

"I'll take a look in just a minute," Erica quickly said.

Cindy's small eyes squinted with surprise. "You've been dying to see these all week. What's more important than your prized swag bag products?"

Erica beamed like the sun. "I want you to meet Jerome Kimbrough."

She'd told Cindy about Jerome two days ago, when she'd come in after court to interview an applicant. Cindy had been skeptical, as was her nature, asking question after question, just as Ashley had done. It was her protective, mama-bear nature, and she reminded Erica of her own mother in that regard.

Cindy looked Jerome up and down, inspecting him through what Erica knew was a very jaded lens. Because Cindy's life had been filled with so many duplicitous charlatans, she was cautious of nearly everyone she met. That was why Erica was shocked when she saw her store manager extend her tiny hand to Jerome, form her lips into an uncharacteristic smile, and greet him as though he was a friend who'd just stopped by for a visit.

"I've heard very nice things about you, Jerome," Cindy said. "It's a pleasure to meet you."

"Likewise, and the pleasure is all mine."

Erica looked on in astonishment as the two continued to exchange pleasantries. She watched as Jerome literally charmed the box out of Cindy's hands, relieving her small arms of the heavy weight. He reached inside, pulled out a jar, and looked at it before handing it over to Erica.

"Wow, this is really nice," he said.

Erica carefully examined her long-awaited product, turning the jar this way and that so she could inspect it from every angle. She was so happy, she could have jumped up and down. The jar, which was heavy plastic that had been fashioned to mimic the look of lead crystal, was embossed with a deep purple, vibrant pink, pale lavender, and cream design that was outlined with small crystal-like gemstones, giving it a sophisticated bling. The combination of soft and bold colors mixed with the dazzling accents transformed the container from an ordinary jar into a work of art.

"It's beautiful!" Erica said in awe.

"I have to hand it to you, kiddo. It's absolutely gorgeous," Cindy agreed. "People are going to want to buy Paradise just for the jar alone. And wait until they actually put it on their skin! It's the best product you've created to date."

"Awww, thanks, Cindy. I hope you're right."

"I always am."

"After all the headaches I went through, this was well worth the long days and sleepless nights. What a way to end the week."

Cindy nodded. "And even better, the trial is over. Didn't you say things would wrap up today?"

"No such luck." Erica briefly explained what happened in court earlier that afternoon.

Cindy folded her arms and shook her head. "That woman is lying to get sympathy and to prolong the trial. She's hoping that over the weekend you'll have time to think about how hard it will be to send a sick woman to prison."

Erica hadn't told Cindy one single detail of the case, yet she instantly reached a negative conclusion. *Typical Cindy,* Erica thought.

"I agree with you, Cindy," Jerome said.

Erica's head swiveled around, and she looked at Jerome, not surprised by his comment, either.

"Let me guess." Cindy smirked. "Our sweet Pollyanna here thinks the woman is innocent and probably wants to send her some get-well flowers."

Erica shrugged. "Honestly, I really don't know what to think. But like one of the other jurors said this afternoon, we have no proof of the woman's medical condition, so on that charge she's innocent until proven guilty."

Cindy scoffed. "Sometimes people have to prove their innocence, not their guilt."

"Ignore her," Erica said, looking at Jerome. "She's really a ray of sunshine once you get to know her."

Jerome smiled and stayed neutral.

"Okay, think what you will," Cindy said. "I'm going to the back so I can inventory the rest of the shipment that just came in." She took the box out of Jerome's hands. "I can tell you're gonna be good for her." She smiled and gave a wink before walking away.

"She's right," Jerome said. "But she left out an important part."

"What's that?"

He moved in close so that they stood side by side, their bodies nearly touching. "I'm also gonna be good *to* you."

Chapter 23

It was dark outside by the time Erica finished looking over the shipment of new products, checked a few e-mails, and called her father to let him know that the jars had arrived. He was busy, rushing her off the phone, embroiled in his own hectic work. But he promised her they'd go out and celebrate next week. While she worked, Jerome browsed the boutique and then walked the block, observing the stores, people, and happenings in the upscale neighborhood.

Now she and Jerome were sitting in her office, trying to decide where they should go for dinner. Tonight was supposed to be their first official "date," with Jerome picking her up to take her out on the town. But their day had been thrown off course ever since Ms. Slater's collapse, and now they had to figure out what they were going to do next.

"I know we never discussed it, but is there a particular restaurant you had in mind?" she asked as she logged off her computer.

Jerome leaned back in the comfortable leather chair in front of Erica's desk. "It's up to you. The whole idea of playing it by ear was so we'd have options. I'm flexible."

"I really don't want to go anywhere crowded, but that's kind of impossible at this hour on a Friday night."

"Something quiet and intimate would be nice."

"I'm with you on that." Erica rose from her chair, came around to the front of her desk, and leaned against it. "Since we know what kind of atmosphere we're looking for, we just need to decide on the cuisine. What do you have a taste for?"

When she saw the unmistakable look of desire dance across Jerome's deep, sexy eyes, she knew exactly what he had an appetite for, and she didn't shy away from returning the same look.

Jerome stood to his feet and came close beside her. "I think we both have a taste for the same thing."

"Well, let's go get it."

Fifteen minutes later Jerome was parking his truck next to Erica's car inside her garage. As they walked through her back door leading to her kitchen, Erica could feel the nervous anticipation building in her body. This was a bold move for her, but she was ready to take it. All her life she'd played by a safe, structured set of rules. Private school, excellent grades, overachievement, perfect manners, don't kiss on the first date—these things were part of the handbook of life from which her parents had taught her. But now she was writing her own script, and tonight she planned to pen her first chapter.

She'd thought about this moment during the quick but congested ride over—finally being alone with him.

"Welcome to my humble abode."

"You have a nice place. Just like I knew you would," Jerome said, looking around before closing the door behind him.

"Thanks. My parents still don't understand why I bought a house in the city. They hardly ever come to visit, because they say the traffic and street parking are just too much."

"You live in a great neighborhood. But back in the day you couldn't pay people to move to Dupont Circle. Now folks can't afford to get in."

Erica opened the refrigerator, surveying its contents. "Yeah, it's a gentrified neighborhood, but I love it here. You can't beat the convenience of all the shops, restaurants, and access to the metro station." She pulled out two plastic containers and sat them on the counter. "It's so convenient."

"Yes, but convenience comes with a price."

She thought about what he'd just said, and she wondered what was behind his statement. She leaned against her stainless steel double sink and watched Jerome as his eyes surveyed her spacious galley kitchen. She knew he was appraising the work. She'd had the room remodeled a few years ago, outfitting it with new cabinets, flooring, countertops, and appliances. The design had been taken from the floor plan of a chef's kitchen she'd seen in one of her favorite cooking magazines.

"So, what do you think of the work?" Erica asked.

Jerome ran his hand across the expensive slate-gray granite countertop. "You didn't scrimp on anything, that's for sure. It's high in quality and design. The work is tight, and your contractor really knew what he was doing."

"Coming from you, that's a huge compliment."

"You think so?"

"Yes, you're a true craftsman."

Jerome tilted his head to the side. "What makes you so sure? You've never even seen my work."

"I don't have to. I know you're great at whatever you set out to do." Erica smiled as she looked into his eyes. It was an invitation that welcomed him into what they both wanted, and he willingly accepted.

Without any words, Jerome walked over to where she stood, planting himself in her space so that their bodies were aligned. Erica inhaled deeply as he pressed himself into her, gently moving his pelvis against hers. She could smell the cinnamon Altoids that lingered on his breath, and it made her feel gloriously dizzy.

Slowly, he raised his hands, cupping each side of her face as he looked into her eyes. "You're so beautiful," he whispered.

Erica's breathing became shallow at his touch. Her body shivered when he placed a slow, soft whisper of a kiss on her forehead, before planting a gentle peck on the bridge of her nose. "So beautiful," he whispered again.

She moaned out loud when his pelvis began to move in a gentle grind as he nibbled the lower part of her earlobe. His hands and body were hard and rugged, but his movements were soft and graceful, like a delicate feather. She threw her head back when she felt his lips slide to the center of her throat, his tongue teasing her skin until her legs became liquid. "Ooohhh," Erica murmured as she exhaled, releasing the desire that climbed up from her core and passed through her lips as sound.

Jerome moved his hands down the small of her back, then slowly eased them lower, gripping her round ass in his large palms. Erica's entire body trembled as he pulled her closer into him, his warm breath coating her skin. She closed her eyes, enjoying the feel of his mouth as it traveled the sweet distance that led to her lips, which he softly grazed with his own.

Over the past week she'd imagined their first kiss and what it would feel like, but her fanciful musings hadn't prepared her for the wanton sensation of his soft, warm lips melting into hers. He parted her mouth, covering it in heat, giving her a taste of his cinnamon tongue. He kissed her sensually, with an intensity that let her know this was what he'd been longing for. She wrapped her arms tightly around him as she moved in sync with the increased pace of his rotating hips.

"Mmmm, baby," Jerome whispered into Erica's ear, pushing himself into her so far that her back pressed against the sink's faucet. "Baby, I want you right here," he breathed heavily, continuing to grind against her.

He held her as they slid to the floor, not missing a beat. The surface was cold and hard, but they kept going, lost in their desires. Erica's back banged against the terrazzo tile, and Jerome's knees scrubbed it like a mop. They worked vigorously to find a comfortable position, but the rough surface proved more a challenge than a romantic venture. Their lust-driven fantasies had led them there in a heated frenzy, but Erica's stiff back and Jerome's aching knees quickly brought them face-to-face with the reality of their mid-thirties.

"How do you feel about a soft bed?" Erica said.

"Baby, you just read my mind."

Chapter 24

With slow and careful steps, Erica and Jerome climbed the stairs, headed to both comfort and pleasure. He nestled his lean, muscular body behind hers, holding her close, lifting one foot in front of the other as they walked as one. Her slender back was pressed against his strong chest while her head rested on his shoulder. They moved upward in perfect unison, relishing the journey. He wrapped one arm around her waist and the other around her chest, finding the softness of her breasts, gently rubbing and kneading her delicate mounds through the fabric of her blouse.

Erica felt his erection rub against her ass, and for a moment they both felt like stopping and making love right there on the stairs, but they remembered the kitchen floor, and the thought propelled them to travel the ten feet to her bedroom.

With Jerome still holding her from behind, Erica stumbled over to the nightstand on the side of her bed and turned on the lamp. They both squinted, adjusting their eyes to the light filling the pitch-black room. It was brighter than was necessary for creating a romantic mood, so she pulled away from Jerome, removed her blouse, and draped it over the silk shade, sending the room into a gentle amber glow.

"Damn, you're sexy," Jerome whispered, smiling at Erica with desire. He walked over to her and enveloped her in his arms, kissing her, holding her, and caressing her soft skin. "I knew your skin would be soft, but, man," he said, anticipation dripping from his voice. "Soft, sexy, beautiful, and you smell good."

They took their time, removing each other's clothes as they inspected one another's body, slowly and purposefully. The sensual heat of their desire made them each pant, kissing and exploring as they went along.

Within minutes they were naked, lying atop the chenille duvet on her king-size bed. Their bodies molded into one fine creation as they picked up from where they'd left off downstairs.

Jerome's hungry mouth journeyed to Erica's breasts. He kissed her soft, supple flesh, circling his tongue around her dark nipples before lightly grazing them with his teeth until she whimpered in pleasure. Erica watched with heated lust as he worked his way back and forth, sucking one while rubbing the other with attentive care.

His hands caressed the soft skin on her arms as he moved down to her stomach, gently kissing every inch of her flesh that his lips could cover. He swirled his tongue around her navel as she trembled and moaned in ecstasy. Slowly, he parted her thighs, situating himself at her creamy center. She was wet and warm and ready.

"I'm going to enjoy this," Jerome softly whispered.

He gently parted her lips with his fingers, taking his time as he rolled his tongue over her glistening skin, stroking her soft folds up and down. He licked and sucked and plied and searched and nibbled and kissed and prodded, darting deep inside her, savoring the tastiness of her sweet juice until she moaned his name.

She bucked her hips, grinding her sensitive flesh against his mouth as she laced her fingers around his sleek bald head. She held him in place, arched her back, dug her heels into the firm mattress, and bore down into an orgasm that made her body spasm and flow like water.

Erica could barely catch her breath. She was drunk with so much pleasure, it made her head spin. "That was so good," she said, panting as she worked to catch her breath. "Now it's my turn to please you."

"You already did. Pleasing you pleases me." Jerome kissed her mouth, his chin wet with the taste of her. He reached over to the nightstand for the condom he'd placed next to her alarm clock. He ripped open the plastic and slid the latex sheath over his rock-hard erection as Erica watched, ready for a thrilling ride.

Jerome parted her thighs with his knee as he prepared to enter her. He went slow, taking his time, letting the tip of his large, swollen head make its way inside her. She gasped when she felt his first few inches—hard and throbbing—enter her empty space. Slowly, he filled her, expanding her walls, spreading himself as far as he could go. Once his entire length was cocooned within her warmth, he began to thrust. He stroked her with loving, gentle force as she wrapped her legs around his waist, moving her hips in tandem with his. He pumped in and out of her wetness, making sure she felt every inch of his desire.

"Oh, Jerome!" Erica cried out, clinging to him.

His strokes became deeper, harder, and more intense. Then he slowed down the tempo, taking hold of her hand, weaving his fingers with hers in a soft grip. They looked into each other's eyes, holding hands, making beautiful love as their bodies rumbled with intense heat, shaking the bed beneath them.

Erica's orgasm was bursting at the edge, waiting to break free. She pushed her hips upward into his thrust as he pumped, keeping her rhythm steady until she felt an intense explosion that made her call out his name, over and over and over again.

Hearing her call his name, and knowing that he'd pleased her, Jerome felt his erection stiffen so hard, he could barely control his movements. His thrusts increased, his excitement escalated, and his body felt the weight of a climax right on the verge of erupting. He charged ahead, and after a few quick strokes he crossed over into paradise, joining Erica in the land of long-awaited pleasure.

Afterward, Erica and Jerome lay in bed, feeling wonderfully exhausted. Jerome looked down at Erica's head resting comfortably on his shoulder and thought about how much he'd changed. There was a time when after he had sex with a woman, the only sound he wanted to hear was the thud of the door closing behind him as he made his escape from her bed—his escapades had rarely, if ever, taken place at his apartment. Very few of his women had even known its exact location. But now he couldn't think of anything else he'd rather do than hold Erica and listen to the gentle sound of her breathing.

He knew he was bordering on what his boys would consider "going soft." His cousin Tiny would shake his head and call him a punk-ass bitch, and Jerome didn't even want to think about what some of the guys at work would say. Ironically, the only person he knew he could share his newfound happiness with was his father, who had been a forgotten ghost until ten years ago.

Jerome had always longed for a relationship with Parnell Kimbrough, who'd abandoned the family when Jerome was a little boy. During the first year after his father left, Jerome used to wait anxiously every night, hoping his father would walk back through their door. But when the second year rolled around, his hopes faded with his father's memory.

Two days after the deadly car accident that had injured Jerome's son, had nearly killed his mother, and had caused him to change his life, his father reappeared. He found out that his parents had never lost touch over the years, but because his father had been so heavily involved in drugs and dalliances with other women, his mother had told him to stay away and never come back. But when word got to Parnell out in California, where he'd built a new life, that Mabel had been badly injured and might not survive, he caught the first thing smoking back to the East Coast and had been there ever since.

In the years that his father had been back in his life, Jerome had learned many lessons from his dad. He'd learned that being a man meant owning up to your mistakes, taking responsibility for and protecting your family, and always living in your truth, no matter how hard it seemed or how much it hurt, because that was what separated the real men from the boys. Theirs was a relationship that was built on the present, not the past, and right now Parnell was the only person Jerome felt he could talk to about the delicate matter of his heart.

"That was amazing," Erica said, pulling Jerome away from his thoughts.

Her dreamy after-sex voice made him want to start round two. He kissed her forehead. "Yes, it was."

"I hope you'll respect me in the morning."

"Baby, I respect the hell outta you right now. You got skills," he teased.

Erica playfully jabbed his shoulder, lifted her head, and looked at him. "I'm being serious, Jerome."

"So am I."

"I don't want you to think that I sleep so quickly with every guy I meet."

"I don't think that. Besides, I'm not every guy, and you're not every woman, right?"

She nodded in agreement. "I just want us to do things the right way, you know?"

"There's no right or wrong when it comes to you and me. We just make it do what it do."

Erica smiled, sat up, and gathered the sheet around her chest.

"Don't cover up," Jerome said, gently pulling the sateen fabric away from her skin, circling her left nipple with his right finger. "I like looking at you. You're so beautiful."

Erica blushed. "I want you to know that I do have moral standards."

"Erica, I know what kind of woman you are. Why you sweatin' this? Are you regretting what we did?" Now Jerome was sitting up beside her, looking at her with a mind full of questions. Erica was the first woman to voice such concerns after sex. In the past, if there were conversations, they were generally quick and involved only questions pertaining to their next hookup, and never their moral code of conduct.

"No, I don't regret anything. I loved every moment we shared, and that's my point." Erica fiddled with the edge of the sheet. "I don't want this to be a hit-and-run type of thing. I was serious about what I said during lunch today."

"So was I. We're on the same page, baby." Although the room was dim, Jerome could see the doubt and questions in Erica's eyes. He saw hurt, fear, and insecurity lingering where there should have been light. A profound awareness came rushing to him, and that was when he realized something that completely blew him away. He loved her. "Erica, don't worry. I got you."

"I'm going to hold you to that." She leaned over and gently kissed him.

"Now, that's what I'm talkin' about. You can hold me to that day and night."

She looked at the clock on her nightstand. "Speaking of day and night, I can't believe it's almost eleven o'clock. We never got to eat dinner."

"No . . . but we had some delicious dessert."

"Yes, we did," she purred. "You hungry? I took some food out earlier, and it's still sitting on the counter. I can warm it up in the microwave."

Jerome reached for her, pulling her back down to the mattress. "What I want to eat is right here." He smiled and slowly slid down to the meeting of her thighs.

Chapter 25

Erica finished slicing the strawberries and then added them to the bowl of fresh blueberries she'd just rinsed in the sink. The English muffins popped up from the toaster just in time for her to place them on the two plates with cheese omelets she'd prepared. It was close to noon, but she was making breakfast because she and Jerome had slept in after making love into the wee hours of the morning.

"My baby's in the kitchen, burnin' this morning," Jerome teased as he walked up to Erica, planting a soft kiss on her lips.

He smelled like the spring-fresh-scented Opulence bath gel that she had taken from the guest bathroom and had given him to use. His jeans and sweater from yesterday hung on him with a well-worn look that Erica thought was more delicious than the food she'd just made.

She was still floating on a mile-high love cloud from last night. She'd experienced passion, pleasure, and a type of sexual freedom that made her feel alive and completely uninhibited. Thinking back, Erica knew she'd had good sex in the past, and she could even venture to say that some of her encounters had been quite memorable. But never had she experienced what she felt last night—the type of sex that Ashley often referred to as "out of this world, make your hair go back, slap your mama dead in her face" kind of sex! But that was exactly what Jerome had given her.

Her body still trembled from his tender touch and gentle kisses. She loved that he was an unselfish lover, and that he wanted to please her more than he wanted to be pleased. "You come first, and that's why I'm gonna make sure that you cum first," he'd told her.

Along with his gentleness and desire to please her, Jerome had allowed her to explore a side of herself that she hadn't known existed. For the first time in her life, Erica experienced what it felt like to let go of her hang-ups, taboos, and sexual insecurities so she could fully embrace what pure ecstasy really felt like. She'd always enjoyed sex, but there was a part of her psyche that had never allowed her to fully release into the moment. She'd limited herself with doubts, worrying if she was pleasing her partner just right, if the cellulite on the sides of her thick thighs was too unsightly, if her round ass jiggled too much, or if her partner would have issues with her aggressiveness if she did let go and get freaky.

But Jerome silenced all her fears and answered her questions by taking them off the table. Nothing was undoable. Nothing was restricted. Nothing was unattainable. With him, she was everything and anything she wanted to be. After so many years of searching, dreaming, hoping, and praying, and then eventually feeling hopeless about the prospect of finding someone special to share her life with, Erica was finally confident she had.

But even though she was in complete rapture, not in her wildest dreams had she ever imagined she'd be dating a man like Jerome, let alone falling into a deep relationship in just one week! Yet there she was, cooking her man breakfast after a night of lovemaking that had made her cry out like an animal in the wild and then sleep like a baby in his arms. He might not possess the degrees or material trappings she was used to, but it didn't matter, because he gave her everything she needed.

"I know you've got to be hungry," Erica said, receiving Jerome's kiss as she balanced their plates in her hands. She walked over and sat them on the small breakfast table.

"I'm starving." He smiled. "I need nourishment because somebody wore me out last night."

Erica laughed. "I think it's the other way around, Mr. Kimbrough."

She poured him a glass of the fresh orange juice she'd squeezed, then passed him the butter for his muffin. They enjoyed each other's company as they ate their breakfast and talked about the day in front of them and the evening ahead, which was sure to be their first big step as a couple.

"I'm so glad you'll be able to attend my brother's event on such short notice," Erica said. "If Ashley hadn't texted me to confirm the time for tonight, I would've missed it, because I put it on my calendar for next weekend. My mind's been in a whirlwind lately."

"No problem. I'm just glad I don't have any projects lined up this weekend. After I leave here, I'm going to spend some time with Jamel, then go home and get dressed so I can be back here to pick you up."

"This is a big step for Nelson, and I'm so proud of him."

After ten successful years as a political lobbyist for an international legal association, Erica's brother, Nelson, had decided to run for a seat on the D.C. City Council. Tonight's party was where he would make his official announcement to kick off his campaign.

"You'll get a chance to meet my family and my friends all in one night," Erica said with excitement.

Jerome gulped his orange juice down in just a few swigs, then took a sip of water. "How do you feel about me meeting your folks? You nervous?"

"No. . . . Are you?"

"Baby, let's face it. The minute your family finds out about my background and what I do for a living, they're gonna have problems."

"Nelson won't," Erica said with confidence, although she wasn't 100 percent certain of her statement.

"Maybe not, but the rest of your family and most of your friends will."

"I thought you said the only people's opinions that count in our relationship are yours and mine."

"They are, but we also have to live in reality. Your family is a big part of your world."

Erica took a bite of her omelet and then spoke. "I'm not concerned about what anyone else thinks. You're who I want to be with. When they see how happy you make me, they'll love you."

Jerome smiled. "You're so believing and trusting."

"I take it you're not comfortable with the idea of going."

"I'm fine with it because I can handle myself in any situation. I just know how much you believe in people's kindness, and I don't want you to be disappointed when you see a different side of them."

"You think my family will treat you badly?"

"Hopefully, not to my face. But I do think they'll wait till you're alone to tell you how they really feel."

Erica thought for a moment, pondering Jerome's words. She knew that her family and friends were of a certain social stratum, and that position and status were important to them. They had high goals and expectations, and they always strived for the best, which was a quality she admired. But she also understood the derisive underlying elitism that existed in their world.

"I'm not naive. I know that some people will raise their brows, but that's their problem."

"I hear you. I'm just trying to prepare you for the attitudes you're gonna run into. I'm from the other side of the tracks, a whole other world away from your fancy upbringing."

"That doesn't matter to me."

"Plus, you're a Daddy's girl."

Erica put her fork down. "What's that supposed to mean?"

Jerome hesitated, looking as though he was choosing his words carefully. "You've told me how close you two are. You're the apple of his eye."

"Yes, and that's why I know he'll like you. Both my parents want me to be happy. They've always supported me in everything I've done, and our relationship will be no different."

Just then their conversation was interrupted by the doorbell.

Erica wiped her mouth with her napkin as she rose from the table. "I wonder who that could be. I'm not expecting anyone."

Jerome sat forward on the edge of his chair, as if on alert. "You sure?"

She saw the concerned look on his face. He'd been involved in crazy love triangles, so she imagined he was probably bracing himself for who could possibly be standing on the other side of her door.

"Don't worry. There won't be any drama here!" she said as she walked toward her entry foyer.

To Erica's surprise and delight, a deliveryman from her favorite florist handed her a beautiful bouquet of vibrant-colored flowers that were beautifully arranged in a crystal vase. After she signed for the delivery and gave the guy a tip, she walked back to the kitchen. "Speaking of my father, look what he sent me," Erica said.

Jerome looked up, still a little on edge. "What's the occasion?"

Erica reclaimed her chair at the table. "Probably to congratulate me for resolving the issues I had at Opulence. He was too busy to really talk yesterday, so this is his way of saying 'Job well done.' He's thoughtful like that, and has sent me flowers from time to time. Let me see what the card says." She pulled the small envelope from the plastic holder, removed the note inside, and then began to read it aloud. "Dear Erica . . ." And that was as far as she got before she stopped. She couldn't go any farther, because the note wasn't from her father. It was from Claude!

Chapter 26

When Jerome heard Erica's voice tighten into a cautious pause and saw anxiety flash through her eyes, he knew something was wrong. She didn't have to tell him that the fragrant flowers she'd just placed in the center of the table weren't from her father, because her expression said it all. He knew that the surprise gift was from a man who either had been with her, was with her now, or wanted to be with her.

He and Erica had talked about his checkered past but had only scratched the surface of her stumbles, which he actually didn't think were many. He quickly analyzed the situation before him and came to the conclusion that the flowers had to be from her ex, the pompous asshole who'd lied to her and deceived her.

Jerome knew it had to be him. For one, he knew that Erica had been too busy over the past few months to start up anything new, and two, it was she who had called off the engagement, not her ex. Jerome knew that as fine and as sweet as Erica was, her rejection would not sit well with any man. They'd definitely want her back.

He watched as Erica finished reading the card in silence, nervously biting her lower lip. He could see her eyes dart to and fro with anxiety, as she knew he was watching for her reaction. He sat back in his chair, waiting, but she said nothing. He decided he would give her five more seconds to explain what the hell was going on before he started asking questions. Luckily, she spoke up.

"I was mistaken. These aren't from my father," she said in a low voice.

"I figured that. So who sent them?"

Erica swallowed hard. He could see her throat move. "My ex that I told you about. Claude."

There was a long moment of silence between them. Jerome waited for Erica to be as forthcoming as he'd been about his past relationships. But instead, she took a small sip of her coffee and then placed the note back inside the envelope.

"You need to start giving me some kind of explanation," Jerome said, trying to maintain a calm voice.

"I'm only silent because I don't know what to say. I'm trying to figure it out myself. . . . It's really very strange," Erica replied, looking into his eyes. "I didn't think anything of it when he called the other night."

Jerome's back went flat against his chair. "He called you? When did this happen?"

"A few nights ago, um, Tuesday. It was when I was waiting for your call, and I thought it was you, so I picked up without looking, and it turned out to be Claude."

"Why didn't you tell me that you two recently talked?"

"Because there was nothing to say. The conversation lasted just a few minutes. Honestly, I was shocked he even called."

"So this guy just called you out of the blue, for no reason?"

"Yeah, kind of. I mean, after I saw him out last week I—"

"Hold up," Jerome said, cutting her off. He was starting to feel heat rise to his head as he spoke. "Erica, why are you just now telling me this? We talked about your ex that first night on the phone, but you never mentioned that you'd just gotten a call from him."

"Because it didn't mean anything."

"The man is sending you flowers. It damn sure means *something*."

"Jerome, I told you, it doesn't mean anything at all. As a matter of fact, he has a girlfriend. When Ashley and I were out at dinner last Friday night, we saw him there with his new woman. Then the next thing I know, he called me a few days later, and now he's sending me flowers."

"What did he say was his reason for calling you after he saw you?"

Erica hesitated. "Um, he claimed he wanted to see if we could get back together."

"Well, there you go. That's why he's sending you flowers during the middle of the day. You must've told him something that got his hopes up."

"The only thing I told him was that I wasn't interested and that he should concentrate on his new girlfriend. I even hung up on him."

Jerome shook his head. "Open the envelope and read the card out loud, please."

Erica's eyes bucked. "Why do you want me to do that?"

"Because I want to know exactly what that muthafucka said to you." He looked at her with steely eyes, so serious she didn't ask the question again.

"Fine." Erica reached for the small envelope and removed the card. "Dear Erica, I miss you so much. Please give our love another chance. Always yours, Claude."

"*Shit!*" Erica yelled at the top of her lungs, but only in her mind. She hated reading Claude's insincere words out loud. It hurt her ears just hearing the slick lies he'd manufactured float into the universe, resting as negative energy. But it was what Jerome had asked her to do, and she felt she had to read it. She couldn't blame him for making the request, because she knew if the situation were reversed, and he received flowers from another woman while in her presence, especially one whom he had recently seen and been in communication with but had not told her about, not only would she ask him to read the card out loud, but she would also demand that he let her see the words on paper with her own two eyes.

Erica wished she had told Jerome about her recent contact with Claude, but she'd honestly thought it was no big deal. In her mind, he was history. Jerome was her present and her future. She knew that Claude had called and sent flowers because he was looking for some type of angle to score with her. As she'd come to learn, Claude never did anything that wasn't tied to something that would eventually benefit him.

Although she didn't know what Claude's motivation was, whatever the scheme, it was messing up her beautiful Saturday brunch with

Jerome, and she was determined to put a stop to it. "Listen," Erica started. "I don't blame you for being a little upset. But please calm down."

"This is fucked up."

"You don't have to use foul language. We can talk about this like adults."

Jerome raised his brow. "Don't tell me how to talk. I'm a grown-ass man, and I know how to express myself."

Erica nodded. "Okay. But I won't tolerate disrespect."

"How can you sit there and talk to me about disrespect when I'm sitting here looking at flowers you just received from another man?"

"It's not like I asked for them or that I was even expecting them. I'm honestly in shock, and I don't know what to think."

Jerome shook his head, taking a deep, heavy breath. "I thought we were building something."

"We are."

"You said you wanted a relationship with me that was gonna lead somewhere."

"I do."

"Then why didn't you tell me that ol' boy's been calling you, wanting to get back with you?"

"Because I have absolutely no interest in him, and besides, I knew he didn't mean it. Claude's the kind of guy who always has an angle for everything. He doesn't want to get back with me. He's just doing this because there's some other thing he's jockeying for. I just haven't figured out what it is."

"You can't be that naive."

"What do you mean?"

Jerome looked at her as if she'd just asked him how to spell *cat.* "I know you always see the good in people and all that fairy-tale stuff, but you can't be that blind. The man wants you back because he still has feelings for you. He told you so on the phone and in that card. What more does he have to do? Come over here and fuck you to make you a believer?"

Erica drew in a deep breath. She didn't like his tone but knew it wouldn't be a good idea to debate it at this point, so she came at him with a different approach. "Do you trust me?"

Jerome leaned back in his chair. "I thought I did."

"Yes or no. Do you trust me?"

He remained silent.

"This isn't going to work if we don't trust each other. There will be obstacles that we'll have to overcome, but I don't want trust to be one of them. If I was trying to hide something, or if I'd had even the slightest idea that those flowers were from anyone other than my father, I would've never walked in here and sat them in front of you, and I certainly wouldn't have attempted to read the card," Erica said. She took another deep breath and then looked directly into Jerome's eyes. "I'm guilty of not telling you about having contact with Claude, and trust me, that won't happen again. But that's all the wrongdoing I'm going to claim."

There was another long stretch of silence, and Erica didn't like the way it felt. She rose from her chair, went over to him, and sat on his lap. She cupped his face in her hands as he'd done hers last night, and again, she looked into his eyes. "You're the only man I want, Jerome Kimbrough. I need you to believe that."

Erica waited for his reaction. Then slowly, she felt his resolve give way to her touch.

"Damn," Jerome whispered, brushing his lips against hers. "You turnin' me into a punk for real, you know that?"

"All I know is that I want you, and nobody else. And I hope you feel the same way."

"You know I do." Jerome's eyes softened. "I told you, I got you, baby."

Erica shifted her body, lifted her legs, and straddled him, sinking her middle into his. She opened her robe, exposed her bare breasts, and started grinding her hips against his already hardened crotch. They shared a kiss of repair, which quickly turned into one of slow, heated passion. For the next half hour they didn't think about old exes or new challenges. All they did was live in the truth of the moment that was in front of them, right there at Erica's breakfast table.

Chapter 27

Jerome was standing at the counter in the Foot Locker athletic store, purchasing a new pair of shoes for his son, when Jamel's buzzing phone cut their afternoon visit short.

"Dad, the fellas just texted me. They want to ball. Can I go?" Jamel asked.

"So now that you're a teenager, you don't have time for your old man anymore? I'm just good for buying you stuff, huh?" Jerome teased.

"It's not like that, Dad. The fellas are ballin' hard today, and the court is gonna be packed."

Jerome looked at his handsome, five-foot-ten-inch son, who looked just like him, save for the tawny brown complexion he'd inherited from his mother. At times, he was still in awe that he'd been blessed with a gift as precious as Jamel. He was Jerome's pride and joy, the one thing he could say he'd gotten completely right in life. He knew that in a few years Jamel's brains, combined with his athletic ability, would no doubt net him a full ride to any university of his choice. And in the meantime, Jerome planned to make sure that his son avoided the pitfalls and potholes that had nearly sunk him during his youth.

"What court are y'all playing on?" Jerome asked.

"Columbia Heights."

Jerome detected a hint of bashfulness streak across Jamel's face, and he knew what had brought about that look. He also knew why his son was so eager to play ball on the other side of town, in Columbia Heights. The boy's nose was wide open, smelling behind Tiffany, the pretty young girl who'd had him grinning like a fool last weekend, when she'd shown up at his birthday party with a pack of giggling girls. Jerome remembered Kelisha telling him about Tiffany, and that the girl lived in Columbia Heights.

Jerome had been talking to his son about sex since the day Jamel turned eleven and had told him that babies were made when a man and a woman hugged real hard late at night. Right then Jerome knew it was his responsibility to school his son in the facts, rather than have him learn the wrong things from his clueless peers. He'd explained that in a few years, puberty would come. "Your body will change, your voice will deepen, hair will grow, and you'll experience erections. It's all part of becoming a man," he'd told Jamel. "And if you ever have any questions, I want you to come straight to me, all right?"

As Jerome navigated his truck down the busy street, headed toward the recreation center, he glanced over at his son, who looked more like eighteen than thirteen, and knew it was time for another talk. He found a parking space on the street adjacent to the building, turned off the engine, and began. "Is that girl you like gonna be here?"

Jamel looked embarrassed. *"Dad!"*

"Boy, don't *Dad* me. I know you breakin' your neck to get in there because that girl from your party last week lives right around the corner."

"Okay, yeah, she's gonna be here."

"You like her?"

"She's cool."

"Tell me why you think she's cool?"

Jamel unbuckled his seat belt and turned to face his father. "Is this gonna be another one of those talks? I already know about sex."

"I know you do. So let's keep it one hundred. Right now your body is filled with urges that you're curious about exploring. Have you had sex yet?"

Jamel looked down at the floorboard. "Kind of."

"There's no such thing as kind of having sex. You've either put your penis into a girl's vagina or you haven't. So are you talking oral?"

Jamel hesitated.

"Son, there's nothing to be embarrassed about. I'm talking to you about this because I want to prepare you with the knowledge to make good decisions, and I don't want you to make the same mistakes I did." Jerome broke the ice by recounting an awkward moment he'd had when he was Jamel's age, and the consequences that had followed.

"Jamel, your grandfather wasn't in my life when I was growing up, so I didn't have anyone to talk to me like I'm talking to you. I had to learn the hard way, in the streets, from guys who didn't know much more than I did. Having sex is a big deal, and it comes with a lot of responsibility. It's not just about the good feeling you get from the act. You have to protect yourself and make smart choices."

"I understand, Dad."

"Do you have condoms?"

"Yeah. Rob's brother hooked me up with some last week, but I haven't used them."

Jerome knew that his son had left the word *yet* off the end of his sentence. The next phase of their conversation was going to require more time than they had right now, parked on the street. "All right, Jamel. Make sure you're ready to go at five on the dot, when your mother comes to get you, and don't make her wait."

"Yes, sir."

"And, son, I want you to remember that you can come to me anytime, with any question about anything. Now, go play ball, and we'll continue this conversation tomorrow."

As Jerome watched Jamel bounce into the building, he thought about how differently his conversation might have gone had his son been a daughter. Females were a whole other headache and mystery to him, and it made him think of Erica.

He'd been mad as hell as soon as he realized that Erica had received flowers from her ex, and to know that she'd been in communication with the man had nearly sent him over the edge. But when she looked into his eyes and explained that she had no interest in rekindling that old flame, he believed her, because he had no other choice. Not only had her eyes told the truth, but his gut had confirmed it, too. But even with the double vote of confidence, Jerome still felt uneasy, because he knew his relationship with Erica was either going to lift him up or drive him crazy.

It was late afternoon as Erica sat behind her large desk in her home office, still wearing her robe from this morning. She was combing through paperwork, getting things prepared for the week ahead. But try as she might, she couldn't focus on the spreadsheet in front of her. All she could think about was Jerome and the near-disastrous hurdle they'd tackled.

She needed to talk things out, so she called Ashley. Within five minutes she carefully explained the situation to her friend.

"I can't believe Claude had the nerve to send flowers to my home!" Erica fumed into the phone. "I haven't heard from him in months, and now that I've moved on and found someone wonderful, he reappears from out of nowhere to cause trouble."

"Girl, that's how Satan works. Busy as hell wreaking havoc."

"You can say that again. But I'm not going to let him mess up things between Jerome and me."

"So you really like this guy, don't you?"

Erica pushed away from her desk and took a seat on the comfy sofa on the other side of the room. "Yeah, I really do, Ash. I know you're skeptical about him, but once you meet Jerome, you'll see why I'm so crazy about him."

"I'm just trying to look out for you, that's all. But really, it doesn't matter what I think as long as you're happy."

"And I finally am!" Erica beamed. "Now I know how you feel when you talk about Jason."

"Humph."

Erica was surprised by Ashley's flat response. "What is that about? You and Jason haven't worked things out yet?"

"The wicked bitch from Vegas flew in on her broom today, so guess who has to work tonight, and guess who has to show up at Nelson's party solo, and guess who's pissed as hell?"

"Oh, no. I'm so sorry."

"But wait. It gets even better. His parents are still coming, so now I'll have to deal with them on my own."

"I didn't know they planned to attend. I guess that's not so good for you, but it's great for Nelson. Tell them to bring their checkbook. This *is* a kickoff fund-raiser, of course."

"Oh, don't worry. Mr. and Mrs. Butterfield are gonna lay down some serious cash tonight. His father is already thinking about the influence he'll have on city contract bids if Nelson gets elected. Strategic, honey!"

"Wow, shrewd."

"You know?"

"It's really too bad Jason can't come. I thought he dropped that woman as a client."

"No, he didn't. Danni Stevens wants to stick around for more than just this deal. Trust me on that. And Jason said the money is so crazy, he'd be shooting himself in the foot if he dropped everything now. This one deal is three times my yearly salary."

"Damn. Why does everything always come down to money?"

Ashley laughed. " 'Cause, my dear, in case you haven't heard, it makes the world go round."

"I thought that was love."

"There's no romance without finance. And that's for real!"

Ashley's statement made Erica think about Jerome. He'd made references to money and status, and the fact that he had neither. He didn't have material wealth, but he made her feel rich and full and loved. The truth of what she'd just realized hit Erica like a bag full of bricks. She rose from the sofa and walked into her bedroom, barely listening as Ashley ranted on. She sat on the edge of her bed and smiled, because in that moment, she knew she loved Jerome.

"Maybe this is just another sign that Jason and I need to put the brakes on things," Ashley said, snapping Erica out of her thoughts.

"You mean call off the wedding?"

"I mean put a pause on it for now and reevaluate what we really want. We're both having doubts."

"That's normal. This is a big, life-altering step you're about to make. Marriage is a serious commitment."

"Exactly, and if we're having problems and doubts before we say

'I do,' it only goes downhill from there. Plus, when you throw temptation into the mix . . . I just don't know."

"How much longer does he have to work on that heifer's project?"

"Another month or so, but who knows? At this point, well, like I said, I just don't know."

"One thing I do know is that the love is there, and if you two really want this, you'll find a way to make it work."

"Girl, the flesh is weak, and once that breaks down, all bets are off."

From the tone in Ashley's voice, Erica wasn't sure if her friend was talking about Jason or herself. But at this point she decided not to ask any more questions or make further comments, because she was there to listen, which was what she knew Ashley needed at the moment.

The two talked for a few more minutes, discussing what they were each going to wear to the event tonight. After Erica hung up the phone, she walked to her master bathroom to start getting ready. As she turned on the shower and stepped inside, she thought about Claude and what his real intentions might be. She knew whatever he was up to, it wasn't any good, and she prayed that today would be the last time she'd hear from him. But as she lathered up her netted sponge, she had a sinking feeling that it was just the beginning.

Chapter 28

All her life, Erica had been punctual, if not ahead of time. It was a habit handed down to her by her father. His philosophy was simple. If you were ten minutes early, you were right on time; five minutes early meant you were pushing it; and an on-time arrival meant you were already late! So when Jerome showed up at her door one hour and fifteen minutes after he was supposed to have picked her up, Erica was beside herself.

When they'd spoken that afternoon, she had impressed upon him how important it was that they arrive early, especially since all her family would be there. This was a huge moment for her brother and for the entire Stanford clan. A sprawling ballroom in the Ritz–Carlton Hotel had been rented out for the event. Elected officials, prominent business executives, community activists, local celebrities, and big money donors would all be in attendance. One of the local news stations was even sending out a camera crew to film the festivities for the weekend evening broadcast.

When Jerome didn't show up early, she wasn't surprised, because she knew he was time challenged. When he was fifteen minutes late, she was irritated, but not too upset. She dialed his phone at the half-hour mark and started to simmer when her call went straight to his voice mail. When forty-five minutes rolled around, she received calls from her aunt Lucile, her mother, and Ashley, each inquiring as to her whereabouts. She'd told them that she'd run into a bit of a problem at work, and that she'd be there shortly. After another fifteen minutes passed, Jerome was officially one hour late, and her simmer escalated into a boil. She grabbed her keys in frustration and was about to head out the door when he called, letting her know he was a few minutes away.

"I'm sorry about running late," Jerome said as they drove down the congested street, headed toward downtown. "I took a nap and overslept. The battery died on my phone, so I charged it and never heard your call. When I realized the time, I showered, got dressed, and rushed here as soon as I could."

All his explaining was falling on deaf ears. Erica didn't want to hear excuses unless they could magically whisk them into the Ritz-Carlton's ballroom that very minute. Luckily, the traffic fairies had sprinkled dust on the busy Saturday night streets and had cleared a path that got them to the hotel in under ten minutes. After Jerome handed the valet his keys, he and Erica walked into the lobby.

She smoothed down the front of her sleek, above-the-knee-length black sheath dress as they marched side by side toward the ballroom. She tried to calm herself with each step she took, but she was still upset. This was an important event, and she felt that Jerome had been inconsiderate, treating her brother's campaign kickoff as if it were a neighborhood barbecue, casually showing up anytime he liked.

"You didn't say two words the whole time we were in the car," Jerome said. "You still mad at me?"

"Can we talk about this later?"

"All right. But can I say one thing?"

She glanced at him, never missing a step as they turned down the hallway. She could already hear music and applause coming from the room at the end of the hall, where they were supposed to have been an hour ago. "Sure. What is it?" she said, mild irritation coating her voice.

"Your fine ass is sexy as hell, even when you're mad."

Erica couldn't help but shake her head and smile as Jerome looked at her with lust in his eyes. He took her hand in his, and they strutted into the room just as Nelson was walking up to the microphone to give his speech.

★ ★ ★

Erica had never been more proud of her brother. Nelson's speech was eloquent, heartfelt, substantive, and honest, everything a politician's promise to their constituents should be, and the rousing applause that erupted throughout the room was evidence that everyone in attendance agreed.

Smooth jazz hummed in the background as Nelson made his way through the crowd of well-heeled professionals. Erica watched her brother in his element: shaking hands, giving hugs, and posing in front of dozens of cameras that flashed like shooting stars. Tonight's event seemed more like a victory celebration than a campaign kick-off. Nelson was a natural.

"Your brother did a great job. He's very impressive," Jerome complimented.

Erica didn't want to spend the remainder of the evening being mad, especially since they'd successfully recovered from their argument earlier that morning. Besides, they planned to go back to her place and spend the rest of the evening making love, and a sour attitude would make that hard to do. So she shed her disappointment, letting it fall away as her lips formed a smile.

"Yes, I'm very proud of him. He's going to make a great councilman."

"Baby, I apologize again. I didn't mean to make us late."

Erica lowered her voice and gave him a sly smile and a wink. "It's okay. You'll just have to make it up to me."

Jerome looked into her eyes and grinned. "What do you have in mind?"

Just as Erica was about to whisper a naughty request into his ear, her parents came walking up.

Maureen and Joseph Stanford were all smiles as they approached, cocktails in hand. They were a handsome, silver-haired couple who carried an old-money look that was steeped in style and sophistication. One glance at Joseph's custom-tailored suit and Maureen's couture dress was all it took to know they were people of a certain class.

Erica greeted her parents, embracing and gently touching cheeks with her mother, so as not to smudge the make-up of either of them, then shared a hug with her father. But right away she sensed that something was amiss. Although they were smiling, she felt an uncomfortable strain between them.

It was no secret to Erica that her parents had experienced their share of marital woes, largely due to her father's promiscuous behavior during his younger years. But age and wisdom had slowed him down. These days he was tame as a house pet and he and Maureen hardly ever argued. And on the rare occasions when they were at odds, they still put on a good face in public. But not tonight. It was as if they were standing miles apart rather than the few inches that separated them.

"Is everything all right with you two?" Erica asked.

Her mother lifted her manicured hand, sweeping an uncooperative strand of her chin-length bob away from her dainty brown eyes. "Yes, um, your father and I were worried you wouldn't make it."

Erica looked at her parents closely. Although her mother was the epitome of grace and beauty, her always perfectly coiffed hair was slightly mussed and her eyes looked tired, like she could use another eight hours in bed. And she noticed that her normally attentive father appeared to be concentrating on something far away. Erica remembered that he'd sounded preoccupied yesterday, when she'd shared the good news with him about her product design. She knew he was a focus-driven man, and his current behavior was a clear indication that something was wrong.

But Erica had to push her worries to the side because no matter her parents' problem, Maureen and Joseph were now eyeing the man standing close by her side, waiting for an introduction.

"Mom, Dad, I'd like you to meet my friend, Jerome Kimbrough," Erica said.

Pleasantries were exchanged, along with cordial smiles. Erica could see that her mother approved of Jerome's *Ebony* centerfold good looks. Even though he had dressed in a rush and had shown up late, his striking sex appeal was right on time. He looked scrumptious, with white teeth sparkling, bald head gleaming, and taut muscles bulging beneath his wool-blend blazer; Erica wanted to take a bite out of him.

She was surprised when she saw her mother actually blush as

Jerome greeted her, and was glad to see her father smile at him with cursory approval.

So far so good! Erica breathed with relief. Until now, it hadn't occurred to her how much she wanted her parents to approve of Jerome, especially after what he'd told her this morning. She'd never had that worry in the past, because all her other boyfriends had come draped in Brooks Brothers, and boasted blue-chip résumés. Fortunately, she saw more good signs of Joseph's and Maureen's approval—the smile her father gave when Jerome offered him a firm handshake, and the respect on both men's faces when they looked each other in the eyes as they spoke. But when Erica saw her father glance down at Jerome's bare wrist and exhibit a glint of disapproval, she felt a small disappointment of her own.

After more pleasantries were exchanged, her parents' interrogation began. Erica was grateful for the backdrop of a crowded room filled with music, because it served to soften the blow of the tense moment as Maureen and Joseph asked Jerome question after question.

"Did you say city *sanitation?*" Erica's mother asked. A long vein strained at the base of her slender neck as her eyes widened at Jerome's words.

"*GED?* As in a high school equivalency?" her father said, squinting his eyes.

Erica practically gulped down her glass of merlot to keep her nerves in check. Although Jerome had told them he was working to start his own business, the only details her parents seemed to hold on to were that he was a trashman who'd dropped out of high school. Their barrage of background questions—which were mainly directed at finding out what he did, instead of discovering who he was—made Erica feel defensive and protective, and she wondered what Jerome must be thinking at the moment.

He was right. Her parents were going to have private words for her about her budding new relationship, and the thought made her mood sink low. She was glad when Nelson's diminutive, no-nonsense campaign manager came charging up, rushing her parents to the front of the room for a photo op with her brother.

"Your folks are real nice," Jerome said once they were standing alone.

"I'm sorry they were so intrusive with all their questions. I appreciate you tolerating their behavior."

Jerome smiled. "It's all right. They're your parents, and they want the best for you. I'd be the same way if I had a daughter and I met the man she was dating."

Erica knew that Jerome was well aware of her parents' particular bias, and she was thankful that he was kind enough to step over their prodding and obvious disapproval of his lack of pedigree. Luckily, as the evening wore on, her other family members and friends renewed her spirits by greeting him with lively, accepting well wishes.

"Well, will you look at what the cat dragged in!" Ashley shouted as she sauntered up to Erica, giving her a perfect air kiss. "I'm glad you finally made it. Wasn't Nelson fabulous!"

"Yes, he was." Erica smiled, glad to see her best friend.

"Your parents are over-the-top proud, too. I was going to come up earlier, but I saw that they had you in the box," she said with a smile, glancing over at Jerome. "That's legalese to say they were interrogating the hell outta you two." And in true Ashley Jackson, straight-no-chaser style, she turned to Jerome and began. "I'm Ashley, and you must be Jerome, the man who's making my friend a very happy woman these days." Ashley grinned mischievously as she gave him a visual inspection.

Erica wanted to laugh when Ashley shot her a "Damn, he's fine!" look. It was a sentiment that had been echoed in the hungry eyes of quite a few women in the room who'd been staring at Jerome. Erica knew she was going to have to stay close tonight, because the piranhas were dressed in Prada.

"Nice to meet you, Ashley," Jerome said in a polite voice. "I'm the happy one, thanks to Erica."

Erica, Jerome, and Ashley stood at a skirted bistro table, sipping wine and making small talk. Erica could tell this wasn't Jerome's thing, because he looked bored and ready to go, but she was glad that he was trying for her sake, and it made her want him even more.

"Ash, I forgot to ask you. Where are your parents? I haven't seen them since we got here."

Ashley took a small sip of wine and pursed her lips. "They both came down with a sudden case of the flu."

"I'm so sorry to hear that," Erica replied with concern. "I hope they feel better soon."

"Girl, they feel just fine. That was an excuse they made up because they knew Jason and his parents were supposed to be here, and they didn't want to deal with them."

"Wow!"

Ashley looked at Jerome. "Just in case Erica hasn't filled you in, my fiancé, Jason, is white, and my parents can't stand him."

Jerome nodded, giving Ashley a look of sympathetic understanding. Erica was glad he didn't let on that he already knew, because she'd told him that tidbit of information during one of their late-night phone calls.

"Jason won't be here, but his parents came," Ashley said. "And, speak of the devil, here they come right now."

Erica and Jerome turned to greet Mr. and Mrs. Butterfield, and that was when the real fireworks began.

Chapter 29

Very few things took Jerome by surprise, but when he looked into the eyes of the desperate housewife who'd tried to proposition him last weekend, he was caught completely off guard.

"So glad you could make it," Ashley greeted as her future in-laws walked up.

Jerome could see the uneasy strain on Ashley's face as he watched her force a light smile with considerable discomfort while she gave a half hug to the woman whom he now knew was Jason's mother, and a genuine embrace to Jason's father.

"Jerome, what a surprise to see you here," Mr. Butterfield said, extending his hand for a firm shake. "It's a small world."

Jerome could see the shock and questions on both Erica's and Ashley's faces, but the desperate housewife's expression was the most telling of all. It was obvious that she was fighting a losing battle to remain calm. Instead, she looked like she'd just seen a ghost. Her boldness from last weekend had been replaced with the worry and fear of being exposed.

"You've already met?" Ashley asked.

"Yes," Jerome answered with a smile as he looked from Mr. Butterfield to the man's nervous wife. "I did some work for these fine people."

"And excellent work, indeed," Mr. Butterfield pronounced. "As a matter of fact, my wife told me just the other day that she'd like you to do some more work for us. Didn't you, honey?" he said, looking toward Mrs. Butterfield.

Jerome watched as the woman nodded slightly, looking as though she was in pain. "Ashley, where are your parents?" Mrs. Butterfield interjected, obviously wanting to change the subject. "I've been looking forward to seeing them."

"You have?" Ashley answered, jerking her neck to the side.

Her response was so matter of fact that Jerome wanted to laugh. He liked Ashley.

"Why, yes, of course," Mrs. Butterfield replied. "We're going to be family, after all."

Everyone, including Mr. Butterfield, looked at the stylishly dressed socialite as if she'd lost her mind.

"They're at home with the flu, but I'll relay your message."

"Sorry to hear that," Mr. Butterfield said. "Yes, please give them our best."

They all stood in awkward silence for a moment, until Mr. Butterfield revived the conversation. "So, Jerome, how do you know Ashley?"

"Through Erica." He smiled and placed his arm around Erica's waist to show they were a couple.

Mr. Butterfield nodded. "You have an exceptional eye for quality and beauty in both your craft and in women," he complimented. "Erica is a fine young woman."

"Thank you, Mr. Butterfield." Erica nodded graciously. "Such kind words."

"True and well deserved."

Jerome was going to chime in when he noticed that the desperate housewife looked as though she'd just inhaled a bad odor. She glared at Erica, surveying her up and down with disdain, as if she was jealous.

"It was lovely seeing you all, but I'm afraid we must be going," Mrs. Butterfield announced, not looking at anyone except her husband.

It was obvious she no longer cared to stand around and endure discomfort. After the couple said their good-byes and then scurried away, the chatter began.

"What the hell was that all about? And give it to me straight," Ashley said, looking at Jerome.

Jerome knew he had to tread lightly with how much information he divulged. On one hand, he wanted nothing more than to call out the desperate housewife for the conniving cougar she was, especially after the nasty look she'd given Erica. On the other, he didn't want to cause waves with Mr. Butterfield, who could lead him to more business. Accusing a man's wife of propositioning you was a serious charge in any situation, so he proceeded with caution.

"Like I said, I did a repair job for them. They paid me, and that's that."

Ashley shook her head. "Uh-uh. There's more to it than that. Mrs. Butterfield looked like she saw someone rise up from the dead when she looked at you. It was clear she was uncomfortable. She even asked about my parents, who she doesn't give a damn about. And then the funky look she gave Erica. Somethin' ain't right."

Jerome knew the desperate housewife's nervous behavior had been obvious, and especially to a lawyer like Ashley. He could also see that Erica was looking at him for answers, too.

"I'm with Ashley," Erica chimed in. "What's the backstory that we're missing?"

Just then, Nelson appeared, giving Erica a big bear hug. "Thanks for coming out, little sis. I'm glad you made it."

Erica admired her handsome brother, all decked out in Armani, looking like two million bucks. She quickly forgot about the strange incident between Jerome and the Butterfields, because she knew by the look on Nelson's face that her parents had already spoken to him about Jerome. She could see his charismatic and observant eyes zero in on her man.

"Good to meet you. I'm Nelson," he said, giving Jerome a strong handshake. "Thanks for coming out."

Erica was thrilled when she saw that Nelson and Jerome clicked right away. Even though Nelson was periodically interrupted by people vying for his time, he managed to engage Jerome in a lively conversation about sports, which eventually led to topics like the economy and black male mentoring. She also noticed something strangely peculiar happening in front of her. Not only was Nelson giving Jerome his attention, but he was taking in the sight of Ashley, as well.

Erica watched as her brother's eyes roamed over, around, and up and down her childhood friend. She knew Nelson well, and she could see that he was inspecting Ashley like a man who was interested in getting more than just her vote. Erica had to admit that her friend looked hot in her body-hugging orange wrap dress and sexy suede stilettos. She knew her brother's taste, and Ashley was right up his alley. He'd always joked that he was an Ivy League–educated, "baby got back" type of brothah.

Erica was even more surprised when she saw Ashley smile, put her hand on Nelson's shoulder, and return each one of his suggestive looks. *What the hell?*

Ashley had always been like a second sister to Nelson. They had grown up together, had been in Jack and Jill together, and had teased each other like any siblings would, so Erica didn't understand what had brought about their more-than-friendly behavior. And given the fact that Ashley was getting married in a few months, and Nelson was running for a highly publicized political office and didn't need the scandal of breaking up an engagement, it was especially baffling that the two were flirting and smiling at each other with innuendo.

Given her parents' uncharacteristically strange behavior, and now her best friend and her brother acting as if they needed to get a room upstairs, Erica wondered what bizarre occurrence was going to happen next.

Unfortunately, her question was quickly answered when she felt a light tap on her shoulder, turned around, and stared dead into Claude's eyes.

Chapter 30

It was one of the very few times that Erica had been so caught off guard, she couldn't find words to speak. All evening she'd been introducing Jerome to everyone who came up to greet them, but standing there, looking at her ex-fiancé, who'd been at the center of her and Jerome's first argument, Erica couldn't find her voice to say a single syllable.

She knew that Jerome had figured out exactly who Claude was, if by nothing else than the look of sheer discomfort on her face. They stood in silence—Ashley and Nelson, she and Jerome . . . and Claude. Erica knew she should probably make the introduction, but she didn't feel that Claude warranted the energy and certainly not the courtesy. She was pissed that he'd even shown up at the event. And the fact that he'd approached her, especially when it was obvious that she was there with someone, made her question his motives even more than she already had.

As if reading her mind, Claude focused solely on her, completely ignoring Jerome. His face brightened into a warm smile. "Erica," he said, "it's great to see you again, and so soon."

Erica gave him a tentative half nod and an even smaller whisper of a smile. If Claude was disappointed in her less-than-enthused reception, neither his eyes nor his demeanor gave any hints. He proceeded to greet Ashley and then Nelson, chatting it up as though he was part of their group. The entire time he spoke, he never acknowledged Jerome's presence. Erica could feel the tension slowly building as Jerome's eyes volleyed back and forth between her and her ex.

"Nelson, my man," Claude said, showing off his Hollywood smile. "I'm going to get in touch with your people next week to co-ordinate a fund-raiser on behalf of my firm, as well as a private event that I'll personally host at my home. I'm going to bundle quite a bit for you."

Claude's boastfulness made Erica want to roll her eyes. His "bundle" comment was meant to reference the fact that because he was so well connected, he had the clout to gather large contributions from individuals and organizations on Nelson's behalf and then present what would no doubt be a hefty sum for Nelson's war chest. Erica didn't want the taint of Claude's paws anywhere near her brother's campaign, but she understood that Nelson needed every penny he could raise in order to wage an effective fight against the incumbent he was trying to unseat.

Nelson smiled and looked Claude directly in his eyes as he re-sponded. "Thank you for your offer, but we've got a number of peo-ple working on various fund-raising strategies for the campaign. If we need your help, which, again, I appreciate you offering, we'll be in touch." He nodded. "If you'll excuse me, I have to say good-bye to a few guests."

And just like that, Nelson shut Claude down. Ashley smiled so hard, her eyes turned into slits. Erica hoped her brother's rebuff would send Claude back to the cave where he belonged, but instead, he di-rected his attention to Jerome.

"I don't believe we've met," Claude said, his smile fading to an acerbic stare.

At that moment, Erica wished she could bore a hole into the floor and jump into it. She knew that Claude was a high-minded ass-hole, but she also knew that Jerome came from the streets, and street folks and high-minded assholes weren't a good mix. She took a deep breath and prayed that hotel security wouldn't have to be called in.

"No, we haven't," Jerome said. His voice was deep, cool, and con-fident.

Neither man took his eyes off the other, and it was almost as if they were staring each other down for a duel.

"Claude Daniel Richardson, the *fourth*," Claude said, never extending his hand or giving a nod or a smile.

No, he didn't just throw out "the fourth"! Erica silently fumed. Claude reserved that suffix for occasions when he wanted to impress, letting people know that he was one of the four generations of prestigious Richardson men, well known among the East Coast Talented Tenth community for their small fortune made as African American industrialists. Erica used to cringe when he did that while they dated, and now, looking at him, she thought he seemed utterly ridiculous in his need to show off his standing.

"Jerome Kimbrough," Jerome said, his reply void of customary pleasantries. "I'm Erica's boyfriend."

Erica nearly swallowed her tongue. She looked at Jerome with a startled expression. She knew they'd talked about building a future, and that they wanted something serious. But hearing him claim her in that way was both surprising and exhilarating, and it lodged a feeling deep in her throat and made her stomach tingle with butterflies.

Claude wrinkled his forehead. "Funny, Erica never mentioned you when we spoke the other night."

"You disrespectful bastard!" Ashley hissed. "Why're you tryin' to start shit?"

Jerome calmly smiled and held a hand up in Ashley's direction. "Don't worry. I got this." He paused, then glared coolly at Claude as he spoke. "This is a nice event celebrating a great moment for Erica's brother and their family, so let's not turn it into anything other than that. I know what's up, so don't try to play me, and don't let my woman's name come out your mouth in front of me again."

Claude balked. "Is that a threat?"

"Yes, it is."

Jerome's simple three-word answer made Erica's heart jump with fear. Even Ashley looked as though she was a bit apprehensive about what might go down. Erica felt she should say something. After all, she'd been standing there silently, not saying a word, since Claude had first appeared. But her voice had gone missing, and she couldn't find it under the building tension.

"Sorry about the interruption," Nelson said, smiling cheerfully as he rejoined the group. "It's the price you pay when you're the host of the party."

Erica could see that her brother had quickly surmised that something unpleasant had happened in the few moments he'd been gone. Nelson was a calm, levelheaded fellow, but when it came to his family, he was more than capable of ripping someone's heart out to protect the people he loved. He'd learned that lesson from his father the night their home was invaded.

"Is there a problem?" Nelson asked calmly, but with serious intent, as he looked from Claude to Jerome and then to Erica.

"Everything's cool," Jerome offered. "Claude was just wishing us good night before he leaves."

Claude looked at Jerome as if he could spit in his face, but instead, he extended his hand toward Nelson, bid him a good night, and walked out the ballroom door.

Jerome and Erica's ride back to her house was just as silent and sterile as their drive two hours earlier had been. At that time it was Erica who hadn't had the need for conversation, but now it was Jerome who preferred silence.

Erica wanted to know what he was thinking and feeling about all that had transpired tonight, especially his interaction with Claude. But she knew it was probably best to let him sort out what was on his mind and then discuss it once they got back to her house.

When they turned onto her block, Erica reached into her small rhinestone-studded clutch for her garage opener, which she'd grabbed before dashing out the door. But when Jerome parked on the street, she paused.

"You're not going around back to the garage?"

"No, I'm parking here so I can walk you to your door and get my overnight bag that I left in your living room."

The streetlights above cast a halo-like glow into the truck, allowing Erica to see the tense expression on Jerome's face. "So you're not spending the night?"

"No."

Without warning or further words, Jerome opened his door and quickly walked around to Erica's side to let her out. He held her hand, making sure her strappy high heels didn't betray her as her feet hit the uneven pavement. Then they walked to her door in silence.

Once they were inside, Erica immediately started talking. "Why don't you want to spend the night?"

"Because I'm upset, and I need to be alone."

"Please don't leave like this. Let's talk about why you're upset."

Jerome walked over to the edge of her staircase and reached for his bag. "You know why I'm upset."

"Okay, well, let's talk about it."

"I'm not in a talking mood, so I'm gonna leave while I still have my temper intact."

Erica trailed behind him as he turned and walked back toward the door. He was about to put his hand on the doorknob when she stepped in front of him, bringing his movements to a stop. "Don't go. We need to talk about this."

Jerome stepped back and looked at her. "Listen, I really think it's best that I leave. That way I won't say anything that I'll regret later."

"I want you to say what's on your mind now. Let me know what you're thinking, what you're feeling."

He took a deep breath and shook his head. "I'm thinking this is bullshit, and I'm feeling like I've been played. You couldn't even introduce me, Erica."

Erica's forehead wrinkled. She knew she should have found her voice to say something to Claude, instead of standing there with no words. But she hadn't wanted to give Claude the satisfaction of an acknowledgment, and then she'd been struck silent by Jerome's public declaration that she was his girlfriend, which had caused feelings she was still processing. "I think you're blowing this way out of proportion. I don't want Claude. I want you."

"Then why didn't you open your mouth and say something? Your brother shut that fool down and wouldn't even accept his damn money. Even your girl Ashley spoke up and had my back and was about to cuss that clown out. But you, you just stood there like a spectator."

Erica folded her arms. "So what was I supposed to do? Get loud and act out?"

"No, you were supposed to acknowledge me. It's about respect and looking out for each other's emotions. I've made myself vulnerable with you because I felt I could trust you. I'm sayin' and doin' sappy shit that would get my ass beat down in the streets. But I allowed myself to go there with you because for the first time in my life . . ." Jerome paused. "You know what? This shit is for the birds. I'm out."

Erica pressed her back against the door, looking at Jerome with pleading eyes. "You're not leaving until we resolve this."

"Erica, please move so I can go home."

"No. I'm not moving until we fix this."

"You're acting like a spoiled-ass little rich girl who's gonna pout till she gets her way. You conned me once today, but that shit ain't gonna happen again."

His harsh words stung Erica's ears, but she wasn't going to let them dissuade her. She loved Jerome, and the thought of him walking out made her heart ache. "I'm not conning you. This is for real. I told you this morning, you're who I want."

Jerome hoisted his overnight bag onto his shoulder. "After what I saw tonight, I don't know what to believe. Now, please move out of my way."

"We have to trust each other, Jerome."

"Trust?" he smirked, his voice rising. "When I told you that I got you, I was telling you that I was ready to go the distance. I poured my heart out to you about my past because I wanted to start things off right between you and me. I've lied and schemed and hustled and whored around in the past, but I don't want that shit anymore. I thought this was gonna be different."

"This *is* different, and I've poured my heart out to you, too. You act like you're the only person in this relationship who's vulnerable and taking chances."

"Maybe it's not worth the risk."

Erica's heart pounded. "Don't say that, and don't let my behavior tonight ruin what we're building. I should've spoken up, and I regret that I didn't. But I've been honest from the start about how I feel about you and what I want, and I'm being honest now."

Jerome looked up at the ceiling in frustration. "I've played this game before. I just got soft and didn't see it coming."

"What are you talking about?"

"I'm talkin' about the game you're playin'," he said, glaring. "With your fancy degrees, bougie family, and expensive lifestyle. You wanted to take a walk on the wild side and try something new. You let me fuck your brains out like those punk-ass dudes you deal with never could, and now that you got your rocks off and you got what you wanted from me, you ready to go back to your neat, clean life, gettin' fuckin' flowers from old boyfriends and shit."

Erica's eyes grew large with outrage. "I can't believe you!"

"Oh, believe it!" Jerome said, his voice rising. "It's all good when we're tucked away in a sandwich shop or in the jury room, and especially in your bedroom. But when it's time to bring me into your world, that's when the shit goes south."

"That's ridiculous, and you know it!" Erica hissed. "If that was the case, I wouldn't have asked you to come with me in the first place."

"You asked me this morning, at the last minute, claiming you forgot until Ashley texted you. How you gonna forget an important event like that?"

"Because like I told you, I programmed it in on the wrong date in my calendar, and with everything I had going on last week, I barely kept up with my own schedule, let alone anyone else's."

"Please get out the way so I can leave," he huffed in an angry tone.

Jerome was breathing so hard, Erica could feel the heat on her skin. The intensity in his eyes wasn't rage, it was hurt, and it was at her hands. She'd brought emotional harm to the one man who'd made her feel safe and loved. The thought made her own baby browns fill with a swell of unexpected tears. She didn't want to cry, and she tried her hardest to hold her tears back, but a stream sliding down her face betrayed her wishes. She wiped her cheeks with the heels of her hands, but her tears continued to flow, despite her efforts to stop them.

"Oh, so now you think cryin' is gonna make me stay?"

Just as she couldn't find her words earlier, they eluded her now. All she could do was look at him with the fear of losing him while she attempted to gather herself and salvage their budding relationship before it ended.

"You might as well stop looking all sad, 'cause your tears ain't gonna work on me."

Erica breathed deeply. "Jerome, I'm so sorry," she managed to eek out as a lone tear fell. "I don't know what else to say except I never meant to hurt or disrespect you. I don't want to lose you." She sniffled, lowering her head. . . .

Jerome looked at her and sighed. "Don't cry, Erica." He let out a deep, labored breath, dropping his overnight bag to the floor. "Please don't cry."

Erica walked over to him, and when she did, he reached for her and pulled her into his arms, holding her close as salt water drenched the front of his cotton shirt.

"Damn it! What the hell are you doing to me?" Jerome breathed out, his words a mixture of confusion and relief.

"I'm trying to love you," Erica said. "Just let me love you."

She planted soft kisses on the base of his neck before searching for his lips. Once her mouth found them, she kissed him hard and deep, hungrily exploring with her agile tongue as she savored the hint of wine still lingering on his breath.

Jerome reached for the hem of her dress, sliding it up the sides of her thick thighs. He hooked his long fingers around the top of her silk thong, tugging at it. The warm feel of her soft skin caused his erection to form a tent at the crotch of his trousers. "See what you do to me," he breathed heavily into her ear, pressing his hardness into her.

"Show me, baby."

He grabbed her ass, held it firmly in his hands, and hoisted her into the air as she wrapped her legs around his waist. He carried her up the stairs, taking them two at a time, then down the hall until he reached her bedroom.

Chapter 31

Erica and Jerome stood close together, removing each other's clothes. They touched and caressed as they tossed their garments to the floor, leaving their heated bodies exposed and naked. Their need for each other was urgent and primal, and they were ready to satisfy it.

Jerome turned Erica around so that her delicate shoulders rested against his broad chest. He gently cupped her breast with one hand, massaging and tweaking her erect nipple, while his other hand explored the depths of her creamy middle. His long fingers plunged deep inside her as a pleasure-filled gasp escaped her lips. He kissed the side of her neck, snaking his tongue up and down her delicious-tasting skin. Then, slowly, he removed his fingers from her wetness, bringing them to his mouth so he could taste her sweet juice.

"You taste so good, baby," he whispered.

Erica threw her head back, absorbed in the moment, flushed at his touch, while he panted hard in her ear. With slow movements, he pressed his hardness against her soft ass, enjoying its plumpness as he rotated his hips in a circular motion, making her moan and shiver all at once.

"Mmmm, yeah, baby." Erica's breath was like a heavy heat wave as she reached down and gently stroked the length of Jerome's thick shaft with the palms of her hands. She quickly turned, dropped to her knees, and took him into her warm, hungry mouth. Sucking, licking, and tasting, letting his fullness fill the back of her throat.

"Yeah, baby, *ooohhh.*" Jerome placed his hand on the back of her head, holding on, digging his fingers into her tender scalp as her tongue teased and circled, then flicked the tip of his swollen head before she released him. She licked her lips, then hungrily engulfed him again, sucking with controlled vigor as she swirled her tongue over his hard flesh. Jerome's pleasure was so great he let out a loud moan.

Slowly, Erica dotted kisses along his body as she made her way back up to his mouth. They devoured each other in a deep, passionate kiss. Their bodies were sleek and wet as they pressed into one another.

"I want to feel you inside me," Erica breathed into his open mouth. "From behind."

Jerome bent down, reached for his pants, which were lying on the floor, and removed a condom from his wallet. He nearly fell over his own feet in his rush to get Erica to the bed. He slipped the sheath over his engorged head as he watched Erica position herself, a careful balancing act as she perched on all fours. Her knees and elbows sank into the plush fabric of the duvet as he came up behind her. Gently, he held her in place with his hands on either side of her hips and entered her with one long, deep, fluid stroke.

"*Yeeesss!*" they both sang out in pleasure at the same time.

Jerome took it slow, sliding in and out of her wetness at a gentle pace, moving his hips in a rolling rhythm. He leaned into her, easing his hands from her hips to her shoulders, holding her as his thrusts became more intense with growing speed.

Erica moaned, begging him to go deeper, harder, and faster as she turned and looked up at him. His face was outlined in sweat and etched with desire as he responded to her call. She watched with brazen lust as he pounded her, creating a sweet pain that made her call out his name. The force of his thrusts was in step with the sway of her hips.

"Yes, baby, yes!" Erica cried out, giving in to a bright electric sensation as she climaxed in a creamy haze.

Jerome laid his body flat atop hers as he continued to pump in and out of her at a heated and steady pace. Her hot wetness sloshed against his leg, creating a sound and a feeling that took him over the edge. He arched his back and swerved his hips, plunging as far as he could go into the soft folds resting between her legs. His pelvis rubbed against her ass, adding to the euphoric feeling spreading through his body as he experienced a release so hot and intense, he collapsed against her back. His body spasmed, his eyes shut tight, and he lay still, completely satisfied.

"I love you," he whispered into Erica's ear.

She moved her head to the side and looked at him. "I love you, too."

Jerome didn't want to move, but he knew his body weight was too much for Erica's delicate frame to hold, so he gently rolled off of her warm back and lay by her side. They were cuddled face-to-face, holding each other close, their bodies wrapped together like they were born that way. He gently stroked the side of her face and kissed her on the bridge of her nose. He loved Erica so much, it scared him. She'd spawned emotions deep inside him that were new and raw, challenging his once ironclad ego.

He'd been pissed during the party tonight. Jealousy and self-doubt had coursed through his body when Erica stood beside him and acted as though she were mute when her ex showed up. Jerome had always worn his confidence like a broken-in pair of jeans—comfortable and easy—but that moment had tested him. Until tonight, he'd never felt threatened by another man. He'd always been sure of who he was and how he appeared in his world. But stepping into Erica's domain, filled with pedigree and status, he'd felt as if he was wandering in an unknown land where all the rules as he'd known them had changed.

During the silent drive back to Erica's house, he'd thought about the fact that this was what he'd said he wanted just a week ago: meeting new people, learning new things, branching out of his comfort zone, and exposing himself to another side of life. But now that he'd stepped into it, he questioned whether he belonged. He'd never wondered if he was good enough for any of the women he'd dated, and when he thought about it, he didn't know if that was a poor reflection on him or them.

Looking at Erica as the light from the window illuminated her body, he thought she was the most precious, amazing creature he'd ever seen. The soft curves of her full hips and thick thighs looked like they belonged on a much larger woman, but it was part of her allur-

ing appeal that held him in her spell, a confluence of consistent con-
tradiction. She was a polished, highbrow sophisticate, yet she was
down to earth and humble. She was a hard-edged businesswoman, yet
she was compassionate and kind. She'd been hurt by failed relationships, yet she still believed in true love and happily ever afters.

She was complex and funny and frustrating, and he loved every
part of who she was.

"That was incredible," Erica said, stretching her arm over his
shoulder.

He kissed the bridge of her nose. "Yes, it was."

"Jerome?"

"Yes, baby?"

"I'm not with you just because you fuck my brains out."

Jerome felt bad when he heard his words repeated back to him,
and coming out of Erica's mouth, they sounded especially biting.
"Baby, I'm sorry I said that. I didn't mean it."

"Yes, you did, and it's okay. I want you to let me know how you
feel so I'll understand how my actions affect you. If we're going to
make this work, we have to be responsible to each other in that way.
What happened tonight . . . I won't let it happen again."

"I have to step up and take responsibility, too. Some of the
thoughts and feelings going through my head had nothing to do with
you. It was about how I feel about myself."

"And how is that?"

"Like maybe I don't measure up. Like you should be with a
brothah on your same level. You know, educated, good job, big fancy
house—"

"Jerome . . ."

"Erica, please, let me finish," he said gently. "I know I'm a good
person. I'm smart, hardworking, honest, and I'll make a great partner.
But right now I can't offer you the kinds of things that you're used
to . . . that your parents think you deserve."

Erica softened her eyes and touched his cheek. "You can't put a
price on happiness or love, and that's what I have with you. You've
given me what I want and what I need."

"So, you're cool with how I am, my lifestyle, and my status?"

"Well, yes and no."

Jerome cocked his head against the softness of the pillow and stared into Erica's eyes.

"What I mean is that I love who you are, but I want you to continue to grow, just like I want to continue to improve my life. And I definitely want your status to change. I want you to complete your GED, start your business, get your company certified, and build projects all over this city. I can help you develop a business plan, and you can help me remodel my boutique. We can learn and grow with each other."

Jerome thought about the things Erica had said and what their future would be like. "You're the first woman I've ever had this kind of conversation with."

Erica smiled. "And I better be the last."

Chapter 32

Jerome sprang up with a force so strong and a speed so quick, he didn't realize he was awake until Erica's cries jarred him into awareness.

"Baby, what wrong? What's going on?" Jerome asked. He looked at Erica for answers, searching for her eyes through the darkness of the room. His heart pounded inside his chest as he reached over and pulled her close against him.

"What's wrong? Talk to me!" he demanded.

Erica trembled in his arms. She was silent. Drenched in sweat. Shaking and scared. Wide-eyed and frightened as a lost kitten. She took deep breaths, trying to calm herself.

Jerome looked into her face and saw that it was covered in horror. She was terrified, and he wondered what awful thought or memory had ripped her so violently from her sleep. He rocked her back and forth, trying to soothe her. "You must have had a bad dream. It's gonna be all right." He stroked her damp hair, pushed it away from her face, and wiped her tears with his hands. "Shhh. I'm here, Erica. I got you."

The early morning sun pumped life in through the side window, flooding the room with soft rays of warmth. It was the start of a new day, and as Jerome and Erica lay in bed, with him watching her sleep peacefully, he thought about what had happened just a few hours ago.

At around 4:00 a.m. he'd awakened to the piercing sound of Erica's cry of "*Noooo! Noooo!*" She had repeated it over and over until she was inaudible. Once she finally stopped trembling, she fell back into a peaceful slumber, sleeping in Jerome's arms as if someone had drugged her.

After Erica's hellish screams had pulled him from his relaxing sleep, Jerome had lain awake until the sun rose, holding her and wondering what had caused her nightmare. Yes, he now knew she'd had a nightmare and not just a bad dream. A bad dream would have meant that she'd had a scary thought that passed through her mind during sleep, leaving her restless and a little uneasy. But a nightmare was much worse. It was terrifying and extreme, and it had left her helpless, as if she'd been pleading for her life.

Her body had shaken so badly with fear that she was nonresponsive. Then, finally, she succumbed to the explosive weight of the experience, causing her to drift away into a deep catatonic-like state. He wondered what kind of awful thing she'd experienced that had made her plead in the night as if she were fighting for her life?

Erica squinted as her eyes fluttered open, adjusting to the brilliant light streaming into her bedroom. She smiled when she saw Jerome staring back at her, and took a deep breath as she inhaled his woodsy vanilla scent, completely amazed by how good he still smelled after a night of heavy sex.

"Good morning," she whispered through pursed lips, shielding him from her morning breath.

"Good morning," he whispered back.

She smiled and stretched herself against his lean, muscular body. But when she looked down at herself, her face drew a tight line of confusion. She realized that Jerome's wonderfully fragrant scent wasn't coming from his skin. It was coming from his T-shirt—which she was wearing! When she'd drifted off to sleep last night, she'd been naked, and now she wasn't.

"You were soaking wet and trembling," Jerome said, tracing his index finger along the contour of her cheek. "I didn't want to search through your things, so I put my T-shirt on you."

She stared at him, and it all came rushing back. She'd had a night-mare, and this time there'd been someone beside her to witness it.

Although she'd spent countless nights in bed with Claude and the other men she'd dated in the past, none of them had ever witnessed one of her heart-thumping, panic-stricken nightmares. But it was only her second night with Jerome, and she'd screamed and cried out, nearly scaring him to death, waking him from his sleep, too. Then something happened mere moments after her frightening episode that she'd never experienced—her eyes closed and she fell into a dead sleep.

Normally, once she was awakened by a nightmare, she couldn't go back to sleep. She'd lie in bed, wide-eyed and exhausted, staring at the ceiling until it was time for her to get up and start her day. But that didn't happen last night. Jerome had held her in the comfort and safety of his arms, and it was that safe place that had allowed her to doze off into dreamland.

She looked up at him. "I had a nightmare."

"I know."

"It was a bad one this time. I'm sorry if I scared you."

"Does this happen a lot?"

Erica shrugged. "Not a lot, but I've had quite a few lately." She sighed and bit her bottom lip. "I've been having nightmares since I was ten."

She went on to tell Jerome about the night that had been living with her every day for the last twenty-five years. She explained that triggers, such as stress, anxiety, or any kind of pressured state that made her feel unsafe or unsure, could bring about a nightmare. "The length of time they last, or even how often they occur, is unpre-dictable," she said. The only thing she knew for sure, as she'd learned from studying dream analysis over the years, was that the episodes were rooted in fear. "I always wake up just in time, though."

"In time for what?" Jerome asked.

"Before I crash to the ground or my heart stops or I suffocate or I'm strangled. Sometimes I'm chased and hunted, sometimes I'm about to have an accident, and at other times I'm just running from danger. But I always wake up before I die in the dream."

Jerome tilted his head and looked at her with concern. "So, is it like the movie *The Matrix,* where if you die there, you die here? I've heard that people can die from dreams, like if you're falling and you actually hit the ground."

"No, that's an old wives' tale. Although I don't doubt that if someone is scared enough or goes into shock or has a weakened heart, it could happen. But generally, no."

"Good."

"Actually, I wish I wouldn't wake up in time. I want to die," she said softly.

Jerome looked visibly disturbed. "Baby, why?"

"I don't mean die in real life. Just in my dream. Usually dreams about death symbolize the end of something, like a relationship or a friendship. It puts an end to whatever trouble is lingering. I think if I actually died in one of my dreams, it might set me free. That's why near the end I always give up and let whatever is happening overtake me. I surrender to it. But instead of dying, I wake up."

"Have you ever considered talking to a therapist?"

"I did once, when I was in college. But it was a terrible experience that left me stale on the idea."

"Don't let one bad experience keep you from breaking through. I'm speaking from personal experience. After I was shot, I was . . ." Jerome paused, taking a deep breath. "I was scared. I didn't even want to go around people I didn't know, because I saw everyone as a possible threat. But the hospital hooked me up with a therapist, and it changed everything."

"I don't know. Maybe I'll look into it."

"Think about it. What you went through as a child was traumatic."

"I felt scared and helpless that night," Erica said. "I saw a man brutally attack and shoot my father. I remember how they struggled and fought, all the blood and the noise." She touched the dark scar on the left side of Jerome's chest, gently rubbing her finger across the slightly raised skin. "You know what it's like."

"Yes, violent memories are hard to shake. They stay with you." Jerome kissed her forehead. "I'm sorry you experienced that as a child, and I'm so sorry I caused your nightmare last night."

Erica shook her head. "You weren't the cause. I've been under a lot of stress lately that has nothing to do with you. You calmed me and made me feel safe. You're the only reason I was able to even sleep."

"But I caused the stress and anxiety that led up to it. I upset you twice yesterday, and I'm so sorry about that, baby."

Erica perched herself up on her elbows, looking Jerome in his eyes. "Did you hear me when I said I feel safe with you? As soon as you held me in your arms, all my fears went away. This wasn't your fault. Yesterday was rough, but our night was wonderful and magnificent," she said, circling her finger on his forearm. "So it wasn't you. I was worried about other things."

"Like what?"

"Last night I could tell there was something very strange going on with my parents. I couldn't put my finger on it, but I got a vibe that something's not right. Then there was that weird, uncomfortable flirting between Ashley and Nelson. I don't know what that was about."

Jerome shrugged. "I know you said she's engaged, but from what I saw, she needs to put that on pause. She and your brother got something goin' on."

Chapter 33

Erica knitted her brow. "You think Ashley and Nelson are fooling around?"

"Hell, yeah," Jerome said, looking at Erica as if she didn't have a clue. "Don't you?"

"Just because they were flirting doesn't mean there's anything going on."

"Trust me on this one. I'm a man. I can tell. If they're not fuckin' now, they have in the past."

"How can you say that, and how are you so sure?"

"Because of the kind of eye contact and body language they had goin' on. It went beyond just flirting. They were very familiar. Nelson looked at her like he's tapped that."

Erica shook her head from side to side. "No. Ashley would've told me. We tell each other everything."

"Uh, apparently not."

Erica thought about what he'd said. "No, I'm sure she would have told me something this important. That's why I can't understand their behavior."

"If it's bothering you this much, you should talk to Ashley and your parents so you can find out what's really going on."

She nodded. "You're right. I'm going to do that this afternoon." She didn't want her questions or confusion to linger, and that thought drew her back to her curiosity from last night. "What's up with you and the Butterfields, and specifically, Mrs. Butterfield?"

She could see Jerome averting his eyes as he shifted his body. "I did a roof repair job for them last weekend."

"Okay. What else?"

Jerome let out a deep sigh. "Damn, pillow talk is dangerous."

Erica's eyes widened. "What's that supposed to mean?"

"It means that some things shouldn't be discussed, not even after a night of good lovin', hell, especially not after a night of good lovin'," Jerome teased as he pulled Erica in closer to him.

"I'm serious," she said. "We just talked about how important it is for us to be honest with each other. Please tell me, Jerome. I want to know."

She could tell Jerome was thinking about what to say.

"Just say it."

"Okay, but you have to promise me you won't run back and tell your girl."

Erica thought about what Jerome was asking. He wanted her to withhold information that could possibly affect Ashley in a negative way, and in her mind, it had to be bad if he was making her take a vow of silence. "If it's something that's going to hurt Ashley, I don't know if I can keep it from her."

Jerome rubbed his chin, and she could tell he was debating what to do. "All right, I'll tell you."

By the time Jerome finished his story, Erica was startled, disturbed, and pissed all at once. "Jason's high-and-mighty mother won't approve of a black woman marrying her son, but she's fine with getting herself some black dick. That bitch!"

"Whoa, baby," Jerome said with surprise. "I've never heard you talk like this."

"When someone messes with the people I love, it's on. No wonder she could barely look you in the eyes. That old heifer should be ashamed of herself."

Jerome laughed. "Damn. I'm gonna make sure I stay on your good side."

Erica shook her head. "I just don't like that kind of fakeness. And you know what? Mrs. Butterfield was kind of obvious. I mean, she was all nervous around you, and she looked at me like she wanted to brawl. I bet you Ashley figured it out on her own."

"You think her husband sensed it, too?"

"Unless he's a complete idiot, I don't see how he couldn't."

Jerome sighed again. "Well, I can say bye-bye to any future referrals from him."

"Maybe not. If Mr. Butterfield's been married to her this long, he probably knows the deal," she said, thinking about the way her own parents operated their marriage.

"You're probably right. Just goes to show you, you never know what goes on when people close their doors."

Erica stretched her arms and legs as she nestled farther into Jerome's body. "I want us to close our doors and walk into peace and comfort." It had taken love a long time to come, but now that it had, Erica knew she was never going to let Jerome go. They shared a gentle embrace and a deep, warm kiss that led them back into paradise.

Chapter 34

Erica pressed her back into the burgundy tapestry of the soft upholstered couch. She'd always loved the comfort of her parents' home. Although it was over six thousand square feet and was decorated luxuriously, her mother's classic, comfortable touch made it feel like a cozy cabin.

It was Sunday afternoon, and Erica and her mother were sitting on the couch in the family room, having tea. She loved the way her mother made an elegant production of everything. Tea wasn't just hot water over dried leaves inside a Lipton bag. Afternoon tea with Maureen Stanford was served on a tray made of handcrafted jade, topped with a crisp linen napkin and an assortment of cookies, scones, and biscotti on the side.

Erica watched as her mother poured steaming water from the neck of the cream-colored ceramic teapot, filling her cup with hot liquid, which turned the bag of Earl Grey into a small black sea.

"Here you go, sweetie," Maureen said, handing Erica the sugar dish from the tray. "Would you like a lemon cookie or a strawberry scone?"

"You know I can't resist lemon cookies." Erica smiled as she scooped two heaping spoonfuls of natural brown sugar into her cup.

Maureen placed a cookie on Erica's dessert plate, then reached for a scone for her own. "Nelson's event last night was lovely, wasn't it?"

"Yes, it was."

"His campaign manager did a fabulous job, and I think she's taken quite a liking to him."

"Who? *Cynthia?*" Erica said with surprise. Cynthia Bowling was a thirtysomething Washington insider who hailed from a long line of politicians and public servants. She had worked on several congressional campaigns and was known as a consummate professional. Stoic and ultrathin, with a stylish haircut befitting a modern business-woman, Cynthia was one tough cookie. Her whispered nickname was the Iron Lady.

"Yes." Maureen smiled as she poured hot water over her bag of peppermint-flavored tea. "Cynthia is an impressive and very accom-plished young woman from a fine family. She's smart and capable, and I can see that she's set her sights on Nelson."

"She may have set her sights on him, but I don't think it's a two-way street. She's totally not his type."

"She doesn't have to be. It's not about love, my dear. This is poli-tics, and it's all about the image."

Erica was completely nonplussed and didn't know what to say. Her mother had always been strategic, practical, and quick with her wits. But her pragmatism was also layered with a generous amount of compassion and care, no matter how bourgeois she appeared to be. Erica's forehead wrinkled with disbelief as she absorbed her mother's unfeeling words.

Maureen took a small sip of her tea, then rested her cup on its matching saucer. "And I'm praying with all my might that Nelson doesn't fall into that trap. In many ways he's just like your father when it comes to appearances. He knows that every politician looks better with a wife and children by his side. But Lord knows, I pray it won't be Cynthia who he chooses to fill that role," she scoffed. "Just because something looks good doesn't mean it is good."

This was the Maureen Stanford that Erica was used to, but at the same time, she was surprised her mother was talking openly about Nelson's personal business. Inserting herself into her children's love lives had never been her thing. "Mom, you're throwing out a lot of stuff. What's really going on?"

"What I'm trying to say is that life is too short to worry about keeping up appearances. All that time spent crafting the perfect image, and for what? In the end there's no happiness in that. You have to follow your heart, no matter where it takes you, or who you decide to take along on the journey with you."

Erica sat her cup on the mahogany coffee table in front of her. "Mom, is there something wrong with you and Daddy?"

Maureen let out a light sigh, uncrossed her legs, and leaned back into the couch. "We won't announce it until after Nelson's campaign is over in the spring, but your father and I have decided to divorce."

Erica's mouth gaped open. She had felt the vibe last night and knew that something was up, but she had no idea that her parents' marriage was about to dissolve. She had never known them to argue or even raise their voices at each other; even though her father's eyes had wandered in the past, it was something that Erica assumed her mother tolerated because she loved him, and he'd afforded her a life of no material want. She loved both her parents, and she didn't judge them for their decisions because she'd made questionable ones of her own.

"I know this comes as a shock," Maureen continued, "but it's a relief for me, and for your father, too."

"Mom, what happened to make you finally call it quits after thirty-nine years?"

Maureen's eyes looked upon Erica's with a mixture of knowledge and regret. "Life happened. Our fortieth anniversary is six months away, and I just couldn't see spending another day pretending."

Erica nodded. "I know this wasn't an easy decision, and I'm a little in shock, but I'm also proud of you for making it."

"It was time. Your father and I grew further apart from each other little by little, year after year. Once you drift too far, it's hard to find your way back to shore," Maureen said, taking a deep breath.

Erica's voice was low. "Wow. I knew something was wrong, but I wasn't expecting this."

"I'm sure you're not going to be alone in that feeling."

Erica nodded. Her parents had been together for what seemed like a lifetime. She was sure that everyone they knew—family and friends alike—would be stunned once they heard the news. "Have you guys told Nelson?"

"No, not yet. He's got too much going on right now with his

campaign, and we don't want this to be a distraction. We'll tell him in due time." Maureen sighed as sadness mixed with relief washed over her face. "I finally woke up and realized that life is too short to live what little time I have left existing in something just because it's convenient.

"When I met Joseph, I thought I'd hit the jackpot. He was smart, handsome, and charismatic, just like your brother," Maureen said with a smile. "I'd grown up middle class, but your father introduced me to a world I never knew existed. Generations of old money and affluence, and I fell into it hook, line, and sinker. We were the perfect couple, with the perfect house, perfect children, and a perfect life. But what I didn't know then was that everything comes at a cost. Don't get me wrong. Your father is a good man, and he has some wonderful qualities. For a time we had a pretty amazing life together. But that ended long ago."

Maureen sat forward and recrossed her legs. "There are just certain things that I can't, and I won't, put up with or settle for anymore . . . not at this point in my life. I refuse to be anyone's afterthought. I deserve love and fulfillment."

Erica understood what that kind of disappointment felt like. She loved her father, but she knew how powerful men could be. "Mom, I love you and Daddy, and I just want both of you to be happy. So if it means being happy apart, then I support you."

"Thank you, sweetie. And I want you to know that I support you, too. Jerome seems like a fine young man. I like him."

"You do?" Her mother was giving her more shock and awe than she could take.

"Yes, from the little that I observed. Let me tell you something. Sixty-four years of living has taught me that love is about what's here." She reached out and placed her soft hand over Erica's heart. "This small organ beating inside your chest is the strongest part of your body, and the wisest. Your heart will lead you where your brain can't follow because your heart is connected to your gut, and your gut is God. And, sweetie, you know you can't go wrong with Him.

"I admire the way Jerome comported himself last night. Your father and I were hard on him, but he didn't back down, and he was more polite and tolerant than most people would've been in his position. That told me that he's a man of character. Then I watched how he looked at you, with love and respect. I could see in his eyes that that man will do anything for you, Erica. And even though you were nervous about us grilling him, I could see that you wanted him to be comfortable, and that you were concerned about how he felt. That tells me that you care deeply for him and you want to protect him."

"I do, Mom," Erica said with a smile. "Even though we've only known each other a short time, it seems like we've been together for years. I love him, and he loves me, too."

Maureen reached for Erica's hand and held it tightly in her grip. "Then you're halfway there. It doesn't take long to spot what you want, if you know what you need," she said with a wink. "Life is a journey, and like I said, you can't worry about what anyone thinks. I'm so happy that you're following where your heart is leading you. It's the only path to true happiness."

Erica nodded with bittersweet emotion. As her new love was beginning, her mother and father's life together was coming to an end. But she knew if her mother had come to this decision, it had been reached after careful thought. "After being with Daddy for so long, it's going to be an adjustment, so if you need me, you just call and I'll be here for you." Erica gave her mother's shoulder a comforting rub. "I know you'll be just fine."

"Yes, I will be." Maureen reached for her room-temperature tea and took a sip. "Now, if we can just get Nelson to see the light."

Chapter 35

Erica walked up the steps to Ashley's well-appointed Victorian row house, feeling a mixture of emotions. Her day had started off with deep conversation and passionate lovemaking in Jerome's arms. By mid-afternoon her mother had thrown her a curveball she hadn't seen coming. And now, as she rang the doorbell and bent to pick up the Sunday newspaper that had been tossed onto one of Ashley's potted red begonias, she wondered what this late afternoon visit to her best friend would bring.

"Hey!" Ashley said, greeting Erica with a big smile.

"I can see you've been relaxing all day. You haven't even gotten your paper." Erica handed Ashley her *Washington Post.* "And look at you, dressed all cute while you're lounging!"

Ashley placed her hand on her ample left hip and struck a sexy pose, highlighting her hot pink terry-cloth pants and matching top. "What can I say? I'm beautiful."

"And don't forget, oh, so modest, at that."

"So true!"

The two friends laughed and hugged as though they hadn't seen each other in years instead of just last night. They walked past Ashley's front rooms, all stylishly decorated in monochromatic colors, with sleek furniture that featured clean lines, and headed back to her den. They settled in, anchoring themselves at either end of her stiff, but fashionable tan-colored couch.

"So what's going on?" Ashley asked. "When you called on your way over, you sounded a little stressed. That asshole Claude didn't mess up things between you and Jerome, did he?"

Erica shook her head. "No, thank goodness, even though he tried. Jerome and I are fine."

"Claude's more arrogant than I thought. He's so full of himself, thinking his shit smells like a bed of flowers. I was so glad Jerome put him in his place."

"And speaking of Jerome, it's truth time." Erica tucked one leg beneath her hip and rested the other on the floor as she attempted to make herself comfortable. "Tell me what you think about him."

Ashley leaned back and paused for a moment, as if gathering her thoughts. "You know, I've been very skeptical, and not because of what he does for a living as much as because of what his checkered background says. I prosecute criminals, and I see the very worst of humanity, so my radar is up high."

Erica nodded with understanding. "I get that."

"You're not used to dealing with folks like Jerome, but I am, and not just because of what I do for a living. Let's keep it real. . . . My family is wealthy, but ours is new, first-generation money, straight from the hood. I grew up behind the gilded gates of Hill Crest Manor just like you, but on the weekends I went to visit relatives who lived in neighborhoods that you've only seen on TV crime shows. You come from a family of people who pride themselves on being born into generations of wealth, education, and social status. You can't even name a single relative who's been in prison, let alone understand the complexities of that world. So, when I got the report on Jerome, I had doubts because, baby girl, you're just not equipped to deal with the kind of life and people he comes from."

"Where he comes from isn't who he is."

"I understand that, but the reality is that he's still somewhat a part of it. Have you been to his apartment yet?"

Erica bit her lower lip. "Not yet. Why?"

"I have his address from the report. I know that area, and it's straight hood."

Erica shrugged. "My man doesn't have a degree or a professional job, *and* he lives in the hood. You may not think he's right for me, but

I know he's the one. I know we'll have challenges, but what couple doesn't?"

"True, but when you mix family into the equation, it brings on a whole other set of issues," Ashley said with a sigh. "I love your family, but let's face it. Most of them are bougie as hell. I saw how your mom and dad looked at Jerome last night. So take my advice, as a person who's having in-law challenges, you better know what you're getting yourself into."

Erica wanted to jump in and tell Ashley a thing or two about her soon-to-be in-laws, but she decided to refrain for now. "I do know, and I'm not going to let either of our families' views dictate our relationship, and I'm not concerned about what anyone thinks of Jerome and me, except the two of us."

"If that's true, why are you asking me what I think about him?"

"Because you're my girl, and I value your opinion. I know you love me just like I love you, and I want your blessing. But if I don't get it, well, I guess I just don't. I asked what you think about *him,* not about *us.* I already know where Jerome and I are headed."

Ashley raised her hand to her chin and thought for a moment. "I'm proud of you, Erica," she said softly. "You're a lot braver than I am."

"It doesn't take bravery to love someone."

"Don't fool yourself."

The two friends were silent for a moment, chewing on their thoughts. "I'll tell you what I think of him," Ashley said. "He's a man's man, straight up alpha male for sure, which I like. I could tell that he's a stand-up guy by the way he handled Claude. I also like that he looks you in the eye when he talks to you, and that says that not only is he confident, but he's also not trying to hide anything. And what's most important is that I could see how much he's into you. Girl, that man would drink your dirty bathwater through a straw!"

Erica laughed. "You think?"

"Yes, and you know he would, too. You got that brothah sprung!"

"And I feel the same way. He's so loving and wonderful."

"And fine as hell! You told me he was handsome, but you didn't say he was a walking, talking piece of chocolate perfection!" Ashley paused and gave Erica a serious look. "Now on to the real question . . . Can the brothah throw down between the sheets?"

Erica leaned back and fanned herself with her right hand. "Yes, yes, and triple yes. I can't even describe how incredible he is."

"Damn! He's fine, *and* the sex is good."

"No, the sex is phenomenal! He knows exactly what to do without me having to tell him. He's gentle and attentive, and he takes his time. But then he can switch it up and give it to me hard and nasty!" Erica purred with a devilish grin.

"Well, all righty then!" Ashley extended her hand, and the two friends slapped high five as they giggled like schoolgirls.

"He's so sweet. Just like last night, I know he didn't want to attend Nelson's event, but he did it for me, and he even stomached all that society nonsense."

Ashley's eyes got big. "Girl, that's what I've been wanting to talk to you about! Did you see the look that Jason's mother kept giving— or shall I say, avoided giving—Jerome? And then, when he put his arm around you, I thought she was going to come out of her skin."

"Yes, I saw," Erica answered. She was treading lightly, just as she knew Jerome had done. She could see that Ashley was dissecting her response.

"You know something, don't you?"

Erica was quiet.

"I knew it! Something's up between Jerome and Mrs. Butterfield. He told you, and he asked you not to say anything, didn't he?"

"I can't confirm anything, but if you ask me a question that I really can't answer, because of privilege, I'll just look away and remain silent. How about that?"

Ashley grinned. "I've taught you well, my friend." She sat on the edge of the couch and fired away. "Jason's mother propositioned him, didn't she?"

Erica turned her head and looked away.

"I knew it!" Ashley screamed. "The nerve of that old bitch!"

"I ain't said nothing." Erica shook her head from side to side.

"That's downright trifling. She snubs her nose up at black folk, but I guess that doesn't apply when dick is involved."

"I said the same thing. Oops," Erica squeaked, covering her mouth. "I let the cat out the bag."

"No, you didn't. It was pretty obvious, and I think Mr. Butterfield knew it, too. That's why he didn't have a problem leaving when she wanted to go. They've been married a hundred years, so he's got to know the deal when it comes to his wife."

"I think you're right. You're not going to mention it to Jason, are you?"

"Do I look foolish?"

"Good. Some things are just better left unknown."

Ashley let out a deep breath. "Wow. This requires a drink. You want something?"

Erica followed Ashley into her gourmet kitchen, equipped with high-end stainless steel appliances and fancy gadgets she never used. She reached into her cabinet, retrieved two wineglasses, and poured Moscato for herself and Erica. They sat on leather bar stools flanking the edge of her granite island as they sipped.

"Let's change the subject back to Jerome for a minute," Ashley said. "Tell me what's up."

"What do you mean?"

"If you don't give a damn about what I think about you and your man, I'm assuming the stress I heard earlier in your voice was about something else. What's going on?"

Erica appreciated the fact that she and Ashley were so close that they knew each other's moods and could talk openly. She didn't want to beat around the bush, so she asked the question that had been bothering her since last night. "Is there something going on between you and Nelson?"

Ashley chuckled. "You think because we were flirting that something is going on?"

"I don't know what to think. You tell me."

"In case you didn't know, I'll fill you in on something. Your brother is hot! And you know me. I love flirting with hot men."

"But it's Nelson."

"Who happens to be hot!"

"What about Jason? He's hot, too. And let me fill you in on something. You're engaged to him. Remember?"

Ashley took a small sip of her wine. "Jason is a great guy, but honestly, I'm torn and I just don't know what to do. I'm not sure that I'm ready to handle the kind of scrutiny and problems that come with marrying outside my race. That's why I said you're brave. You're willing to step outside your social class and pedigree for love."

"I'm not gonna sit here and say that race doesn't matter, or that we've evolved into a completely accepting society when it comes to it, because we both know that's not true. Your fears are valid. But you knew that going in. Any relationship is going to have its obstacles."

"I know, and that's my point. I understand about facing challenges. I get that. But when you throw race, class, raising biracial children, and families that don't accept you into the mix, it makes for a crowded pot. It's just a lot."

Erica nodded. "I talked to my mother just before I came here, and you know what she told me? She said I shouldn't worry about what society, our family, or anyone else thinks about my relationship with Jerome."

Astonishment swept across Ashley's face, forcing her to set her wineglass on the counter.

"Yeah, you heard me right," Erica said. "My bourgeois mother told me not to worry about appearances or what might seem unacceptable, not even to our family. She said I should follow my heart because it won't lead me wrong. I believe her, and I think you need to do the same."

"The theory sounds great, but the practical application isn't that easy. After last week I knew that Jason and I had a lot to work through, but I thought, 'We'll see how this plays out.' Then that bitch from Vegas came to town yesterday, and we had an argument about her, and he and I haven't spoken since."

Erica frowned. "You haven't? That's not good. Have you tried to call him?"

"No, and he hasn't tried to call me, either."

"You two really need to talk. Communication is key, and I'm just afraid that if you let things go, they might spiral out of control. Marriage is a big step."

"I never, ever thought I'd get married, and quite frankly, I'd never really wanted to until I met Jason. Now I'm up to my eyeballs in plans for a big fancy wedding. My parents are pissed. Jason's parents are pissed. I feel pressure. He feels pressure. And I'm not sure if I can do this, or even if I want to."

"Flirting with Nelson isn't going to solve your problems."

"Does it bother you? The thought of Nelson and me as a couple?"

Erica thought about the question. Not in her wildest dreams had she ever considered Nelson and Ashley as a possibility. They were family. But then she thought about how much she loved both of them, and about what her mother had said earlier about following one's heart. "It would take some getting used to. But if that's what you two wanted, I would be happy for you." Erica cleared her throat. "Are you two fooling around?"

Ashley took a sip of wine, shifting her weight on the bar stool.

"Ashley, are you and Nelson fooling around?" Erica asked slowly for a second time. She took a deep breath, and then something caught her eye. She looked down the hall toward Ashley's coatrack, and when she saw Nelson's leather jacket hanging on the hook, she got her answer.

Chapter 36

Jerome and Jamel sat across from each other in a small booth, enjoying their Sunday afternoon lunch. They were at Ben's Chili Bowl, a D.C. institution famous for its savory pork and beef sausage Half-Smokes and it's legendary chili. Jerome took a bite of his Chili Half-Smoke as he listened to his son talk about his new girlfriend, Tiffany Macey.

"We kinda made it official yesterday," Jamel said, trying to withhold the silly grin that threatened his lips. "She's cool, Dad."

Jerome nodded. "That's good, and this is the second time you've said that about her. So tell me why you think she's cool?" He wanted to see where his son's head was. He knew the boy was raging with hormones, and that simple fact, along with the young girl's pretty face, had both contributed to her coolness. Jerome saw this father-son time as the perfect opportunity to start teaching Jamel what qualities he should look for in a woman and how he should conduct himself as a young gentleman. These were things he'd never been taught or even thought about growing up.

Jamel stuffed a handful of fries into his mouth, chewed for a minute, and then spoke. "She's smart. She makes good grades. And she's really nice to everybody. She's easy to talk to, not like most girls, and she knows a whole lot about sports."

"Those are good qualities. Especially that she's smart and treats people nice. That's very important, because the kind of young lady you choose can either help or hurt you. Always look for someone who's trying to do good things with her life."

Jamel smiled. "Yeah, she's looking at colleges now and studying for the PSAT. She said she's gonna help me with mine when it's time for me to take it."

Although Jerome had never thought about taking the college entrance exam before he dropped out of school so many years ago, he still knew what it was, and he understood that seventh graders generally didn't take the test for at least a couple more years. "What grade is she in?"

"She's a sophomore," Jamel said with a prideful grin. "Tiffany's fifteen, Dad."

Jerome rested his half-eaten food on his plate. He didn't know whether to high-five his son or caution him. A two-year age gap wasn't a big deal, but going from thirteen to fifteen was like going from zero to one hundred. Jamel had been only twelve up until last weekend, and now he had condoms and a girlfriend.

Jerome was more than a little unsettled by the rapid developments in his young son's life. But then he remembered that he'd long lost his virginity by the time he was Jamel's age. And that was what worried him. He didn't want Jamel traveling down the same road.

Jerome decided to remain neutral until they finished their meal, giving his food and his thoughts enough time to digest before he laid down the law on their ride back home.

"I still can't believe how fast he's growing up," Jerome said to his father as he drank from his tall glass of iced tea. "But he's a good kid, so I think he'll be all right."

"Sure he will. He's a chip off the old block. You're doin' a fine job with Jamel," Jerome's father said.

Jerome was sitting on the floral-print couch across from his father, sharing a late afternoon conversation, just as he'd done with his own son earlier that day. This was what he'd always wanted, a relationship with his father, and it still amazed him that his childhood wish had been answered nearly three decades later.

After Parnell left the family, Jerome had prayed every night for a full year that his father would return. And even though he'd stopped the nightly devotion when year two rolled around, he'd never given up on the dream or desire of having his father in his life.

Parnell Kimbrough's journey back to his family had been a precarious one. Tall, dark, and so handsome that women literally swooned over him, Parnell had been a natural playboy and a smooth charmer. He'd also been a natural-born street hustler, preferring to walk a crooked line over what was right and just. His long-standing weakness for beautiful women, coupled with his growing, and often dangerous, involvement in the streets, had left him a wayward man. When his wife, Mabel, couldn't take his philandering, hustler ways any longer, she told him to get out of the apartment they shared with their two children.

At the time, Parnell saw it as his ticket out of a load of responsibilities he'd never wanted. But life without his young wife and children had proven to be hard, eventually landing him in jail for one petty crime after the other. Finally, during one of his long incarcerations, he experienced a spiritual awakening that changed his life. He began studying the Bible and eventually gave his life over to God. Once he was released from prison, he tried to contact Mabel, but she refused to return any of his phone calls. He sent her several handwritten letters apologizing and asking for her forgiveness, but within days of mailing them, he would receive them back, unopened, with RETURN TO SENDER in Mabel's handwriting across the envelope.

Finally, after several months of futile attempts to reconnect with his family, and with no job offers in sight, he decided to travel out west, to L.A. He'd been given an opportunity to join a small ministry that was run by the brother of the inmate who'd led him to the Lord and, in turn, to his salvation.

Parnell thrived out west and grew closer to the Lord in his spiritual journey, eventually starting a small church of his own. And although Mabel had not found it in her heart to forgive him, he wired money to her bank account each month without fail. When he heard about her and his grandson's car accident, he dropped everything and headed back to D.C. He stayed by Mabel's bedside during her two-week hospitalization, and once she was released, he faithfully chauffeured her to and from her physical therapy appointments over the next four months. By that time, it was clear that Mabel and Parnell were back together again, and this go-round it was for good.

It had taken Jerome a while to get used to his father being back in his life. He'd prayed for it, but he hadn't expected the resentment and anger that had come forth each time he looked into Parnell's eyes. It didn't matter that Mabel had told him to leave. Jerome knew from experience that if a man wanted to stick around, there was nothing a woman could say or do to get rid of him.

Father and son had to take baby steps toward healing the wounds of abandonment that Jerome felt, but eventually, they found their way back to each other. Today their relationship was strong, and Jerome was thankful for it.

"When he told me his little girlfriend was fifteen, I thought, 'Damn. She's gonna turn him out,'" Jerome said, shaking his head. "He's already got condoms and everything. But he's still just a kid, and he's not ready."

"No, he's not. The responsibility that comes with it is something young people can't fathom. I know I didn't."

"I don't want him out there gettin' all caught up, so I need to keep an extra pair of eyes on him. But at the same time I can't be there to watch his every move or control what he's doing."

"True. There's only so much you can do."

"I just pray he makes smart decisions and takes precautions. I broke everything down for him, real talk, and I told him not to let any of those knucklehead friends of his pressure him into anything. The sign of a real man is how much self-control and independence he has."

Parnell nodded. "I'm proud of you, Jerome. You're a much better father than I ever was."

"You're here now, and that's what counts."

"Not a day goes by that I don't regret leaving you all the way I did. So many wasted years that we can't get back." Parnell sighed and shook his head. "But I'm thankful because despite my shortcomings, God blessed me with a second chance. Not too many people get those."

"You're right." Jerome took a long gulp of his iced tea, swishing the ice cubes around in his mouth. He sat his glass on the coaster atop the side table and glanced over at his father. "I met someone."

Parnell raised his brow. "Oh yeah?"

Jerome knew his father was shocked. In the ten years since Parnell had reentered his life, Jerome had never introduced, let alone talked about, any of the women he'd dated to his parents. On the rare occasions that he sought relationship advice from his father, he never called any one woman by name, and the conversation was usually very general in nature. But with Erica, it was different, and he found himself telling his father all about her. He tried not to smile like a love-struck kid—as he'd seen Jamel do—but he couldn't help it. The mention of Erica's name and the thought of her soft, sweet-smelling skin brought about feelings that were hard for him to hide.

"She's special," he said. "I see a good future with Erica."

Parnell said with a smile, "I'm happy for you, son."

"Thanks, Pop. She's definitely the one. I'm just glad that I'm ready for her. You know what I mean?"

Parnell nodded. "I know exactly what you mean. Your mother is the best woman I've ever known, but it took losing her for me to realize it."

And as if on cue, Mabel walked into the room. "What'chall in here talkin' about all quiet like?" she asked. She leaned over and gave Jerome a quick kiss on the cheek, then sat her cane on the side of the couch as she took a seat next to her son.

Jerome looked to Parnell to see what he would say, and was surprised when he glimpsed a smile holding up each side of his father's mouth. It was aimed at his mother. Parnell looked at Mabel with a kind of affection that Jerome had never seen, or perhaps had never taken the time to notice until now. He didn't know if it was the maturity he'd achieved by virtue of age and experience, or the raw feelings and emotions that Erica had stirred in him, or the reality of his son's coming-of-age, but he recognized through the glint in his father's eyes what real love looked like.

"I was telling Pop that I met a really special woman," Jerome said to his mother.

"Oh yeah?" she replied.

Jerome chuckled. "That's the first thing Pop said."

" 'Cause he was probably just as shocked as me. I know you not as bad as you used to be, but you still got a lot of women, and we ain't never heard you mention anybody outside of Kelisha."

Whereas Parnell was more reserved and laid-back, Mabel was extroverted, if not boisterous, and would let you know exactly what was on her mind. She was a Southern woman who came from a different kind of South, one void of the legendary genteelness associated with the region. Rather, she'd been raised by women who couldn't afford the luxury of living as polite belles or shrinking violets. They were more the steel magnolia breed—strong enough to raise an entire family without a man's presence, yet gentle enough to soothe and comfort anyone in need.

Jerome shook his head and laughed. "Now, how do you know about who I'm seeing or what I'm doing?"

"A mother knows her child, and you always have loved women," she answered.

"Stay outta his business, Mabel," Parnell cautioned.

"He the one bringin' up his love life, not me."

"You're right, Mom," Jerome said, leaning back into the couch. "But I've changed more than you know. I'm ready to settle down with a good woman, and I believe I've found her." Jerome went on to tell his mother about Erica, how they'd met, and that she was a successful business owner.

"That's good that she got her own store and runs things herself. She got spunk," Mabel said.

"Yes, she does. She makes me want to step up my game."

"Where's she from?" Mabel asked.

"She grew up in PG County."

"That's real nice. She got any kids?"

"No. No children."

"She ever been married?"

"No, she hasn't," Jerome answered. He could see the wrinkle line appear across his mother's otherwise smooth forehead. It was a crease he was familiar with. It always appeared when Mabel was in serious thought. "Go on and say what you're thinking."

Mabel crossed her plump arms over the girth of her stomach. "I been readin' about how hard it is for young black women to find a man, get married, and have kids. A lot of 'em startin' to date outside the race, just like y'all black men been doin' for centuries."

"That won't be Erica's problem any longer," Jerome replied.

Parnell and Mabel looked at each other and then at their son. Jerome could see that he'd shocked them both again. Talk of a commitment coming from his mouth was like hearing him speak a foreign language. He had to admit that it was startling, even to him. But he knew what was in his heart, and he was ready to go for it.

Jerome was satisfied with his day and couldn't think of the last time he'd felt this good. He'd awakened beside the woman he loved, starting the morning off with good conversation and even better lovemaking. Then he had spent quality time with his son and had opened up another facet of their relationship. He'd rounded things off by visiting with his parents and shocking them before they ate his mother's delicious Sunday dinner meal. And now, as nighttime had descended, Jerome lay in bed and dialed Erica's number.

"Hi, Jerome," she said, picking up on the first ring.

The sound of his name coming out of her mouth made him smile. "Hey, you. Did you get the call from court?"

"Yes, I did. I'm glad Ms. Slater is feeling better. Now we can get her testimony tomorrow and hopefully be done with the trial."

"We'll see. What're you doin'?" he asked.

"Lying in my big empty bed, thinking about you. What are you doing?"

"The same."

"We need to be doing it together."

Jerome looked at his alarm clock. It was 9:00 p.m., and Erica's house was only twenty minutes away on the other side of town. "If that's what you want, I can make that happen."

"You can come over?"

"I'll pack my overnight bag now, and I'll be there soon."

Chapter 37

Erica hung up the phone with butterflies humming in her stomach. She'd had a full day, and seeing Jerome was the perfect way to spend the rest of her evening. She hopped out of bed, pulled on her purple velour robe, and slipped into her matching slippers before she headed downstairs.

She knew that Jerome's "I'll be there soon" could easily turn into an hour or longer, so she took her time preparing for him. She loved the spontaneity of their lovemaking, but tonight she wanted to make their time together extra special by planning a romantic evening. She opened her refrigerator and removed four different cheeses from the crisper and pulled out a bundle of grapes. Then she searched through her pantry, selecting a box of whole-grain gourmet crackers.

"This will be a tasty treat," Erica said out loud as she removed a mahogany serving tray from the stately sideboard in her dining room. After she draped it with a colorful napkin—which was her mother's signature move—she arranged the goodies she'd prepared, along with a bottle of wine and two glasses, atop the tray.

She walked upstairs with a light spring in her step, excited about spending an evening with her man. She peeled out of her robe and gown and was about to take a shower when her cell phone rang. She walked over to her nightstand and saw Jerome's name illuminated and let out a sigh. They'd had a serious conversation about his lateness before he left that morning, and she'd made him promise that if he found himself running behind schedule, he would call to let her know. She'd just spoken with him fifteen minutes ago, and she hoped he wasn't calling to say it would be another hour before he got there.

"Hey. What's going on?"

"I'm turning down your street. Can you open your garage so I can park?"

"You're here?"

"I told you I would be."

Erica was happy but stunned that Jerome was on time. She'd planned on his lateness, and now that she'd miscalculated, she wouldn't have time to shower and make herself as alluring and sensuous for him as she'd wanted to.

"Okay. I'm headed downstairs now."

A few minutes later Jerome was walking through Erica's back door, headed for the kitchen.

"I missed you while we were apart today," she said, nestling herself in his strong arms as he hugged her.

"I missed you, too." He looked over her shoulder at the tray sitting on the counter. "That's nice, baby."

"I thought we'd have a romantic evening together."

Jerome kissed her lips and whispered in her ear. "All right. Let's take this upstairs."

Erica watched Jerome as he placed the tray on the bench in front of her bed and then sat his overnight bag on the other side of it. "I was on my way to take a shower before you came." She smiled and walked toward her master bath. "I'll be right back."

Jerome strolled over to her, hooking his arm around her waist and then pulling her close to his body. "Let me join you."

A wicked grin formed at the edge of her lips. "Follow me."

Erica adjusted the water, putting her hand under the flowing stream to make sure it was just the right temperature for a relaxing and sensual shower for two. Once it had reached a pleasing point, Erica flipped the lever to create a waterfall from above. She turned and looked at Jerome, who was already undressed, standing in nude perfection, hard and incredibly irresistible.

"You want to feel it to make sure it's not too hot?" she asked.

"The temperature doesn't matter. I just want to get wet with you." He walked over to her and loosened the sash of her robe, letting it fall to the floor.

When he traced his long fingers around the outer part of her right nipple, then tweaked its tip, Erica let out a soft moan. Slowly, they stepped into the shower; Jerome in front and Erica in the back.

"I didn't put on my shower cap," she said.

"Don't worry about getting your hair wet. Let it go back to Africa," he teased.

"Are you going to style my hair so I'll look presentable in court tomorrow?"

"I'll do whatever you want," Jerome breathed, pulling her in close.

Erica's worry about her hair quickly faded to a distant place when she felt Jerome's hard body and the warm water caress her skin. He kissed her long and deep, swirling his tongue around the depths of her mouth as he held her against his body. Carefully, they switched positions, placing Erica in the front lines of the water. She leaned back into Jerome, feeling his hardness press into the lower part of her back as he rubbed it from side to side against her skin.

Erica reached for her pink netted sponge and poured a generous amount of shower gel onto it, then handed it to Jerome. She relaxed as he washed her from head to toe. Her body tingled with delight as he ran the sponge over the sensitive skin of her underarms, then onto the surface of her stomach, before moving down to the softness between her legs and then sweeping lather up and down her thick thighs. She enjoyed every moment of his attentive care.

"You're so beautiful," he whispered into her ear.

Erica slowly ran her hands over Jerome's body, scant of soapy lather because he'd said he didn't want to smell like a girl. His manly scent was pleasing to her senses either way, so she took pleasure in the mix of water and lust that her fingers washed over him.

Once they finished, they took turns drying each other off and then walked back to the bedroom.

"Let's eat by candlelight," she said as she lit two scented candles.

"Damn, you're sexy." Jerome looked at Erica and smiled. "How about a relaxing massage?"

"You're not gonna get an argument out of me." Erica walked back to her vanity table, retrieved a plain white plastic jar, and then lay across the bed beside a waiting Jerome. She unscrewed the lid and handed him the jar. "This is Paradise."

Erica watched as Jerome sniffed the fragrant body butter and smiled. "This smells really good. I mean really, really good."

"You're not just saying that?"

He cut his eyes at her. "You know me by now. I'm straight up, and I really do like it. It's soft, but strong enough to leave an impression, and it's clean and fresh, but also sensual. I'm diggin' it."

"I need you to do a commercial for me," Erica said with a smile.

"You got it. But for now, lie on your stomach and let me take care of you."

Jerome's strong hands melted the tension in Erica's back, which had been caused by months, weeks, and recent days of stressful work demands. She forgot about her parents' pending divorce, about Ashley's troublesome love triangle, and about the feeling that Claude was waiting in the wings to cause more trouble. She let her body sink into the softness of Jerome's touch and the promise of their future as she enjoyed the beginning of another journey into pleasure.

Erica and Jerome bolted up at the same time when they heard her alarm sound on the nightstand, waking them from their slumber.

"Good morning," she purred.

"Morning." Jerome kissed the back of her neck as they lay back down on the soft comfort of her mattress, with him spooning her from behind.

"I put the snooze on for five more minutes. Let's just lie here before we have to tackle the world," Erica said in a sleepy voice.

But their peaceful moment was interrupted when Erica's phone began to ring. It was 6:00 a.m., and she knew the only kind of call that came at that hour of the morning was one of bad news. Even before she reached for her phone, she had a sinking feeling about who awaited her on the other end. She lay still for a moment, bracing herself.

"You're not gonna answer it?" Jerome said, a mixture of concern and suspicion breaking through in his voice.

Erica could tell that he'd snapped into full alertness and that he must've sensed the same unwelcome trouble lurking with each ring that she did. Slowly, she reached for her phone and saw Claude's name and number light up the screen.

Chapter 38

Jerome sat next to Erica in the jury box, feeling a mixture of emotions that ranged from pissed off to regretful. He hadn't been able to shake the unsettling mood he'd been in ever since Erica's ex-fiancé had called her at the crack of dawn. It seemed that every time he and Erica stepped back on a good footing, something would crop up and put them at odds with each other again. For a relationship that he felt was meant to be, it seemed the universe was leaving him small clues that he should take a second look, and despite what he'd told his parents just yesterday, he was beginning to doubt his own instincts for the first time.

He thought about the events of the past few days. Claude had sent Erica flowers, then had shown up at her brother's event, and now he was giving her early morning phone calls. Jerome knew the intention behind those moves, because he'd done a few of them himself, and he also knew that if a man was putting in the kind of time and effort that Claude was demonstrating, he had to be after something.

Jerome wanted to believe what Erica had told him—that she'd cut all ties with the man—but the evidence of Claude's presence in her life made that claim a bit questionable. Even though she'd appeared irritated at the sight of her ex Saturday night, Jerome wondered if there was more to the story than she'd let on. Something about the whole situation didn't feel right to him.

When Erica had hesitated to answer the early morning call, his antennae went up right away, as he knew that it had to be a man on the other end, and in particular, her ex.

"It's Claude," she'd said, turning to him with a look in her eyes that he couldn't place.

With involuntary reaction, Jerome took the phone out of her hand, sat up in bed, and pressed the talk button. "Hello," he boomed in a stern, no-nonsense tone.

"I'm trying to reach Erica," Claude said with smug confidence.

Jerome knew that Claude had recognized his voice, yet he had the nerve to still ask for Erica. "Erica isn't available. Why're you calling her this time of the morning?"

"Why are you answering her phone?"

" 'Cause I'm her man, muthafucka!"

When Jerome heard the dial tone sing in his ear, he wanted to jump through the phone and whup Claude's ass. "Why's that muthafucka callin' you all times of the morning?" he asked, his breathing starting to quicken. "What the hell's goin' on between the two of you?"

"Nothing! I don't know why he's calling me or what he's up to." Erica sat up beside him and put her hand on his shoulder, rubbing it gently. "You have to believe me. I have no reason to lie."

"Maybe you want to have your cake and eat it, too. Hell, you're gettin' the best of both worlds. An Ivy League business dude to show off in public and a roughneck to sex you under your expensive sheets."

Erica twisted her mouth and pulled the comforter up to her chest. "I know you're not going to start with that again."

"What am I supposed to think? You got this punk callin' you, sending you flowers and shit, and showing up at family functions."

"Nelson's campaign kickoff was a public event that anyone could've attended who wanted to, and I guess he wanted to."

"Yeah, right."

"You know what? I'm sick of justifying and defending myself to you just because you feel insecure about who you are. If I didn't want to be with you, you wouldn't be in my bed right now."

"I can fix that." He rose to his feet and started gathering his things.

"What are you doing?"

"Gettin' out of your bed."

"Don't be ridiculous."

"Don't talk to me like I'm a child."

"Stop acting like one."

Jerome stopped in his tracks and glared at Erica, but when he saw her glaring back at him with the same intensity, he lost it. "Just like I said the other night, this is some bullshit! You might have a fancy degree, come from a rich family, and have a lot of money, but you bring just as much fucked-up drama as any of the hood rats I used to deal with."

Erica stood to her feet, butt naked and pissed. "Get the hell out of my house right now!" she yelled. She pulled on her robe, then reached for the boxers and T-shirt he'd tossed to the floor the night before. She walked over to him, calmly placed his clothes in his hand, and then walked toward her bathroom. "I have only two things to say to you. Don't ever answer my phone again, and please don't be here when I come out." She closed the bathroom door behind her and never looked back.

Jerome was so mad, he could have hurt someone. But instead of storming into the bathroom to exchange more angry words, he quickly dressed and left.

Back in the present, Erica shifted in her seat beside him, drawing his mind to the here and now. *What is this woman doing to me?* he asked himself. He was a man who, until recently, never lost his temper and always remained calm. Even after he'd been shot twelve years ago, he'd still managed to stay in control of his emotions. But now one week with Erica had made him curse and nearly yell over things that wouldn't have normally phased him. Before, if he suspected that a woman whom he was seeing was double dipping with another man, he'd just leave her alone and go on to the next female waiting in the wings. It was no sweat off his brow.

He was used to being the person with the upper hand in his relationships. But now the power had shifted, and the hold that Erica had on him made him feel vulnerable and weak. Those emotions had had no place in his life until recently. But the moment he met Erica, things changed, and if indeed she was "the one," he had to figure out how to make things right again.

Chapter 39

Erica rubbed her hand across the top of her head as she walked in line back to the jury room. She'd had to use water and gel to slick her hair down into a neat bun this morning, after getting it soaking wet in the shower last night. *All because of him!* she shouted in her head. She could feel Jerome's eyes blazing through her as they walked the short distance down the hall. Half of her wanted to turn around and hug him, but there was another part of her that wanted to yell, kick, and scream in his face. That was how much he'd frustrated her.

She had read romance novels, articles, and had even seen movies that depicted the challenges of star-crossed lovers who came from different worlds. She'd known what she was getting herself into when she first met Jerome, and she was ready because her heart and her gut had told her that he was worth the work.

She remembered the beautiful love they'd made last night. The way he'd rubbed her back gently before giving her pleasure that made her moan like a woman gone wild. She touched her lips, remembering the way he'd fed her grapes as they lay in bed and talked about their future. She was impressed with his parenting skills when he told her about the way he'd educated his son on the facts of life and the responsibilities that came along with growing into young adulthood. It had made her think about what it would be like to have a child with him, and how they would parent together. But as she entered the jury room and took her seat, all she could think about at the moment was the growing confusion in her head.

Erica looked at Jerome out of the corner of her eye as he eased down into the chair beside her. He was wearing the same dark denims and cable-knit sweater that he'd had on yesterday, and she suspected that he hadn't showered, either, because he wouldn't have had the opportunity to go across town and still arrive in court on time. She marveled at the fact that despite all this, he looked as fresh and crisp as brand-new money. She didn't' want to feel anything for him, but she couldn't deny the irresistible urge creeping up inside her to place a kiss on his soft lips. *What is this man doing to me?* she asked herself.

But Erica didn't have time to answer questions about her complicated relationship, which seemed as though it was coming to an end. So she concentrated on what was at hand—the fact that she and her fellow jurors were about to deliberate Ms. Slater's fate.

Because Jerome always seemed to be in control and he'd calmed everyone down last Friday, his fellow jurors had voted to make him the foreman. Erica beamed inside, feeling proud and confident in his ability to lead them, even if she was unsure about his stability within their own fleeting relationship.

"I think she's guilty," one juror said. "She couldn't answer any of the questions the prosecution threw at her, and I still think she faked that attack last Friday."

Maude spoke up. "The doctor said she was suffering from fatigue and stress. She was probably feeling the effects of the trial."

"She should've thought about that before she swindled her company out of all that money," another juror said.

Jerome raised his hand, calling order back to the room. "Let's take emotions out of this and look at the bare facts," he said in a commanding voice.

Every person in the room was rapt in attention at the sound of his words. Erica was so turned on that she wanted to walk over to him, sit on his lap, and go for a pleasure ride. She listened as Jerome outlined details about the testimony of each eyewitness, as well as that of Ms. Slater.

She was in complete awe of him. She didn't know how Jerome

did it, but he recounted details and corrected jurors about the facts that had been stated under oath by each witness who'd taken the stand, along with reciting the pointed questions that both the defense and prosecution had asked. All this from a man who had not written one single word of notes during the entire trial.

Although Erica had been not so secretly rooting for Ms. Slater from the start, it became clear after two hours of debate that the woman was guilty. Erica had tried to argue, along with Ms. Maude, that the defendant could have mistakenly hit the wrong computer keys and entered incorrect numbers on her time sheet. But when Jerome pointed out that 80 percent of her time sheets indicated she'd worked more than seventy-five hours a week, there was nothing left to say.

Erica had to admit that Ms. Slater's testimony was less than convincing. The woman seemed not to be able to remember what she did from day to day, yet when the prosecution asked her to describe her duties, her interactions with coworkers, and even certain assignments she'd been given, she'd recalled each one with vivid clarity. All this and she couldn't give definitive answers about her time sheets.

"I believe we've reached a verdict," Jerome said after counting each juror's ballot, and seeing that it was unanimous. "I'll let the bailiff know we're ready."

Erica watched Jerome as he walked to the door. She drank in every ounce of him, from his straight back to his squared shoulders and up to his royal head held high. When their eyes connected, she saw the glimmer of a look on his face that echoed what she was thinking—*I'm sorry.*

The trial was over, and everyone was relieved, except Ms. Slater, who, after being found guilty, was scheduled to report back for sentencing in two weeks.

"I wanted to believe she was innocent," Ms. Maude said. "But after Jerome and the others laid out the facts, it was hard not to see that she was guilty."

"I feel the same way," Erica said.

"That young lady reminded me so much of my daughter." A

small tear fell from Ms. Maude's eye. "My Tammy was a good girl who got caught up in the wrong things by hanging around a bad crowd. I stuck by her side and believed her until the very end, too. But just like Ms. Slater, Tammy was guilty."

Erica's eyes questioned the old woman's. She wanted to know what her daughter had been guilty of, but didn't know how to ask.

"My daughter was involved in a robbery," Ms. Maude said, answering the question Erica couldn't ask. "They sentenced her to ten years, but she only served three months before she took her life. I saw the same look in Ms. Slater's eyes that I saw in my daughter's," she said with a sniffle. "I just hope that poor woman lasts longer than my Tammy did."

Erica put her hand on Ms. Maude's shoulder. "Are you going to be okay?"

"Yeah, I'm a tough old woman. I'll be fine."

"You have my number, so please use it. Call me whenever you need to talk, okay?"

Ms. Maude nodded. "You're such a sweetheart. I appreciate you being so kind to an old lady like me. And I'll be by your store in a few days to get me some of those nice-smelling body creams."

"Ms. Maude, it's on the house."

"Well, thank you! I can't wait. And listen, be sure to send me an invitation to the wedding." Ms. Maude wiped the last of her tears and smiled as she looked from Erica over to where Jerome was standing and talking to another juror on the other side of the room. "You two are gonna be good together."

"You think so?"

"I know so. I might've misjudged Ms. Slater's innocence, and even my daughter's, but this is one thing that I know I'm right about."

Instead of getting into a discussion about her complicated relationship with Jerome, Erica nodded and gave Ms. Maude a big hug, promising to keep in touch. She stood for a moment, watching her new friend as she walked out the door, and thought about what the old woman had said. She'd actually predicted that she and Jerome would get married.

Erica didn't know about a wedding, but she was sure that she loved Jerome, in spite of everything that had happened that morning. She also knew there wasn't any hurdle that love and honest communication couldn't overcome. She remembered the struggles she'd had trying to open Opulence, and she understood that if you wanted something, you had to fight for it. She wanted Jerome, and she was determined to get her man.

Chapter 40

Jerome and Erica walked out of the jury room and into the hallway at the same time. Although the quick glance they'd exchanged earlier had held the promise of an olive branch, they hadn't spoken to each other since their terrible argument.

Jerome regretted not holding his temper in check and accusing Erica the way he did, and he made up his mind that he was going to step up like a man, as he'd always told Jamel to do, and apologize. He was about to take Erica by the hand and pull her over to the side when Sasha came up, swaying her imaginary hips beside him.

"I like the way you handled things today. You impressed me," Sasha said, flipping her hair off her shoulder.

Jerome wanted to tell her that he didn't give a damn about impressing her, but instead he nodded. "Thanks."

She placed her hand on his muscular bicep and leaned in close. "Let's let bygones be bygones, okay? How about you and me go get a drink to celebrate the end of this trial? I know a nice bar a few blocks from here that has a great happy hour special that's starting in a half hour."

When Sasha lightly squeezed her hand around Jerome's arm, he bristled, especially knowing that Erica was walking right beside him. He also knew that Sasha hadn't slept on the fact that he and Erica had been chilly to one another all day, and she probably saw their small rift as an opportunity to get what she'd wanted since she first saw him during jury selection. Experience had taught him that women like her were more dangerous than firearms, and he knew he had to cut things off before they jumped off.

"No, I can't. My girlfriend and I are getting ready to go to dinner," he said, taking a hold of Erica's hand.

When he saw Erica's eyes widen with a smile, he felt as though he could breathe comfortably once again. He turned his attention back to Sasha, who looked as though she could bite through steel. After the day he'd been having, the last thing he needed was a scene. So as much as he didn't want to be polite to her, he knew he had to diffuse the situation by extending her a little unearned courtesy.

"Take care of yourself, Sasha," he said, giving her a cordial smile.

Sasha narrowed her eyes at Erica and then at him. "You think you're slick, but I got your number."

Jerome couldn't figure out what her problem was. *Maybe she's just psycho, like her crazy cousin,* he said to himself. Whatever the case, he wasn't going to allow her to phase him. "I'm going to let that slide," he responded in a calm tone. "Like I said, take care of yourself, all right?"

By now they had approached the escalator leading downstairs to the courthouse entrance. Jerome made sure that Sasha stepped on in front of him and Erica, because after witnessing her erratic behavior, there was no way in hell he was going to stand with his back to the woman.

He was still holding Erica's hand as they walked out the front door of the courthouse. The brisk afternoon chill greeted them as they smiled and made quiet apologies to each other. Jerome breathed with relief, thankful they were getting back on track and also glad that he'd just avoided a potential scene with Sasha.

He couldn't wait to start his evening with Erica and continue making up, but his romantic thoughts were interrupted when he saw Sasha, who was walking several paces in front of him and Erica, turn around and slowly strut toward him.

She smiled at Jerome and extended her hand. "I want to apologize to you, and to you," she said, looking toward Erica. "What I said was wrong, and I'm sorry."

Something told Jerome not to trust her words. She'd already

proven that she was unstable. A person had to show their ass to him only once to make him a believer, and Sasha had done it twice. Rather than shake her outstretched hand in a truce, not knowing what she might do, he simply nodded. "No need to apologize. Everything's cool."

Sasha smiled and quickly leaned in close before Jerome could stop her. She whispered in his ear, "If you think Tawanna fucked you up, you ain't seen nothin' yet." She stepped back, gave Erica a warm smile, and then turned and walked away.

"What did she just say to you?" Erica asked.

Jerome never lost the cool composure that was nearly always imprinted on his face. He looked at Erica and squeezed her hand, which was still resting inside his. "She said she hopes we have a nice evening."

Erica stared at him with doubt. "She looks like she has an ax to grind. There's something about that woman that makes the hair on my arms stand up."

"Don't worry about Sasha," Jerome responded, even though her last words had made him feel the same way. "That's the last we'll see of her. Let's concentrate on you and me and enjoying the rest of our evening."

Up until that moment, Jerome had been honest with Erica. But now he'd just told her two lies within thirty seconds. He didn't like dodging the truth. However, given the circumstances, he felt his small indiscretion was necessary and would ease Erica's mind. After the rocky road they'd just traveled, all he wanted was peace, and telling her that Sasha was crazy and that this wasn't the last they'd see of her were two truths that would only make things worse.

Erica stopped by Opulence, checking in to make sure things were running smoothly. LaWan was looking low and slightly disheveled again, no doubt because of her new man, while Christopher was still angling to tag along for the Tracy Reese fashion show next week. Erica knew she'd have to have a talk with LaWan tomorrow and get her straight about her appearance. This was the second time the young woman had dragged herself into the boutique looking as though she'd just stumbled out of bed, which was completely unac-

ceptable. But for now, Erica let it go in favor of greeting the customers who were perusing the shelves.

After she took care of business at the boutique, Erica went by her
house and packed an overnight bag. She was excited because she was
going to spend the night at Jerome's place and get a chance to see
where he lived. She was backing out of her garage when her cell
phone rang.

"Hey, Ashley," she said, feeling bright and springy.

"You said you were going to call and let me know the verdict, so
what happened?"

"We found her guilty, just like you said we would."

"I know you wanted to believe in that woman's innocence, but,
girl, sometimes people just don't do right. When criminals see an
angle, they take it."

"Unfortunately, that's true." Erica's mind jumped to Ashley's own
sticky predicament. "How're you doing? Have you spoken with
Jason?"

"He's leaving his office in an hour and then coming over here so
we can talk."

Erica could hear the anguish in her friend's voice. "I don't know
what's going on between you and Nelson, or you and Jason, but I
want you to know that whatever you decide, I'm in your corner and
I support you."

"Thanks. I needed to hear that right about now. I'm feeling so
many different emotions. But I know I have to be honest with Jason
and tell him about Nelson. He deserves that."

"Yes, he does." Erica steered her car onto the busy street. "One
thing, though. If you decide to start seeing my brother, I absolutely
will not indulge in conversations about your sex life. That would just
be too much!"

Ashley burst into laughter. "But some of our best conversations
are about sex!"

"That may be true, but talking about it when it involves my
brother . . . uh, I don't think so."

"I'll say this. Nelson can put it down, girl."

"What did I just say?"

"Okay, okay," Ashley teased. "Speaking of putting it down, how are you and Jerome doing?"

"I'm in the car, headed over to his place now."

"I hope you packed a gun, because you might have to shoot your way into and out of his neighborhood."

"Stop that, Ash." Erica felt defensive, even though she was slightly wary of driving around in that unfamiliar part of town at night.

"I'm serious. It's rough over there, and I know firsthand. Just be careful, okay?"

Erica didn't want Ashley's fear to fuel her own growing trepidation, so she quickly ended the call with the promise that they'd talk tomorrow. As her GPS led her closer to her destination, she saw what Ashley had meant by her crass but true comments.

Even though Erica had grown up in the D.C. area, had been living in the District for nearly ten years, and had traveled around the city to all eight wards, she'd never been to this part of Southeast. This was the side of town that gentrification had forgotten, but hard times and blight had kept close to their bosom. As former mayor Marion Barry, better known to Chocolate City residents as "Mayor for Life," had said, it was the land of the least, the last, and the lost.

It was cold and dark outside, and Erica was trying to take in all the elements of her new and dangerous-looking surroundings. She felt nervous when she came to a stoplight where several young men were milling around on the corner. She watched as their eyes peered at her from the curb, sizing up her black Mercedes sedan. It was a limited edition model that she'd purchased for herself last Christmas to celebrate a very prosperous year for Opulence.

Erica's car had given her a sense of pride and accomplishment, but now it was drawing unwelcome attention and she wished she was driving a hooptie instead. One of the thugged-out, saggy pants–wearing young men began raising his hands, yelling in her direction. Even though her windows were rolled up and her music was down low, Erica could hear him talking loudly to his buddies, telling them he liked her car and that he wouldn't mind taking it off her hands. She bit her bottom lip and prayed the light would turn green.

She thought about her privileged background and hated that she was stereotyping the young men based on the images she'd seen in rap videos and on the evening news. For all she knew, they were just hanging out, shooting the breeze, and simply admiring her car. But as quickly as that thought entered her mind, it made a hurried exit. Right now she couldn't blame the media for her fear, because it wasn't the Channel 7 news that picked up a rock, hurled it at her car, and yelled, "Get the fuck outta my hood, bitch!" just as the light turned green and she stepped on the gas.

When Erica finally found a parking spot on Jerome's busy street, he was standing there to meet her at her car door. She'd called him in a nervous panic right after the rock had crashed against her passenger side door.

"You okay?" he asked, hugging her close.

"A little shaken up. But I'm all right."

Jerome retrieved her overnight bag from the backseat and then walked around to the passenger side of her car to inspect the damage. "Those muthafuckin' cowards!" he hissed. "I wish I'd been in the car with you."

Erica touched the lower part of his arm, looking from her left to her right. "Let's just go inside." Although his street was quiet, there were random people walking by, all eyeing her car. She pressed the alarm and followed Jerome up the steps to his apartment.

Erica wasn't sure what she'd expected, but when she walked through Jerome's door, she was pleasantly surprised to see how neat and organized his place was. Even though his physical appearance was always immaculate, she knew that just because a man looked good, it didn't mean he kept a neat house. Even Claude, in all his sophisticated refinement, would have lived in squalor had it not been for his house-keeper who tidied up once a week.

Another thing Erica hadn't expected was the diminutive size of his apartment. He'd told her that his place wasn't large by any stretch, but she had no idea it would be so small. From what she could see at first glance, the space in which he dwelled was a fourth of the size of the first floor of her home. The living room, dining room, and nearly nonexistent kitchen were all in one cramped space, which was attached to an equally cramped hallway that led to what she imagined were two cramped bedrooms in the back. The apartment that she and Ashley had shared in college was twice the size of Jerome's.

Even though it was just him, and occasionally his son if Jamel spent the night, Erica couldn't understand why Jerome lived in such a tiny place, one that didn't match his large and commanding presence. A part of her felt sad that at thirty-five years of age, he had very little to show for all his hard work. He rose at dawn every morning and labored over the discarded remnants of other people's lives, he worked on home repair projects when they fit into his schedule so he could build his contracting business, he studied for his GED exam in between, and he still managed to spend time with his son and his parents. He was a good guy, and she wanted better for him.

Thinking about the kind of man she'd fallen in love with made Erica feel proud. He might not have possessed the material things she thought he should, but she knew he was rich in so many other ways. She made up her mind that instead of concentrating on what his home was lacking, she would find things to praise. Like the fact that when she breathed in deeply, she noticed that the room was awash with the hypnotically fragrant smell of soothing incense. When she looked around, she could see that everything was neat and in order, from his books, which she was glad to see were many, to his CDs and old-school vinyl record collection. His floors were clean and free of clutter, and the lone couch, the scratched-up coffee table, and the flat-screen TV were all situated to maximize space in the small room.

"This is where I call home," Jerome said, looking closely at her.

Erica knew he was scanning her face for signs of disapproval, and she wanted him to know that he had nothing to worry about. "You're a pretty good housekeeper. I was expecting a bachelor pad filled with stinky drawers and beer cans," she teased.

Jerome laughed. "C'mon now, you should give me more credit than that." He led her a few steps over to the couch. "Let's sit for a minute."

Erica removed her coat and took a seat. She hadn't realized that her hands were still shaking until she placed them on her lap. The concerned look in Jerome's eyes told her that he was worried about her.

"You want something to drink?" he asked.

"No, I'm good."

"I'm sorry those knuckleheads did that to you. You sure you're okay?"

"I'm sure. I guess it's just been a long day and those young boys sent me over the edge."

Jerome took her hand in his and held it gently. "I'm sorry about the things I said this morning."

"Me too."

"You only reacted the way you did because of what I said. I led you down that road." He paused, then took a deep breath before continuing. "You were right. I felt insecure, and I let it take over. Feeling vulnerable is a new thing for me, Erica. I want to be with you, and I don't want you to look at me as any less because of my current circumstances. I'm working hard to make sure I can give you the things you want and deserve."

Erica kissed the bottom of his chin. "I work hard every day, just like you, and it's no secret that I make a good living. I can buy myself practically anything I want and need. But in just a short amount of time, you've given me things I can't purchase, like joy and fulfillment and happiness and butterflies and safety and love."

"I do love you, baby."

"I love you, too."

When Jerome took her in his arms, the residual fear and doubts she'd been carrying were erased by the passionate kiss he placed on her lips. One by one he undid the buttons that held her silk blouse in place. Then he slowly removed her arms from each sleeve to reveal her lavender-colored lace bra. He held his arms up as Erica lifted his cotton knit sweater over his head, exposing his hard pecs and sexy six-pack. She leaned back, allowing Jerome to slowly ease her down so that she was lying on the couch. They kissed again, creating a rhythmic beat with their tongues, which swirled and glided, caressing each other's mouths as their bodies danced below.

Erica lifted her hips as Jerome slid her skirt down her legs, planting gentle kisses on her softly scented skin. She let out a gasp when he rolled his tongue around her knees after removing her tights and panties. She unzipped his pants and pulled them down the length of his muscular legs, letting her palms graze the skin on his taut thighs.

She hooked her fingers around the elastic band of his boxers and released his rock-solid hardness as she rubbed it gently.

She could barely contain herself as he reached for a condom. She opened her legs wide, watching him slide the latex glove over his impressive erection. When he entered her, slow and deep, their fingers laced and they never lost eye contact. They looked into each other's heart as they kissed, caressed, and made love on his couch.

Chapter 41

Jerome was happier than he'd ever been, and as he reminisced about the past few weeks, he knew he had a lot to be thankful for. His relationship with Erica was progressing so fast and so smoothly, he felt as though angels were guiding them on their way. Not since their Monday morning blowup nearly a month ago had they experienced one moment of discontent or strife. They were like glue, sticking together to form a tight bond that couldn't be torn apart. They communicated openly and honestly whenever their differences threatened to cause a problem, and they helped each other grow in ways that complemented each of them, and for that, Jerome felt Erica was making him a better man.

He was proud of the accomplishments she'd recently achieved, and even though her days had been like a whirlwind since the Tracy Reese fashion show, they'd still managed to spend quality time together. Paradise had been a hit, and everyone who'd used the luscious body butter had raved about it, so much so that Erica had appointments lined up to meet with buyers from several department stores who were interested in carrying her products. The beauty editor at *Essence* magazine had even contacted her to arrange an interview and photo shoot so that they could feature Opulence in their big holiday issue.

And for his part, Jerome was doing equally well. He had gotten a pay raise at his regular job with the city and had received his GED, and his home repair business was picking up, thanks to his hard work, his dedication, and the Web site Erica had helped him create. She'd also been instrumental in assisting him with organizing the necessary paperwork he needed in order to file for his D.C. business license and obtain certifications that would legitimize JK Contracting as a fully operating entity.

And best of all, Jamel was doing well in school and had been responsible in his actions with Tiffany. Jerome was glad that so far as he knew, Jamel hadn't had sex with the girl. But he understood it was coming, so he planned to prepare himself to cross that bridge when it rolled around.

When he thought about all the great things that were happening in his life, Jerome couldn't stop himself from smiling several times a day, and he knew that Erica was a major reason for his good fortune. Gone were the days when he'd been eager to hang out in the streets and hook up with several women in one night. Now the only woman who he wanted to come home to was Erica, and he couldn't imagine spending one day without her.

He'd thought long and hard one night before coming to a powerful decision that he knew would change his life permanently for the better. He'd decided he was going to propose to Erica during the upcoming Christmas holiday. Given the fact that it was a time for year-end celebrations, Jerome couldn't think of a better present than the promise of spending their lives together. He also knew that if he planned to marry her, he needed to introduce her to his family right away.

He was nervous at first, because he'd never introduced a woman to his mother. Even when he'd been dating Kelisha, he had just brought her over one day when he was passing through, and had casually said, "Mom, this is Kelisha. She's pregnant with my baby." Mabel had been left dumbfounded, and Jerome didn't want that to happen again. This time around there was no pregnancy tying him to a woman, only love, and love changed a multitude of things.

Jerome planned a Saturday afternoon dinner meeting at his parents' favorite soul food restaurant so they could meet Erica. He knew that a good meal helped even the most uncomfortable of situations go down smoother. And to his relief, Erica and his mother got along so well.

Erica broke the ice by bringing his father a black leather travel bag filled with Opulence shaving cream, raw soap, and body oil, and for his mother, she'd put together a colorful basket filled with fresh flowers and bath products fit for a queen at a ritzy spa. The two women talked like mother and daughter, and by the time the meal ended, they'd exchanged phone numbers so they could keep in regular contact.

The next step was introducing Erica to Jamel and Kelisha. Jerome knew Jamel would love Erica, because he was such an easygoing kind of kid, plus, he knew his son wanted him to be happy. But Kelisha was another story altogether.

Even though he'd ended their turbulent relationship two years ago, Jerome knew that Kelisha was still hoping they'd eventually get back together. Whenever they spoke by phone—which he limited to subjects that involved only Jamel—she always tried to extend their conversation, hinting and flirting until he had to bring the call to an end. Whenever she saw him at Jamel's school activities or sporting events, she always made sure she strutted her curves in front of him. And each time his birthday or the holidays rolled around, she gave him gifts, even though he'd repeatedly asked her not to.

Kelisha's actions were the reason he wanted to meet with her in a public place when he told her the news. But to his discomfort, she insisted that he come over to her house, saying that after a long day of doing nails at the salon, she didn't feel like going anywhere except her couch. Not wanting to argue, he agreed to come over on her day off.

Jerome entered Kelisha's house, feeling almost like a stranger. It had been more than a year since he'd been inside, and judging from what he could see, everything still looked the same. Kelisha had moved into the well-kept row house when her grandmother died a few years ago and left her the property. It was located in a sleeper community in the northwest section of the city, known for its clean streets and conscientious residents.

"Usually when you want to talk about somethin', you just pick up the phone and tell me what it is," Kelisha said, placing her hand on her round hip as she greeted Jerome. "But you comin' over in person, so somethin' must be up. What the hell's goin' on?"

"It's good to see you, too," he replied in a calm tone, bracing himself for attitude.

Kelisha motioned for him to follow her into the living room and have a seat on the couch. "So what's up?"

Jerome settled his body onto the love seat across from her. He didn't want to be there any longer than he had to, so he got right to the point. "I wanted to let you know that I'm going to introduce my girlfriend to Jamel."

Kelisha was quiet for a long moment. She leaned forward and stared at him as though he'd just asked her a multiple-choice question. Right then, Jerome knew there was going to be some drama.

"I don't think that's a good idea," she asserted, then sat back and crossed her legs.

"No disrespect, but I'm not asking your permission, Kelisha. I'm giving you the courtesy of letting you know that I'm going to introduce her to Jamel."

"How you gonna come up in my house all big and bad and tell me what you gon' do with my son?" Kelisha's voice was elevated, but Jerome knew that it could travel several octaves higher before their conversation ended.

"Jamel is a teenager now. It's not like he's a kid. And even if he was, I'm trying to do the right thing and be respectful by coming to you first."

"That's some bullshit! The respectful thing to do would be to let me meet her first so I can see what kinda woman you bringin' around my child."

Jerome had originally planned to do exactly what Kelisha had just suggested, but after thinking it over, he'd decided against that course of action. He knew that Erica could be a saint sent straight from God who fed the hungry, clothed the needy, and healed the sick, and Kelisha still wouldn't approve of her. She would find a reason not to like Erica and would try to poison Jamel's mind against her. But if Jamel met Erica first and liked her, there would be little that Kelisha could say.

Jerome knew she was trying to be difficult just for the hell of it. "Like I said, I'm coming to you first to let you know. But if it'll make you feel more comfortable, you two can meet her together."

"Uh, that's not happenin'."

"Why not?"

"You run the streets, and I don't know what kind of female you tryna bring around me and my son. I know how these scandalous females are."

"As long as Jamel has been alive, I've never brought a woman around him, and that's because I'm very selective about who I choose to expose him to. You know that, so stop trippin'."

"You the one trippin'. You called like you wanted to talk about you and me, and then you walk up in here with this bullshit."

Damn. Here we go! "Do you really want to take it there?"

Kelisha sucked her teeth and rolled her eyes. "Yeah, we can take it there and back again!"

It was classic Kelisha, and it used to irritate the hell out of Jerome. But now, instead of getting upset, he simply thought her gestures were childish and just plain sad. He knew he hadn't given her any false impressions during their brief phone call.

Jerome had wished for some time that Kelisha would start dating and find happiness of her own, instead of waiting around on him. She was still young, attractive, and in just as good shape as she'd been when they met in their twenties. She was the head nail technician at the salon where she worked, and when she wasn't being loud and disagreeable, she actually had a good sense of humor and could be fun to hang out with. He knew she could easily find a man, and he hoped that now that she'd seen there was no possibility of them getting back together, she would move on.

"I'm a good woman," Kelisha said, shifting her weight to one hip as she rested her elbow on the edge of the couch. "But now that you got a big raise on your job and you startin' your own business, you gon' just piss in my face and get wit some society chick. You a damn sellout."

Jerome shook his head. He wasn't surprised that Kelisha already knew about Erica, especially since Sasha, who was from the old neighborhood, had no doubt put his business out there for whoever would listen. "It's not like that. I was hoping we could have an adult conversation about this."

"Oh, so now I'm not mature enough for you, huh?" she said, enunciating each word in a clipped, proper tone.

"Kelisha, please."

"I put up with your bullshit for all these years, and this is how you wanna step to me?" Kelisha huffed. "I raised your son when your ass was out in the streets, whorin' and fuckin' everything movin' in a skirt, and now that you movin' up in the world, you just gonna forget about me."

Jerome stared at her, his eyes holding her heated gaze. "Now, hold up. I'll be the first to admit that I wasn't there for Jamel in the beginning like I should've been, but you know that ever since the car accident, I've stepped up. I spend quality time with my son, and there's not a day that goes by that I don't talk to him on the phone. And don't I send you money every month and give you extra even if you don't ask for it? I bust my ass so my son can have better than either one of us did. I may have been out in the streets with women, but I've always taken care of my responsibilities."

"And what about your responsibility to me?"

What the hell is she talking about? Jerome was so confused by her comment that he squinted his eyes, as if it would help him better understand her irrational-sounding thoughts. "This isn't about you. This is about our son, and me coming over here to let you know that I'm going to introduce him to the woman in my life."

"This is some bullshit."

"No, this is life, and it's about moving on and being happy." Jerome leaned forward, positioning himself closer to Kelisha. "What we had was over a long time ago, but we were blessed because God gave us Jamel. My commitment to my son and helping you with whatever you need for him won't change."

"Last month you was tryin' to holla at me at Jamel's birthday party, actin' all nice and helpful and shit, and now you comin' at me with this!"

Jerome looked at Kelisha in disbelief. "You gotta be kidding me. Just because I offered to help you clean up after the party, that didn't mean I was trying to get with you. What the hell's wrong with you?"

"I stuck by you through all these years. You ain't never heard about me with no other dudes, either."

"That's on you. I never asked you to wait around for me. I told you that the last time we were together. Honestly, I hope you find someone who will make you happy, because you're just bitter."

Kelisha stared at him. "Get out."

Five minutes later Jerome was in his truck, driving down the road. He turned off the volume on the radio so he could think about the conversation he'd just had with Kelisha. He knew she was irrational, but her behavior this afternoon had been over the top, even for her. He couldn't put his finger on exactly what it was, but his gut was sure there was something stirring. But he had to block it out of his mind because he was headed to Erica's house to spend a quiet, drama-free night.

Chapter 42

Erica lit the two candles in the center of the table, admiring the beautiful flowers in the lead-crystal vase and the elegant place settings she'd set side by side in preparation for a romantic dinner with Jerome. The delicious smell of herb-roasted chicken, rosemary and dill risotto, and fresh asparagus filled the room with a scent that made her want to devour the food now instead of waiting for Jerome, especially after the long day she'd had at Opulence. But she contained herself because she knew her man would appreciate the effort she'd put into making their night together special.

The past few weeks had been unbelievably wonderful, and she didn't want the incredible feeling to end. She and Jerome had been busier than ever, with each of them experiencing highs in their careers, as well as in their relationship, which had blossomed into a romance that Erica thought was almost too good to be true. But unlike the fairy-tale courtship she'd been lured into with Claude, which had turned out to be a huge sham, she knew what she and Jerome had was as deep, real, and true as the lines on the palms of her hands.

Jerome was everything that no other man in her life had been. He loved her, and he didn't shy away from telling her verbally or showing her through his actions and deeds. His love was a verb, an adjective, a noun, and a simile all rolled into one feeling that had Erica believing for the first time that fairy tales really did come true.

When Jerome told her that he wanted her to meet his parents, she'd felt honored, because she knew his mother, as well as his father, meant the world to him. Mabel had been his rock his entire life, and his father had shown him that second chances were possible. They were two great people, and she knew that getting their approval was pivotal in her and Jerome's relationship.

She'd been nervous at first, but both Mabel and Parnell had fallen in love with her, just as she had with them. She and Mabel had even talked on the phone a few times about body lotions, food recipes, and life in general. And now she couldn't wait to meet Jamel, which she knew was going to be an even bigger step than meeting Jerome's parents. If his parents were his world, his son was his universe.

Erica admired the fact that Jerome was such a dedicated father and that he was very careful in everything regarding his son, and the fact that she was going to be the first woman he'd ever introduced to Jamel spoke volumes about where their relationship was headed. He'd assured her that Jamel would love her just as his parents did, but she worried about the big albatross hanging over them, which was his baby mama, Kelisha. Although Jerome didn't speak much about his ex, Erica couldn't help but feel the woman might be trouble down the road.

"Don't even worry about her," Ashley had said. "Just concentrate on the happiness that you and Jerome have, and you'll be fine."

Even though Ashley couldn't manage her own personal dramas and was now balancing her feelings for two different men, Erica knew her friend always gave sound advice from the heart. Plus, Ashley had dealt with baby mamas in the past, so she knew what she was talking about.

Erica sat a basket of bread on the table and then turned on the stereo to let Kem's voice serenade the room. She was getting ready to call Jerome to make sure he was on his way when her doorbell rang. She wasn't expecting any Friday night guests, and she wondered who it could be. When she peeped through the hole and saw Claude standing on the other side of her door, she felt her stomach tighten. *What the hell is he doing here?*

Erica's first reaction was to let him stand outside in the cold until he went away. But then she knew that Jerome was on his way over, and she didn't want Claude there when he arrived. She placed her hand on her hip and opened the door. "What do you want, and why are you popping up on my doorstep?"

Claude smiled and smirked at the same time. "I see that hanging around with a certain element is beginning to rub off. Where has your graceful etiquette gone? Can I at least get a proper greeting?"

"What do you want, Claude?"

"Despite your caustic attitude, you look beautiful."

Erica removed her hand from her hip and folded her arms at her chest. The royal purple sweater dress that hugged her curves was one of Jerome's favorite outfits on her, and she knew he'd love seeing her in it as they ate by candlelight, and she knew he'd love the fact that she was completely naked underneath. But right now she felt less than sexy in it, and she hated the fact that Claude could see her erect nipples standing at rapt attention, a sight that wasn't meant for him.

"My boyfriend is on his way over. You need to leave."

Claude didn't flinch. "I can believe you're serious about seeing this guy. I mean, c'mon, Erica. He's a trashman, for Christ's sake!"

"And he's also a good, honest, decent man." Erica glowered at him and took a step forward. "Which is much more than I can say about you. I'm not sure what you came here for or what you're up to, but I'm gonna end this little visit right now."

Claude threw up one hand in defeat, then raised the other to meet Erica's folded arms. "Here. This is the purpose of my visit," he said, handing her a flyer.

Erica looked at the familiar 8½ x 11-inch paper and rolled her eyes. She didn't move her hands to accept it, and now she was getting pissed. "You came here to give me one of Nelson's campaign flyers?"

"I'm canvassing the neighborhood. I've left them with every neighbor on your street."

"Canvassing at night?"

"Anything to get the job done."

Erica was suspicious. She knew that Claude wasn't a grassroots, door-to-door kind of guy. His political involvement was relegated to fancy dinners and swank fund-raisers, not boots-on-the-ground efforts. She knew something was up, and she was determined to get to the bottom of it. "Okay, let's cut the bullshit. I know you don't have real feelings for me, so what is it that you're really after?"

Claude shook his head. "You're beautiful, even when you're angry."

"If you want to see angry, stick around five more minutes. When Jerome gets here, you'll see real anger." Erica glanced at her watch, praying that Jerome would be late, because she didn't want a showdown at her front door.

And apparently Claude didn't, either. He stepped back and smiled. "You have every reason to be skeptical of my intentions. I didn't know what a good thing I had until it was too late. I messed up royally," he said, looking genuinely sincere. "But I know you and I are right for each other, Erica. We speak the same language, we like the same things, and we're both ambitious. We were good together, and if you give me another chance, I'll show you how great we can be. I've changed, and I'm ready now."

Claude's snake oil tactics almost made her laugh, but she pulled back on the joviality when she saw Jerome's truck coming down the street.

Erica's heart pounded rapidly against the wall of her chest when she saw Jerome double-park in front of her house and put on his flashing lights. Normally, he parked his truck in the garage around back, but she knew the minute he saw Claude standing at her door that he'd come charging up.

"I told you to leave, and now it's too late," Erica hissed at Claude.

Claude turned to face Jerome just as he was approaching. "I'm sure Candidate Stanford already has your vote," he said, "but it never hurts to ask." He held out the campaign flyer in Jerome's direction. "You do vote, don't you? But wait. Are convicted criminals allowed to vote in the District?"

Jerome dismissed the flyer and looked past Claude. "Are you okay?" he asked Erica.

"Yes. He was just leaving."

"Why are you coming over to my woman's house when you know you're not welcome?" Jerome asked in a steely voice, turning his attention to Claude.

Claude stuck out his chest and glared at Jerome, looking as though he was ready to attack at any moment. Erica held her breath, not knowing what kind of physical confrontation might come next.

She watched as Claude walked down her steps to where Jerome was standing.

"Don't ever question me about anything I do," Claude growled.

Jerome calmly smiled. "I'll do whatever the fuck I wanna do."

"Typical gangster language." Claude smirked and looked at Erica. "Think about what I said." And with that, he breezed by Jerome, leaving him fuming at the foot of Erica's steps.

Chapter 43

Jerome was so mad, he could have punched something, but he knew that wouldn't solve anything at the moment. He walked into Erica's kitchen without saying a word and sat his overnight bag on the floor. "What did he say to you?"

Erica blinked. "What?"

"The muthafucka said, 'Think about what I said.' I want to know what he said to you, Erica."

She lowered her voice, as if she didn't want anyone else to hear her words. "Crazy talk about us getting back together. But, baby, I don't know why he's doing this. I haven't encouraged him or given him the slightest indication that I want to be with him. He just started this out of nowhere."

Jerome leaned against the counter and looked at Erica. He wanted to believe that she was telling him the truth, but it still didn't make sense to him why a man of Claude's social and financial status would publicly hound a woman who didn't want to be with him. He knew that men who possessed enormous egos like Claude would rather walk over hot coals than sweat a woman, especially if the woman had moved on to a new man.

The sound of Erica's voice broke his thoughts. "The next time Claude calls me or shows up at my door or initiates any kind of contact, I'm going to get the authorities involved. This is just too strange, and I don't understand it."

Jerome nodded. "That's a good idea, 'cause next time I might not be so calm. I was ready to fuck him up, and he knew it. But he also knew that a brothah like me can't afford any trouble with the police. I ain't about to get arrested in this neighborhood, no way, and that's why his punk ass went off at the mouth the way he did."

"Speaking of trouble with the police," Erica said, looking at Jerome through confused eyes, "what did he mean by that convicted criminal comment and you not being able to vote?"

Jerome shook his head. "He's obviously taken the time to check out my background, and that's another reason I know something's up with the dude."

"But you've never been convicted of a crime, right?"

"No, baby. I've had arrests, but no convictions. He just said that bullshit to get a rise out of me."

"This doesn't make any sense. Why is he doing this?"

"The man wants you, and he's doing some crazy shit to prove it."

"But like I said before, he doesn't really want me back," Erica protested. "I know Claude, and I know there's something up his sleeve."

Jerome shook his head. "You know, I thought the same thing after my conversation with Kelisha this afternoon." He could see the concern sitting between Erica's knitted brow, so he quickly gave her a rundown of the tense meeting he'd had with his ex. "If I didn't know any better, I'd think the two of them were conspiring."

"And you're sure you haven't given Kelisha any mixed signals that might make her think you wanted to rekindle things?" Erica asked.

"Have you given Claude any?"

Erica wrapped her arms around his waist and laid her head against his chest. "I'm sorry I sounded accusatory. I guess I know how you feel now. This is just bizarre."

"It is, but, baby, you're the only woman for me."

"I love you, Jerome."

"I love you, too." He kissed the top of her forehead and inhaled the sweet scent of her skin, which always managed to comfort him.

"I guess this is a test, huh?"

Jerome smiled. "It ain't nothin' but a thing. They're gonna have to come harder than this to break us up. We're solid. But still, I ain't gonna sleep on either one of them." He kissed her on the bridge of her nose, then on the center of her soft lips.

"That's right," Erica agreed. "And I'm not going to let your ex or mine ruin our evening, especially since I spent the last two hours making us a romantic dinner. You hungry?"

"I sure am. Everything smells good, too!"

"All right. Let's eat."

Jerome tugged at the hem of Erica's purple dress, sliding it up the sides of her legs as he dropped to his knees in front of her. "I want to start with dessert." He smiled with seduction. Slowly, he gently placed his mouth on her heated flesh. "This is the kind of sugar I like."

As Erica lay in bed, listening to the sound of Jerome's soft snores, she took deep breaths of her own, trying to calm herself. She'd just awakened from a bad dream. She hadn't experienced a nightmare in almost a month, but now the terrifying episodes had returned.

Quietly, she slipped out of bed and went into her bathroom. She ran a cloth under the cool water and then applied it to her forehead. Although this nightmare hadn't been nearly as severe as most of them usually were, it had been nonetheless frightening.

She'd been chased down a long, winding hallway that didn't seem to end. Then, finally, just as she'd seen the light at the end of the proverbial tunnel, a hand reached out to grab her, pulling her back into the darkness. She hadn't put up much of a struggle before she let the force overtake her. She had been prepared to rest in the black silence of an unknown world when she awoke in a sweat.

She'd been glad that Jerome was knocked out in a deep, satisfied sleep; otherwise, she knew he would have been upset to see her in such a state and would probably have brought up the subject of therapy again.

After Erica calmed herself, she slipped back under her warm sheets. As soon as she slid her body next to Jerome's, he reached for her. He kissed her on the nape of her neck as she nestled in beside him.

"You okay?" he asked in a half-asleep, half-awake voice.

"Yes, I just had to use the bathroom. Go back to sleep," she whispered.

When she felt his warm breath caress her skin, her fear and anxiety slowly melted away. But deep inside, she wondered how long that sense of comfort and all the goodness they'd experienced together would last. And more important, she had a bad feeling about whatever both their conniving exes were really up to.

Chapter 44

Erica was excited, nervous, and anxious all at once. In a few hours her home would be flooded with a flurry of people and activity. It was Thanksgiving Day, and she was hosting a huge feast that would bring together the Stanford and Kimbrough clans and their friends. Erica knew this was an ambitious feat, but she thought there was no better time than the present to introduce the two families, which she was certain would eventually become one.

Though it had only been three months since she and Jerome had started dating, they were confident in the fact that they wanted to spend the rest of their lives together. Erica often laughed when she thought about the line Jerome frequently quoted from the song "The Light," by one of his favorite musical artists, Common: "It don't take a whole day to recognize sunshine." She knew that was indeed a true sentiment, because it had taken her only a week to know that Jerome was special and less than two to fall in love with him.

For the first month or two of their relationship, Erica had been waiting for the other shoe to fall—for something bad to happen—particularly given the strange behavior of Claude and Kelisha. But a few weeks ago half her worries had been laid to rest when she learned the real reason behind Claude's insistent pursuit of her.

One evening Claude had been volunteering for Nelson's campaign, sending out e-mails to potential donors, seemingly doing all he could to help propel the Stanford campaign to victory. He'd also sent out an e-mail to his fellow partners at his firm, all but guaranteeing political influence for their company on government contracts because he was dating the future councilman's sister. Not only was sending that blatantly untrue e-mail an unethical and stupid thing to do, but it proved to be a huge blunder, because he accidentally forwarded it to a potential donor, who in turn forwarded it directly to Nelson. After that, it was a wrap for Claude.

Erica had been disgusted and relieved all at the same time, but ultimately, she was glad to finally put Claude's nonsense behind her. It seemed as though she and Jerome had hurdled over every barrier that had come their way . . . except one, and that was Kelisha. Erica had known the woman was going to be trouble, but she'd had no idea how much, and the fact that Kelisha was resentful of the relationship she and Jamel had established only added more strife to the bothersome brew.

Jamel loved Erica, just as Jerome had said he would. The two instantly bonded, as if she'd been mothering him his whole life. She helped him with his math homework whenever he ran into tough equations, and she talked to him about his "girlfriend issues" when he didn't feel comfortable confiding in Jerome or Kelisha. In return, Jamel helped her on the weekends at Opulence, earning extra spending money by stocking shelves, cleaning the break room, and making sure the windows and hardwood floors were polished to a sparkling shine. Their relationship was smooth and easy, much like the one Erica shared with Jerome. But her relationship with mama bear was an entirely different animal.

When she and Kelisha finally met last month at one of Jamel's soccer games, Kelisha had made it clear that she didn't want anything to do with Erica. She'd refused to even shake Erica's hand when Jerome introduced them, and she'd nodded a terse "hello" only because Jamel had been standing next to them. Once he left to take his place on the field, Kelisha dismissed her completely. But at the end of the game they had to come together again, and that was when Kelisha took the opportunity to let Erica know exactly how she felt.

Jamel's team had won the game, and they were set to go to Pizzeria Uno afterward to celebrate.

"I'm so proud of you, baby," Kelisha said, giving Jamel a big hug.

"Jamel, you were a star out there!" Erica enthusiastically cheered.

"That's my boy," Jerome said, giving Jamel a customary brother-man dap.

All seemed to be going well as Jerome and Jamel walked and talked side by side while they headed toward the parking lot, with Erica and Kelisha strolling a few paces behind. Erica saw this as her opportunity to break the hard sheet of ice that her man's ex had formed.

"You and Jerome have done a great job with Jamel. He's a wonderful young man," Erica complimented with a smile.

Kelisha stared straight ahead and unleashed a quiet fury, which had apparently been simmering inside her for weeks. "Let's get one thing straight from the jump," she hissed in a low voice. "Just 'cause you the new woman in Jerome's life, that don't mean jack. Yeah, you the first one he's introduced to his mama and daddy and Jamel, but that don't mean nothin'. I've seen his women come and go, and I've outlasted them all. Believe me when I say that once you gon', I'll still be here, havin' his back."

Erica controlled her anger and outrage as she spoke. "With all due respect, which you haven't had the courtesy of giving me, I'm sorry you're so bitter about the fact that Jerome and I are happy together. But like it or not, I'm not going anywhere."

"You think you better than me just 'cause you talk all proper and you got money and a fancy degree. But let me tell you somethin', Miss Thang," Kelisha replied, rattling like a deadly snake. "I'm the one who had his baby and got his back, and it's been that way since before you came along. He just fascinated by you, that's all, and when it wears off, we'll see whose bed he gon' come runnin' back to, just like he always do."

"Why are you so bitter? Just move on," Erica said, her anger ratcheting up.

Kelisha continued to stare straight ahead as she delivered her next set of biting words. "You the one who's bitter and barren. You ain't never had a man or a child of your own, and you ain't about to now. You one of them women who got to go out and take somebody else's."

"Y'all all right back there?" Jerome called out, turning slightly as he looked between Erica and Kelisha with a cautious stare.

"We fine. Just doin' a little girl talk." Kelisha smiled.

Erica wanted to say, "No, we're not fine. This crazy bitch is talking shit, and I'm about to slap her ass into next week!" But she didn't want to cause a scene in a parking lot full of parents and children, so she smiled and kept her mouth shut.

Now, as Erica stood in her large dining room, putting the finishing touches on her beautifully decorated table, she tried to push Kelisha out of her mind. The sad reality was that Kelisha would be a part of her life through Jamel. In a short amount of time she'd grown to love the adorably sweet teenager, despite his hellion of a mother, so she knew she had to accept what came along with the package of a blended family.

Erica returned to the kitchen and grabbed two oven mitts from the counter. "Perfect," she said as she carefully removed the twenty-two-pound turkey from the oven. She looked around at her countertops, which were crowded with food, and praised herself for a job well done. She'd been cooking since yesterday, and now she was ready for what she hoped was going to be a joyous Thanksgiving celebration to remember.

"Everything is delicious," Erica's mother sang with delight as she bit into a stuffed spinach puff. "I can't wait to taste the main course. You've outdone yourself, sweetie."

"Thanks, Mom." Erica smiled, happy that everyone was having a good time. She looked around her living and dining rooms, surveying the crowd. Her parents, who were distant but cordial, entertained opposite ends of the house with their family stories from yesteryear, while Nelson and several cousins regaled each other with their funny childhood memories. It was a scene straight out of a Norman Rockwell painting, only with a little chocolate sprinkled in.

Erica was having a ball playing hostess supreme, making sure that everyone's glass was full and their appetizer plates were replenished as they waited for the full-course meal. But if there was one disappointment she felt, it was that Jerome's parents had yet to arrive. Mabel and

Parnell were the prized guests she'd been waiting for, and the reason why the abundant meal she'd prepared was on hold. She didn't want to sit at the table and carve the turkey until they got there. She couldn't wait to introduce them to her parents and the rest of her family.

"Baby, I can't believe you cooked all this food by yourself," Jerome said, finishing the last bite of his mushroom and red pepper crostini before he planted a light kiss on her cheek. "This food is on and poppin'."

Erica smiled. "Thanks. It would be even better if your parents were here. Where are they?"

"I know, and I'm sorry about that. I guess CP time runs in the blood. My pops is always late."

Just as Jerome was making his statement, Erica's doorbell rang.

"They might be late, but they're right on time," Erica said with relief as she walked toward her front door, with Jerome following behind her. "Happy Thanksgiving!" she greeted with a big smile as she welcomed Mabel and Parnell into her home.

Mabel smiled so wide, she looked as though her mouth had stretched across her entire face. "Same to you, sugar! Sorry we're late." She apologized and gave Erica a firm hug. "Parnell's always making us late for everything," she said as she tossed her husband a playfully cross look.

"Sorry, Erica," Parnell said. "I wish we'd have come earlier, 'cause it smells some kinda good in here!"

Jerome took his parents' coats and hung them in the front hall closet. "We've killed most of the appetizers, but wait till you see the spread Erica made for dinner. My baby threw down."

"Well, let's go," Parnell said with enthusiasm.

They walked from the foyer to the living room, laughing and talking as Erica introduced them to her family members one by one. She could see that Mabel and Parnell were impressed when they learned that Nelson Stanford, whom they'd seen a picture of in the paper, was her brother. It was obvious they weren't in the know, and Erica smiled with pride as Nelson wrapped them around his finger, displaying his signature charm and newly acquired political sway.

"Where's Mom and Dad?" Erica asked her brother as she searched the room.

"Right behind you."

Erica turned around and gave her parents the same bubbly smile that Mabel had greeted her with. "Mom, Dad, I'd like you to meet Jerome's parents, Mr. and Mrs. Kimbrough."

The pleasant greetings and hearty smiles that Erica had expected them to exchange fell flat, and she saw a look of shock and surprise flash through both her parents' eyes. She watched as her father stood in disbelief and her mother's hand flew to her mouth in horror.

"You're Jerome's father?" Maureen said, the color draining from her lovely caramel-colored skin.

Jerome and Erica, along with Mabel, looked to Parnell for answers.

"Oh, God," Parnell said, his voice sounding like a distant whisper.

"What's going on?" Erica asked, instantly knowing she wasn't going to like the answer.

Joseph zeroed in on Parnell, staring as though he could slice the man in half with his thoughts. "This is the son of a bitch who shot me twenty-five years ago!"

Chapter 45

Erica felt as though she'd fallen into a bottomless hole as she stared into Parnell Kimbrough's face. She didn't understand how this could be. She'd laughed with this man over a nice meal, talked with him over the phone, and listened to his stories about how precocious and strong-willed Jerome used to be when he was a little boy. She wondered how the God-fearing, gentle man before her could be the same cold-blooded animal who'd broken into her house, shot her father, and then left him for dead.

"I don't understand," Mabel said in a panic-stricken tone. "Parnell, what are these people talking about?"

Joseph spoke through clenched teeth as he stared at Parnell. "It was twenty-five years ago. You've changed, but not that much. I'll never forget the eyes of the man who tried to kill me."

"Is this true?" Mabel asked. "Parnell, say something! Is this true?"

Parnell lowered his head, barely able to keep his balance, and sank down onto the couch. He looked up into Maureen's eyes. "I'm so sorry, Reene. I'm so sorry."

"Reene?" Joseph said, almost in a whisper. He turned to Maureen, looking at her as if he'd just seen a long-forgotten ghost. "This is *him*? Maureen, please tell me that this isn't *him!*" he shouted.

Maureen closed her eyes and shook her head. "This can't be happening. . . ."

"What the hell is going on?" Nelson asked, looking from his parents to Parnell.

By now, all conversation in the room had come to an abrupt halt, and all eyes were trained on the man sitting on the couch and the people standing around him. Maureen, Mabel, Nelson, Jerome, and Erica looked as though they were frozen in time, but Joseph was livid.

"For Christ's sake, Maureen!" Joseph spat out.

"Mom?" Erica pleaded, anguish lacing her voice as she touched her mother's arm. "What's going on?"

Maureen shook her head and ran up the stairs in tears, leaving a room full of people wondering about the answer to the question Erica had just asked. What the hell was going on?

It took only a few minutes to clear nearly twenty people out of Erica's home. What had started off as a holiday celebration of family and good cheer had ended in turmoil, hurtful realizations, and a scandalous secret that was obvious, but that no one wanted to touch. After everyone had gone, Nelson offered to drive his father home, seeing that he was in no condition to get behind the wheel. Jerome talked to his father to get his side of the story, while Erica went upstairs to see about her mother.

When she opened her bedroom door, Erica found Maureen sitting on the plush bench at the foot of her bed. She walked over and took a seat close beside her. They sat in silence for a long while before Maureen finally spoke.

"What I'm about to tell you is going to be hard to hear. Are you sure you want to know everything?"

"Yes. Start from the beginning."

Maureen took a deep breath and began. "Your father and I had grown apart. I was young and attractive, with a big, fancy house, two beautiful children, and all the material trappings I wanted at my fingertips. But I was lonely, and I was tired of waiting at home for Joseph night after night, knowing he was in the company of other women, some of whom I even knew. One day when I was in the city, having lunch at Union Station, I met a handsome man who swept me off my feet. He was charming, funny, and he showered me with attention. It was clear that we were from different worlds, but that was part of what attracted me to him.

"He understood that I was married, and I knew he was, too. I never knew his last name, and he never asked mine. I called him Parry and he called me Reene, and that was all the understanding we needed. We'd meet once a week in a hotel in downtown D.C. It lasted for a year before things went bad. I knew that Parry used drugs occasionally, but I didn't know he was an addict. When money turned up missing out of my purse after we'd been together, I confronted him. He denied taking anything, but I knew it had to be him, because there had been no one in that hotel room besides the two of us.

"I found out he'd developed a taste for heroin, and the effects began to show. As much as I didn't want to, I told him we couldn't see each other anymore. That's when things got out of control. He followed me home one day, and somehow he got the phone number to our house. He started calling me, begging to see me. One time your father picked up, and Parry was so high, he asked for me, saying, 'Is Reene there? I'm in love with your wife and I want her back.' Your father and I had a terrible fight that night. It was okay for him to roam, but not for his wife. I was frightened because Parry knew where I lived, and I was in constant fear that he'd show up and all hell would break loose. Well, eventually he did, and he brought the disaster I'd feared right along with him."

Erica looked at her mother. "The night of my birthday."

Maureen nodded. "Yes, sweetie. That was the most awful night of my life. I've been carrying around that secret and so much guilt ever since. I brought harm to my family because of my reckless behavior, but I couldn't say anything, because I was so ashamed. Parry never breathed a word to the authorities about how he came to target our house in a gated community. I guess he felt sorry for what he'd done and he didn't want to implicate me or cause me any more trouble."

"Is that why you've put up with Daddy's crap for all these years? Because you felt guilty?"

"Yes. Everything that happened that night was my fault. If I'd never had an affair with Parry, none of that would have happened."

"I can't believe this."

"Funny thing is, when I met Jerome, it was like looking at a young Parry all over again. But I dismissed it, thinking it wasn't possible. Parry had told me that he and his wife didn't have any children, which I now know was a lie. Jerome was the same age you were."

Erica stood up and walked over to her window. She looked out into the cold darkness, her heart feeling heavy. "All these years I've been having nightmares, running from the bogeyman lurking in the shadows, and now I find out that he's sitting downstairs in my living room."

"Erica, I'm so, so sorry." Maureen broke into tears again. "I wasn't strong back then. I let you all down."

Erica sighed loudly. "Mom, please don't cry. This is an awful situation, but I know we'll all get through it."

Maureen looked at her daughter through red eyes as she sniffled. "Always the optimist."

"I really don't know what I am right now. I'm so much in shock, I can't process it all, and . . . damn! I don't even know what I'm going to say to Jerome. They're still downstairs."

"I'm sure Parry, um, Parnell, has told him exactly what I told you. You need to go talk to him."

"This is so freaking unbelievable."

Maureen rose from the bench and walked over to her daughter. "You can do it. You're so much stronger than you know. I've always admired that about you. You see the good in everything, and that takes courage."

Erica shook her head. "Funny, I've never felt strong at all."

"You're the most fearless Stanford in the entire clan. Your father always wanted to start his own business, but he never had the guts to take the leap like you did. Nelson's always wanted the approval of others, so now he's seeking votes, instead of letting life play its hand the way you have. And me . . ." Maureen smiled. "I've always hidden behind my secrets and fears, never trusting anyone the way you do, which is the reason why you're so loved by everyone who knows you."

"Try telling that to Kelisha."

"Who?"

"It's a long story," Erica said with a shrug.

Maureen walked over to the bench and took a seat again. "You mind if I stay here tonight? I really don't feel like driving home, and I don't think I can face Joseph."

"Sure. The guest bedroom is all yours." Erica walked past her mother toward the hallway. "I'm going downstairs."

As she descended the stairs, taking them slowly, one step at a time, Erica braced herself so she'd have the strength to stare her nightmare in the face.

Chapter 46

Jerome knew his ears were working properly, but he felt as though his mind was stuck in quicksand, sinking with each detail he learned from his father. He knew that Parnell had led a wild, irresponsible life in his younger days, and that he'd been in and out of jail for petty crimes before abandoning the family, but he never imagined that his father had served seven years in prison for breaking and entering and attempted murder.

That the crime had been perpetrated against Erica's family was a hard blow to take, and worse still, the fact that he'd had an affair with Erica's mother was almost too much to handle. It was also more than Mabel wanted to deal with at the moment, so she'd gone into the kitchen and busied herself by covering all the untouched food that Erica had left out on the counter.

Talking with his father one-on-one, Jerome sat in disbelief as Parnell described the way he and Reene had met—seeing each other by chance and connecting right away. Her beauty and their natural chemistry had captivated him, and whether it was love or his addictive personality, he couldn't bring himself to stay away from her. A passionate romance quickly ensued but then spiraled out of control.

The rest of the story unfolded like a movie, only it was real life. Real people were hurt, and lives were scarred. Jerome thought about the nightmares Erica had struggled against all her life, and he felt a sorrow in the bottom of his stomach that unsettled him, knowing her misery was at the hands of his father.

Parnell hung his head low. "I've spent so many years trying to make up for the terrible things I did in my past, but I guess it's true that you can't outrun your secrets. They always come back to haunt you. I never wanted my sins to burden you, and I'm so sorry they have."

"This is . . ." Jerome paused, trying to articulate his jumbled thoughts. "I don't know what to say to Erica. I can't imagine what she's feeling right now." He looked up when he heard footsteps on the stairs, which came to a stop. He stood and went over to Erica, cradling her in his arms, hugging her close to his body as he stroked her back. "Baby, I'm so sorry. Are you okay?"

"I don't know," she whispered in a low voice. "This is a really bad situation."

"Seems like every time we get past one problem, another one pops up."

"This is a big one."

Jerome took a deep breath. "I know. But we can get through it."

Erica looked past his shoulder in the direction of where Parnell was sitting on the couch and cringed. She stared at him for a long stretch of time. Her body stiffened, and she moved away from Jerome's firm hold. "Maybe this is a sign."

"What do you mean?"

"It shouldn't be this hard," Erica said through weary eyes. "Loving someone, having a relationship, it shouldn't be this damn difficult. Every time we turn around, something pops up that prevents us from having peace. We keep ignoring the signs while they beat us over our heads."

"Erica, I know this is an awful situation, but—"

"This is too much for me to deal with right now. I need some time and space."

Jerome looked into Erica's eyes. "Baby, we can get through this, like we always do."

"Your father is the man who attacked my father and turned my whole world upside down. I've had nightmares that he'd come for me since I was ten. I can't be in the same room with him right now." She backed away. "I think you and your parents need to leave."

Jerome called his mother on her cell phone to make sure she and his father had arrived home safely after the traumatic Thanksgiving dinner that never was. He felt relief wash over his body when Mabel told him that they were okay and had settled in for the evening. Next, he called Jamel to see how his dinner at Kelisha's aunt's house had turned out.

"Everything's cool, Dad. I'm gonna spend the night here at Aunt Deena's and hang out with Pooch," Jamel said, referring to the nickname the family had given his cousin Dale.

"Okay. I'm glad you're having a good time, son."

"How're things going over at Erica's? Did she throw down on the food?"

"Things went all right," Jerome lied.

"Dad, are you okay? You don't sound so hot."

"I'm fine. Just tired. Getting ready to head home and call it a night."

He and Jamel talked a few minutes longer before they ended their call. As Jerome steered his truck toward his apartment, he called Erica again, but all he got was her voice mail. This was his seventh attempt in less than an hour, and it was clear that she didn't want to speak to him. She'd never ignored him like this, and the fact that she couldn't bring herself to communicate with him made the sorrow he'd felt in his stomach earlier rumble even more.

"Out of all the women to screw and the houses to rob!" Jerome lamented about his father's deeds. "Damn!" He entered his apartment and kicked the edge of his sofa on his way over to his small kitchen. He retrieved a bottle of Cîroc from his cabinet, then opened the refrigerator in search of cranberry juice.

Jerome mixed his drink as he thought about the night's events, still trying to take in the hard reality of his hidden connection to Erica and her comment about this being a sign. *Is that why we were drawn to each other?*

An hour later, Jerome was lying across his sofa, nursing the last

drop of liquor in his glass. He knew that drinking himself into a stu-
por was a bad idea, but at the moment it was the only thing that
numbed the disappointment and loneliness he felt. All he could think
about was Erica, what she must be going through, and how he
wanted to be by her side but couldn't.

His eyes blinked in quick succession when he heard a pounding
knock at his door. He was startled because he rarely, if ever, had any
visitors, and he wondered who it could be at this time of night. Then
it came to him—Erica! She'd come to be with him and to work
through the terrible mess that had been made back in the past.

Jerome slowly stumbled to his feet, his head feeling as though it
was spinning round and round like a hula hoop. He was in no shape
to stand, let alone walk, but somehow he managed to prop himself up
against the door for support. This wasn't the state he wanted Erica to
see him in, but at this point it really didn't matter, because all he could
think about was being with her and easing her pain.

When he looked through the peephole and saw Kelisha, he had
to do a double take to confirm that his eyes hadn't betrayed him. He
looked a second time as he blinked again, and there was no mistaking
that it was Kelisha's hard fists pounding on the door.

"Jerome, I know you up in there, 'cause I seen your truck parked
on the street. I talked to Jamel, and he said you didn't sound good.
Open up."

"I'm fine. Go home."

"No, you ain't, and I can tell you been drinkin'. Open up!"

Jerome didn't need the headache of dealing with Kelisha, but at
the same time he didn't have the energy to stand at the door and
argue until she went away. He needed to get back to the couch before
he fell to the floor, which had begun to spin beneath his unsteady
feet. He unlocked the dead bolt and then stumbled back to the couch,
letting Kelisha make her own entrance.

"What the hell is wrong with you?" she asked, surveying the
room. "It smells like a liquor house in here." She picked up the empty
Cîroc bottle next to the couch. "You drank this whole bottle by your-
~'?"

        ~'t full when I started."

    ~uch did you drink?"

Jerome was growing tired of Kelisha's voice, and all he wanted to do was sleep next to Erica in peace and quiet. "Listen, I'm tired. It's been a long night."

"I can see." She stood over him at the edge of the couch. "You don't even roll like this anymore. Somethin' bad must've happened to make you so upset that you went back to drinkin' like this."

Jerome's stomach and head felt as though they were in a losing battle with his body. His eyes began to feel heavy, and he could barely hear Kelisha's nagging voice any longer.

"Let's get you to bed," Kelisha said with a smile. "I know how to take care of you. Like I was just saying the other week, I always got your back."

Chapter 47

Erica awoke to the smell of bacon and eggs. "Mom's down there cooking," she said through a sleepy yawn. She stretched and yawned again, feeling as though she hadn't rested, despite the fact that she'd gotten a full eight hours' sleep.

She sat up at the edge of her bed and rubbed her tired eyes with the heels of her hands. She felt exhausted and anxious, the way she usually did after a bad dream, only her nightgown wasn't soaked with sweat and her heart wasn't racing in her chest.

For a brief moment she thought that maybe she had indeed been dreaming, and that the drama that had brought her holiday celebration to a standstill was all make-believe. But she knew every horrible detail from twenty-five years ago had unfolded in real time, right in the middle of her very own living room. The fact that her mother was downstairs instead of in her own house let Erica know it was real, and the fact that Jerome wasn't lying beside her when she awakened confirmed it.

"It happened, and now I have to get on with life," Erica said aloud. She wrapped her warm terry-cloth bathrobe around her body and went downstairs.

"Good morning," Maureen greeted. "You're just in time for breakfast."

Erica took a seat at her kitchen table as her mother placed a plate in front of her. "You didn't have to cook, Mom. There's tons of food in the fridge that we never touched yesterday."

"You can't eat turkey and dressing for breakfast. That's just unnatural."

Erica unfolded her napkin and laid it across her lap. She wanted to eat because she hadn't had a meal since yesterday's breakfast. Her stomach was growling, but she didn't have an appetite, so she drank her orange juice instead. "How do you feel this morning?"

"Surprisingly, I feel pretty good. Thanks for letting me spend the night. It's the first good night's sleep I've had in years. It's like my insomnia vanished."

"Really? I didn't know you had trouble sleeping."

"There are a lot of things I've kept to myself over the years," Maureen said in a low voice. "That's the thing about secrets. You can lock them away, but they'll eat at you little by little, until either they consume you or you set them free."

Erica thought about the wisdom and truth in her mother's words, knowing they applied to her own life, as well. When she'd finally drifted off to sleep, she'd been afraid that a dangerous nightmare would break her slumber, which usually happened after experiencing the kind of drama she'd gone through yesterday. But instead of waking in a panic, she'd slept through the night without opening her eyes even once. Now that she'd faced the bogeyman, she no longer had anything to fear. She was free. Just as her mother had said.

"Your father is moving out of the house," Maureen said, breaking Erica's thoughts. "We talked before I came down to make breakfast. It's such a relief. We were just keeping up appearances, and now we don't have to."

Erica nodded. "I still can't believe everything that's happened. I mean, what are the odds that I'd be dating the son of the man who traumatized our family and who . . ." Erica paused, not knowing how to say what she was thinking other than to blurt it out. "Who you had an affair with. It's going to take a while for it all to really sink in."

"Yes, I know. It's a lot to absorb. After Parry went away to prison, I didn't think I'd ever see him again. But that shows you how strange life is. I never in a million years thought he'd end up being my in-law."

Erica put down her orange juice and looked at her mother with surprise. "I think you're jumping the gun."

"And I think you're fooling yourself. Sweetie, don't let the past mess up what can be a happy future. Parry paid his dues for that night. . . . We all did," Maureen said, a hint of sadness coating her soft voice. "It's a brand-new day, and it's time to get on with the business of living. You and Jerome are good for each other. Don't let love slip away from you, because sometimes you don't get a second chance at it."

Erica rose from her chair, walked around the small table, and kissed her mother on the cheek. "Thanks, Mom. You can let yourself out. Just call me when you leave so I can set the house alarm from my phone," Erica said as she headed down the hall.

"Are you going out to do a little Black Friday shopping?" Maureen called out.

"Nope, I'm gonna take your advice. I'm going to see my man!" Erica yelled back. She walked up the stairs with a mission—get dressed and head over to Jerome's house. She was going to put the gloomy past behind her so she and Jerome could have a bright future.

Jerome's head felt as though balls were bouncing around inside it. He was stretched out on top of his bed, eyes shut, mouth dry, and his body feeling as though he'd been up all night.

"Here. Drink this," Kelisha said as she handed Jerome a glass.

"What's in this?"

"Alka-Seltzer." She smiled. "I found it in your cabinet."

In my cabinet? Who the hell told her she could go through my stuff? he thought. He wanted to call her out on rummaging through his cabinets and probably his drawers, too. He could only imagine how much she'd snooped around while he'd been asleep. There were things he certainly didn't want her to find. But the deafening ringing inside his head quieted his fight. "Thanks," he whispered instead.

Kelisha sat on the edge of Jerome's bed, smiled, and gently stroked his forehead. "I'll always have your back. I'ma take care of you."

"Please don't do that," Jerome said, moving Kelisha's acrylic-laced nails away from his head.

She threw her hand in the air. "I can't believe you. I took care of your pissy drunk ass, made sure you got in the bed, and cleaned you up in the shower this morning. But now you don't want me to touch you? What kinda bullshit is that, Jerome?"

Jerome hadn't suffered from a hangover in so long, he'd forgotten how awful it felt, and Kelisha's presence wasn't making it any better. He appreciated the fact that she'd taken care of him, but he knew the singular motive behind her kindness, and he knew that the slightest contact with her could lead to trouble. He wanted to beat himself up for getting drunk and letting his guard down in the first place, because now he had to contend with the consequences.

He barely remembered falling asleep last night in a booze-filled haze. The last thing he felt before closing his eyes was Kelisha's arm draped over his shoulder, her breasts pressed against his back, and a sense of regret, which he'd been too tired to fight, but now he wished he had. He didn't want Kelisha thinking that just because they'd slept in the same bed—he was glad that sleeping was the only thing they'd done—it entitled her to take certain liberties, like she'd obviously done this morning.

When he'd awakened, he was naked, standing in the shower with water beating down on him and Kelisha hovering an arm's length away. She'd tried to towel him off, but he'd rebuffed her actions. After he lumbered back to his bedroom, it was all he could do to pull on his pajama bottoms and fall onto the mattress for a few more hours of sleep.

Jerome was disappointed that he'd allowed this situation to even happen, and he knew he had to fix it right away. "Listen, Kelisha, I appreciate what you've done, but you didn't have to come over here and I didn't ask for your help with anything. I'm not trying to be disrespectful, but c'mon, you know I'm in a relationship. And you and me, we ain't like that anymore."

Just then his cell phone rang on his nightstand. He saw Erica's name flash across the screen and debated whether he should answer. He wanted to hear her voice so badly, but he knew he couldn't risk talking in front of Kelisha, who he was sure would purposely say something in the background so Erica could hear her on the other end.

"I'll walk you to the door," he said.

"Oh, no, your black ass didn't!" Kelisha nearly screamed. "You gonna put me out just 'cause she callin' you. I don't understand you, Jerome! First, you say you want to get back wit me, and now you playin' me off for some uppity bitch and——"

"Hold up. I never said I wanted to get back with you."

"That's not what I heard."

"From who?"

"Who you think?" Kelisha spat. "Oh, just forget it. I ain't got time for this bullshit. I'm out!"

Before Jerome could question her further, Kelisha slammed his front door behind her. He didn't want her leaving in a mad fit, but he was relieved that she was gone. He picked up his phone and hit Erica's number. He waited as it rang and rang, until the call finally went to her voice mail.

"Hey, baby. It's me. Sorry I missed your call. Hit me back." He saw that she'd left a message, so he quickly retrieved it.

"Hey, it's me. I'm actually parked outside your building, getting ready to come up. I guess I'll just knock on your door. See you in a few seconds."

"Shit!" Jerome hung up and rose from his bed. He walked over to open his mini-blinds, and when he looked out his window, he felt as though all the life was draining from his body. He shook his head at the scene taking place two stories below—Erica and Kelisha, standing toe-to-toe.

Chapter 48

Erica's eyes bucked wide when she saw Kelisha staring at her with a smile as she strolled out of Jerome's building. At first she wondered why the heifer was there and who else she knew besides Jerome who lived in the building. But that thought quickly faded because the bounce in Kelisha's step and the satisfied look on her face practically shouted the name of the person she'd been there to see.

How can this be? Erica thought. Her mind quickly went to work imagining possible scenarios, and she determined that this hadn't been just a quick drop-in to say hello. For one, even though they'd met only once, Erica knew that Kelisha wasn't the type of person who walked around with a smile on her face, especially the kind of schoolgirl grin she was now sporting. And second, it was only 9:00 a.m., and the only logical reason she'd have for leaving his apartment at this time of morning was that she'd spent the night.

Erica stood in front of her car, which was parked just a few spaces behind Kelisha's, and tried to stop her emotions from building. The clouds above were threatening rain, looking as though they were about to burst open just like her anger. She locked eyes with Kelisha, who was casually strutting up to her, looking happier than a kid who'd just been given a slice of cake.

"You should get back in your fancy car and leave," Kelisha commanded with a sly smile. "I took care of him real good last night, so your services are no longer needed."

"What's wrong with you? Why can't you leave us alone and let us be happy?"

"Hey, he's the one who called me over here last night."

"I don't believe you."

"You just need to go," Kelisha said, keeping her voice low as she looked over her shoulder.

Erica didn't want to be one of those stereotypical women who fought over a man or, worse still, who fought over a man who was in the wrong! When she was in college, she remembered shaking her head more than once at girls who'd squabble over a cheating boyfriend while the dog in question sat back and went on to eat the meat off another bone. Erica had too much pride to be one of those women.

She looked Kelisha in her eyes. "The only place I'm going is straight upstairs to Jerome's apartment to hear what he has to say."

"He just gon' lie to you."

"You're the one who's lying."

"Bitch, I know you didn't just call me a liar," Kelisha snarled, taking an aggressive step toward Erica.

Erica surprised Kelisha, as well as herself, by making her own equally threatening advance as she spoke. "Don't let the degrees and the smile fool you. I'm not gonna get into a crazy catfight with you, but I'm not gonna stand here and let you call me out of my name, either."

"What you gon' do?" Kelisha smirked, putting her hands on her hips.

"I'm going to call Jerome so he can come down here and we can settle this. I want the truth." Erica reached into her large handbag, pulled out her phone, and hit Jerome's number.

Kelisha huffed as she started walking at a fast pace around to her car. "Bitch, I already told yo stupid ass what happened. He asked me to come over, and we slept together. That's all you need to know."

"That's a damn lie," Jerome said, startling both Erica and Kelisha as he walked toward them. "Erica, baby, she's lying."

Small raindrops had begun to fall, making the chilly air feel even colder. Erica looked at Jerome and didn't know what to believe. He was standing in front of her in a pair of loose-fitting pajama bottoms and the sweater he'd worn yesterday. The faint smell of alcohol wafted up to Erica's nose, causing her to take an inventory of his bloodshot eyes and the uncharacteristically ashen color of his skin.

Erica folded her arms across her chest. "Jerome, what in the hell is going on?"

"I'm outta here!" Kelisha said, hurrying to open her driver's side door.

Jerome walked up to her. "What's your rush? You were talkin' all that shit just a minute ago, and now all of a sudden you ready to go?"

"I don't have to take this," Kelisha yelled.

"First, you didn't want to leave my apartment, because you were tryin' to start trouble, and now you want to go 'cause you're lyin'. Tell the truth," Jerome demanded in an angry voice.

"I already told her what happened. You and me slept together, and you know it!"

"Nothing happened between us last night. That's what I know. Why the hell are you doin' this, Kelisha?" he said.

"Because you told Sasha you wanted me back!"

"What?"

Jerome and Erica both looked at Kelisha with surprise. He'd known that he hadn't heard the last of Sasha after her departing threat in front of the courthouse, and now this explained why Kelisha had been acting so strangely. This had *crazy* written all over it, and the one thing he knew was that Sasha was definitely crazy.

"She told me everything," Kelisha said with a smug look on her face.

"What exactly did she tell you?" he quizzed.

"That while y'all were in court on that trial, all you could talk about was me, and how bad you wanted to get back wit me. But you had to be careful 'cause of that bitch right there," she spat out, looking at Erica. "She crazy just like Tawanna was, and you didn't want her to go off. But you know what? I ain't scared of her!"

Jerome would have laughed if the scene wasn't so messed up, and now he actually felt a little sorry for Kelisha, but only a little. The fact that she'd tried to take advantage of him when he was drunk and then make it seem as if he had called her over and had sex with her quickly riled him back up again.

"You should know by now that if I don't want to be with someone, crazy or not, I know how to cut them loose. Erica is my heart. Plain and simple, and she ain't goin' nowhere."

Kelisha rolled her eyes and shook her head, pointing her acrylic-filled fingernail at Jerome. "That don't change the fact that you and me had sex last night." She breathed hard and then glared at Erica. "And I gave it to him real good." And with that, Kelisha hopped into her car, started the engine, and sped off down the street.

Erica stood in the rain, drenched from head to toe as the heavy drops pounded everything in their path. She looked at Jerome as he stood just a few feet away from her. "What really happened last night?" she asked.

Jerome slowly walked up to her. "Let's go inside."

Chapter 49

Erica sat on the edge of Jerome's small couch, shivering and numb. The startling scene that had unfolded in her living room yesterday had been bad, but now here she was, sitting in the middle of another shit storm. She felt as though she was trapped in a bad reality TV show.

She watched as Jerome went over to the thermostat and adjusted the heat. "You need to get out of those wet clothes before you catch a cold."

"I'm fine. Tell me what Kelisha was doing here."

"Baby, you need to change out of those clothes. You're soaked."

"Your baby mama just said you called her over here and you two had sex. You smell like liquor, and I'm pissed. I want to know what happened."

Jerome came over to the couch and sat beside her. "After everything that went down at your place yesterday, I came home and got drunk. Kelisha showed up last night, bangin' on my door, so I let her in, 'cause I wasn't in the mood to argue."

"She just showed up here for no reason?"

Jerome shook his head. "She talked to Jamel, and he told her that I didn't sound good, which I probably didn't, so she came over to check on me."

Erica took a deep breath, looked down at her feet and then at

Jerome. "Did you sleep with her? Wait, let me correct that. . . . Did you have sex with her?"

"Uh, yes and no. We slept in the same bed, but nothing happened."

"You really expect me to believe that?"

"Baby, it's the truth! She helped me back to my bedroom, and I guess I passed out, because the next thing I knew, I was in the shower this morning."

Erica cut her eyes at him and held up both her hands. "What? How the hell did you end up in the shower with her?"

"She wasn't in there with me. When I came to, I remember standing in the tub with the water coming down on me. She was standing to the side, and when I realized what was happening, I asked her to leave."

"You expect me to believe that your ex-girlfriend tucked you into bed all nice and neat last night and then served as your personal bath butler this morning . . . all without anything happening? Really, Jerome? *Really*?"

"When I walked outside, I heard you tell Kelisha that you didn't believe her lies. So why can't you accept what I'm telling you now?"

"I told her that because I wasn't going to stand there and let her shake me up. But she did, and now I don't know what's true and what isn't."

"Baby, I know it sounds hard to believe, but nothing happened. I can't deny I made a big mistake by letting her in, especially because of my condition last night. But I love you too much to do anything that would hurt you like that. I didn't have sex with her."

Jerome went on to explain in detail all the events that had led up to Kelisha's bald-faced lie. "Erica, I promise you that's all that went on. I know it sounds suspicious, but believe me when I say that you're the only woman I want. Kelisha knows that, and she's trying to drive a wedge between us. You see how fast she left when I came out there. She wanted to get away so she wouldn't get busted, because she knew she was lyin'."

Erica sat in silence, trying to wrap her brain around Jerome's story.

"You believe me, don't you?"

"I received flowers and a phone call from my ex, and you hit the roof, questioning me like I had something to hide. But this . . ." She sighed and paused. "I just don't know what to make of it. I came over here to talk to you about your dad and my mom and all the craziness that ties us together. I wanted to get it all hashed out so we could move forward. But I wasn't expecting to find even more drama. How do you think I felt when I saw Kelisha bouncing out of your building, disrespecting me, calling me a bitch, and saying she slept with you? Do you know how humiliated I felt?"

Jerome eased his body close to Erica's and took her hand in his. "I'm sorry you went through that. But don't worry. I'm gonna get Kelisha straight about the shit she tried to pull."

"Is this what it's going to always be like? Drama every other month? Dysfunction and chaos at every turn? I can't operate like this, Jerome."

"No, it's not gonna always be this way. Sometimes relationships go through bumps and tests. We're just getting ours out of the way early. From here on down the road it's gonna be smooth sailing."

Erica looked into Jerome's eyes. She believed what he'd said about Kelisha because in her heart she knew that he loved her and that he wouldn't do anything to hurt her. But she wasn't completely convinced about his prediction of smooth sailing. They were from different worlds, which had collided even before they met.

"Our past was rocky before we ever laid eyes on each other," Erica said, almost in a whisper. "All last night I kept wondering whether what happened twenty-five years ago was a sign that we were destined to be together, or if it meant the universe is telling me that I need to stay the hell away from you."

Jerome rubbed his hand across the light stubble on his otherwise smooth chin. He shook his head and chuckled lightly. "While I was drinking last night, I was thinking the same thing. I said to myself, 'I finally found a woman who I'm completely in love with, so why is there always some shit tryin' to pull us apart?' But that's when I remembered what my mom always used to say. 'Nothing worth having comes easy.' "

Erica looked at Jerome's strong hands entwined with her own. His words were what she needed to hear. "I've forgiven your father."

Jerome let out a deep breath. "Thank you for saying that. I don't know if he's ever forgiven himself, though. I'm so sorry about all this. But I know through it all, you and me, we're supposed to be together."

Erica wondered what had happened to her always bright optimism. She'd forgiven Parnell for his past aggression because she believed in the power of redemption. So she couldn't understand why her mind was sending her into such a state of doubt when it came to Jerome, a man who made her feel as though nothing was impossible. Yet all she could see was pitfalls.

"Think about all the good times we've had over the past few months," Jerome said as he smiled and squeezed her hand.

Erica smiled with a gleam of love in her eyes. "We've had some amazing times."

"Even right now, with all the shit that happened yesterday and the scene that Kelisha caused this morning, we're still together, sitting here on my couch, soaked to the bone, getting ready to go back to my bedroom and get our freak on."

Erica laughed as Jerome lifted her up from the couch and into his arms. They stood and kissed, their tongues embracing in heated passion. They began to remove each other's clothes, leaving a trail of wet garments on their way to his bedroom. Jerome was about to lay Erica across the bed when she stopped him.

"We need to change these sheets," she said with seriousness. "Just the thought of that woman being in here, in your bed . . ."

Jerome paused and looked at Erica with an undeterminable expression. He opened his mouth to say something, but nothing came out. Without another word he went to the small closet in the hall and came back, holding a fresh pair of sheets.

"Are you okay?" Erica asked with concern.

"Yeah, I'm cool."

But she could see that he clearly wasn't. His brow was scrunched, as if he was deep in thought, and his eyes darted across the room. Erica wondered if she'd offended him with her request, which she thought was well within reason given the circumstances. She watched as he stripped the mattress of its brown sheets and replaced them with

green ones. He still hadn't said a word, and now a look of worry shad-
owed his face.

Damn. What kind of drama is getting ready to happen now? she
thought.

"Jerome, what's wrong? Why are you so quiet, and why do you
look so worried?"

"I'm not worried. I'm just thinking."

She was standing next to his bed, wearing nothing more than an
aqua-blue thong and a frustrated look on her face. The romantic
mood she'd felt when they first entered the room was gone, and she
could tell he felt the same way. He was standing shirtless in his wet pajama bottoms, looking as though he was in a debate with himself. The
tension was starting to unsettle Erica.

"I know something's wrong, so whatever it is, just tell me so we
can deal with it."

Without warning, Jerome dropped to his knees and reached for
Erica's left hand. "I never believed in love at first sight until I met you.
I didn't even think real love was possible, 'cause I've been through so
much. But you changed all that. I love you with everything I have.
You are my world," Jerome said, looking into Erica's big brown eyes.
"I don't want another second to go by without you knowing how
much I want to make you my wife."

Erica was so stunned that it took a minute for her to fully dial
into the moment. Jerome was proposing to her! She took a deep
breath and looked back into the eyes that were staring into hers, eyes
that held truth, honesty, love, and hope.

"You want to marry me?"

"Yes, baby."

Erica knelt down and hugged him tightly. "Yes! I will marry you,
Jerome Kimbrough!"

They hugged and kissed and hugged and kissed some more until
they found their way to the surface of his freshly laundered bedsheets.

"I love you so much," Jerome said between soft kisses.

Erica beamed and smiled as she held out her left hand. "I said yes,
but as the song says, you're gonna have to put a ring on it!" she said
with a playful laugh.

"Oh, I got so carried away, I forgot." Jerome reached behind his nightstand, looked on the floor, pulled out a small black box, and smiled.

All Erica could do was smile back through happy tears, which had begun to trickle from her eyes. Just a few months ago she'd awakened on a bright sunny day to nightmares and fears. And now her cold, gloomy morning was filled with rainbows and shooting stars. She felt blessed beyond measure, and her heart was filled with love that she'd only dreamed about. She smiled as Jerome slipped the beautiful diamond solitaire onto her finger, removing her from the 42.4 percent and leading her into the happily-ever-after she'd always dreamed of.

BREAKING ALL MY RULES

Trice Hickman

ABOUT THIS GUIDE

The questions that follow are included to enhance your group's reading of this book.

Thank you so much for reading *Breaking All My Rules!* I hope you enjoyed the story! Here are some questions I believe will enhance your reading experience and spark some interesting dialogue. If you're a member of a book club, I'd love to join you at your monthly meeting, in person, by phone, or by Skype. (I *love* book clubs!) If you're interested, please visit me at www.tricehickman.com, and we'll make it happen! Happy Discussion!

1. Erica and Jerome were born into different worlds and lived different lifestyles, yet they found their way to each other. Although they were seeming opposites, what were some of the similarities they shared?

2. How likely do you think it is for well-established women/men to date outside their comfort zone, i.e., outside their social/economic class, race, age group, etc.?

3. Which do you think is more challenging—a relationship in which the man is well-to-do and the woman is blue collar, or the reverse? Explain how you arrived at your conclusion.

4. Ashley and Jason seemed to have the perfect relationship, yet they began to struggle. Although there were obvious challenges, what do you think were some of the more subtle problems they faced?

5. Both Erica's and Jerome's parents had turbulent marriages. How do you think their parents' relationships affected their views on love and fidelity?

6. Erica witnessed a violent episode as a child, and Jerome struggled with the absence of his father growing up. Can you point to incidents in the story where each of these events affected the characters' actions?

7. Erica and Jerome were physically attracted to each other at first sight. How important do you think physical attraction is in a relationship?

8. Do you think it's possible to have a successful relationship with someone who treats you well, even though you are not physically attracted to them?

9. Who was your favorite character and why? Who was your least favorite character and why?

10. After the last page of the book, what do you see happening next for the two main characters?

Don't miss more Trice Hickman in

Unexpected Interruptions

On sale now!

Chapter One

*N*ot Necessarily In That Order . . .

"**W**hy is my life so damn complicated?" Victoria asked herself as she steered her car past her circular driveway, toward the car pad in the back. She turned off the engine and sat for a few minutes, reflecting on the last twelve hours of her day. Work and men, not necessarily in that order, had thoroughly wrecked her nerves.

She grabbed her handbag, leather attaché, and umbrella from the passenger seat, took a deep breath, and readied herself for the cold Atlanta rain that had been falling all day. Looking overhead at the evening sky, Victoria could see that it was just as unsettled as her mood. She stuck out one leg, planting her size-nine, black Ferragamo onto the cold, wet pavement. *"Damnit, it's days like this that I wish I'd never turned the garage into a home gym,"* she cursed, quickly pushing her umbrella open as she made a mad dash for the door. She fumbled with her key until it slid into the lock.

"Home sweet home," she said out loud. Each time Victoria walked through her door she felt an immediate sense of comfort. After patiently saving money, buying high-end furniture, scouring antique stores, and then garnering her treasured finds in a storage unit she'd rented, Victoria had finally found her dream home. This month made one year since Sherry Smith, Realtor extraordinaire, had led her to 1701 Summerset Lane.

"Sherry, this house is beautiful!" Victoria had marveled, pulling her long black hair behind her ear as she and Sherry approached the large Tudor-style house.

"I came by first thing this morning to check it out for myself," Sherry smiled, flashing her perfect, cosmetically whitened teeth. "This home is a lovely split level with three large bedrooms including a master suite. There's even an extra bonus room that'll be great for a home office. Victoria, I know you'll just adore the large living and dining rooms; they're perfect for entertaining. And wait 'til you see the hardwood floors, high ceilings, and crown moldings throughout. Believe me, this house is *you,* dear," Sherry gushed, already calculating her sizeable commission.

Things had been very different twelve months ago when Victoria walked into her dream home—out of a recent nightmare. And as she replayed today's events in her mind, she had a funny feeling that her life was about to take an unpredictable turn. Her day had begun with an interesting twist when Ted Thornton knocked on her office door.

Warm Cinnamon Sugar . . .

"Hi, Ted, how are you?" Victoria smiled, startled to see him as she looked up from the stack of papers on her desk.

"I'm well, thank you," he smiled back, allowing his eyes to quickly dart over both Victoria and her office.

Ted Thornton had been hired at ViaTech seven months ago. Lamar Williams, the Founder and CEO of the company, had successfully wooed him from Asco Systems, one of their toughest competitors. Lamar was retiring next spring, and had handpicked Ted as his successor to run the company he'd built from a small storefront into a telecommunications powerhouse. Ted was well known and highly regarded throughout the telecom industry, which made Lamar confident in his choice of the man he both admired professionally and respected personally. It was even rumored that Ted had negotiated a deal with Lamar to become part owner of the privately held company once he assumed the permanent CEO position next spring.

For a man of forty-five, Ted looked younger than his years. He was very handsome . . . one could even say outrageously so. His ocean blue eyes, tall, lean body and confident allure attracted all the women at ViaTech, many of whom boldly flaunted themselves at him. He could have his pick of women, but he was careful, never giving them so much as a second glance. His nonchalance served to make him even more intriguing to his many admirers, particularly since it was no secret that his marriage of over twenty years was about as sunny as London in the fall.

"Victoria, do you have a minute?" Ted asked.

"Sure, have a seat," she said, motioning to the chair in front of her desk. Victoria had only seen Ted twice in the seven months he'd been with ViaTech. Their first encounter had been during her department's senior management meeting. He'd only been with the company for less than a week, and no one had expected him to attend department meetings so soon, or without warning. He had come in, stayed for a few minutes, then left as suddenly as he'd entered.

The second time was two months later when he'd requested individual meetings with senior staff in the Atlanta headquarters office. Their meeting had gone well. They'd started out discussing business strategies and ViaTech's future, then shifted to a more casual conversation: his adjustment from L.A. to Atlanta and her preference of Atlanta over her hometown of Raleigh, North Carolina. They even touched on their personal lives. Nothing too deep. Just nice get-to-know-you questions—Where did you grow up? What are your hobbies and interests? Their meeting ran well over the scheduled thirty minutes, and even Jen, Ted's personal assistant, had said that was a good sign because Ted Thornton wasn't a man prone to wasting time on idle chatter. But up to this moment, Victoria hadn't heard from him since that day many months ago.

Now, he was standing in her office and her mind raced to figure out why the hell he was there. She knew it wasn't every day that the acting CEO just happened to pop in for a visit. Victoria watched as he pulled out one of the leather chairs in front of her desk, unbuttoned the jacket of his gray, custom-made suit, and took a seat. Even though most telecom companies practiced a relaxed dress code, ViaTech employees, save for the engineers, dressed like Wall Street investment bankers. *He's very handsome,* Victoria thought to herself, watching him settle comfortably into the chair.

"You have an incredible office," Ted observed, surveying the room. "The way you've decorated with art on the walls and plants all around . . . it feels more like a room in your home than an office at work. And it smells good too."

Victoria smiled. "It's my job to make our employees feel comfortable when they come to me with problems or concerns, and I believe a welcoming environment helps to foster that." Although she appreciated his discerning eye and obvious good taste, she thought it was an unusual observation to make, given that most of the men at ViaTech could care less about her office's décor and had never commented on the fragrant smell that filled the room. But she noticed that Ted had taken in every detail.

"I like your style, Victoria," Ted smiled.

"Warm cinnamon sugar," she spoke up.

"I beg your pardon?"

"That's what you smell, it's warm cinnamon sugar–scented potpourri."

"Ahh . . . very nice." Ted paused, giving himself a moment before proceeding with the speech he'd been rehearsing for days. "Victoria, as you know, ViaTech is the number two telecom company in the region. But our goal, and my plan, is to make us number one. The only way to hit that target is through the strength of our human capital. Only the best and the brightest can lead this company forward."

Victoria nodded in agreement, but wondered where he was going with the conversation.

"Five years ago the executive management team developed a highly selective year-long mentoring program to identify individuals who show great leadership potential. You're familiar with the program, are you not?" he asked.

"Yes, I'm very familiar with the Executive Mentoring Program. Our department handles the announcements." *Who doesn't know about EMP?* Victoria thought, letting out a frustrated sigh—but only in her head.

The EMP nominations for the upcoming year were due to be announced next week. Victoria was sure that Patricia Clark, the senior director of compliance, would be nominated from their department for the prestigious honor. But she couldn't figure out why Ted had come down to her office to share that information.

"Then all that's left to say is congratulations, Victoria. I'd like to personally nominate you for the program," Ted smiled.

Victoria sat in stunned silence. At thirty-three, she was one of the youngest senior directors in the company. She'd started in the marketing department when she came to ViaTech six years ago after leaving Queens Bank. But after working for a short time in the all-white, male-dominated department, the only upward mobility she saw available required a willing libido, which for her was out of the question. So when the HR department posted an internal search to replace the director of employee relations, Victoria seized the position. A few years later she was promoted to senior director. She excelled in her job, which was a piece of cake compared to the rigors of having worked for Queens Bank. In return for her hard work, ViaTech rewarded her with a handsome salary, bonuses, and perks.

But despite her corporate success, Victoria longed for something else entirely. Her plan was to leave ViaTech next summer and do what her heart had been calling her to do for as long as she could remember—open her own event-planning and catering business. She'd started Divine Occasions a year ago, shortly after she bought her house. Slowly, she'd begun to build a client roster and was putting plans into motion to run her business full-time. Being nominated for EMP was the last thing she'd expected, or wanted for that matter.

"Ted, I'm . . . um . . . honored. I really don't know what to say," Victoria stammered. She came from behind her desk as Ted rose to his feet on her approach. She sat down in the chair beside him, crossed her long legs, and quickly tried to organize her thoughts.

Ted carefully inspected her from the top of her head to the tips of her pointed toe shoes, all done so smoothly she didn't even notice. Her silk blouse, slim fitted skirt, and double strand pearls and matching earrings gave her a decidedly feminine look he loved. "Just say you'll accept my nomination," he encouraged.

"Well, it's just that I'm really shocked by this . . . I wasn't expecting it at all." Victoria's mind raced. All she could think about were her plans to leave ViaTech.

She knew that start-up costs for her business would be high, so she'd decided to work until next June so she could stash extra money under her belt before fleeing the corporate dungeon. Victoria knew that her father would gladly give her as much financial backing as she needed, even without presenting the business plan she'd been working on for months. His guilt, if for nothing else, would dictate that. But this was something she wanted to do on her own. So instead of accepting his money, she planned to apply for a low-interest loan just like any other bank customer. Besides, she knew that her cousin, Jeremy, who was now helping to run Queens Bank, which her father owned, would probably demand a perusal of her business plan. In Victoria's opinion, Jeremy was a first-class asshole.

She knew she had to ease out of the EMP nomination without giving away her plans. Her father had taught her the golden rule of corporate America—never let them know all your business!

Ted sensed her trepidation. "Victoria, you seem a little hesitant?" He was trying to figure out why a go-getter like her wasn't jumping at the golden opportunity he'd just laid before her.

"Actually, I am. The truth is, I have a lot on my plate right now." She could see the surprise on Ted's face, but she continued. "It's just bad timing. I believe in giving one-hundred percent, and if I don't see that it's possible for me to do my best, I don't commit. That's why as much as I'm flattered by the nomination . . . "

"Victoria," Ted interrupted, "I understand your concerns. And yes, committing yourself to this program will require extra hours and projects, in addition to your normal workload. But I'll see to it that you have the support and resources you'll need."

Ted hadn't planned on Victoria turning him down, and now he was scrambling to convince her to accept his nomination. He'd been looking for a way to spend time with her since the first day they met. But without a legitimate work-related project, the acting CEO couldn't spend leisure office time with one of his many employees unless there was a damn good reason.

Initially, Ted questioned his decision for choosing Victoria. Was it because he was attracted to her, or was it because she deserved to be in the program? In the end he realized it was both. Her outstanding reviews, high praise from the executive team, and her record of achievement made her a prime candidate. And an added bonus was that he would finally be able to spend time with the woman he'd been thinking about and desiring from afar.

"Ted . . . again, I appreciate the consideration and vote of confidence. But as I said, it's bad timing."

"I must say, I'm disappointed." Ted leaned back in his chair, quickly plotting his next move. "The nominations won't be finalized until next Friday. I'd like you to take a week and think it over," he asked, masking his desperation. He stood and buttoned his suit jacket, signaling that he was about to leave.

Victoria rose on cue. "All right, I'll think about it," she said, even though she knew her answer wouldn't change.

As she watched him walk out of her office, she could feel there was something arrestingly different about him. He wasn't like most executive types she knew. He seemed familiar, almost like she knew him, even though this was only their third encounter.

Just as she returned to her desk to finish her paperwork, Denise, her administrative assistant, walked through the door. She stood there, arms crossed and staring. "Girlfriend, what kind of excuse are you gonna come up with for not accepting that man's EMP nomination? Telling him you can't dedicate one-hundred percent is some bullshit that ain't gonna fly."

"Have you been out there listening?"

"Absolutely. You know I gotta get the 411," she grinned.

Victoria pictured Denise standing outside her door with a glass cupped to her ear like a detective in a 1960's spy movie. Denise called Victoria by her given name in the presence of their colleagues, but when they were alone she affectionately referred to her as "Girlfriend."

Denise was impeccably dressed, well-organized, and knew her job inside-out. She was an unabashed woman who could read you like last week's news, yet be gentle as a lamb when the occasion warranted. There were three things about Denise that were constant: She always smelled of Chanel No. 5, her pretty, apple-shaped face always boasted a smile, and she always shot straight from the hip, never sugar coating anything. She had an Associate's degree in Administrative Office Technology and a PhD in common sense. She was sharper than a J.A. Henckels carving knife, and Victoria relied heavily upon her insight.

"Denise, why didn't you tell me that Ted Thornton was coming to my office? I was completely caught off-guard."

"Sorry. He must've come by my desk while I was in the copy room," Denise said, handing Victoria a thick stack of papers. "When I came back your door was half-closed. I was going to come in and see what was going on, but then I heard you two talking, and well . . . I listened because Mr. Thornton never comes down to anyone's office," she said, placing her hands on her ample hips.

"I'm shocked. I just knew that Patricia had the nomination in the bag, at least that's what she's been telling everyone. Can you imagine how embarrassing it's going to be for her when she finds out that she's not one of the ten nominees?"

"That's *her* problem. This is one time she can't throw her legs open to get what she wants. That woman is so shady, I wouldn't trust her with the keys to the shit house."

"Damn!" Victoria laughed. "You're right about that. But seriously, Ted Thornton can give me a week or even a month, I'm not going to change my mind."

"And you shouldn't. You've put your dream on hold long enough. You have to make yourself happy, Girlfriend."

"Tell me about it. I'm tired of running my business on the side and trying to maintain this job at the same time. It's really taken a toll over the last year. I just wish I'd had the courage to make this decision sooner," Victoria lamented.

"Things don't always work out the way we want them to. Things happen over time, not overnight."

"Yeah, that's true. And it's time for me to stop letting other people's expectations and my own fear impede my happiness," Victoria said with confidence, thinking about the sacrifices she'd made to please others, like when she wanted to attend culinary school after high school graduation.

She could still hear her father's words ringing in her ear. "No child of mine with a near-perfect SAT score is going to school to learn how to cook and throw parties for a living. What kind of profession is that anyway? Your mother and I want so much more for you. Who knows, maybe one day you'll take over the bank," he'd hinted.

"But Daddy," Victoria challenged, "event planning and catering can be a lucrative profession, just like any other service . . . like the bank. Besides, I'm good at it. Look how well the homecoming party turned out that I planned. Everyone said it was the best party Alexander Prep has ever seen!"

"Planning a homecoming party in a gymnasium and mapping out your future are two entirely different things," her father cautioned. "Victoria, you're my little Queen, and it's my responsibility to make sure that I prepare you for the real world."

After months of arguments and listening to her mother's pleas of intervention, Victoria appeased her father. She enrolled at Spelman College, majored in finance, and minored in coordinating birthday parties, graduation celebrations, and any other kind of festive event she could plan. After graduation, she went on to earn her MBA from Wharton, her father's alma mater—again, obeying his wishes. She'd surprised herself when she discovered that she actually enjoyed the curriculum, knowing that her training would come in handy one day when she started her own business. But in the meantime, she put her dreams on hold and went to work at her father's bank, which he'd named in honor of her and her mother—his two Nubian Queens.

Victoria focused on marketing and community relations at the bank. She planned and executed promotional campaigns, community outreach events, and employee programs. She frustrated her father by doing what he called "fluff work" instead of digging into the "meat" of the bank—dealing with operations and finance. After they butted heads one too many times, Victoria decided to leave. She dusted off her resume and started looking for a new job. Within a month she landed a position with ViaTech. She packed her bags and moved to Atlanta, putting her back in the city where she'd gone to college and the city she'd grown to love.

"Girlfriend, you know I got your back and your front, whether I'm helping you with memos here or planning a party with Divine Occasions," Denise said.

"Thanks, you're such a good friend."

"No need to thank me, you're my girl. Now, you better get ready for your lunch date with Mr. Might-Be-Right."

"I just hope he's Mr. I-Am-Sane! I'm really not up for any drama."

"This is your first date in over a year. Just be positive. You know that saying . . . we get back what we bring forth."

"Preach, Oprah," Victoria teased as they broke into laughter.

You Like Adventure, Don't You? . . .

I hope he's gonna be worth me getting out in this cold rain, Victoria thought as she glanced at her Baume & Mercier dangling from her wrist, and realized she was running late for her lunch date.

"Victoria, I know you'll love him," her friend Debbie had said with enthusiasm. "Vincent is tall, handsome, and *really* nice. Now, he's a little on the shy side and doesn't talk a whole lot, but he's very sweet. And oh yeah, he's a consultant. I know you two will hit it off!"

Debbie and her husband Rob had met Vincent a few weeks ago at the gym, and she thought he'd be perfect for Victoria. Debbie Long was a professor in the art department at Emory University, and one of Victoria's closest and dearest friends. They'd been roommates in graduate school, helping each other labor through insanely demanding course work. But after a semester of Probability and Statistics, Debbie decided that business school wasn't for her. She changed her major, breezed through the History of Art curriculum, then accepted a faculty position at Emory. When Victoria had moved back to the area, Debbie was thrilled that they were in the same city once again.

Victoria was both nervous and excited as she turned her silver Audi into the restaurant's parking lot. This was truly out of character for her. She'd never been on a blind date, let alone agreed to go out with someone she'd never even spoken to over the phone. Debbie had set up everything because she was afraid that if left to Victoria, the date would never happen. She knew her college buddy would just find another excuse for not getting back into the dating scene, and Debbie thought it was high time her friend jumped back in with both feet.

Boy, this is a nasty day. But at least it's Friday, and who knows . . . this lunch date might be the beginning of a good weekend. Just think positive, Victoria encouraged herself, walking into the restaurant with a spring in her step. She shook out her umbrella, ran her fingers through her long, silky mane, and looked around for Vincent. Debbie told her that he'd meet her at the hostess stand, so Victoria knew that the first tall, handsome, black man she saw standing up front would be him. She saw a man coming toward her.

"Whassup baby, you must be Victoria. Damn, a sistah's fine!"

Oh my God. How does this man know my name? Victoria wondered.

"I'm Vincent Frank," the man said, extending his hand. "I been waitin' about ten minutes, but now I see it was well worth it," he grinned, looking Victoria up and down like she was an item on the menu. "C'mon baby, let's get our eat on." He motioned for Victoria to walk in front of him as they followed the hostess back to their table.

Victoria was in shock and had to remind herself to breathe. The hostess seated them and gave Victoria a look that said *"you poor thing"* before walking away.

"Well, well, well, I hit the jackpot witchu', baby. Debbie said you was beautiful and all, but you know how some white folks be thinkin' that just 'cause you a sistah, that you all exotic and shit. So they think you look good, know what I'm sayin'? But, baby, she was right about you . . . you a stone cold killa!"

Victoria bristled at his words, feeling as though the air had been sucked out of the room. *Breathe, breathe,* she told herself. Vincent was talking, his lips were moving, but she couldn't hear a word he was saying. She was too busy trying to process the visual before her eyes. He was wearing two-tone alligator shoes and a green suede pantsuit. A playboy bunny medallion dangled from a thick gold rope chain around his neck, so big she could have snatched it off and started a game of Double Dutch. His gold tooth was centered in the front of his mouth, and each time he smiled it gleamed against the flickering light of the votive candle on the table. When he lifted his hand to stroke his goatee, Victoria nearly choked at the sight of his large, diamond encrusted gold watch, accented by a gold nugget ring on his pinky finger. The crowning touch were his two-carat diamond studs, blinging loud in each ear. Victoria stared at him, feeling faint.

She thought about Debbie's description of Vincent, and so far she was only half right. She'd said he was tall, handsome, shy and educated. *He's tall and cute, in a slick, bad-boy, hustler-on-the-street kinda way. But he's definitely not shy, and he doesn't sound educated. Come to think of it, Debbie never mentioned where he went to college.*

Victoria had just assumed that because he was a consultant, he must have an MBA and work for one of the major firms. Her mind was swirling with confusion.

Snap, snap! Vincent popped his fingers, breaking Victoria's trance. The server was standing at the table, ready to take their order.

"Hey, baby, I know you captivated and all," Vincent smiled, using his hands to showcase himself like a game show prize, "but let's get some drinks goin' on."

"What will the lady have to drink?" the server asked.

"I'll have a glass of Pellegrino, please."

"I like a woman who ain't afraid to get her drink on durin' her lunch hour. You like adventure, don't you?" Vincent winked.

"It's not alcohol, it's sparkling water," Victoria blinked with disbelief.

"Oh, you a sophisticated sistah," he grinned. "I'll have a Bud."

Oh my God! I'm gonna kill Debbie! Victoria repeated in her head. *But wait . . . slow down. Maybe I'm being too judgmental. He's not the kind of guy I usually go for, but maybe I should give Vincent a chance.*

"Yeah, I think we gonna hit it off real nice, know what I'm sayin'? You tall, dark and luscious and I'm the real deal. You lookin' at a total package right here, baby," Vincent said, making a fist and pounding his chest.

Can this get any worse? Victoria was beginning to think that her first impression had been right on target.

"I usually date redbones, but you look so good I'm willin' to make you the exception 'cause that body is tight. And I love a sistah wit' good hair all down her back." Vincent grinned. "Yeah, I can tell it's real. It ain't no weave, that's all you, baby . . . you the shit, you know that?" Vincent smiled, licking his full lips. He leaned against the side of the booth, pleased with himself, like he'd just given Victoria a real compliment.

Did his simple ass just say what I think he said? This fool is clearly hauling around a heavy load of plantation luggage! Victoria was pissed. "I didn't know you had a hair and skin-color requirement, or was that a back-handed compliment you just slapped across my face?" she said in her best *go to hell* tone. Vincent's complexion was the color of light caramel, sufficiently qualifying him to pass the dreaded brown paper bag test.

Vincent threw his hands up in surrender. "Whoa, whoa, baby girl. You fine as hell, no matter what the color. I'm just tryin' to be real about my shit. I usually date light skinned babes, know what I'm sayin'? But wit' all that junk in yo' trunk, a brothah's got to get wit' that!"

Okay, this jackass has lost his damn mind! Victoria tried to restrain herself by taking another deep breath. She cleared her throat before she spoke. "Debbie gave me the impression that you were . . . well . . . not as *extroverted* as you appear to be," she said, struggling to hold back her displeasure.

"I like the way you use them big words," he smiled as Victoria's eyes bucked wide at his statement. "Well, you know how you gotta play the role wit' white folks, talkin' all proper . . . like you sound. You know, make'em feel comfortable and what-not. But witchu' . . . you family, I can be myself, know what I'm sayin'?"

What the hell? Okay, that's it! Victoria looked at Vincent with near disgust. She was ready to leave, but being a human resources professional she had to know what reputable firm was foolish enough to hire the asshole sitting in front of her.

"Tell me, Vincent . . . what firm are you with?"

"Oh, I work for my family's company."

"And that would be?"

"Franks' Pest Control," he said with pride.

Victoria looked puzzled. "But Debbie said you told her that you're a consultant?"

"Yeah, I am. You see, I go to a client's house and evaluate what kinda pest or rodent problem they have and then I consult wit'em on how to treat it. Know what I'm sayin' . . . I'm a consul'ant, baby."

Oh, hell no! Victoria couldn't take it any longer. Vincent's racial snides, profanity, misrepresentation, and flashy jewelry had all pushed her well beyond her limit.

"Mr. Frank, my name isn't baby, it's Victoria . . . Ms. Small to you." And with that, Victoria grabbed her belongings and started to slide out of the booth.

"Where you goin'?" Vincent asked with surprise.

"Anywhere you're not!"

"I can't believe you snooty, educated bitches! Y'all sistahs always cryin' the blues 'bout how you want a good black man, but when you get one you can't handle us. Don't know how to 'preciate a good brothah. I got a good job, ain't got no kids, ain't never been arrested, and I got a top of the line Sentra parked out front . . . fully loaded. I got females sweatin' me left and right tryin' to get wit' this," Vincent said loudly, pounding his chest again.

People sitting at the surrounding tables and booths began to look in their direction. Just then, the server came back with their drinks as Victoria pushed past him and stood. "Your stupid ass is crazy," she hissed, just loud enough for Vincent to hear.

"Go 'head then, step off. I'm tired of dealin' wit' sistahs that be trippin' anyway. That's why I'ma get me a white woman. They know how to 'preciate a good man," Vincent sneered, taking his glass of beer from the server's tray.

Mortified, Victoria let out a small gasp. She looked over her shoulder and saw a gray-haired older white woman put her hand to her mouth in shock. She wanted to grab her glass of sparkling water and throw it in Vincent's face, but instead she simply held her head high, walked away and never looked back. The server just stood there—speechless.

Isn't It Incredibly Cool? . . .

"What were you thinking, setting me up with that jackass?" Victoria asked Debbie, speaking into her hands-free headset as she drove back to work.

"What're you talking about? Vincent is a really sweet guy."

"Yeah, about as sweet as strychnine! He was putting on an act for you. He's not shy at all. He was just quiet around you so you wouldn't find out how crazy he really is."

"I don't get it . . . what did he do to make you so upset?"

"Well, for one thing he was wearing a green suede pantsuit, and tons of jewelry. He looked like a reject from a low-budget rap video."

Debbie shook her head on the other end of the line. "God, Victoria. You've always been picky as hell when it comes to clothes and men. Loosen up, why don't you?"

"You've got to be kidding!" Victoria nearly screamed. But what did she expect from a woman whose wardrobe consisted of tie-dye shirts and broomstick skirts. Debbie was a free spirit and liked guys with an edge. She'd stunned her family and friends when she settled down and married a guy as straight-laced and normal as Rob. The truth was, the only reason Victoria had agreed to the date was because Rob had given Vincent his stamp of approval. Victoria loved her friend, but she knew that she and Debbie had very different tastes.

They were complete opposites. Victoria was tall, African-American, and refined. Debbie was short, Caucasian, and a wild, artsy-fartsy kinda gal. Victoria wore heels, while Debbie wore Birkenstocks. Victoria ate sushi, while Debbie preferred Ramen noodles. Victoria sipped mocha lattes, while Debbie drank hot water and valerian root. But over the years they'd become as close as any blood sisters could be.

"When I met him he was wearing the cutest T-shirt and shorts," Debbie countered, trying to defend Vincent.

"That doesn't count. It's hard to foul up workout gear!"

"Okay, so what if he's not the best dresser? You can't just throw out the baby with the bath water!"

"Debbie, he had a *gold* tooth."

"I know, isn't it incredibly cool?"

"I don't believe you just said that," Victoria strained. She had one hand on the wheel and the other on her head. Things like this brought up their differences. To Debbie, a gold tooth was *incredibly cool*. To Victoria, it was the equivalent of the grim reaper's kiss of death.

"Victoria, I think you're overreacting. You need to be more open-minded."

Victoria ignored her statement. "Debbie, he was loud, obnoxious and completely uncouth. But I've saved the best for last. Let me tell you the absolute *worst* part of this bullshit date, and the real reason why I'm so upset! That idiot told me he was making an exception by going out with me because he normally only dates light skinned women, but because I have a nice ass and *good* hair, I get a pass. Then he told me that he puts on his 'good guy' act for white folks . . . like you . . . to make *y'all* feel comfortable with his stupid ass," Victoria huffed. "I should've walked away when I first saw him, but *nooooo*, I was trying to be *open-minded!*" she shouted, ending her tirade.

"Oh shit," Debbie whispered in a low voice. "Victoria, I'm so sorry. I had no idea Vincent was like that. I guess I made a terrible, terrible mistake."

"I can't believe Rob thought that asshole was cool. He usually has better judgment about people."

"Well, actually . . . um . . . he and Rob only played basketball one time. Vincent's in my aerobics class, and honestly, he seemed so nice. When I found out he was single, I immediately thought about you. You know, because it's been so long since you've gone out with anyone. Not since . . . "

"Don't say his name," Victoria snapped.

"I wasn't going to . . . Victoria, you're my friend and I care about you. It's been a year . . ."

There was a silent pause.

Debbie was one of the most sincere and caring people Victoria knew, and was sensitive to a fault. She knew that her friend meant well, and she felt bad for yelling at her. "I guess I should've talked to that fool myself before agreeing to go out with him. And you're right, I do need to start dating again, this just wasn't the guy to do it with," she said, softening her tone.

"I'm really, really sorry," Debbie apologized again. "So . . . do you forgive me? Are we cool?"

"Yes, I forgive you. And we're always cool, you know that."

"Good," Debbie breathed with relief. "Hey, are you still meeting us at Sambuca tomorrow night? You better say yes, I'll even buy all your drinks. . . . It's the least I can do."

Damn, I forgot about tomorrow night, Victoria sighed to herself.

She'd promised her friends she would join them, and she knew that if she bailed out once again she'd never hear the end of it. "It's time for you to start going out again," she could hear them saying. So in spite of her reluctance, she told Debbie she would be there.

After ending their call, Victoria pulled into the ViaTech parking garage and headed into the building. She tried to brush off her frustration as she rode the elevator up to her office, but all she could think about was the name that Debbie had almost called out, and the pain that still lingered from the man tied to it.

The Nerve . . .

Victoria sat at her desk and checked her e-mail as she filled Denise in on the details of her horrifying lunch date.

"Girlfriend, tell me you're lyin'!" Denise said, shaking her head.

"I lie to you not."

"Humph, that's a damn shame for anyone to act that way. His attitude was loud and wrong. My grandmother always said to stay clear of people with two first names . . . can't be trusted."

Victoria nodded, but then frowned as she read her most recent message. "I just got an e-mail from Patricia. This woman is so obnoxious."

"What does it say?"

"Brace yourself for this," Victoria said as she read the e-mail aloud.

Date: Fri. October 1 2:01 p.m.
From: patricia.clark@ViaTech.net
To: victoria.small@ViaTech.net

Subject: SME Report: URGENT!

I want to make sure you have the SME report on my desk before the Wed. Oct. 6 deadline. I need to get started on this project ASAP, as my workload will increase once the EMP nominations are announced. Naturally, my nomination will dictate that I spend the ma-

jority of my time on program related issues. Make sure you get this
to me on time.
PC

Patricia Clark had always considered herself a perfect ten. She
loved her creamy porcelain complexion, super thin body, and
Angelina Jolie-like lips. She thought her only shortcomings were her
small eyes, outlined with crow's feet, and her slightly wrinkled neck,
announcing her membership in the forty and over club. That
notwithstanding, her crowning glory was her platinum blond hair,
compliments of L'Oréal, and her big boobs, compliments of Dr. Jerry
Steiner & Associates Surgical Center. *What more could you ask for?* was
her attitude. She didn't have a college degree, but she'd managed to
work her way up the corporate ladder with what she called "friendly
ingenuity," or sleeping her way to the top, as everyone else accurately
pinned her tools for success.

Patricia had it in for Victoria from the first day they met. When
Victoria turned in her reports, her work was error-free, which made
Patricia suspicious. She believed that Victoria was getting other
people to do the work for her. *How else could she do such a good job?*
she often thought, discounting the fact that Victoria held an MBA
from one of the top business schools in the country. And she didn't
understand how Victoria could work twelve-hour days and still find
time to bake homemade treats to bring to the office. Everyone loved
Victoria, and Patricia couldn't stand it.

"The nerve," Denise fumed. "Like she's even being considered for
EMP. I wish you would accept Mr. Thornton's offer just so I could
see her shit a brick. She's more fake than those flotation devices she
masquerades as breasts. She's one sneaky bitch. I'm telling you right
now, you gotta watch her."

Victoria knew Denise was right. That's why she decided she
would come in this weekend and work on the SME report to make
sure it was ready in time for the Wednesday deadline.

And that was how her day had gone . . . so far.

Catch a sneak peek of Trice Hickman's

Keeping Secrets & Telling Lies

On sale in July 2013!

Chapter One

Still Going Strong . . .

"Listen," Victoria whispered. "Did you hear that?"

"V, it was nothing," Ted whispered back in a low moan, breathing hard into his wife's ear as he pressed his hard body against her soft curves.

"No . . . listen. I think she's up."

Knock, knock, knock.

There was no mistaking the faint sound of small knuckles rapping on the door. Victoria quickly adjusted the spaghetti strap of her silk teddy as she sat up in bed. She could still feel Ted's warm body next to hers as she gathered the sateen sheet around her waist.

"Mommy, Daddy . . . it's morning time!" Alexandria called out in a high-pitched squeal, peering into her parents' bedroom through the crack in the door. "Are you up?"

Ted sat up beside Victoria and sighed. As much as he loved his precious little daughter, he also cherished his alone time with his wife, especially since it was something they seemed to have very little of lately.

Over the last several months he'd been spending extra-long hours at the office in preparation for taking his company public next year. ViaTech had survived the telecom industry's downturn several years back and was now poised to make a strong initial public offering next spring. And Victoria's days were just as long and hectic, because her business kept her equally on the go. Divine Occasions, her event-

planning and catering company, was in its sixth year of full-time op-
eration and had established her as one of Atlanta's most sought after
event coordinators.

But despite Ted's and Victoria's jam-packed work schedules, they
always made sure to carve out time for their daughter. She was the
single most important part of their lives. On evenings when Victoria
didn't have an event to oversee, she was diligent about spending quality time with Alexandria, making sure that she prepared dinner so
they could eat together. And most nights when Ted wasn't out of
town on business, he managed to return home from the office just in
time to tuck her in and read her a bedtime story. After their professional and parental duties ended for the day, they'd steal a few treasured moments together before falling off to sleep.

"Yes, we're up, sweetie," Victoria answered.

With that, Alexandria came barreling into the room, ponytails
flying and a grin on her face as big as the sky. She ran up to her parents' large four-poster bed, using the antique mahogany footstool as a
springboard to hop in between them. She giggled hard as she made an
indentation where she landed in the soft jacquard-print comforter.
"It's morning time, Mommy and Daddy!" she shouted again, full of
all the excitement that a combination of Saturday morning cartoons
and the promise of an afternoon playdate could bring to a five-year-
old.

Ted put his hand to his chest and fell back onto the bed, pretending to suffer an imaginary attack. "You yelled so loud, I think you
gave me a heart attack," he teased.

Alexandria stopped grinning and stared at her father. Her face
carried an odd, serious look. "Daddy, are you all right?" she said softly,
putting her small hand on his broad chest. "Don't have a heart attack,"
she whispered, peering into his deep blue eyes.

Ted couldn't help but let out a laugh. Alexandria Elizabeth
Thornton was the joy of her parents' hearts and, as they had both
come to agree, was one of the most serious five-year-olds to ever own
a pack of Crayolas. She was playful and exuberant, yet incredibly mature and cerebral for someone who could claim only graduating from
preschool as her highest level of academic achievement to date.

She was what her nana Elizabeth called an old soul. "That child has been here before. Any child who has that much common sense has walked this earth and seen things in another lifetime," Victoria's mother often said.

"No, sweetie. Your father's fine," Victoria reassured. "You just startled us. What have I told you about using your inside voice?" she lightly scolded.

Alexandria didn't answer right away. "Daddy, your heart's not right?" she said, tilting her head to the side, making it sound more like a pronouncement than a question.

Victoria didn't know why, but something in her daughter's tone put a chill on her arm.

"Daddy's fine, princess." Ted smiled, grabbing Alexandria and tickling her until she dropped her frown and began smiling along with him.

Victoria tried to smile, too, but she felt unsettled by Alexandria's comment and reaction to what should have been a playful moment. She looked into her daughter's eyes, wanting to reassure her again. "Sweetie, your father's fine. He was just playing around, okay?"

Alexandria nodded in compliance but still didn't look completely convinced. "Can I watch Big Bird?" she asked in her small, high-pitched voice.

"Sure, princess. I'll set it up for you downstairs." Ted reached under the comforter, pulled his pajama bottoms up to his waist, then leaned over and whispered into Victoria's ear. "When I get back, we'll pick up where we left off." He winked, then scooped Alexandria off the bed and headed downstairs.

Victoria watched her husband and daughter as their heads disappeared down the long hallway. She marveled at the way Alexandria had Ted wrapped around her finger. It reminded her of the relationship she'd shared with her own father when she was growing up. Alexandria was Ted's little princess, just as she'd been her father's little queen.

Victoria stretched her arms high above her head and thought about the busy day that lay before her. First on her list was dropping off Alexandria at her first Jack and Jill playdate, then making a quick trip to her office to go over the remaining details for a large celebrity wedding she was coordinating next weekend. After that, she planned to head back over to pick up Alexandria, drive across town to pick up Ted's dry cleaning, and then swing by the grocery store before she took Alexandria to their neighbor's house for a sleepover.

At times, Victoria felt as though she didn't have time to think, let alone breathe. She always seemed to be going to this, hurrying there, or coming from that. Running her business required her to put on a good face for the public, even when she felt crappy. Motherhood demanded that she appear eager and attentive, even when she felt exhausted. And being a wife meant she had to master the delicate art of compromise, even when she wanted to do her own thing.

But she knew there were worse things than having a busy life, and she knew that a lot of women would gladly trade places with her in a heartbeat. She was blessed to have a happy, healthy daughter who was as smart as a whip, and whose loving spirit made her a joy to raise. And even though she wished her husband spent more time at home and less time away on business, and had fewer late nights at the office, she knew that he loved and adored her. She lived in a custom-built home in an exclusive gated community. Her child-care service was reliable and trusted, and she was fortunate to have neighbors and friends who gladly pitched in to help. She had quit her corporate job several years ago to pursue a passion she'd had since childhood, and to top it all off, she was in good physical health. Yes, she knew she was blessed, and she knew there were worse things than busy days.

After Ted secured Alexandria in front of the TV, with her juice box in one hand, the remote control in the other, and her favorite DVD playing, he hurried back upstairs, taking the steps two at a time. When he walked into the bedroom, a smile slid across his face.

Victoria was waiting for him, perched on her knees in the middle of their king-size bed. Her silk teddy and lacy thong had been tossed to the side, and the look on her face said she remembered his parting words. She was ready to pick up exactly where they'd left off.

Ted was struck by the fact that even though he had seen his wife's naked body a million times, her sensuous allure and striking beauty never failed to stir him. He loved the velvety smoothness of her deep chocolate brown skin, which always felt soft to the touch. He took pleasure in running his fingers through the silky thickness of her long black hair, which draped the slender elegance of her neck. And he felt he could lose himself in the gentle curve of her lower back, which gave way to the seductive pull of her soft, round behind. Motherhood had given her slim figure slightly more weight and an added sexiness that he loved.

"Damn, you're beautiful," he said, removing his pajama bottoms. He pulled the door closed behind him and walked toward the bed.

Victoria smiled, enjoying the look that always came over Ted's face when they were about to make love. It let her know that he wanted her. He climbed into bed, covering her naked body with his. She embraced the feel of her husband's tall, muscular frame as she prepared herself for the pleasure to come.

He kissed her slow and deep, gently tweaking her hardening nipples with his fingers before moving down, alternating between his hands and mouth as he suckled her soft mounds of flesh. He eased his way farther down her body, placing small kisses along a man-made trail, until his head rested between her legs.

"I love it when you're this wet," Ted breathed, gently rolling his tongue over her throbbing tenderness. Victoria threw her head back, digging her heels deep into the mattress as she clenched the bedsheet between her fists. He placed one hand under her hips and the other at the center of her warm middle. He worked with diligence, licking, sucking, and gently kissing her glistening folds. He took his time, devouring every inch of her sweet spot until she shuddered into a creamy orgasm that made her tremble. She released a deep, ecstasy-filled moan that rumbled in the back of her throat.

After a brief moment, Victoria regained her senses, ready to give Ted the same intense pleasure she'd just received. She secured her hands around him, holding him in her firm but gentle grip as she stroked his hardness, massaging him with care. A long, slow "mmm" escaped his lips as Victoria worked her magic. She opened her mouth wide and swallowed him, sucking and licking with controlled precision. When she squeezed the tip of his head deep into her tightening mouth, he could barely hold on any longer.

"Ooh, V," Ted moaned, perspiration dampening his skin. He shifted positions, gently laying Victoria on her back as she wrapped her long legs around his waist, arching her pelvis into the air to meet his. He slipped inside her with smooth, even strokes as they made love. Her body received him as he moved in and out, delighting and electrifying her all at once. Their rhythm was a slow and easy grind that flowed into a growing and heated frenzy as Ted went deeper, increasing the speed of his thrusts. Victoria moaned, clinging to his sex-drenched, sweaty body while she worked her hips at an equally hungry pace. Finally, they both surrendered to a second wave of pleasure.

Victoria reveled in her husband's ability to fulfill her sexual desires. He knew exactly how to please her, anticipating her wants and knowing her most intimate needs. Over the course of their six-year marriage, even though the frequency of their lovemaking had slowed, he had never left her wanting. This was yet another one of her many blessings, and again, she knew there was a multitude of women who would kill to be in her shoes.

She had heard more than a few of her friends and clients complain about their dead sex lives, citing disgruntled husbands, over-active children, and underactive libidos as major culprits. One of her best friends, Debbie Long, who was like the sister she'd never had, had recently confided that since the birth of her son seven years ago, her love life with her husband had dwindled to a state of near nonexistence.

"We're like roommates," Debbie had told Victoria a few months ago. "We love each other, but the passion is gone. We're just going through the motions. As a matter of fact, I can't remember the last time Rob and I made love," she'd complained.

Victoria had been shocked to learn that Debbie and Rob's marriage had shriveled into the dull, sexless picture her friend had painted, especially since she and Rob had always been romantic and affectionate with each other. Aside from her parents' strong and lasting union, Victoria had regarded Debbie and Rob's relationship as the gold standard by which marriage could be measured.

But as Victoria would soon come to learn in the weeks ahead, time and circumstances were instruments that could change the tune of one's life in shocking and unexpected ways.

Looking at her own relationship made Victoria feel grateful that she and Ted were still going strong. She knew their marriage wasn't perfect, but they had love and trust as their anchors. The sex was hot, and he made sure that he pleased her. He was in excellent physical health, and his age-defying good looks made him appear a decade younger than his fifty-two years. His vanilla-hued skin had a hint of olive and was taut and supple, with hardly a trace of wrinkles, and the subtle hints of gray that now peppered his thick black hair added to his outrageous sex appeal. He kept his muscles strong and well toned with regular workouts, and jogged several times a week to round out his physical fitness regimen. Having a mate like Ted was what Victoria had always dreamed of, and again, she knew she was blessed.

After making love, Victoria lay next to her husband, running her fingers across the faint dark hairs on his broad chest. "Alexandria's movie is probably half over by now," she said.

"Uh-huh," Ted answered in a dreamy, after-sex voice.

"I'm gonna take a shower and go downstairs to make Alexandria's breakfast. We have a busy day ahead, and I need to run a few errands before I drop her off at Susan's later this afternoon."

"Another sleepover?"

"Yep."

Ted pulled Victoria on top of him and grinned. "That means we'll have tonight all to ourselves."

"Mmmm, we sure will." She nodded.

They enjoyed a long kiss before Victoria rolled out of bed.

That Thing . . .

Fresh from the shower, Victoria headed downstairs. She walked into her large family room, adjacent to the gourmet kitchen, and found Alexandria engrossed in the classic *Big Bird's Big Adventure*. The movie held her complete attention. It was a treat for Alexandria, because Victoria and Ted didn't allow her to watch television on weekdays unless it was educational programming. Weekends were her time to "veg out," as they liked to say.

Victoria poured Alexandria's Cheerios into her cereal bowl and sat it on the breakfast table, along with a glass of orange juice. "Alexandria, come and eat your breakfast, sweetie," she called out.

Alexandria walked slowly toward the breakfast table, pulling out the chair closest to the family room, angling it so she could see the large-screen TV from where she sat.

"Wash your hands before you eat, young lady," Victoria said as she split a bagel and popped it into the toaster.

"Yes, ma'am." Alexandria made her way over to her step stool by the sink, singing along with the song that Big Bird was belting out.

A few minutes later Ted walked into the kitchen, still wearing his pajama bottoms and a T-shirt. He came up behind Victoria at the large granite island and rubbed his pelvis against her curvy backside. He lifted her heavy mass of hair to the side and kissed the crook of her neck.

"Ted, your daughter's right over there," Victoria playfully cautioned, tilting her head to where Alexandria was sitting at the breakfast table.

"She's so into that DVD, she doesn't even know we're here."

"You're probably right," she laughed. "Didn't you get enough this morning?"

"Not hardly." Ted held Victoria close and kissed the side of her neck again. She was his second wife, but his first and only love.

After being trapped in a miserable marriage by a conniving, gold-digging wife for more than twenty years, Ted had given up on the possibility of emotional happiness, let alone the idea of love. Instead, he had concentrated on his career, successfully achieving the professional goals he'd set for himself by following in his father's giant footsteps. But after moving from Los Angeles to Atlanta seven years ago to assume the position of CEO and part owner of ViaTech, one of the Southeast region's leading telecommunication companies, his plans all changed the day he met Victoria Small.

At the time, she worked in ViaTech's human resources department. When he first met her, it was literally love at first sight. She was tall, elegant, and startlingly beautiful. Everything about her had captivated him. She had earned an MBA from Wharton, which told him she was smart, and in a few short years she had risen to become one of the company's youngest senior directors, which meant she was am-

bitious and business savvy. They were qualities he admired, and she ignited a fire in him that wouldn't go away until he had her.

He had spent months trying to get close to her under the guise of
developing a professional working relationship, and his plan to woo
her would have succeeded much sooner had it not been for Parker
Brightwood. Parker had come into Victoria's life one weekend and
had swept her off her feet. Ted cursed himself for not acting sooner or
telling Victoria exactly how he felt about her from the beginning. But
he had been caught in a delicate situation. He was her boss, and at
the time he was still married.

He removed the largest obstacle by filing for divorce, ending the
paper-thin facade he had called a marriage. But there was still the
sticky proposition of having an office romance, so he used discretion
in his pursuit. Then there were the other issues: age and race. He was
twelve years Victoria's senior. It wasn't a significant age gap and didn't
seem to bother Victoria in the least. But what Ted soon discovered
was that the larger issue at hand was his race. He was white, she was
black, and she'd made it clear that the two didn't mix in her romantic
dealings.

Initially, Ted was disappointed to learn she felt that way. And to
compound matters, his mother and Victoria's father had both expressed contrary views on the subject. He almost felt defeated because
Parker had an automatic leg up by consequence of birth. His ethnic
heritage guaranteed him a seat at the table. But after nearly a year of
quiet, yet patient pursuit, Ted finally won Victoria's heart. He knew
the love they shared was real, and it conquered a world of challenges.

Victoria and Ted joined their daughter at the breakfast table, and
soon each of them was immersed in their own world: Alexandria
chomping down on her cereal in between songs and giggles with Big
Bird, Ted reading the *Wall Street Journal* while trying to balance his
bagel and coffee, and Victoria checking her BlackBerry in between
sips of her peppermint tea.

After a few minutes, Ted lowered his paper and turned his attention to Victoria. "What time does that thing start today?"

Victoria stopped in mid-text and stared at him. She knew exactly
what he was talking about, and she didn't like the way he had just referred to Alexandria's first Jack and Jill playdate as "that thing." She

knew that Ted was still uncomfortable about their daughter's membership in the elite social organization for African American children. It had taken several discussions on the matter before she finally convinced him to let Alexandria join.

They'd gone round and round about the issue. "Ted, growing up, I was a member of Jack and Jill, and it was a wonderful experience," Victoria had told him several months ago, when she filled out Alexandria's legacy membership application. "This will give Alexandria a chance to interact with kids who look like her, and it'll expose her to social and cultural experiences that I know you'll appreciate once you give it a chance."

For Victoria, their daughter's membership in the organization wasn't an issue that was up for debate. Alexandria was one of only a handful of black children in the exclusive neighborhood where they lived, as well as at the preschool she had been attending for the last two years. And while Ted was as white as any white man could be, thanks to Victoria, Alexandria's complexion clearly provoked questions about her racial background. She was a lightly toasted cream color, and she stood out in the sea of white faces that surrounded her every day.

"It's not a *thing*. It's a playdate," Victoria said with slight irritation, "and it starts at eleven. They'll have games and lunch for the kids, and then I'll pick her up around two this afternoon."

When Alexandria heard the word *playdate,* she turned her attention from her movie to her parents. "Will there be lots of kids for me to play with?" She brightened.

"Yes, sweetie." Victoria smiled. "There will be lots of kids there."

"Yea!" Alexandria cheered. She was an only child, and she eagerly jumped at any opportunity to be around other children.

Ted shifted his weight in his chair. "Will there be other kids there like her?" he asked, this time with a little irritation in his voice, too.

Again, Victoria knew exactly what he was hinting at. "Certainly, all the children attending today will be in her age group, and from what I've been told, there's almost an even number of girls and boys. She'll have a ball." Victoria smiled, leaning over and tickling Alexandria on her side.

"That's not what I meant."

"I know exactly what you meant," Victoria responded in a sugary sweet voice, cutting Ted a look that contradicted her tone. She was happy that, for once, her naturally intuitive daughter was so caught up in the excitement of her impending playdate that she hadn't picked up on the tension that had just blanketed the room. She pushed Alexandria's empty cereal bowl to the side. "Sweetie, why don't you go upstairs and start brushing your teeth. I'll be up in a minute to help you pick out a nice outfit for today, okay?"

"Okay, Mommy." Alexandria obeyed. She hopped down from her chair and headed upstairs.

Victoria and Ted sat in silence until they were sure their daughter was out of earshot.

"What's wrong with you?" Victoria asked, peering into Ted's deep ocean-blue eyes. "How could you ask a question like that in front of Alexandria?"

"V, you said that you wanted her to join this organization so she can be around kids like her. Well, she's not just African American, you know." Ted folded his newspaper, placing it to the side. "Will there be any white kids or biracial kids there?"

Victoria let out a huff. "We've been through this before. You know full well that it's a black organization."

"My point exactly. I don't understand the necessity of her joining Jack and Jill. She's already in a playgroup at her school," Ted pointed out. "I thought we decided a long time ago that we weren't going to expose Alexandria to anything that was exclusionary."

Victoria threw up her hands, taking a deep breath as she looked out their large bay window. "Well, we better put the house up for sale. Take a good look around you."

"This neighborhood isn't exclusively white, but Jack and Jill *is* exclusively black," Ted responded.

"Other than the two black families in this neighborhood—whose children are in high school, by the way—and half a handful at her school, Alexandria's always in the minority in her everyday environment. I know what that's like, Ted . . . but you don't. And even though Alexandria just turned five, she sees the difference, too."

"What do you mean, she sees the difference?"

"You know that she's always been inquisitive and is a bit more knowing than the average child her age. . . ."

"Yes, I know, but what are you saying?"

Victoria put down her BlackBerry, locking eyes with her husband. "The other day Alexandria asked me, 'Mommy, if you're black and Daddy's white . . . what am I?' "

They sat in silence again, staring at each other. Ted was at a temporary loss for words. He had been warned by his mother that this day would come, and logically, he knew this was a natural question for Alexandria to ask. But he hadn't anticipated it to come so soon. His little princess was still so young.

"What did you tell her?" he asked.

"I told her the truth. That yes . . . Mommy is black and Daddy is white, and that she's the best of both of us," Victoria said, leaning back in her chair. "It seemed to satisfy her, but, Ted, whether you want to face it or not, society has already labeled our child. There will be times when she *will* have to identify."

"Why do you always think she's going to have to choose one over the other?"

"Why do you think she'll never have to?" Victoria countered, shaking her head.

This was an issue that sometimes left them at odds, the struggle over their daughter's racial identity. Victoria knew that the discord would only grow as Alexandria matured in age, and the thought of having to constantly fight to infuse her African American roots into her daughter's life was something that she knew would wear thin.

"Because we live in a global world," Ted continued. "Things have changed since we were Alexandria's age. You act like we're living in the Jim Crow era."

Victoria smirked. "Hah, Jim Crow was blatant. What I'm talking about is the subtlety of twenty-first-century racism. It's cloaked so well that you don't even see it. Hell, it's got you drinking the Kool-Aid. You haven't been ostracized in your social circle for being married to me, but it's only because of *who* you are and the economic status you hold. But trust me, they've talked about us under their breaths."

Ted shook his head, turning his eyes away from his wife, knowing she was right.

"As much as you love Alexandria and me, and as open-minded as you are, you still have a blind spot when it comes to race. Are you just that oblivious, or do you purposely choose to ignore it?"

The air between them became thick with discomfort.

"I'm not oblivious about how things work," Ted answered. "I'm immersed in corporate America, remember? I understood the prejudice we were going to face long before we got married," he said, squaring his shoulders. "We simply have different views on the subject. Alexandria's just five years old, V . . . five years old," he stressed. "I don't want her to feel like she has to choose anything right now."

"But, Ted, we've been teaching her how to make choices since she was old enough to speak her first words. Please, let's be clear about this." Victoria paused. "You don't want her to have to make choices when it involves race."

"V—"

Victoria interrupted him. "Before we got married, I told you my concerns about us raising children and the struggles we would face, and you were the one who said you were ready to deal with anything that came our way, remember? Well, it's time to start dealing."

Ted let out a deep breath filled with frustration. He didn't want to argue so early in the morning, especially after they had gotten the day off to such a good start. He decided that it wasn't the time to tackle such a delicate debate, so he reached over and put his hand on top of Victoria's. "I love my family, and I'll do whatever it takes to protect you and Alexandria. I'm not oblivious, and I won't make blind decisions that will hurt us. This is just something I feel strongly about."

"And so do I."

Ted leaned in close, prepared to give in, but only for the moment. "I hope Alexandria has a good time today." He smiled. "I really do."

Although Victoria knew that he meant every word coming from his mouth, what he just said didn't arrest her worries, because she knew what her husband didn't—that this was just the beginning. She wished she could wave a magic wand and change the last three hundred fifty years of American history. This was a war she had been suited up to fight all her life, but it was a new battle for Ted, and she knew that he would never fully understand the complexities of what it meant to be black in America.

"I'm heading upstairs, because we've got to leave soon," Victoria said. She grabbed her BlackBerry and rose from the table. She leaned over and kissed Ted lightly on the lips. "We'll work through this, together."

Ted kissed her back and nodded his head. He watched his wife as she walked out of the room, and thought about the question his daughter had asked. *What am I?*

He's Quite a Catch. . . .

Victoria's stomach was a bundle of squiggly lines and nervous jitters. It had been that way since she had arrived at Hilda Barrett's house a half hour ago. She looked down at her watch. *Damn! Thirty minutes to go.* That was how long it would be before she could get the hell out of there!

She couldn't wait to make a beeline out the door and head straight to her car. Even though she would have to return in a few hours to pick up Alexandria from her first Jack and Jill playdate, she knew that she needed to leave now, before her temples throbbed any harder.

She was sitting on a large paisley-print sofa with her legs crossed, trying to concentrate on the information that Hilda, the current chapter president, was delivering to the parents of the newly minted crop of young Jack and Jill darlings. Even though Victoria knew the information like she had written it herself, she tried to focus hard on the words coming out of Hilda's mouth. Focusing would help take her mind off the man sitting across the room. The one causing her nerves to fray at the edges.

She'd spotted him as soon as she and Alexandria had arrived. He'd been bent down on one knee, whispering something to an adorable little boy who looked like his "mini me." He rubbed his hands over his perfectly shaven bald head, then over the child's thick mass of black curls, which mimicked the ones he had briefly sported several years ago. When he stood, he looked as handsome and sexy as she remembered. His neatly creased trousers and white polo shirt hung well on his tall frame. She couldn't help but notice and admire the fact that his golden-colored skin was still smooth and his dimples were still alluring. His brown eyes were still piercing, and his muscular body was still in tip-top condition.

He had looked at her, then down at Alexandria, before focusing his enticing baby browns back on her again. He stared for a few uncomfortable moments before Victoria finally looked away. His gaze made her feel flushed and nervous.

"Mommy, what's wrong?" Alexandria had asked, tugging at the lightweight material of Victoria's sundress, sensing the change in her mother's mood.

"Nothing's wrong, sweetie," Victoria softly reassured her. When she looked in his direction again, she saw that one of the other parents had just come up and engaged him in what looked like a deep conversation, taking his attention off of her.

After one of the parent volunteers escorted Alexandria and the rest of the children back to the sunroom, Victoria had tried to make casual conversation with two other mothers in attendance. They were standing in the large living room, nibbling on fruit, waiting for Hilda to start the welcome meeting.

Victoria zoned in and out of the ladies' mindless Q&A. "Where do you live?" "What do you do?" "What sorority did you pledge?" "Are you a legacy?" All the typical questions in that type of circle, which usually bored her to tears. It wasn't until she caught the tail end of what one of the women was saying that she realized the conversation had shifted to *him*.

"He's the top gun in charge at the Carlyle Fraser Heart Center at Emory," the chatty woman said. Her name was Roberta Stevens. She was short and superthin with a whiny voice, the kind that was primed for nagging. "He's one of my husband's top clients . . . with Merck, you know." She smiled with a wave of her fragile-looking hand. "He's also president of the Association of Black Cardiologists, on the board of the Boys and Girls Club, and he's very involved with his son. He's quite a catch."

Tasha, the other woman who rounded out their group, looked across the room at him with hungry eyes. "So, he's single?"

Victoria quickly glanced down at Tasha's bare ring finger. There was something about her that was off-putting, a crooked line in her otherwise well-put-together countenance. She was attractive, and her style of dress was hip and sophisticated, masking the ugliness that lay beneath. Victoria had known women like Tasha—ruthless! The cunning type who would stop at nothing to get what she wanted.

"Oh, yes," Roberta answered with a quick nod. "He's single and very much available."

"*Really?*" Tasha said, pepping up, looking around the huge living room full of parents. "He's one of the few fathers who showed up here today, and probably the only single man in this entire room," she added, calculating. "But I bet he won't be single for long . . . if I can help it." She grinned and gave a seductive purr. "So, what's the story on his son's mother?"

Victoria could see that Tasha was probing hard, probably already thinking of ways to make dinner plans with her intended prey.

Roberta shook her head. "They never married, but they share custody. She's general counsel for a huge lobbying firm downtown . . . a real workaholic, if you ask me. That's why she's not here today. She's out of the country on business. The two of them used to fight like cats and dogs, but lately they've been getting along, which is a blessing for their son's sake. Poor little guy." Roberta sighed, shaking her head again. "What could be more important than spending time with your only child?"

Tasha nodded in agreement, but Victoria was motionless as Roberta went on. "She used to try to use the boy as leverage to get a ring . . . like that would ever happen."

"I thought you said they were getting along now," Tasha remarked with raised brows. "You don't think there's a chance of reconciliation?"

Victoria could see that Tasha was hoping there wasn't.

"Maybe when hell freezes over." Roberta smirked. "They're being civil for their son's sake. Besides, he's kind of, um . . . What's the word?" She scratched her head. "Commitment phobic, that's it. I don't think he's the marrying type, if you know what I mean. In the years I've known him, I can't recall him ever dating anyone for longer than a couple months at a time."

Victoria remained silent, as though the details of his life were of no concern to her.

"You seem to know a lot about him," Tasha said, still keeping her eyes on the handsome man.

"Yes, Parker and my husband, Alvin, are quite close, and our sons used to attend the same preschool. We do playdates and sleepovers all the time," Roberta responded. "That's his name by the way. Parker . . . Dr. Parker Brightwood."

Tasha grinned. "That's good information to know."

"Looks like someone's got their eye on the good doctor," Roberta giggled.

Tasha flashed a smile in Parker's direction, which he seemed to return. "You could say that."

"Well, just be forewarned," Roberta advised. "He's a hard nut to crack, so good luck."

Back in the present, the other dozen or so parents looked on, actively engaged in Hilda's presentation. But Victoria felt as though she was sinking in her seat. She wanted so badly to get up and leave, to walk outside into the late morning sun to clear her mind. But she knew it would be rude to interrupt the session, and she certainly didn't want to draw any attention to herself.

She focused on Hilda's speech so she wouldn't be tempted to look at Parker's sexy, soft-looking lips. She glanced up at the lovely silk taffeta drapes hanging above his head so her eyes wouldn't accidentally land on one of his deliciously inviting dimples. It had been six years since the last time she had seen him, and she still remembered his words from that day. "I'm gonna fight for you," he'd told her. "I'm not giving up on us."

He had devastated her with a betrayal that had hurt worse than her first broken heart. She uncrossed her legs at the thought, then nervously recrossed them, realizing that she was slowly melting away.

She wondered if Parker was as uncomfortable as she was, if he was sitting across from her, thinking the same thoughts that were running through her mind. She almost smiled to herself, remembering what a smooth operator he was. He could be sweating bullets, and one would never know; that was how cool and controlled his outward appearance always seemed to be.

She wanted to steal a glance to see if she could discern his mood, but she was afraid he'd catch her in the act. Unlike him, nearly every move she made was obvious, because she wore her feelings on her face. It made her think back to the night they first met. They'd been at one of her favorite restaurants, The Cheesecake Factory. She'd been alone, and he'd been on a blind date. The entire evening he had stolen glances at her. Remembering that night made the smile she'd been trying to hide slip out before she could catch it. *Why am I thinking about this?*

But the truth was that she knew exactly why those thoughts, along with others, were floating through her head, and it frightened her. It brought back to mind the recurring dream that invaded her sleep every so often, and the disturbing knowledge that she had never quite gotten over him. *I've got to get out of here right now!*

Just as she was about to rise from her seat, Hilda concluded her presentation. Victoria was relieved and tried to make a dash for the door, but just as she was heading out, Roberta stopped her.

"Victoria," Roberta said, smiling. "We should get together for lunch sometime. Do you have a card?" she asked, handing over one of her own.

"Oh, sure." Victoria tried to smile back as she fished through her overstuffed handbag for her silver-plated business card holder. She panicked when she looked up and saw that Parker was approaching. His eyes were fixed on her, as if he was taking inventory of her thoughts. Victoria quickly handed Roberta her card. "Call me, and we'll get together," she said in a hurry.

Instead of thanking the hostess for her time and hospitality, or standing around and mingling with the other parents, Victoria headed straight for the front door.

Part of the Package

Ted looked at his watch and rubbed his tired eyes. It was late afternoon, and he'd been in his office since he left the house that morning. He was sitting at his desk, reviewing projection reports for an upcoming strategy meeting. He pulled off his reading glasses and leaned forward in his high-back leather chair, tapping his signature engraved Montblanc against a small stack of papers.

He was still thinking about the conversation he'd had with Victoria over breakfast. He didn't like arguing with his wife, but he knew the topic they'd discussed was one that would most certainly come up again, especially as their daughter grew in age. He hated the thought of Alexandria having to face the ugly prejudice of the world. She was his only child, and he wanted to protect her.

He let out a heavy sigh, pushing his papers to the side of his desk. This was what Victoria, and even his own mother, had warned him about; it was part of the package that came along with being married to a black woman and raising a biracial child. When he and Victoria had first learned they were expecting a baby just a month after they married, he'd been elated. He couldn't wait to see a miniature version of the two of them running around the house.

But during Victoria's sixth month of pregnancy, she began to verbalize her concerns more and more. "Ted, you're fooling yourself if you think that our child won't be treated differently," she had told him.

Victoria had been speaking from a foreign place that he knew nothing about, and it had scared the shit out of him. He knew how racist the world could be; he'd worked in corporate America long enough to see it firsthand. And he had witnessed it up close and personal in his own family when he learned about some of his Back Bay relatives' reactions to him marrying Victoria. But he had convinced himself that they were in the minority, and that things would be different for *his* child. His station in life had afforded him certain privileges that he intended to pass along to his son or daughter.

Ted had always prided himself on being a man of great will and prodigious determination. He was the son of Charles Thornton, legendary Boston businessman and real estate developer. He was a man's man, strong and immune to weakness, and like his father, he was always cool under pressure and calm in the face of adversity. But the thought of his child having to endure discrimination and cruelty simply because of the color of her skin was something he was ill prepared for.

Ted leaned back in his chair and looked at the two pictures on the edge of his desk. One was a photo of Victoria, Alexandria, and himself, taken last Christmas, all smiles and cheer. The other was his favorite picture of all they had ever taken as a family. He and Victoria were smiling as they held their tiny daughter in their arms, joy and gratitude spread over both their faces. It had been a tender moment his mother-in-law had captured with her digital camera shortly after Victoria and Alexandria arrived home from the hospital, two weeks after Alexandria was born. They were all smiles and cheer in this photo, too, but instead of celebrating the holidays and the miracle birth of Christ, they had been celebrating the miracle that both mother and daughter were alive.

Ted rested his chin in his hand as he thought back to those days. They had been the roughest weeks of his life, each day presenting the possibility that he might lose the two people who mattered most in his life. Victoria had suffered complications from an emergency cesarean, and Alexandria had been born with health problems. That had been a bleak time, and it was only after his wife and child were safe at home, both out of danger, that Ted got a good night's sleep—his first in fourteen long days.

As Ted reminisced over those events, a thought sprang into his mind. It was something he'd heard one of the ladies say when he'd passed the nurses' station in the neonatal unit on his way to Victoria's room. "That Thornton baby is so beautiful, like a little black baby doll," the sixty-something, mocha-colored nurse had said to one of her coworkers. Then his mind took him back to small things he'd brushed off when he'd been out with Alexandria, taking her to the park or out for ice cream when Victoria had weekend events to oversee for Divine Occasions. He thought about the quizzical stares that people had given him when they saw him with his daughter.

It was something that used to irritate him, and he had attributed their behavior to plain ignorance, like the time, a few months ago, when a blond woman who was sitting across from them in Baskin-Robbins leaned over, looked at Alexandria, and told him that she thought adoption was a great thing.

Which dress to wear? Which boy's offer to accept to the prom? Which college to attend? Which academic major to pursue? Those were the kinds of decisions he saw in Alexandria's future. Not what race she would claim. The thought pissed him off, and the fact that he knew there was little he could do frustrated him.

Right then and there, Ted made up his mind. Up to this point he had been largely silent and ambivalent about the issue whenever Victoria brought it up. But now he was going to have to face the cold, hard truth that he realized he'd been avoiding. He knew that his daughter would need support and reassurance in ways that her everyday environment couldn't adequately afford her. He decided that when he returned home tonight, he would talk to Victoria and let her know that Alexandria's membership in Jack and Jill was just fine with him.